The Cold Shoulder

Also by Bill Blume

West of Apocalypse

The Dragon Spy

Gidion's Hunt

Gidion's Blood

The Deadlands: And Other Stories

The Cold Shoulder

Bill Blume

Time Killer Publishing

Trigger Warnings: alcohol, amputation, animal death, assault, attempted murder, blood, bones, cults, death, fire, gore, hostages, kidnapping, misogyny, murder, poisoning, profanity, prostitution, religion, sexism, violence

1

A Perfect Ambush

A man as tall as Aden intimidated others. He loved it as a child, but now, he cursed it. A man could only sit and slouch so much to avoid notice. He even concealed every weapon he owned, from his daggers to his shakta.

He didn't look at all like a man intent on murder.

Orin Gregane, on the other hand, preferred to walk about as if an armory with feet. A sword rested on each hip with a third, shorter sword slung over his back. A pair of gaudy daggers rested within sheaths on his belt buckle. Like any gentleman from Salendar, he'd fit more than a dozen piercings in various places on his head that defied explanation save for a lack of anything better to do in a place where the warmest point of summer still allowed for a light snow.

This guy made a perfect target. Even with business slow this night at the Stray Dog Tavern, the entertainment value of Orin's self-mutilated face reduced Aden to a shadow.

All Aden needed to do was wait for an opening.

Orin flung his ugly knives at a circular target hanging on the wall opposite from the bar. The number of deep cuts into the wall suggested this town had plenty of strong arms with lousy aim. Aden noted with some discomfort that his target's daggers landed close to the center.

"You want more ale?" one of the younger serving girls asked Aden. He guessed she might be sixteen, almost a decade younger than he was. He shook his head, making one mug of ale his limit tonight. The young thing's shoulders drooped in disappointment. She wouldn't liquor a healthy tip from him. He needed his wits sharp, and the pouch sewn to his belt was too light to afford more.

Another dagger slammed into the center of the target. The wooden circle rattled against the wall but stayed in place.

As a child, he assumed the life of a bounty hunter was filled with travel, women, and lots of money. Three years chasing men like Orin, he'd reached his fill. Travel? He'd seen enough dust pits like this one to know that most places were little better. As for women, his talent for killing didn't translate into any skills for wooing. And then there was the money... the price of a human life averaged somewhere between pitiful and pathetic. More often than not, they paid you less to kill a man than to take another alive.

Every once in a while, an Orin Gregane came along, though. Praise the Spirits for the wicked people! Months ago, the walking armory had murdered a wealthy Salendaren merchant's only son in a bar brawl. Salendar's government wasn't part of the Astesian Empire and couldn't afford the court fees Astes demanded for detaining and handing over a prisoner, certainly not one this far east of the empire's borders. Fortunately, the merchant had the money to spare to see Orin dead, in or out of the Astesian Empire. Dark! For the six hundred silvers the merchant offered, Aden would've risked all the monsters of the West to put Orin in the ground.

Damn that was good money! He'd be able to eat meat for an entire year with enough coin left to rent a decent room he didn't have to share with strangers. The thought made his mouth water as he pushed away the bowl of thinned chicken broth that he'd emptied all too quickly.

Orin downed his third mug of ale for the night. "More!" He flung the empty vessel at the bartender, who used his body to shield the fractured mirror behind the bar.

Aden held in the groan that might give him away. Would the man never piss? Orin finished off the fourth mug of ale almost as quickly as the serving girl delivered it. That he wasn't stumbling like a bird on a tree limb in a hurricane baffled Aden.

"I want another waiting when I get back!" Orin said, as if the news he was about to visit the tavern's outhouse warranted a herald for the deed.

The walking armory stumbled a few steps on his way out the back door. A little too much ale, after all.

Aden paid his tab and marched out the front door onto the street. The memory of his old mentor's voice chased after him, warning that a person without immediate purpose walks with patience. He once assumed experience would make it easier to conceal his intentions, but many lean months peppered throughout the past three years disproved that. He ran from his mentor's advice as he rounded the corner of the tavern. The space between the tavern and the neighboring bakery, which smelled more like a tannery, provided enough space as long as he kept his body turned sideways.

With all the ale in his body and that ridiculous belt buckle, Orin wouldn't get his pants down to do his business that easily. That gave Aden the time needed to get back there and make the kill.

A perfect ambush.

His hand itched to remove the wooden stick from his jacket's breast pocket. Three slices of his soul resided within his shakta. With that weapon, he could rip Orin apart with a single thought, but the mess left behind would leave no doubt what weapon had done the deed. Like Orin, Aden lived with a bounty promised to anyone who made his life shorter. Each use of his shakta planted a sign post for an assassin to follow.

He pulled out a dagger from his jacket as he reached the back of the buildings. Only a pitiful bit of light from the rear windows of the tavern offered any aid to see. The outhouse turned out bigger than Aden expected. He should have checked that before going into the tavern, and his old mentor's voice nagged him for his laziness. *No kill is a simple kill.* Aden pushed the old cat's voice aside and focused on the task before him.

An outhouse that size could accommodate two people, and that wasn't unheard of for a public privy. That could place Orin to the right or left, giving him a few more seconds to react. Aden needed to move faster.

A groan came from the outhouse. Aden stifled his chuckle. Seemed Orin's business in there provided a better distraction than Aden had hoped. *Finish him, and then ride hard for those six hundred silvers,* Aden thought.

He readied his grip on the dagger, then flung open the door. He never stepped into the outhouse. Orin's vacant eyes stared up at Aden, already dead or close to it. The hilt of a dagger stuck out from the center of his chest.

A thick, wooden board cracked into Aden's head. He dropped his dagger as the fire of his mind snuffed out for a near fatal span of seconds. No useful wisdom from his dead mentor entered his thoughts. A second swing of that board caught him on the forehead. In the dark of the back alley, he couldn't count his attackers. They kicked his back, stomach, and head—didn't give him a chance to defend himself. Blood spilled from a cut to his forehead, gushing down into his eyes, obscuring the world.

He heard a dagger jerk free of its sheath. The familiar sound warned him these men meant to finish him for good. He used his arms to shield his stomach and heart. He rolled back and forth as the blade stabbed hard into his torso. Once, twice, a third time. He lay still upon the dirt muddied by his blood and urine. Something warm and wet splattered against his right temple, and only after the fact did he recognize the sound of his attacker spitting on him.

"Jha veet est! Bayot!" he heard one of the men over him say. Aden didn't recognize the language.

Hands as rough as his attacker's boots rifled through his clothes. Aden fought for silence, not wanting to give them a reason to stab him again. The cuts to his upper torso demanded his screams, but he clenched his teeth and allowed only stifled grunts. He heard his attackers run away, followed by a pair of screams. Then his mind flickered out.

2

The Healer

Aden awakened to a sickening scent that reminded him of rotted mint. That alarmed him less than the darkness of this room. He'd been stripped and placed in bed. A thin sheet covered most of his body. He was alive, if not well.

The only light came through an open window which permitted a gentle spring breeze. He thought the horrid smell came from outside, but then he realized it was drifting up from his mouth. The taste on his dried out tongue offended him just as much. What had his absent caretaker shoved down his throat?

He took his time to sit up. Bandages made of linen were wrapped around his stomach where the dagger had buried into him. Still hurt, but the cuts seemed to have healed. He'd been out a while.

The air coming through that small window felt humid, suggesting a recent shower, something this desert town didn't get that often. Goosebumps covered his arms as he climbed out of the bed.

The signs of regimented sterility assured him the room belonged to a practiced healer. Aside from the bed, the room had a dresser and a chair. He found most of his belongings, except his weapons, inside the dresser. His senses reached out for the familiar hum of his shakta, but silence answered. That only meant it wasn't near him. Only a powerful mage could damage or destroy a shakta, so he wasn't worried about that. With any luck, it might even be in this house.

You keep thinking those happy notions, his thoughts taunted him. Maybe they'll eventually be right, for a change.

His would-be-killers had dug through his clothes. Had they taken his shakta? Only the person whose soul resided in the stick could wield that weapon, so what would be the point?

He picked up his purse. It felt a few coins lighter, but not empty. A bad sign. Muggers didn't settle for half a purse.

He donned his shirt and pants, doing so as quietly as he could manage. He hadn't heard anyone else move within this house, but that didn't mean he was alone. A glance out the window at the empty street let him know just how late it was. He was still in Crestnal, only a few buildings down from the tavern. Now that he realized he was upstairs, he lightened his steps in case anyone was beneath h im.

The door to his room opened without making any sounds. Thank the gods for that much. A small house, he discovered. There was only one other room on this floor, on the other end of the hallway. He glanced down the stairs but only saw darkness.

Aden crept toward the master bedroom's door. It stood ajar, but not enough to let him see anything. He pushed open the door. Even in the limited light, he recognized the shape of a woman on the bed.

As he stepped into the room, something from beneath the bed growled. Aden didn't speak its language, but any man with half a brain knew when a critter was telling him to stay still or get his balls chewed off.

"Her name is Castine." The woman didn't bother to lift her head from the pillow.

"Named for the goddess of retribution." Yet another reason not to antagonize that critter. Aden didn't know much more of the religion tied to Castine. It had spawned during the past decade and gained in popularity among the empire's elite.

The woman in the bed sat up. The dark reduced her to little more than a shadow's outline, but it was enough to tell her body was slender. "You should go back to bed."

"Better I got on my way," he said.

"Better you let me and Castine sleep."

"And you would be?"

"Miriam." She sounded less pleased with him than her dog. "You can leave now, if you like. You'll be leaving without your weapons, though, and I get the feeling you'll need them."

That last barb hit the mark, reminding of the silence he felt when he tried to sense his shakta. A part of his spirit twisted with a growing panic the longer that silence persisted.

He considered trying his luck with the dog, assuming that's what Castine was. Not knowing what manner of creature she might be provided plenty of reasons not to pick that fight. Also, Miriam's statement suggested she intended to return his weapons to him, just not right away. The stitched cuts to his torso ached as he turned to leave, adding one last reason not to pick a fight tonight.

"Good night, Miriam... Castine."

Neither woman nor beast acknowledged him. He returned to his room, slipped off his clothes and climbed back into the bed. Sleep didn't reclaim him so easily. He listened for his shakta, his soul reaching as far as he could. The silence that answered scared him far more than Miriam's beast.

The next time Aden's eyes opened, the sun had replaced the moon. The stink of minty medicine remained but mingled with something far better. After he dressed, he followed his nose downstairs. Miriam was awake and cooking breakfast.

"I hope you like sausage," she said, confirming his nose's intuition. "There's some hot tea already brewed over on the table."

Damn, Aden thought. He despised tea, but he wouldn't complain. Gods, when had he last eaten a decent piece of meat?

"Where's Castine?" Aden would expect the animal to pester its owner for a bite.

"Upstairs sleeping." Miriam smirked without looking up from the frying pan. "She'll come along soon as I'm done. She's simple-minded, but she's wise enough to wait for a greater reward, unlike most."

Aden took her subtle jab in silence, the other night having given him ample practice. Pain flared from the wounds in his lower torso as he sat. He wondered how long he'd need to recover.

Miriam flipped the sausage patties within the black skillet atop her stove. A long metal pipe funneled the smoke out the side of the house. Wiping her hands on the apron tied about her waist, Miriam turned to look at him.

"You've got your color back," she said, her manner rather indifferent. "Take your shirt off. Let's have a look at those wounds."

He complied, adopting Castine's wisdom lest he lose out on a bite of that sausage.

Miriam's hands felt good, even if she was only shifting his bandages. Damn, he'd gone a long time without a woman's touch, not that he was in any shape for that sort of thing. Fortunately, Miriam's disapproving scowl deterred that line of thinking. She appeared middle-aged, with only a hint of wrinkles at the corners of her pale blue eyes. The brown hair that flowed down to the middle of her back didn't show any signs of turning white or grey.

"You're healing well enough. No sign of infection." She poured herself a mug of tea from the steaming kettle atop her kitchen table. "You're a lucky man. Stabbed thrice and not one vital organ hit."

"That wasn't luck," he said without any bravado.

"Oh really?" She sat at the table with him. "I suppose you meant for those boys to stab you. Most impressive." If she'd laid the sarcasm any thicker, she might have bottled it for jelly.

"If I was really good, the bastards wouldn't have gotten the chance to cut me." His old mentor's voice berated him for getting sloppy. "But yes, I took the blows as best I could."

He slipped back into his shirt, moving slow enough to avoid antagonizing his wounds.

Having expected to finger the trio of cuts to his shirt, he realized his hostess had cleaned and mended his clothes. Oddly considerate of her, given she appeared more annoyed with him than anything else.

Miriam's eyes shifted to the stairs. "The sausage must be ready." He looked over his shoulder and got his first look at Castine. *That's what scared you back into bed last night, bounty hunter!* his old mentor's voice laughed. The bitch wasn't big enough to lick his knees, not even standing on her hind legs.

He made quick work of the sausage and biscuits Miriam served him. By the time he'd made it halfway through his food, Miriam had only cut into her first few bites. Castine, the dog of retribution and sage patience, sat a few feet from her owner's chair waiting for a bite.

"They found you in the alley behind the tavern about," Miriam paused as if to examine a calendar within her mind, "five nights ago. Lucky for you, the screams brought the constable before anyone had a chance to make off with your belongings."

"I'm missing some money."

That arched one of her eyebrows, a slender line of that wonderful, dark brown hair. "You're only missing five coppers."

"You took my money?" His accusation lacked conviction as he forced the words around one of the first mouthfuls of meat he'd had in weeks.

"A healer values all life, but not charity," she said. "Though five coppers comes close to it. Be glad I didn't empty your whole purse."

"Why didn't you?"

This woman didn't lack for money or so it seemed. Her furniture wouldn't impress any nobles, but in a remote town like Crestnal, her home looked luxurious.

"I've just enough money to provide for myself and Castine," she said. "Don't need another mouth to feed. Left you enough coins to be on your way once you're better."

"That'll be this morning. I've lost enough time here as it is."

"Already?" Apparently, she'd expected him to freeload from her a little longer and even sounded a little disappointed, though that was probably his imagination. "And where are you in such a hurry to go?"

"Going to see your constable, for starters," he said." Don't suppose he caught the guys who stuck that dagger in me."

Miriam barked out a laugh and stopped short of taking a sip of her tea. "Oh, Dellem caught them all right."

"Good." Aden smiled at this bit of news. "Might let me answer a few questions."

"Only if you recognize them," she said. "Found both of them dead less than ten feet from you."

The nerves he felt from the absence of his shakta reawakened with that news. "What about Orin?"

"The one in the outhouse?" A nod from Aden answered her question. "Constable said he was dead when he found him."

"Buried them yet?"

"After five days? Of course." She offered him a sympathetic quirk of her brow as if to ask how a man this dimwitted had managed to stay alive so long. "And they don't waste money on a box for men like that."

Aden sighed and sought what solace he could in his last bite of sausage. "I'm gonna have to dig up those bastards just to get a look at them."

"You won't."

"Why's that?" He rubbed his bruised forehead as he decided he'd reached his fill of surprises.

"Just go see the constable." She glanced at a drawing of the town hanging in a simple, wooden frame on her wall. "You'll need to anyway. Dellem collected your weapons."

His body chilled, despite the warm food and drink he'd consumed. He hoped this constable didn't know what a shakta looked like, because if he did, then getting out of this small town would get a lot more complicated... and bloody. "I assumed you had my weapons here," he said, hoping his fears weren't too obvious.

"I don't care for weapons in my home. Don't need them." She tossed a piece of her uneaten sausage to the floor where her dog snatched it up. "After all, I've got Castine."

3

The Constable

The town of Crestnal offered little more than a place to rest between the cities of Gorman and Ostice. The larger markets in those two places stunted growth for this town. Beyond its one main street with about twenty buildings on each side, the only other reason Crestnal managed a place on a map was a couple dozen surrounding farms.

The houses didn't offer much for the eye to see. Their flat, off-white walls matched the sand of the surrounding desert. That made the jail stand out. For a bunch of farmers, they built one mean-looking lockup.

"Built it myself." Constable Dellem Arkreus gave Aden a small tour. The silver-haired fellow looked like he'd seen his share of fighting. Even two heads shorter than Aden, the constable's hard lines made him just as intimidating. "Took about ten years to put this thing together. Until then, we didn't even have one."

"Gods, what did you do with your prisoners?" Aden asked.

"Didn't take any. Simple laws for simple towns. Anything required a constable either got you kicked out of town or hanged."

"What changed?" Aden asked as Dellem led him down a hallway with a pair of cells in it.

"Got too expensive not to have one. Astesian law requires all towns to have a functioning jail or they charge a steep prisoner tax."

"Well, you did a nice job." Each wall looked a good two feet thick. Even had a courtyard with a double layer of barbed bars to let prisoners out for some sun but without a chance of climbing out. "You built all this yourself?"

"Some friends helped me with the things I didn't know how to make, but for the most part." Dellem smiled. "Was an engineer during the Samanthan Crusades. Grew up wanting to build palaces, but spent most of my life tearing things down to keep the West from getting a foothold. She's not a palace, but this was the first time I ever got to build something. Figured I'd make the most of it."

Dellem led him into what Aden took for a courtroom. The design resembled a typical Astesian court with a slightly elevated platform in the center of the room with a lectern for the judge, which Aden assumed to also be Dellem. Benches, three rows deep on each side of the podium, took up the rest of the space.

The constable headed up to the podium. "Have a seat." Keys jingled within his hand. He opened a lock in the small twin, steel doors in the wall behind the podium. As he pulled back the doors, Aden saw an organized set of shelves. Wooden boxes, some flatter than others lined the top two shelves. The bottom row belonged to some thick books. Astesian lawbooks, most likely. The Astesians had always said the gods rewarded those who embraced order, and in the process, crafted one of the most damned confusing set of laws in the world.

The book Dellem pulled out certainly didn't contain any laws, though. "Here we go." Bits of paper stuck out of the leather-bound journal in all directions. Dellem cracked the journal open. Aden expected all the paper to fall out, but Dellem held it together. He filed through the pages with his fingertips and pulled out two sheets.

"These are the two boys I found dead in the back of the tavern with you."

Dellem set the pages down on the bench next to Aden. Boys turned out a rather accurate description. The first picture captured a young man, with just a hint of fuzz for a beard. Narrow face, nose like a beak and thin eyes... the look of a predator. *Turned into the prey, though, didn't you?* Aden thought to himself with an ironic twist of sympathy. Was that a sign he was getting older, when he could even feel sorry for a boy who tried to kill him?

He diverted his attention to the second picture. Not much difference. This one just had bigger lips and a slightly smaller nose. Unless he missed his guess, these boys were brothers.

"You drew these?"

"Didn't just want to build palaces," Dellem said with the same pride he'd shown for his jail, "wanted to design them. Meant I needed to draw them first, so I spent a lot of time practicing as a child. Did better when I was in the crusades, but my eyes were better then, too."

Aden wondered if Dellem had drawn the picture of the town hanging in Miriam's house, but he let it be. "How were they killed?"

"How about you first tell me if you recognize them?" Dellem's tone made it clear he already suspected what Aden would say.

"I couldn't even say for certain if either of them attacked me." Aden shook his head, ignoring the silent nagging of his old mentor. "Didn't see either one of them coming. These boys laid a nice trap." *Or whoever hired them did.* Aden suspected the same person killed them, too. "So, how were they killed?"

"Something ripped out part of their chests."

The constable's words sent a chill into Aden's heart.

"Ripped out or chewed out?" Aden saw the answer in Dellem's face. They were thinking the same thing. "Ever seen what a dar'jiat wraith does to its victims?"

"No," Dellem said, "at least, maybe not until the other night. I heard enough stories about them during the crusades when I was in them, though. Take it you have?"

Aden nodded. "Two problems come to mind if it was, though."

"Never heard of a wraith this far east?"

"That's one." Aden studied the pictures of the dead boys. "The other thing? Damn things are near invisible at night—perfect predators. So why waste a dar'jiat wraith on these boys? Why even hire the boys? Just send the wraith after m e."

The questions went unanswered. To think a wraith got that close to him... D amn.

"Someone got a reason to hate you that much?" Dellem asked.

"To send a dar'jiat wraith? Enemies I've got to worry about don't usually make deals with the West."

"Seems you got one now."

Aden couldn't argue with that. Couldn't do much with what he knew either. "Where's Orin buried?"

"The pin cushion?" Dellem chuckled. "Dropped him in a hole with the other two in the cemetery behind the church. Planning to pay your last respects?"

"Something like that. Anyone mind if I dig him up?"

"Dig him up?" The constable stepped back from Aden. "Why in Dark would you want to do that?"

"Unfinished business," Aden said. "That and I'd like a look at those boys to make sure what killed them."

"Long as you put them back in the ground and bury them when you're done." The constable's pale eyes studied Aden as if to realize he'd missed something about this young bounty hunter. "Just let the priest know before you start digging. He'll probably let you borrow a shovel, too."

"Good. Can I have my weapons now?"

The constable nodded as he picked up the pictures of the two boys and slid them back into his art journal. Once that went back onto the shelf, he pulled out one of the flatter and wider wooden boxes and set it down on the bench. "There you go."

Aden looked over the items. His daggers, sword, and whip were there. He sifted through all the weapons and looked back to the shelf. The silence in his soul made his hands shake.

"Something wrong?" Dellem asked.

"My—" he said, then stopped. "A throwing stick. A white, ribbed stick."
"Stick?"

Those damn boys! They'd taken it when they'd dug through his jacket's pockets.

"I think they took it," he pressed. "Did you find anything like that on one of the boys?"

"Sorry, lad."

Spirits burn! Aden could replace all this shit, steal it if he needed to. Where was his shakta? Where was his false sword?

4

The Grave

A flurry of curses, some in languages to which Aden knew no other words, filled the consecrated ground of the cemetery. For two hours, he stabbed his borrowed shovel into the ground. The recent spring showers had turned the dirt into mud, much of which now covered him. Thankfully, he'd exercised enough foresight to take off his newly cleaned shirt.

His anger increased with the growing pile of dug up dirt. A green, leather-skinned courser he'd "borrowed" from one of his previous bounties yawned its indifference in the shade of a nearby tree. Getting this large cat-like creature back from the local stable cost him nearly every coin Miriam left him. He'd need his ride, though, assuming he found what he was looking for at the bottom of this damned hole.

"Look like you could use a drink."

The priest stood over the ever-deepening hole. He held a wooden pitcher and a mug.

"What's that?" Aden asked as he planted the shovel into the dirt deep enough so that it stood on its own. "Water?"

"No, I brought you ale." The priest smiled at him. "You don't strike me as the type to favor water."

Aden shook his head. He was tempted, but even Miriam's cooking hadn't been enough to ease the queasiness in his stomach. Whatever medicine she'd given him must have been pretty potent. The rejection of the ale displeased the priest, judging from the twist of his lips.

"You look awful young for a priest," Aden said.

"I was raised to the gold robe just a few weeks ago and sent here." He gestured with open arms towards the church house. The building itself wasn't much to boast about. The white boards lining the outside of the house were showing early signs of rot. Four sigils representing mountain, fish, flame, and cloud, hung over the door. The sigil for cloud looked damaged. Hard to say if it had fallen and been remounted or if someone vandalized it. The most telling thing about this church was how small it was. "What can I say? More senior priests are rarely given small flocks."

"That must have hurt," Aden said.

"Pardon?"

"Your hand." He pointed to the priest's right hand, which was missing its pinky finger. "You lose a fight with one of your flock?"

The priest laughed. "No, no. Was giving some scraps to a stray dog. He was a little hungrier than I'd realized. Fortunate he didn't take the whole hand." The priest held up the pitcher of ale. "Sure you don't want some?"

"No, I'll be fine." Aden lifted the shovel from the dirt. "Best I finish this before dark and be on my way. I'll put the shovel back before I go."

"Of course." The priest scowled as he walked back inside his decaying church.

Aden returned to his digging. Impatience to put this town behind him made him reckless. He reached the bodies moments later, but he only realized it once he shoved the point of the shovel into the boy with the beaknose. The shovel slit open the stomach, exposing his decayed guts and all the vile insects that relished the taste of carrion. A wonder he didn't retch at the sight alone, but the stench to match shot a taste of that recently-relished sausage, now basted in bile, up from his stomach to burn at the back of his throat.

He fought to get his breathing under control. "Should have become a carpenter." Then he laughed. Like he knew anything about building things. He envied the constable's skills, because since he was a child, he'd been trained for one thing: the chase.

The Order raised him to spy and kill. Now that he'd rejected the Order, gone his own way, he found his skills useless for most work. Any government might have paid dearly for a man with a shakta to work for them, but none of them would trust him and would just as likely kill him. The Order turned spycraft and betrayal into an art, and with every member of the Order willing to kill him on sight, he brought too much baggage with him to any job.

With his sense of smell finally deadened to the stench of the bodies, he cleared away the rest of the dirt covering the boy's chest. The sight of the wound, peppered in loose dirt and gnawed upon by the many eaters of the dead, confirmed his suspicions. The sight of a wraith wound murdered his stomach's resolve. He turned away and vomited onto the ground outside of the hole.

"Oh... gods," he whispered as his stomach settled. A damned wraith... no doubt about it. He knew enough to imagine how that boy died. A hand and fanged mouth, melded into a single appendage, would start wide and then clamp down. Hundreds of tiny, shark-like teeth ripped out flesh and muscle, spitting out the bones.

Aden's gaze slid up to the sky. The sun hung at its zenith, still somewhat low given summer was far off. Was that bloody wraith still out there? What even greater horror held its leash? Something that dark couldn't survive in daylight, so where was it hiding? This town sat in the middle of flat country.

Calm down, he chided himself, *think. If the damn thing wanted you dead, then you'd be in this hole, too.*

He looked down at his feet.

"Shit, I am in this hole."

That pulled a weak laugh out of him, more like half-laugh, half-dry heave. The rest of his laughter erupted more freely after that. His fit gave him the serenity to finish what he'd started, clearing the dirt away from the other boy. He searched the pockets on both of them. Nothing.

That meant the wraith had taken his shakta, but everything he'd ever been taught insisted that wasn't possible. A creature of Shadow couldn't hold a weapon fashioned from Light.

"Someone else took it," he muttered to himself. Someone in this town? He doubted it. Few who ever saw a shakta up close lived to share the knowledge, and anyone who might recognize what his forbidden weapon was would just as likely know it wouldn't work for them. *Once you give it up, you don't get it back,* the mage told him before he shaved off a bit of Aden's soul to empower the carved stick of wood, turning it into a weapon.

The "why" of it all and, just as importantly, the "who" went unanswered by the time he'd uncovered Orin's body. He used his hands to wipe off enough dirt to see Orin's face, piercings and all. Killed in an outhouse. "Well, I suppose you did go in there to clear your bowels," Aden said under his breath. He forced Orin's pants down until his privates were exposed. Right there on the tip, yet another piercing. How did a man pee with that thing there? For that matter, why would a man do that to himself? Warriors had probably spent half the world's currency finding ways to protect their manhood with armor, and these idiots actually shoved a piece of metal through theirs. With a grimace, he reached down to pull out the piercing. He somehow managed to do it without touching Orin's decayed skin and held up his prize to examine it in the sunlight. Engraved on the barrel in Salendar script, *Orin Gregane, Son of Orin and Nala.*

"Six hundred silvers." He dropped the piercing into his purse. Part of him hoped to find the piercing gone, because then all that business behind the Stray Dog Tavern might have been nothing but another bounty hunter chasing after Orin for the reward.

No, this was about Aden, about his shakta, and he didn't have a damn clue why.

While Aden shoveled dirt back into the hole, the priest came back out and offered to let him stay for dinner and the night. He refused. Instead, he rode his courser around the town, listening for a sign that his shakta might be here. The silence that answered terrified him.

He left town with a little less than half a day's light left to him, pushing his courser hard towards the west. Once he reached Gorman, he could figure out what to do next.

Someone had stolen a part of him, and whatever it took, he planned to find it.

5

The Player

Heralds claimed Gorman was once the most beautiful city in all of the eastern continent. Those same tale spinners also blamed war for turning the place into some madman's unfinished maze. Aden considered that shit, not the part about war making it a mess, but that it had ever been beautiful.

Only locals who knew their way around dared to go out at night. Even regular visitors such as himself limited how far they ventured within Gorman after sunset. The streets twisted about like the twin of some drunken spider's web.

Then there were all the damned walls, and this was where war took fault. Centuries of wars resulted in constant wall building. Only the damn builders never accounted for the city getting any bigger. Go down a street far enough, and you'd likely hit a dead end where the war-battered remains of some wall had refused to fall. The crazy bastards who lived here took pride in all the dead ends, said they symbolized their resolve. Never made any damn sense to Aden since a fragment of a wall meant the rest of it had fallen. Of course, most Gormans didn't understand they'd ever been conquered. He supposed their government changed so often, they accepted it as the norm.

This place didn't belong to any government, though. Gorman belonged to the thieves. Bandits left the roads to Gorman alone, which was why Aden had slept with ease during the three days journey here. Better for thieves to let idiot travelers make it here and then end up lost forever.

With all that in mind, Aden supposed an inn named "Go Further & Get Lost" made perfect sense. The place belonged to a man only a little older than Aden named Will October. Five minutes with him and you were convinced you knew all there was to know about him. After a few years, Aden realized he knew next to nothing about him.

Aden stabled his courser and went inside. Will's inn attracted an odd crowd. A shadow-haired lady bedecked in jewels and rolls of sky blue fabric climbed the outside stairs. A man of equal stature escorted her. The upstairs belonged to the wealthy, and Aden suspected he had as much chance of ever affording a dinner up there as he did of farting fog.

He belonged downstairs. Mercenaries, bounty hunters, and smugglers came here to conduct business with Will October as host and negotiator. Some well-paid guards kept everyone in line. Get thrown out of the Go Further & Get Lost, and you never came back. A person who didn't do business in here had a hard time doing business in Gorman.

Pipe smoke filled the place thick enough to limit Aden's visibility to no more than fifteen steps in any direction. Good luck finding Will in this crowd. The sun had called it quits a good hour ago, and the party was well underway. He heard much more than he saw. A group of musicians played nearby, with a man shouting out some crude lines sure to please anyone actually listening. Laughter, from a woman with a smoke-roughened voice, erupted somewhere to his left. A loud crash followed by cheers suggested a particularly rough arm-wrestling contest somewhere on the far side of the inn. All that and the buzz of too many conversations.

The smell of food cooking and the heat of the fire led him to the bar, which ran in a half circle along the left wall. A pair of cooks, each a tall man with thick arms, held a pair of wooden sticks and used them to shred and stir the meat and vegetables cooking upon a round metal grill the diameter of a man's height. His stomach ached as he watched the closer of the two cooks toss some strips of lamb onto the heated metal. The smell of the seared meat and spices sprinkled upon it distracted him from his purpose. A tendress, looking as sweaty and dirty as the cooks, blocked his view of the meat and brought him back to his purpose.

She strained her neck to look up at him. "What do you want?"

"Looking for Will," he said.

"Check the dart boards."

Aden worked his way back through the crowd. He ran into half a dozen people before spotting the audience clustered about the dart boards. A hand brushed against him near his purse. Aden grabbed the short thief by the shirt and shoved him away. Damn pickpockets. Not that he had anything for the bastard to steal. He felt for the purse just to be safe. Thank the gods. Last thing he needed was to lose that damn piercing after all he'd been through to get it. He'd need the money to search for his shakta.

He reached the outer edge of the spectators at the dartboards. Will always put on a good show, and everyone who spent any time in the Get Lost knew it. Most of the onlookers were women. No shock there. Will stood in the center of the clearing. Not the tallest man, but Will's height must have been the only average thing about him. Black hair, cut short with just enough down in his face to give him a boyish charm offset with a well-trimmed beard. He dressed with a taste for the expensive but never gaudy. The garnet shirt might appear plain from a distance, but a closer look revealed a textured design that hinted at the work of an expert tailor.

Two young women in front of Aden whispered to each other, their attention focused all on Will. "I'm telling you," one whispered to the other, "that man's legs are the finest sin in the East and West."

Will was a dog, self-admitted, and women loved him all the more for it.

"I need a volunteer." Will raised his voice to ensure all of his audience might share in his play. Those brown eyes groped the crowd, pausing for the barest hint of recognition as they spotted Aden. "You, my lady." He snagged one of the young women in front of Aden by her hand and pulled her to him. Leave it to Will to find the prettiest thing among the throng. A wonder he picked one in pants and not a skirt.

"Just stand here," Will said as he turned her until her back faced the wall with the three square targets. Darts, one group blue and another red, littered the boards and suggested Will faced a challenge tonight. Aden wondered who that might be, but the opponent was hidden among the crowd for now.

"Now," Will's voice thundered with wicked merriment, "just spread your legs, and I promise this won't hurt a bit." With a flourish worthy of a dancer, he placed his red dart in his mouth. He turned around, bent over, and flipped up onto his hands. His feet reached for the ceiling as he walked on his hands until he faced his volunteer. He slipped his calves about the lady's neck and pulled her close as if to hug her with his legs. Using her for support, he lifted his right hand up to remove the dart from his mouth.

"This isn't your first time, is it?" Will flashed that demon's smile, making the crowd laugh again. "Just don't tell me your name. It's better that way in the morning."

If he took himself seriously, people would hate him, but one look told you he was laughing at himself as much as anyone else.

Will aimed between his volunteer's legs, and those gathered about hushed.

The dart shot through the lady's legs and stabbed into the center of the middle target. Cheers erupted with cries of "Yes!" from those who had gambled wisely and groans from those who had not. The other woman still in front of Aden shouted, "Me next!"

Will flipped back onto his feet. He spun around once in celebration, then took his volunteer's hand into his, bringing it slowly to his lips. Where as a gentleman might kiss a woman on the back of the hand, Will suggestively kissed her palm. The women went quiet as the lucky lady's face flushed. Aden noticed the men shaking their heads, likely sharing the same thought as him, *How does the dog do it?*

"My lady," Will said, his eyes never leaving hers as he let her hand linger close to his lips, "my thanks." He surrendered his assistant back to the crowd and bathed in the applause.

"Very well, Will," a woman said, managing to be heard above the adulation, "my turn."

She looked no less beautiful than the first lady, but where the one had been soft, this one was polished stone wrapped in reddish-brown, leather armor.

That armor wasn't just for looks. Not only was it practical, offering the required protection, but it still showed off her figure, suggesting it was custom-made. Hints of damage, where a dagger or sword had kissed the leather, left little doubt she'd seen her share of fights.

Just as Will had stolen the eyes of the women, this lady held every man and some of the women in thrall. She walked over to Will and slid her arms about his neck like a comfortable lover moving in for a kiss.

"Don't move." She flicked a wing of her blue dart across Will's lower lip. Aden found himself so caught up in the woman that he only realized in hindsight that the one man not bewitched by her was Will himself who just smiled and enjoyed his continued place within the center of attention, even if he had to share it.

The woman turned Will until her back was to the boards. Then she wrapped her legs about his waist and leaned backwards. She hung there, upside down, her long blonde hair teasing the floor. Aden watched her legs, though. That red leather was wonderfully tight, enough to let him see her legs quiver as her muscles strained to keep her body still.

"Now, I know this isn't your first time." Her quip got plenty of laughs, including Will's. Her comedy cost her, though. Her dart shot across the room as Will laughed, and the dart embedded itself just left of center.

The crowd still cheered. The woman was good—damn good. Aden wanted to know who she was, but one look told him enough. He had nothing to offer a woman like that. He'd learn her name, if nothing else. *Learn that and be satisfied,* he told himself, knowing full well it wouldn't be enough.

She scowled at Will once she was back on her feet. "You moved."

"Sorry, I've just never met a woman who actually wanted me to stay still while I was between her legs." He held out his hand, and she stared at it. With a sigh, she dropped five gold coins into his palm. Damn! She could afford to gamble away five golds! She had to be something more than a simple mercenary to have that kind of money.

She disappeared among the onlookers as she walked away. Money exchanged hands and people dispersed. A few ladies lingered long enough for Will to kiss their palms, but for once, he appeared more interested in business.

Will stopped in front of Aden and looked him down and up. "You've either gotten taller or thinner."

"Thinner," Aden said.

"Let's get you a drink."

"You just got paid five golds to have that woman wrap her legs around you. You can buy me dinner, too."

Will grinned. "Just remember, no meal is ever free."

"I'll pay you back." Aden meant it, but he knew he'd never be able to keep the promise.

Will glared at the mug sitting in front of Aden at their table.

"I offer you a free drink, and you order ale," he said. "Only thing costs less is the water."

"The ale's safer than the water in this city," Aden said.

"That's not the point."

Aden chewed a piece of lamb and swallowed. A little too seasoned for his tastes, but he wasn't about to complain. "You'd rather I ordered something more expensive?"

Will picked up his wine glass and tapped the rim, producing a chime discernible even amid the buzz of conversations.

"Wine." Will spoke the word with an uncharacteristic crispness. "I sell the finest wine in the East, and you order the ale."

Something had Will on edge. The way he acted, one would think he was the one at this table who'd lost a piece of their soul to a monster in the desert. Aden had never seen Will like this.

"I like ale." Aden shrugged.

"Ale tastes like piss." Will slammed the flat of his hand on the table. "You hear me? It's not only piss. It's bloody bad piss! You want to save money? Don't even buy the ale. Just take a mug and piss in it."

"All those women whose hands you go around kissing," Aden said as he set down his lamb, "do they realize you know what piss tastes like?"

Will glared at Aden as he tapped his left temple with a long finger. "Drink your damn ale."

"Thank you." Aden lifted the mug as if to make a toast but then resumed his attack on his lamb.

After much food, ale, and wine, the conversation turned to business as Aden knew it would. Will's mood improved with the change in conversation, and he left both of them laughing with his misadventures, all the funnier for being true. A life like Will's required no embellishment. Aden returned the favor, and until he filtered the past few days through his healthy buzz of ale, he'd not realized just how humorous they'd been. Will had doubled over laughing as Aden told him about digging up Orin's body.

"The inn looks like it's doing well," Aden said as their laughter calmed. Sobriety and the early hints of a morning hangover had worked their way into his skull.

Will picked up a cigar that one of his servers had delivered. "Expectations for war tend to help my business."

"War?"

Will nodded and leaned forward to light his cigar on the table's candle. The tip of it glowed brightly as the tobacco burned. A stream of smoke flowed from his lips with a sigh of satisfaction. He didn't lean back, instead he lowered his voice. "The Astesian emperor was assassinated two nights ago." He paused, and Aden got the impression Will was measuring his reaction. His friend's smile suggested he was relieved by what he saw. "I didn't think you'd heard."

Aden leaned forward and lowered his voice, mimicking his friend's discretion. "Who's taking the blame?"

"Last I heard? You are."

6
Framed

Aden wanted to throw up.

Will made a reputation as many things, a prankster among them, but as a source of reliable information, he had few peers. The hard look in Will's eyes as they studied Aden's reaction confirmed his latter nature was speaking.

"No one has named you as the assassin," Will said, "yet."

"Then how—?"

Will stared at him through the haze of his cigar's smoke. "Sure you want to know?"

Aden nearly cursed him for asking a ridiculous question, bu this "yes" froze against the back of his throat as he tried to make sense of this. *The ignorant make the best victims,* his old mentor's voice chastised him.

"Tell me what you know," Aden said.

"Those boys took your—*sword*—didn't they?"

The certainty in Will's statement slapped him into silence. Will smiled. How long had he known about Aden's ties to the Order? A denial meant nothing now, not with the look of shock he'd failed to hide. He couldn't manage a word, only a nod.

"Well, whoever took your weapon killed the emperor with it."

"That's not possible!" Aden said, the last word turned into a hiss by his whisper. No one could use his shakta except for him.

"I'm no mage," Will said, "but nothing kills a man quite like a shakta. Your weapon was found in the castle. An obvious plant, but an excuse an emperor's successor won't hesitate to use to secure a claim."

"Secure his claim?"

"Actually, probably 'her.' Most of the contenders are women. The Council of Elders will certainly favor one who delivers an assassin's head on a plate."

Aden felt his head spinning again but not in the pleasant way the ale had managed. Thoughts were alighting through his head faster than he could track them. Most absurd of all was to wonder how he'd ever reach Salendar to collect his six hundred silvers.

"I don't understand," Aden said. "How could they trace that shakta to me? It's not as if I have my name writ on it."

The look Will gave him reminded him of the healer in Crestnal, that expression that begged to know how such a fool had lived so long.

"I've known you were on the run from the Order since I first met you. For all your faults, you make a good hunter, but if I've seen through you, then others have, too."

"If I'm so obvious, then why hasn't the Order caught up to me?"

Will's smile, that damned smile, said it all. The bastards wanted him loose.

"They're framing me." That thrust the last dagger in his back, one of many that had led him to leave the Order in the first place.

"Perhaps," Will paused to release another plume of cigar smoke into the air between them, "or perhaps someone else has been looking after you. Mayhap they've guarded you from your hunters to let you take the fall for this?" He shrugged as if to say the theory was as good as any other.

Aden wondered if that was even possible. "That's three years of covering my back."

Will nodded. "Bad sign if that's the case. Means the one to blame is patient. If they're making their move now, then they're certain you're already wearing the noose."

Aden looked about the inn, still packed solid with the night more than half gone. Any of these people might be watching him. How the Dark could he figure out which one?

"A lot of this doesn't make sense. What about that wraith?"

"Did you see it?" Will pointed the ash end of his cigar at him as if he meant to burn his point into him.

Aden shook his head. "Saw the wounds, though."

"Five days after the fact." Will shrugged. "What was that pinhead you were chasing after doing in Crestnal anyway?"

"Business." Aden's turn to shrug, because he knew little more than that.

"In Crestnal?"

"What I was told."

Will puffed out a ring of smoke, then flashed another of those smiles. "And who told you that?"

My neck is in a noose, and this piece of courser shit is still putting on a show. Aden shook his head but kept his thought to himself. "Found out from one of your stable boys. Orin was bragging about the money he was going to make from whoever he was meeting in Crestnal. Was going to make a fortune sitting on his..." The words died away as he saw Will's smile shift into a scowl. "Spirits burn. The bastard was getting paid to draw me there."

"The stable boy," Will said, "short and thin, dirty blond hair, voice as squeaky as a mouse?"

"Couldn't get out more than four words without his voice cracking," Aden said with a laugh drawn more from dread than humor. Already, he felt a stirring in his stomach, like a snake swimming in circles.

"Constables found the boy's body in an alley near here just three days ago. Constables said a thief killed him. No witnesses."

"Gods."

Will nodded his agreement. He retreated behind the grey smoke of his cigar as he contemplated that. "The people who set you up are covering their tracks. Orin, the two who stabbed you, my stable boy."

Every muscle in Aden's gut clenched, and he suddenly realized this was more than a case of nerves. He groaned and tried to stand, a desire to run taking hold as fear overpowered all thought. His world tilted, and his hands latched onto the table for support.

"Aden!"

He looked up at Will. "Oh... gods." His tilted world lurched in the other direction, and he altered his footing to compensate. His senses had betrayed him, though, and his misstep dropped him to the floor. His right side lost all feeling, as if dead weight welded onto the rest of him. His stomach heaved. Will, his smile gone, rushed to his side and cried out something Aden couldn't understand. Aden's mind fell into blackness as it had a week ago, and he wondered if this time he would ever wake.

7

Poisoned

Nothing told a person they were alive better than pain. At least, Aden prayed he was alive, because if the pressure pounding in his head indicated what eternity would be like, then he hoped for an after-afterlife.

"Told you." Will laughed. "Even demons won't take that one."

Aden opened his eyes and groaned. What little light there was in the room made his head hurt worse and prevented his eyes from focusing. He couldn't decide if something was pushing against the inside or outside of his skull. Maybe both.

"Think I drank too much ale," Aden said. "Next time, I'll go with the wine."

Aden needed a moment to realize he was in a bed and stripped of his clot hes... again. Just once he'd like to have this happen and find an equally naked woman next to him.

"Sit up," a stranger said as he came over to the left side of the bed. He looked twice as old as Will and Aden combined. The old fellow moved spry enough, though. He picked up a mug from the nightstand next to the bed and thrust it towards Aden. "I said to sit up."

"I'm working on it." Aden winced at his own words, each syllable pounding into his skull. "Feel like my head might falloff."

He took the mug and sipped it. "Death and daggers!" Aden said. "What is that?"

"Tea, y'jackass," the stranger said. "Wouldn't hurt you to drink it more often by the looks of you." A healer, Aden decided. Had to be. Will must have sent for the man after he passed out. Knowing Will, he'd sent for this reed-thin stick of wrinkles second. Probably called a lady healer first and had her sleeping quite satisfied in his own bed.

"I am not drinking that," Aden said. The tea had a familiar burn to it that had nothing to do with it being hot."

"You'll drink it if I have to shove it down your throat through your nose," the healer said.

Aden wondered how that worked but decided it best not to ask and drank. "The ginger in it will settle your gut." That explained the burn to the tea.

The pain pushing in and out of Aden's skull lessened the longer he remained upright but only a little. He rubbed his forehead as if to squeeze the pain out of his ears.

"Usually handle my drink better than this," he said.

"Idiot," the healer said, "don't you know the difference between a damn hangover and..."

"Mateen," Will said, cutting off the healer, "will he be all right?"

"Yeah, just make sure he sticks with tea for the next few days. Should flush him out."

"Thank you. You have a good night."

"Night? It's bloody morning, y'damn boy." Mateen snatched a leather bag off the nightstand. "Debt's paid. Y'hear me? Paid." With that, he stormed out.

Aden realized he must be in one of the rooms of Will's inn. Hell of a way to get a private space.

"Never met a less pleasant healer," Aden said, thinking more fondly than ever of Miriam.

"Mateen doesn't like to work for free," Will said. "I know few men worse with a set of cards in his hands. He ends up owing me every few months."

Aden's forehead throbbed again. "He might be right about the tea. Never had a hangover this bad."

"That's no hangover." Will lit up a half-used cigar. Might have been the same he'd started during their meal. "You were poisoned."

"Poisoned?"

"Mateen says you were." Will blew out a stream of smoke. "And that's good enough for me."

"Something in the ale?"

Will shook his head. "Probably a few days ago. Said you must still have it in your body, that the ale aggravated it."

"That means it happened in Crestnal."

"Sounds like a good place to start," Will said. "Get some rest. We'll leave tomorrow morning."

"Thanks, but I won't need the help. You've got your own problems."

Will sucked on that ugly cigar and let the smoke filter out of his smile like a lazy fire. "I've my own reasons for going." Aden didn't waste his time asking what those reasons were. Even if he answered, Will never tipped his hand, and whenever he did, Aden always felt as if the cards changed the instant he hid them again.

8

Bad Medicine

A troubled mind kept Aden from more sleep. He sat in the bed and puzzled over what he knew. Ambushed and left for dead, poisoned, and framed for an assassination.

"And I know less than a deaf confessor."

Will meant to dive into the thick of it. How did he know so much about all of this? He'd known the man for three years, but he knew little more about him than anyone else. Will disarmed people with his smile and wit. Only a fool took Will at face value.

Poisoned. Will said it wasn't in the ale, but as he thought back to the conversation with the healer, Aden realized the healer had never actually he'd been poisoned. He'd hurried out with his tale between his legs and a purse no longer in danger of losing weight. Will hadn't let him talk about the poison at all.

He needed answers he could trust, and he wasn't going to find them sitting in a damn bed.

Aden dressed and was relieved to find all of his weapons, what was left of them, with the rest of his belongings. He wondered what he would say if Will saw him leaving the inn, but he knew from past visits to the Get Lost that its owner slept away his mornings to stay sharper at night.

He stepped out into the hallway and walked to the main room of the inn. Less than a dozen people were left here, two of whom were passed out at their table. Inns tolerated a lot so long as the customers paid their tabs. A woman behind the bar was cleaning off the bar top. This lady looked older than the one from last night.

She looked him up and down. "You're a tall one." Hard wrinkles pinched the corners of her eyes and lips, suggesting a life that had overindulged in smoke and drink.

"What can I get you?" she asked.

"Looking for a healer, the old fellow that was here earlier," Aden said. "Name was Mateen."

"Mateen? A healer?" The lady laughed. "I suppose he does well enough to be called that."

Aden wondered what that was supposed to mean. "Where do I find him?"

"He works at the Third Guard Wall."

"The Third Guard Wall?" Aden said. "Is he a constable or a healer?"

"Oh, he's definitely not a constable. Just go there. You'll find him," she said. "Anything else I can do for you?" Those old eyes were marking Aden with obvious designs, so he didn't linger.

He expected sunnier skies to greet him outside the Get Lost, but the day was all heavy clouds and no rain. He found the Third Guard Wall with little trouble, running into only one dead end along the way. Still made for quite a walk, and by the time he saw where the building's walls met the street, his exhaustion made him wish he'd stayed in bed.

A pair of constables who looked much fresher than Aden marched past him. They were probably starting their rounds. Each wore an orange scarf about the neck. The image of a black sun was stitched into the visible corners of the scarves. These men enforced the law in Gorman. A city this big required a lot of constables, and they used more than one building to house their men. The constables in this part of the city used the remains of an old gatehouse.

Aden noticed the ground was smooth as he passed through the gate. He shifted his gaze up at the spear-like points of the raised portcullis above him. A long time since they'd bothered to lower the gate, given the lack of holes in the ground. He wondered what condition it might be in and couldn't help but think the bloody thing would choose the moment he was beneath it to drop and kill him. More like a mercy killing at this point, he thought. His head ached less than it had, but the pain remained like a bad memory that refuses to fade.

"I'm looking for Mateen," Aden said to another passing constable. He thought this one rather short, but as tall as he was, he made a poor judge of stature or rather the lack thereof.

"Over in the stables." The constable pointed to the right, then walked out the gate. Aden watched him leave and wondered how a man that short managed to intimidate anyone enough to enforce those damn Astesian laws.

The Third Guard Wall stood like a timeline. He could read the age of each structure of stone and wood. Unlike the wall with the gate he'd just gone through, the other walls looked much younger and stood half as tall, maybe fifteen feet. A cage more fit for animals than men took up the left end of the courtyard. A single-story building reminded Aden more of a small house. He half-expected a little boy and girl to run out the front door with a pet lizard nipping at their heels. The tiled roof suggested it was built here before anyone thought to reuse the gate and its tower for the city's constables.

The stables appeared a much more recent addition and a hasty one. The timber used on the right half of the stables had a darker stain than the wood on the left. Gorman always reused what it had. All that wood might have belonged to condemned buildings or even a row of outhouses. Could easily be both or m ore.

A courser rushed out of the stable's open doors. Sharp paws dug into the dirt, shooting a brown cloud into the air to mark its path.

"Come back here, dammit!" Mateen yelled from inside the stables.

Aden whistled after the courser, and the lithe creature curled around to a stop near the center of the courtyard. Its grey ears perked up like tiny hands reaching for the heavens. The large catlike head canted as those yellow eyes, with their slit pupils, narrowed on him. What grabbed Aden's attention was the lack of a harness. Without that harness, the bloody thing might attack him or anyone in its path.

He steadied his nerves, no small task after last night. His stomach still felt weak, and none the better for the flutter he felt as the courser ran its tongue across its teeth. Giant muscles tensed beneath the large cat's grey, leathery skin.

The courser charged him. Aden reached into his jacket for his shakta and cursed when he realized it wasn't there.

Too late to do anything else, Aden winced in anticipation of the courser's bite. He shut his eyes as the courser's landing stirred up a large cloud of dust. He expected fangs and claws to tear into him. Instead, he felt a heavy, gentle push against his stomach. He peeked open one of his eyes to see the large cat's head nudge against him. A deep purr rumbled from its throat. The purr grew louder as Aden reached down to scratch behind the courser's ears.

"I'll be damned," a young voice whispered from the stables, one of four boys standing in the doorway with Mateen.

The old gambler looked less impressed than the boys." Just one damn animal saying hello to another."

Aden tried to channel Will with the most confident smile he could manage. Maybe he could bluff Mateen into thinking he had control of the cat.

"Apparently, it doesn't like you as much as me, Mateen."

"You want to impress everyone, then let's see you get that thing back into a harness and in its stall." He then scowled at the tallest of the four boys. "Get the harness. Imagine it's where you dropped it."

"Thought you were a healer," Aden said.

"Ain't no healer, y'idiot." Mateen took a few steps closer, but kept a safe distance. "Just know when a man's fucked."

"So why'd Will call you?"

Mateen laughed. "Son of a bitch calls me, because I don't cost him anything. Think he stacks the cards against me just to keep me in debt."

Aden didn't think Will needed to go to the trouble. A gambling man's constant desperation eroded a body, and Mateen wore the look like a tailored shirt.

"So you know anything about healing, or do you just kick a downed man until he gets up?"

"Just get the courser inside."

"Not yet," Aden said over the courser's purr as he continued to scratch behind its ears. He hoped he didn't tickle the wrong spot and tick off this giant cat. "I've got questions, and unless you want to chase this courser around the city, you're going to give me answers."

Mateen crossed his arms and rested his weight on his left leg, the gambler weighing the odds. "What do you want to know?"

"You actually a healer?"

"No, but I know enough. Come from a long line of debtors. Helped my mom patch up my dad and granpy."

That might account for a bruise or broken arm, Aden decided. "So how do you know anything about poisons?"

Mateen smiled, and Aden didn't like the looks of it. "Poison's just another word for bad medicine. Course, that just depends on how you use it."

"Get to the point or I stop petting the cat. Do you know anything about poisons, or was that stuff you told Will a load of shit?"

"No, you were poisoned all right. Y'see, my mom was a healer, so I learned a thing or two from her." He lowered his voice. "Also learned how to use some of that bad medicine to settle some debts, if you take my meaning."

"You poisoned the people you owed money to?" This was the kind of man Will called on to heal him.

"No, y'jackass." Mateen looked ready to strike Aden but then glanced at the cat and had second thoughts. "Keep your damn voice down. Have y'no clue where we are? More than a half dozen constables in earshot and you go mouthing off like a damn herald. I just sell bad medicine. My mom told me all the things they can do. I sell the information and the medicine. What they do with it then ain't any of my damn business."

"That's why Will called you," Aden said, "because he suspected I was poisoned."

"Of course. Might not be the healthiest fool I've seen, but a man like you doesn't just fall over. Even that arse Will October knows better'n that."

Aden looked past Mateen, wondering where the fool stable hand was with that harness. He kept telling himself not to scream each time the courser shifted against his legs. "So what was I poisoned with?"

"How much you gonna pay for it?"

That brought Aden's attention back to Mateen with a glare. The reminder of how empty his purse was had lit his temper. "You want this courser loose again?"

"Jackass," Mateen said. "Fine. Could be a few things. Fellan and scarrus will both fuck your gullet for days. Gotta take those in small doses, though. Too much, too fast will kill a man."

"No."

"Drink anything that tastes like maron fruit? Most folks slip that in your drink. Makes your shit thin as water, too. Got a man old and sick enough, that alone'll kill him"

"No."

"Suppose there's schist, but you usually got to get that into a person while they're asleep."

"Asleep? Why?"

"Well, you coat the roof of the mouth with it. Y'inhale the fumes until it wears off. Do that, person will stay out for days. Can't kill a person, though, not even to starve to death. Body gets hungry enough, it'll force 'em to wake up sooner than most."

The more Mateen described that particular "bad medicine," the more Aden felt as if someone had danced upon his ashes. "This schist, what does it taste like?"

"Nasty. Don't want to use it on someone who knows about it, because there ain't no hiding it. Soon as they wake up, they'll know. Kind of like a cross between mint and piss."

Aden wondered how all these people knew what piss tasted like. If this was some bizarre rite of manhood he'd missed, he didn't plan to correct the oversight.

"Hard to get, though."

"How hard?"

"Only place the stuff grows is Salendar, and who wants to go there? Some of their priests use it to hibernate through winter like bears. There are merchants from there who'll sell it to you, but they'll make you pay enough to build a mansion."

How Aden kept his eyes from falling out of their sockets, he hadn't a clue. The merchant had been in on it! Aden had been set up from the start.

By the time the stable hands secured the harness to the courser, the sun had dropped low enough to touch the top of the city's outermost wall. Aden wanted to drink himself into oblivion, and from what Mateen said, getting drunk during the next few days might kill him if he wasn't careful. Will hadn't sent for a healer, though. That troubled him. Had Will just made a good guess, or did he know more than he was sharing? He couldn't shake the feeling the latter was more likely.

The street crowded in around him as he walked back to the Get Lost. Hundreds of Gorman's honest workers closed the doors to their daylight duties and headed for the taverns or home. Bodies brushed against him. He placed a hand over his purse, just in case.

He was replaying the past week through his mind when he recognized, too late, the hiss of air from a crossbow's bolt. He spun around when he heard the repulsive "thunk" of metal burying into someone behind him. The victim, a large man not more than two steps behind him, dropped to his knees. The bolt stuck out of the left side of his head. The stranger glared at Aden as if he had shot the bolt himself, then his eyes glazed over, already a corpse by the time he fell flat upon the ground. Others cried out, running for anyplace other than this stretch of street. Aden stood there just long enough to see an assassin's dagger gripped within the dead stranger's left hand.

Aden spotted two more hooded figures running against the tide straight towards him. The faces beneath their dark green hoods wore black masks he knew all too well.

The Order of the Hunt had found him.

9
Hunters

Aden pivoted to take in his surroundings and then ran for the nearest open door. He found himself in a forest of hanging rugs. A half dozen pairs of eyes looked up from their looms as he ran past them.

The weavers shouted protests he recognized more from their tone than the words themselves. The shouts increased as the two hunters dashed in after him.

He found the stairs in the back and ran up them. The wall shattered behind him. These hunters were using their shaktas! He didn't turn to see the strands of life, fueled by the power of their souls as they burrowed through wood and brick. If he'd been a second slower, the damn things would have split open his right thigh.

A shakta contained three strands of the wielder's spirit, and a trained hunter could unleash those strands to take a variety of shapes to defend or destroy. He felt the vibrations of just how close each of those strands were. If Aden could have spared a moment, he might have been able to see the formation of the attack and gauge just how skilled these hunters were with their shaktas.

His mentor's voice demanded he pace himself. Everything else in him screamed to run as if a dar'jiat wraith was about to bite his arse.

He reached the upstairs and thought his chest might explode. That damn poison had corrupted his body's strength. He couldn't outrun these bastards. He needed to stand and fight, but without his shakta, he didn't stand a chance.

He sprinted down the hallway, buying a few seconds beyond the view of the two hunters. He ran through an open door, slammed it shut and then pulled it open a few inches. The door slam might confuse them, make them more likely to check the rooms with closed doors first and give him more time to think of a way out of this mess.

A bed barely large enough for one body filled most of the narrow space in this room. The mattress was thinner than some blankets. Whichever rug weaver downstairs called this home, he needed a bigger window. The shutters were open, but Aden knew he couldn't squeeze out of that small space.

The heavy footfalls of the hunters stopped. They'd made it upstairs. Aden pulled out a dagger, a piss poor defense against two shaktas, but what choice did he have?

He planted himself as far against the wall as he could manage so that the partially open door would conceal him. He adjusted his grip on his dagger and waited. Now he wished the bastards would hurry. If they searched separately, he might stand a chance, but if they stayed together... Best not to think about it.

The creak of the floor warned him one of the hunters was close, but he couldn't decide if he had one or both outside the room. A light tap of wood on wood let him know the fool was pushing open the door with his shakta instead of his hand. The smooth, rounded tip came into view.

Aden grabbed for the shakta and threw all his weight against the door. He prayed this worked. If not, the shakta might take off his hand like a hundred arrows striking a target at once.

He jerked the hunter's hand into the room and slammed the door against his wrist. Bones crunched, and the hunter screamed. The shakta pulled free. Aden tossed it out the window. The hunter's hand dangled, reminding Aden of a tree branch too alive to break off but just as useless.

Aden threw open the door and charged the hunter with his dagger in hand. The hunter's brown eyes widened at the sight of dagger, but Aden didn't plan to cut him. He pushed the hunter against the far wall. His forearm crushed the hunter's windpipe. A gasp assured Aden he'd struck his target.

The other hunter ran into the hallway from a room at the far end. Aden threw the wounded hunter towards his partner. Nice if they collided, but not likely. The wounded hunter still made a useful barrier against the other man's shakta.

Aden darted down the stairs, taking four steps at a time. His lungs ached, and his muscles, stiff from his initial run upstairs, refused to comply. He thought a muscle in his left thigh might pull, but by the time he made it back downstairs, his muscles had loosened.

A weaver shouted at him in his foreign tongue. The angry wave of his arms made it clear what he was saying was for Aden to leave. He gladly complied. The injured hunter would keep the other from chasing Aden. *You never abandon your own,* his old mentor told him. He just hoped the uninjured hunter adhered to that dictum better than Aden ever had. If nothing else, they wouldn't leave the shakta he'd tossed out of the window sitting on the street for anyone to find. Aden wished he could recover his own shakta half as easily.

The same crowd that fled from the crossbow attack had returned to gather about the body of Aden's would-be-killer. He wanted another look at the body, but too many people surrounded the dead man. Best to run until he'd gotten far enough to know he wasn't being chased. He went straight for the Get Lost or as close to straight as one could manage in the maze of Gorman.

Daylight had vanished. A haphazard smattering of streetlamps, the ones not doused by the city's busy thieves, offered little light to guide him. He made enough wrong turns to reach Will's tavern well after the nightly party had begun. If he'd had the strength, he'd have mounted his courser and left Gorman to memory. Instead, he found his room and collapsed into the bed. Damn that poison. He could barely catch his breath. Just a little sleep, he promised himself, then he would leave. Even he didn't believe that, but that didn't stop him from closing his eyes. The last thought that went through his mind was of the man with the dagger. That man didn't belong to the Order. Aden wanted to know why that stranger wanted him dead and who killed him to save Aden's hide.

10
Return to Crestnal

The next morning started little better than the previous night ended. A rough kick to his bed sent Aden bolt upright. The booted foot belonged to Will's left leg.

"Gods!" Aden said. "What was that for?" Awake less than a minute, and his mood had already soured. Startled as he was, he'd reached into his jacket for his shakta which still wasn't there.

"Seems you've overstayed your welcome," Will said with that gift for sarcasm that made everyone want to smile with him even when they were the butt of his joke, not that Aden was smiling.

"Yeah, I got that impression."

"Word has it you nearly got a dagger in your back. Your name hit the streets yesterday afternoon along with a healthy reward to bring you in very unhealthy."

More good news. "A pair of hunters tried to get me, too."

"The Order of the Hunt?"

Aden was surprised Will hadn't heard about that, but then the Order made a habit of covering their tracks well. He would know.

Will had some coffee and breakfast delivered to the room as Aden recounted what happened for Will's benefit.

"Would appear your unseen guardian does exist," Will said. "And a good shot with a crossbow, too."

"But why protect me now?" Aden asked. "They've framed me and put a bounty on my head. Why not just kill me and be done with it?"

"The person protecting you is working with his own agenda. A lot of people want to be the new emperor. Some might see you more valuable alive."

"Lucky me."

A knock came from the door. Aden reached for his dagger on the first try this time, instead of going for his absent shakta.

Will held up a hand for Aden to stand down. "He's one of mine." He pulled the door open and waved a young boy into the room. Aden recognized the boy as one of Will's stable hands. He held a lantern that only added to the tired look on his face. Aden wondered how Will had known who was at the door. Just another of the many mysteries about him.

"Coursers are ready, sayer," the boy said, using the local title of respect for a man.

"Thank you," Will said. "We'll be leaving in just a moment."

The door closed, shutting away the light of the boy's lantern.

"What time is it?"

"Not even sunrise yet," Will said. "Best we get you out of here before then."

"You're still coming?" Aden meant for the question to sound more conversational, but the suspicion he felt betrayed itself.

"As I told you before, I have my own reasons." Will spread his lips in one of his disarming smiles. Aden found it less than reassuring in this case. Knowing Will, Aden's suspicion probably flattered him.

"You ever been to Crestnal?" Aden asked.

"Always a first time," Will said with a sly purr to his words. "Hoping I might buy this lady healer of yours a drink while we're there."

Cloudless skies accompanied Will and Aden as they rode their coursers back east to Crestnal. More than once, Aden brought up the topic that brought them out here, but Will waved off each attempt at serious discussion.

"Tell me about this woman," he said with a wicked merriment. "Spare no details. Just how pretty was she?"

"Too motherly for your tastes, I think," Aden said.

"That kind is sometimes the best. Sure, they'll look down their nose at you, but treat them with the proper respect and well..." Will laughed. "Best of all, they want nothing to do with you later. All the fun with none of the obligation."

Aden considered debating Will's opinions of women, but then he thought better of it. Women just acted differently with Will.

"So, you still haven't answered my question," Will said. "How pretty was she?"

"Dress her up, and she could pass for nobility. Had that regal, I'm-better-than-you air. Still liked her, though."

"And just how old was she?" Will asked. Aden got the impression that was somehow important to his rather venal friend.

"Not sure," Aden said. "Never asked."

"Wiser not to," Will said. "If you had to guess?"

"Somewhere shy of four decades."

Will grunted. By now, he'd pulled out a dark blue blanket from his pack and rolled it out. He was lying on the blanket and staring up at the stars as if to contemplate which one was brightest.

The servants at the inn had packed them food and what some would consider necessities. Having been tight on money for so long, Aden's definition of a necessity had changed a great deal during the past three years. They'd packed more than enough food to make the trip from Gorman to Crestnal and back several times. Another sign Will had planned for more than flirting with Aden's one-time healer. That was fine, because Aden had plans for her, too.

The town of Crestnal looked much as Aden remembered it. Houses painted in white and illuminated by the orange-red rays of the setting sun lined both sides of the street. People moved about as they had before, most heading to their homes, others to taverns... daily lives that never changed.

One thing differed, and the sight of it chilled Aden's blood.

"Burned down the night after you left," Dellem said. The old constable had been walking back into town from the opposite direction when Aden and Will arrived. Their separate paths converged in front of Miriam's house. Only black timber remained.

"Looks like it started by the stove," Aden said.

Blackened support beams, those that remained, leaned inward as if that spot had sucked in the entire house.

"Whoever set it wanted it to look like an accident, make us think she'd gotten careless with her stove." The edge to Dellem's voice added a few years to his appearance.

"What makes you sure it wasn't an accident?" Will asked.

"Fire doesn't spread like that." Dellem pointed to a trail of heavy burn marks that led over to where the breakfast table had been. "Probably used something like wine to give the fire a path to travel across the floor. Fire goes upward, not outward."

Will walked through the skeleton of the house. Aden watched from where the front porch had been.

"What about Miriam?" Aden asked.

"Found her body, what was left of it." Dellem shook his head. "I ever find who set it, I'll kill him on the spot."

The vow surprised Aden, but then he recognized it for what it was. Even older men could carry a torch for a pretty lady. Probably explained the drawing Aden had seen hanging in Miriam's home. He wondered if Dellem had ever declared his feelings, but something in Dellem's demand for justice made Aden certain he never had. The missed chances always stung more than the rejections.

"What about her dog?" Aden asked.

Dellem shrugged. "Hope she got out, but nobody's seen her. Her ashes are probably in there somewhere. Only the gods know where."

"Shit," Aden said under his breath. The woman had probably poisoned him, and he wanted to know why. He considered asking Dellem what kind of woman she'd been, but he questioned what kind of opinion a man in love, or even just lust, would offer.

"How long had she lived here?" Aden asked.

"Not long," Dellem said. "Moved here about two months ago."

"Where was she from?"

Dellem shook his head as he stepped closer to the house. "No idea. Rather private woman. People usually come to a town like this to get away from something. Most have had their fill of trouble and want some quiet. The ones who haven't don't stay long. Ones who stay take a while to open up."

"Anyone ever visit her?" Will asked as he stepped out of the ashen debris.

"Not that I noticed."

Aden looked at Will and could tell he was thinking as he was. Miriam had made certain she left as little evidence of herself here as possible. Convenient, especially for whoever killed her.

"Constable!" A boy, probably no more than ten, ran flailing his arms as if his shouts weren't enough to ensure every eye on him. The child's face glowed as if a ghost possessed him.

Dellem walked to the boy, his calm manner a contrast to the boy's excitement. Another sign, Aden decided, that this man had seen his share of action during the crusades. Some of the best soldiers and hunters he'd ever met made themselves calmer when faced with the unexpected.

"What's wrong, little Castus?" Dellem asked, placing a hand on the child's shoulder.

The boy panted for breath. Despite the pale glow to his complexion, dirt covered him from head to toe and sweat had drenched the front of his shirt. He'd scraped his hands and the knees of his brown pants; he'd taken a fall or two.

"I—I was going to the Cavanagh farmhouse. Needed some money, so I was going to see if they needed me to clean their stables. I went—"

"Castus, just tell me what's wrong," Dellem said, his manner firm and gentle.

"Somebody killed all of them!"

"Are you sure?" Dellem asked, but judging by the look on his face, he trusted this boy's report.

"Yes, sayer."

"The ones who killed them?"

"Didn't see anybody else." The boy's pallid skin shifted to a greenish hue. "They look like they've been dead a while. They were all gross."

Dellem nodded. "All right. Go home. I'll head out there and take a look. You've done well."

The boy smiled, a child's hero worship for authority. In spite of his liking for Dellem, Aden felt a dagger of cynicism twist in his gut at the sight of it. He'd once felt that same admiration for the Order of the Hunt.

"I can help, if you want?" the boy said.

"No, you run home. Come by my house tomorrow, though. I'm sure I can find some work for you. That'll earn you close to two coppers, but only if you stay clear of the Cavanagh place. You understand?"

"Yes, sayer," Castus said. "Thank you, sayer."

Dellem patted him on the back just before he ran off.

"Mind if we go with you?" Will asked.

The constable regarded them, probably weighing whether it was coincidence that they'd arrived at the same time as the news of these bodies. Had he been in Dellem's place, he'd have probably said to stay put.

"You can come," he said. "Just mind what I say."

"As you wish, constable." Will sounded a little pleased with himself. "Our best behavior." Aden eyed him, wondering why he was so giddy.

11

Short One Body

They stopped by the church before leaving town. Dellem asked the priest to bring his wagon for the bodies. While the priest hooked a beast of burden to the wagon, Dellem led Aden and Will east along a dust-covered road. A full moon asserted its dominance as this day's sun, reduced to a slice on the black horizon, burned its last breath of life. Aden thought about the dar'jiat wraith, the screams from the two boys who attacked him. This road made him feel exposed.

Desert crocs warbled and growled as if to mourn the sun's death. They prowled in packs at night and killed anything in their path. Those nasty creatures, small but thickly armored, skittered across the desert floor. Their yellow eyes glowed as they eyed the three men walking past.

Dellem pointed in the direction of those yellow eyes. "They'll leave us alone on the road."

"Warded?" Will asked.

"Yeah, town pays a mage to cleanse the road every spring. Makes a small fortune off people who live outside of town to do the same for their properties." Dellem pointed to a large rectangular silhouette a hundred paces off the road to the north. "That's the Cavanagh house."

"Not a single lamp lit," Aden said.

Will pointed up. "At least we have a full moon."

"Won't do us any good if someone is waiting inside." Dellem gestured to the flat terrain, absent of any plants, between them and the house. If anyone waited for them inside, then they'd certainly see the three of them approach.

Aden spotted a herd of fat tabucks roaming about a fenced-in area behind the house. Their moans gave them away. Sounded hungry, suggesting quite a few days since they'd been fed.

"I'll take the back." Aden jogged ahead.

"Don't forget about that wraith." Will sounded less concerned than his warning suggested, but that did little to undo the knot of Aden's stomach.

"See you inside." Aden kept his eyes on the house, looking for any movement. Not so much as a wind shifted the curtains in the open windows. He vaulted the fence, a length of wooden beams linked by posts every five feet. The dull tabucks gave him a dirty look for entering their yard without bringing any food. A second fence separated the back of the house from the tabucks. A small barn occupied the northeastern corner of the property. He considered searching the barn, but decided to stay with the house.

The back door sat open. Nothing suggested anyone had forced their way inside, not from the back. Aden remembered Dellem's philosophy about simple laws for simple towns, and suspected these people never bothered to lock their doors. Odds favored a tabuck might stumble into the house long before anyone broke in. *Didn't work out that way, though, did it?* Aden thought. Odds also favored whoever did this was long gone, but he wouldn't take any chances.

Aden paused outside the door that led into the kitchen. The house had a dirt floor. The walls were bowed with age. A stove similar to the one he'd seen in Miriam's home was placed in the corner, its insides cold.

Flies buzzed from within the kitchen. Their chorus, a sickening hum from deeper within the house, gave him all the warning he needed that Little Castus' description of "gross" would do little justice to what they found.

He pulled out his dagger and entered. The stench suffocated him as he crossed the threshold. You couldn't hide a body in a house, not unless it had been long dead and even that wasn't a guarantee. These kills were too fresh, and to Aden's nose, not fresh enough. He found what was left of a grown man in the main room of the house, most of his rib cage chewed open. Chunks of bone were spit up next to the body.

Aden spotted movement to his left and relaxed as he saw it was Will and Dellem. They checked each room, finding three more bodies, more of the Cavanagh family, all children.

"Gods!" Dellem whispered. They didn't say anymore. None of them wanted to breathe any more of this air than needed. They retreated outside and didn't stop until the smell of the death faded.

A fruitless search of the barn took little time.

As they walked back to the front of the house to wait for the priest's wagon, Will lit a cigar. He offered one to Dellem and Aden. Dellem gladly accepted, but Aden refused. One lesson his old mentor hammered into him, *Keep your breath pure.*

Dellem took a few deep pulls from the cigar before he said anything. "Thought those two boys I found with you were bad."

"Looked like one wraith." Aden stared at the ground trying to avoid looking at the house. "He was there a while, fed on the bodies for a few days. At least we know where he was hiding."

"I didn't see Amella Cavanagh in there," Dellem said. "I've heard tales that those wraiths will eat a whole body, not leave a bit of evidence behind."

Will laughed. "I've heard better, but none of it's true. They don't like the bones. Might pick a body clean, but they always spit up the bones."

"Dar'jiat wraiths don't behave this way on their own. They sure as Dark don't leave the West unless someone makes them." Aden clenched his fist, frustrated by the wooden shakta that wasn't in his grip. "Someone's holding the leash."

Dellem didn't reply right away. He focused on his cigar instead.

Aden had seen that before. Mundane tasks could settle a man's nerves. This constable had seen his share of war, but he'd gone many years without it. Aden envied that. He knew no quiet towns awaited him and old age even less likely.

Dellem cleared his throat. "Only strangers been through town lately were you and that Orin Gregane fellow. Any chance the wraith took Amella Cavanagh somewhere else?"

"Whoever controls that wraith probably took her," Will said around the cigar in his teeth. "Doubt they took her alive, though."

Aden pointed towards the house he refused to see. "Know anyone in their past that would want them dead?"

"Those people have lived here for more than ten generations." Dellem shook his head. "Wouldn't half nod to a person on the street that wasn't born here."

"So why take her and leave the men?" Aden asked.

"Sure you don't want one, Aden?" Will held out an unlit cigar to him. "Hard part's about to start." He pointed to the road. Aden heard the wagon, the sound of the tabuck's hooves dropping in a steady pattern on the packed earth. The priest without the pinky finger had come to collect his gods' due.

Aden accepted Will's cigar and lit it just before they went back into the house. They all kept their cigars between their teeth as they lifted the bodies onto bed sheets and wrapped them. Foul as the smoke drifting up into their nostrils was, better that than the stench of rot they carried to the priest's wagon.

"Too late for you two to get a room at the inn. You can stay at my place."

Dellem's offer startled Aden out of his thoughts. To move those bodies, he'd "separated soul from body" as his mentor liked to call it. Sometimes, a person couldn't let themselves think about what they were doing or it wouldn't get done. He'd occupied his thoughts instead on where the wraith's master had taken that woman and why. That he couldn't remember anything between going back into the house and the priest's wagon pulling back onto the road was a blessing.

As uncomfortable as the idea of staying with a constable might be, Aden didn't see that he and Will could refuse. "Appreciate the offer, constable."

"Just call me Dellem." He waved for them to follow. "Come on. I'm not far from here."

"Got anything to drink?" Will asked.

"Brandy suit you boys?"

Aden growled, wondering how long he'd need to wait for this poison to work its way out of his body. What he wouldn't give for a mug of ale.

"You got something against brandy, son?" Dellem asked. An easy smile parted his lips.

Will laughed. "He's just pissed about his involuntary abstinence."

"His what?"

"Pour me a glass of brandy, and I'll tell you all about it," Will said. "Just make sure you brew him tea."

12
War Stories

Dellem prepared dinner and spared nothing. Aden had thought his appetite dead after their work at the Cavanagh house. The tabuck steaks Dellem grilled changed his mind. Aden didn't recognize the long, orange vegetable slices on the side, but they resembled a squash and were sweet with a spicy aftertaste.

Aden enjoyed the old constable's stories from his war days. To hear Dellem tell it, both sides of the Crusades won most of their battles on dumb luck. Men could plan a battle all they wanted, but wars rarely suffered order.

"So this captain was convinced he could lead the charge to victory. There he is, one pants leg flapping in the wind like a fart had popped it off, and he's shouting some business about 'For the *gory*, boys!' He was always getting his words wrong, especially when he got nervous. He takes off running, and just then the general's horn orders the retreat. The lieutenant gets halfway across the battlefield—"

"I thought he was a captain?" Will sounded a little sauced, as well. He'd had more brandy than Dellem.

"Captain, lieutenant, whatever." A loud burp capped off Dellem's laugh which he followed with a muttered apology before he continued. "Poor fool makes it halfway across the battlefield before he realizes nobody's with him. Flaming arrows are chasing after him like a black cloud raining brimstone. Lucky he was so skinny. They just couldn't hit him for anything. Never did either. Unfortunately, he gets halfway back, trips, and lands his arse on one of those arrows. Soon as he gets back on his feet, he realizes his loose pants leg is on fire. He takes off like a cat running from its own tail. Doesn't realize he's going the wrong way, gets past the enemy's lines and accidentally sets off their entire store of fire powder. Luckiest man I ever met."

"Lucky?" Aden laughed. "How do you figure that?"

"He took out half of the Garfidian soldiers with that explosion. The rest of them scattered like roaches caught in daylight. The general even promoted him! And believe me, she was stingy with promotions."

Will started to speak, but realized he still had his cigar in his mouth. He pulled it out and continued. "You're saying he survived that?"

Dellem raised a hand as if to swear an oath. "We found him in a farmhouse half a click away passed out in a pile of hay with his pants blown clean off. I'm not saying the blast tossed him all that way, but he also couldn't explain how he got there, so..." He shrugged.

Will and Aden almost laughed themselves out of their chairs. They spent most of the night on Dellem's front porch. Dellem owned a small house on a stretch of land just outside of the town. Nearest neighbors were beyond sight, and if they were lucky, beyond hearing, too. They traded stories and laughed like fools into the thinnest hours.

Dellem stumbled his way back into the house. He'd muttered and giggled a good night before the front door swallowed him whole. Before the brandy had its way with him, he'd thought to get some blankets for his guests.

Their laughter subsided with Dellem's departure. Aden thought Will might have fallen asleep if not for the infrequent rings of smoke he puffed into the now chilly air.

"So," Will said, his voice pulling Aden from the brink of nodding off, "have you figured it out yet?"

Aden stared at him. He felt more drunk from exhaustion than Will must have been from brandy. How could Will even think by this point?

"What are you talking about?"

"Miriam," Will said, "the healer." Aden could not have missed the sarcasm placed on the woman's vocation had he drunk as much as Will and Dellem combined. "Well?"

"I don't have a clue what you're talking about." Aden waved some of Will's cigar smoke out of his face as it drifted his direction.

"Gods, Aden... think about it." Will took another pull on his cigar, then blew out a ring of smoke. "I'll even offer you a hint. She's not dead."

"If she's not dead, then whose body do you think they pulled out of her house?" The question led his mind to the answer before Will could give it, and he saw the satisfaction on his friend's face as he recognized Aden had pieced it together.

"How long have you known?" Aden asked.

"Suspected it soon as we found the place burned down, but I knew it once we got out to the Cavanagh place and that lady's body was missing."

Aden shook his head. He hadn't wanted to believe Miriam was involved in any of this, that perhaps she'd been forced to poison him. If her death had been faked and that family slaughtered by a wraith to cover it, then little doubt remained. Was she the one controlling the wraith? He considered the woman who tended to him and compared it to the image of a cold-blooded killer. The two didn't blend well in his mind. Something was missing, something that might explain it all, but damned if he knew what.

"You haven't told Dellem," Aden glanced over his shoulder through the open front door. "Don't trust him?"

"I don't get the feeling he's involved in this, if that's what you mean," Will said.

Aden knew exactly what Will meant, and he nodded his agreement. "He's carrying a torch for the healer."

Will laughed. "If that woman's a healer, then I'm the bastard son of a king." He didn't say anything more after that, not for a while, at least. Aden had nearly dozed off again by the time Will continued with his thoughts. "I like Dellem, and mark my words, the man plans to go with us. He wants the dogs who 'killed' this Miriam. Problem is when he finds out she's not dead." Will pointed at Aden with the ash end of his cigar. "Which side will he take then?"

"Let's hope his blood's going to the right head when the moment counts," Aden said.

Will stared at him, blinked, and then burst into laughter. Aden suspected all that brandy had more to do with Will's reaction than his attempt at wit, but he laughed along with him.

Talk of Miriam ended there. They traded a few more jokes and then they went inside for some much-needed sleep.

Aden woke with a sore back and the headache Will should have suffered. Will had taken the floor with the blanket from his pack as a mattress. Aden had taken the couch.

Dellem's house offered quite a few contradictions. The condition of the place wasn't the best, an aged house preserved by patchwork. The mismatched color of wood on the walls and ceiling reminded Aden of a pair of some child's pants held together by a half dozen bits of fabric of varied patterns so that little of the original material remained. He thought back to the jail and wondered how much of the work on this house Dellem had done, using what limited resources he could afford.

The furniture offered the same disparities. The couch he'd taken appeared in pretty poor shape with three clawed legs and one straight leg. The newest-looking piece of furniture was the plush chair Will had draped himself over, perhaps a gift from the folks in this town, maybe even someone's idea of a bribe.

"Been a long time since I slept on the floor." Will sounded amused and without a hint of a hangover.

"We slept late." Aden rubbed at his eyes to clear the crust off them.

"No, you slept late. I've been awake a while, but I figured you needed the rest after being poisoned." Will glanced out the window towards the town. "Dellem ran out earlier. Wanted to put somethings in order."

"So he is going with us." Aden wondered if that was a good thing. "Still don't trust him?"

Will sat up in his chair and lit what was left of his cigar from last night.

"Men in love always cause trouble." Will paused for a drag of his cigar. "If we leave him here, he'll just follow anyway."

"True enough, and just going by the looks of him, he'll be good in a fight if we run into trouble."

"If?" Will laughed and nearly choked on his smoke. "If we run into trouble? Damn, you are an optimist."

Aden walked over to a window. He could see the town in the distance and make out the shapes of people walking along the street. A mail coach, pulled by two coursers headed east, towards Ostice.

"You considered where we're going next?" Aden asked.

Will nodded. "Take it you have, too."

"Not much of a choice," Aden said. "Suppose I could head for Salendar and throttle that merchant until he gives up who paid him to hire me."

"Probably doesn't know anyway," Will said. "Give a person enough money, and they'll gladly overlook little things like names."

"And you can bet whoever wants me will be looking for me there, too."

"Narrows down your choices, doesn't it?" Will sounded amused that Aden wanted to take the time to think it through out loud.

"Ostice." Aden shook his head at the thought of going to the Astesian capital, the place where the emperor was assassinated and every guard had probably burned a sketch of his face into their memory. "Just how much are they offering for my head?"

"Highest offer I heard before we left Gorman was five-hundred golds," Will said. "Rumor has it there's more than one party offering a reward for you. Imagine the price is going up each day you're still loose."

"How high before you turn me in?" Aden asked.

Will smiled, his cigar dangling between his teeth until he removed it to speak. "Some want you dead, others alive. Whoever was offering five-hundred golds is among the latter."

"I still don't understand why they didn't just kill me," Aden said. "Seems like that would have been easier."

"Actually, I'm still trying to figure out why they didn't kill Dellem or the priest here in Crestnal," Will said. "Why kill as many as they have to ruin your alibis but leave those two alive?"

"They aren't going anywhere, Will." Aden laughed that he had to point that out. Will prided himself on being so bloody clever. Aden supposed a person used to a large city like Gorman where people came and went every day forgot others sometimes stayed in one place. "At least, they didn't expect them to. Didn't count on Dellem's feelings for Miriam."

"Maybe," Will said.

Aden rolled his eyes. Will couldn't accept anything clever without a question for it... not unless it came out of his own mouth.

"Can't help thinking there's more to it," Will said.

"There he is." Aden pointed out the window. Dellem walked with an easy stride. Strong winds kicked up some dust clouds in his path. By the time he made it through the front door, he looked as if he'd been rolling on the desert floor instead of walking across it.

"See you boys are awake." He brushed the dirt from his pants legs.

"Don't suppose you've got anything for breakfast?" Aden asked.

"Breakfast? Closer to lunch," he said and barked a laugh. "Got a loaf in the kitchen and some fruit. You didn't need to wait."

"Haven't been awake that long," Aden said.

"Any trouble getting a courser?" Will asked.

"No, Marden Fellis sold me one of his. Picking it up later." Dellem reached for his purse. "Took your advice and only needed half the money you gave me."

Will grinned at that. "Flattery and alcohol," he said. "Few things weaken a negotiator better."

"Here." Dellem offered him the small purse of leftover coins.

"Keep it," Will said. "Good chance you'll need the money later."

They gathered around Dellem's kitchen table as he pulled out the food and set it on the table. They grazed on the bread and prickly pears.

"Take it you boys already have a plan?" Dellem said and then spit out a seed.

"We're heading for Ostice," Aden said. "Whoever's framing me and burned down Miriam's house is most likely there."

"Makes sense." Dellem cut into another pear. "Once we're there, what then?"

"Oh, I've got a few ideas." Will said, his eyebrows waggling with mischief. "Tell me, Dellem. How would you like to earn an easy five hundred golds?"

13

The Oasis

Aden, Will, and Dellem left for Ostice the next morning. The Aiman Desert stretched a distance that required four hard days to cross. At Will's insistence, they packed as much water as possible for them and their coursers.

"I want to avoid stopping at an oasis, if we can," Will said as he tied two of their water skins to the back of his courser's saddle.

"What if we run out of water?" Aden asked. Their coursers carried two skins each, but given how hot it was as they prepared to set out, he wondered how long even that would last.

"If we need the water, then I or Dellem will get some, but that will only give us four skins full of water," Will said.

"Why only four?" Dellem asked as he mounted his newly acquired courser. The cat glanced back at Dellem as if to ask who this stranger was on its back. "Seems we could at least make a courser carry twice that for a short trip."

"No, if I was a bounty hunter looking for me, something like that would catch my eye, make me suspicious," Aden said. "And if the bounty hunters don't think it's odd, the constables will."

The road to Ostice offered plenty of company, more than they wanted. For Aden, that meant wrapping his head in a scarf as if he was protecting himself from being burned by the sun. Enough people on the road did the same to keep him from standing out because of it.

Most of the other travelers had the look of mercenaries drawn by the news of impending war and eager for the steady supply of food an army man received. Thinking back to his lean days of broth dinners, Aden appreciated how they felt. He'd eaten better thanks to Will's company and Dellem's, but if not for his hunger, he might not have awakened as soon as he had from the poison.

Now that Aden suspected Miriam, her behavior after he woke made more sense. His decision to leave so quickly had startled her, too. He saw that clearly in hindsight. She'd played her hand with caution, perhaps overplayed it. Her feint of irritation that he'd freeload had backfired. She'd meant to keep him there until someone showed up to take him away as a prisoner. The truth left too many damned questions, and the longer he traveled, the fewer answers he realized he had.

By their second night, they knew they couldn't make the trip without a stop at an oasis. They were going through their water too quickly.

"The Thoran Oasis is just over the next rise," Will said after they'd found a place off the road to rest. "I'll take my courser and refill two of our skins. While I'm there, I can check for any contacts of mine to see what I can learn."

There was just enough moonlight for Aden to see Will and Dellem. They opted against a fire, not wanting to draw any unwanted company who might want to partake in a fire's warmth. While the temperature didn't drop anywhere close to freezing, after baking all day, it felt as if they should be able to see their breath.

"Better wait until morning," Dellem said. Will opened his mouth to protest, but the constable caught him short. "If something as simple as going in there with more than two skins will draw attention, then you leaving in the direction from which you came won't go unnoticed."

"You're right," Will said. "I'll leave early in the morning. By the time you both get past the oasis, my business should be done, and I can catch up to you."

"Sounds like a plan," Aden said. "I'm going to get some sleep." Gods knew he needed it with all the traveling they'd done. His exhaustion had just as much to do with the poison in his system.

He bundled up in his thin blanket as best he could and tried to sleep.

Will set off at sunrise, leaving Aden and Dellem to enjoy their cold breakfast. The stale bread filled their stomachs, but Aden thought it offered little else to satisfy a body. He longed for another of the steaks Dellem had served the other night.

Conversation ran thinner than the first rays of morning light. Not until Will had disappeared behind the upward curve of the nearest dune did Dellem even speak.

"How long you known him?" he asked.

"Three years," Aden said. "He arranged some of my first jobs. Recognized I was a pity case the moment he saw me."

"Had a few people approach me about doing some mercenary work after the wars," Dellem said. "Tried it for a while, but a few months of that was all I could stomach. Then I found out the constable back home in Crestnal had gotten killed, and town was looking to hire. No one else local had any experience or desire, so they would have had to pay someone to move there. They don't like outsiders, so I knew I'd be a lock for it."

"Sounds nice," Aden said.

"You ever think of settling down for something steady?"

"Not an option." Aden avoided the constable's eyes. He scooped up a handful of sand and let it spill out between his fingers. "No opportunities like that back home, and they sure as Dark wouldn't take me anyway."

"You know, I can account for you," Dellem said. "I know you didn't do what they're accusing you of doing. I might come from a small town, but I'm a constable sworn to the law."

"Thanks." Aden clapped his hands together to knock off the remaining grains of sand. "Won't work, though, and we both know it. Assuming anyone even believed you, then the ones framing me would kill you before you got the chance to clear me or frame you as a co-conspirator."

Dellem packed his saddlebag. Aden did the same. He sensed Dellem wanted to say or ask something, even as they mounted their coursers. Their beasts were lazily traipsing across the desert, with sunrise working its way towards midday, when Dellem asked the question Aden expected days ago.

"So why'd you leave the Order of the Hunt?" He said it as casually as anyone might, but Aden recognized the unease behind the words. Hunters were missing a piece of their souls, Aden more so than most with his shakta missing. Dellem had taken Aden's admission better than expected. His desire to avenge Miriam likely had more to do with his open-mindedness. "Thought the only way out of the Order was death."

"They don't much like that I'm the exception," Aden said. "They've tried to amend that a few times."

"Any chance they're the ones setting you up? Order serves Mirite. Those people wouldn't lose any sleep over an Astesian emperor being assassinated."

"Considering the rumors of war brewing, I'll wager they're losing plenty of sleep." That his first instinct was to defend the homeland he'd turned his back on annoyed Aden.

The oasis interrupted their conversation. A path from the main road led down a steep ravine to a massive camp of large and small multi-hued tents cast about a pool of crystal blue waters. Aden had heard of these desert pools, and in sight of one, he finally appreciated why some thought them mystical. How in Dark did water stay that blue?

"So you never answered my question." Dellem sounded less impressed with the oasis. Of course, he'd probably seen it many times. "Why'd you leave the Order?"

Aden liked Dellem, but the tone of his reply lacked any kindness. "Family matter."

Dellem dropped it and all attempt at conversation. Aden felt guilty about that. The old constable had taken on a great personal risk by helping him. Sure, he had his own reasons, but Dellem now knew Aden for a fugitive, twice over. The Order wanted him dead for deserting and the Astesian Empire would

execute him for his ties to the Order. Never mind the bounty on his head for an assassination he didn't commit.

What he wouldn't give to get back his shakta. He felt only half alive without it. He'd gladly remain a wanted man within this country's borders if he could get his hands on it again.

Thoughts of his weapon distracted him for several hours. Dellem's nosiness had opened up the well of his memory. How much longer could he keep ahead of the Order? If Will was right, then he could only last as long as his "shadow benefactor" deemed him worth the effort to protect.

"He should have been here by now," Dellem said when the midday sun had come and gone. They'd spent hours on the eastern side of the dunes surrounding the oasis. Travelers had ambled by on the road to Ostice, some observant eyes noticed them but if they thought anything odd, they kept moving. Aden wondered how long that would last.

"We can't stay here," Aden said with a shake of the head.

"Only two choices really," Dellem said.

"Head for Ostice or go down into the oasis." Neither option suited Aden. He found it difficult to imagine Will in a situation he couldn't handle. The man's luck bordered on the unnatural—in all matters.

"Just how well you actually know this boy?" Dellem asked.

"Well as anybody, I imagine."

"Meaning?"

"Let's just say if he planned to make a fast coin off of me, he could have done it a long time ago." Aden hated the taste of that admission. "The Order would have paid him nicely for my arse, and he's the kind they'd trust to keep his mouth shut about it."

Dellem sighed. "Well, if we're going down there, then we better do it before sunset. You can't walk around with a towel wrapped about your head when the sun goes down."

Aden nodded and went about concealing his features with the long white linen he'd gotten before leaving Crestnal. He'd worn it most of the ride along the road and found it damned uncomfortable.

"Do we have anything remotely resembling a plan?" Dellem asked.

"We look for one of two things," Aden said. "First, we keep an eye out for Will's courser."

"What's the second thing?"

"Large gatherings of women."

Dellem laughed. "If that bastard's been getting laid, I'll kill him myself."

Aden wouldn't put it past Will to take care of his business in the oasis and bed at least one woman along the way, but to take this long... No, that wasn't like Will. He'd sooner con the woman into coming with him than linger in one place.

Dellem raised a hand to his head like a visor as he glanced towards the sky. "Probably got about three hours of sun left."

"You ever been here?" Aden asked.

"I've transported a prisoner or two to Ostice. The Thoran Oasis is just one big tent pit. Can find a couple hundred people here at any given time, but only about three dozen of them actually live here. Most are merchants. The layout of the place changes daily. Makes it damn confusing to find anything, even for the locals."

They fell in line behind a merchant's caravan made up of six wagons. A mirden pulled each wagon. The foul-smelling creatures were each three times as large as a courser and taller than any man. Their maroon, leather hides glistened with thick sweat, the source of their stench. They lumbered into the oasis, but that served Aden just fine. Anyone in their path would be too busy keeping out from underneath the round, flat hooves of those mirdens toeven look at him or Dellem.

Dellem's description of the oasis proved true enough. Try as Aden might, he didn't see a single permanent structure among the many tents. He wondered if the constables here even bothered with a jail, Astesian laws be damned.

"They have one." Dellem's tone conveyed his low opinion of it. "Wouldn't trust any constables here, though. They get paid to look the other way. Lot of 'legal' smugglers stop here."

"Legal smugglers?"

"Means they're dealing in contraband, but they're working for some noble in Ostice. Never matters what they're shipping to the capital, just who they're shipping it to."

"True enough," Aden said. "Where's the jail?"

"Usually keep it closer to the water," he said. "Easy enough to get a peek inside, but we better be careful doing it."

They parted ways from the caravan. With the stench of the mirdens behind them, Aden could smell the fresh, clean scent of the water as strong as any wine's fruit-filled perfume. After a moment, he realized that was Dellem's guide to the jail rather than any landmark.

"I've heard the waters here are enchanted."

"Plenty of debate on that," Dellem said." Figured you'd know better than I would. I deal in what I can see and touch, measurements and pen strokes. Enchantments aren't something I care to mess with."

There was no missing the unease in Dellem's stare. How much more nervous would he be if Aden had his shakta. *Of course, if I still had my damn shakta, I wouldn't be in this mess,* he thought. Between the first time he left Crestnal and finding out from Will he'd been framed for killing an emperor, a part of him had wondered if losing his shakta might grant him some peace, make the Order lose interest in him.

A damn fool's hope that was.

Three years gone and he still wasn't free of the Order. The pair of hunters who chased him in Gorman proved that. He'd dodged these bastards all that time, and only after his shakta went missing did they find him. Thinking on it in that light, he sensed how wrong that was. If it wasn't coincidence, then what did it mean?

Dellem brought him out of his contemplation. "There it is."

The jail barely qualified as a tent. They'd built it from a brown fabric faded by the sun and abused by dust devils until it matched the very hue of the sand. The wooden beams, most warped and weather-worn, were the only thing permanent about the place. The tent's fabric only formed three walls, and while it also offered cover up top from sky, there were plenty of holes in it. Where a fourth wall might have gone, the guards had left it open to the elements.

"Part of the punishment." Dellem pointed to the eight sets of stocks, lined up into two rows. "Not a place you want to find yourself in the middle of a sandstorm."

"Like your jail better." Aden made no effort to conceal his disdain for the constables who called this oasis their home.

"Inhumane is what it is," Dellem said. "They round up as many trouble-makers as they can find just before a sandstorm hits. They joke that it's the best weather forecast for the oasis. People even place wagers on how many prisoners will survive each storm."

"Guess they're expecting clear skies." Aden counted one man locked up within the stocks. The withered-looking fellow had been stuck here a while, judging from his red face and shoulders.

"Don't stare." Dellem focused on the street formed by two rows of tents. "A constable spots you staring, they'll assume you got a reason to be in there, too."

"At least we know Will hasn't gotten himself thrown into the stocks," Aden said.

"Would've been simpler if he had."

The question of where to look next troubled Aden into silence. No longer speaking, Aden felt something alive and ephemeral in the air. Such a faint thing that he only reacted to it by instinct. If he hadn't caught himself reaching into his jacket for the shakta that wasn't there, he'd never have realized it until too late.

"Oh, gods!" Aden said.

The constable jerked his courser to a stop. "What is it?"

"Hunters." Aden struggled to keep his voice to a whisper.

Dellem's head jerked back and forth. "Where? I don't—"

"They're communicating with their shaktas," Aden said. "They're all over the damned place."

"What are they saying?" Dellem's head wouldn't stay in one place, jerking his courser right to left with each turn of his head. "Have they seen us?"

"Keep still!" Aden said.

Dellem quit looking about, but his old flesh was stretched tight with tension.

"I can't tell what they're saying," Aden said, not mentioning that if he'd had his shakta, he could have listened more easily. A hunter could vibrate the soul strands, mentally pluck them like the strings on a musical instrument, to produce a sound that no human ear might recognize. The other hunters would detect it, because their shakta's strands would react to the vibrations. Aden's ability to sense the vibrations even without his shakta was a secret he'd managed to keep most of his life, but without his shakta, he couldn't hear the conversation clearly enough to understand anything.

What made it easy for him to look calm was how natural it felt to be surrounded by the noise. His anger burned deep as he realized he missed it. "They're tracking someone."

"Suppose it's too much to hope it's not us." Dellem reached for his sword's hilt.

"Keep your hands on your reins," Aden said. "Sword won't do you a damn bit of good anyway."

"We either stay and look for Will or run," Dellem said. "Got no wish to die, least of all on the receiving end of a shakta."

That mystical buzz to the air pestered Aden. The conversation he could no longer decipher grew more insistent. Then the buzzing stopped, and Aden knew what that meant.

"Shit! Ride, Dellem!"

Aden pressed his heels into the courser's sides, launching the large cat into a sprint. The lithe beast kicked out its legs, scampering across the sand. A growl rumbled beneath the leather skin. Aden felt the ripple of the courser's muscles beneath its flesh as it bounded away like some tomcat caught rummaging through back-alley trash.

People shouted curses as he and Dellem forced them out of the way. He trusted the constable followed and didn't dare look over his shoulder to confirm it. Aden darted his eyes left and right searching for the hunters he sensed, but he saw only pissed off people. Was he jumping at shadows?

Strands of silver light burrowed into the ground just before him and confirmed his worst fears. Sand erupted from that spot into a large plume. His courser leaped high into the air. Aden grabbed his saddle's pommel so he wouldn't fall.

The courser made it past the attack and charged down the street. Where the Dark were they going? These damned makeshift streets formed a maze.

"Gods!" Dellem shouted. "We circled the damn oasis!"

Sure enough, the three-sided tent of the jail was coming into view ahead of them again.

"This way!" Aden jerked his courser to the right and through the front opening to a large tent. *Let's see the bastards anticipate this*, he thought. He might have picked better. They charged straight into a makeshift brothel. Half the people abandoned their clothes to the floor of the tent as they ran out to the street and hurled curses at him and Dellem.

Aden kicked his courser into running to the far end of the tent. His courser reared as it reached the back wall, and its front claws ripped at the fabric to make a way out. They raced back into the light on a street Aden didn't recognize. The buzz of shaktas raged about him. How many hunters were chasing them, and where were they?

"Don't slow down!" Aden shouted to the constable. A long green scarf had snagged onto the hilt of the old man's sword and fluttered like a flag.

"Aden, stop!" The shout didn't come from Dellem, but a woman. The sun disappeared for a split second as the black silhouette of another courser jumped over Aden from behind and landed in his path. The large cat roared its challenge, and Aden's green balked as it skidded to a stop in a dust cloud of its own making.

Two more coursers landed, one on each side to deny Aden any escape. He didn't pay those two a bit of interest, though. His eyes locked on the woman atop that first courser.

"Stand your ground," she said.

Dellem pulled his courser up beside Aden's. He held his sword's hilt, the flimsy scarf still clinging to it, but he didn't draw the weapon.

"You know her?" Dellem asked.

"Yes," Aden said, still in shock.

The black mask and hood that all hunters wore hid her face, but he recognized her red, leather armor. The one time he'd seen her was in front of the dart boards of the Get Lost with her legs wrapped around Will. She no longer held a dart in her hands, but a black, ribbed stick. Aden sensed the power within her shakta and knew she was ready to use it if either he or Dellem moved.

Aden's heart slid down within his chest. Three years he'd managed to stay ahead of his former brothers and sisters. Few lasted half as long apart from the Order, but the chase had finally ended.

Her grip on her shakta tightened, but in the moment he expected her to strike, she lowered it. "Be at ease." She slid the sacred weapon into her jacket. "Make no move against us, and we'll make none against you."

"Then what do you want?" Aden asked.

Shouts came from the direction of where they'd been.

"Not here." She looked past him. "We've a quieter place to conduct our business. Follow us, and you'll live to see another sunrise."

"And Will?" Aden asked, confident they'd found the reason for his disappearance.

His demand received a smirk, one he heard in the woman's voice even if he couldn't see it. "Oh, you'll see him soon enough. He's been treated well."

Dellem grunted. Aden shared the constable's sentiment. He no more trusted this woman than he would a dog foaming at the mouth, but the shouts of the local constables left him little choice. He'd seen how they would treat him, and he didn't wish to become part of the forecast.

14

No One Ever Leaves the Order

The hunters led Aden and Dellem to the far side of the oasis. With sunset near, the population increased. The same streets Aden's courser had easily raced through only moments ago thickened with a blend of foot traffic and wagons. Barkers bathed in fresh torchlight peddled before their tents with promises of exotic performers and fine wine. More than one man they passed latched his attention on the beauty in the red leather armor, but a single glare from her sent their hopes elsewhere.

They stopped once they reached a pair of large tents. One reminded Aden of the jail, with one side left open. This tent belonged to the coursers and a single stinking mirden. The mirden's burden, a wooden wagon rested between the two tents. An older gentleman stepped out of the tented stables.

"Little Aden Murai." The old man hacked out a laugh. "The Cold Shoulder returns."

"Greetings, Argus," Aden said. Three years hadn't changed the courser master much. Once upon a time, he'd been a hunter, as well. He lost his left eye and his shakta during a mission to the West, back when Aden was just a child. In his shame, Argus had accepted the role of servant to other hunters. He still looked strong as any hunter, though, and his disposition as foul as ever.

"The Cold Shoulder?" Dellem asked.

"It's what we call your friend," the lady in the red leather said with mocking amusement, "but not in public. Courser master, see to the beasts. You two... wait out here with the Shoulder's friend."

"Dellem stays with me," Aden said.

Her pink lips smirked at him. "Scared we'll kill him?"

"Hunters aren't known for letting others live who've seen their faces," Aden said.

"True, but we have better uses for that one alive," she said, "for now."

Dellem rolled his eyes. "That's a comfort."

Aden dismounted his courser. The large creature curled up on the ground by the stables and licked its paws. He envied the animal's ambivalence. Coursers had good instincts, though. Perhaps that boded well for Aden, that or the cat was looking forward to not having someone as big as Aden on its back.

The woman in red leather led Aden inside the other tent. The outside gave the impression of wealth, but the inside turned out sparse in its furnishings, which didn't surprise Aden. He might have been gone for three years, but he still knew the Order's ways. Some sheets were hung to create the illusion of rooms within the tent. The woman pushed aside one of the sheets, and there was Will, sitting on a rug. Two more hunters, both men, stood watch over him.

"Aden, nice of you to join us." Will raised a glass of red wine in mock toast. "As you can see, your old friends have been keeping me company."

"You all right?" Aden asked.

"We don't make a habit of killing our associates." The woman removed her cloak and placed it on a hook attached to one of the support beams.

"Associates?" Aden looked from the lady to Will, who had the decency to look at least somewhat embarrassed. If he had his shakta, Aden wondered if he could have resisted the urge to use it on his friend.

"Did you really think you left the Order?" The woman walked over to a dresser with a bottle of red wine and empty glasses. "Leave us." The two guards obeyed her order without a word, but when their back was to her, one of them rolled their eyes. Clearly he didn't care for the one in charge.

The woman poured herself some wine, her back to Aden as if he offered not the slightest threat.

"I did leave the Order," Aden said.

"We let you believe that." She paused for a sip from her glass. "But you've been working for us from the moment you broke your oaths."

"I'm sorry, Aden," Will said, "but it's true."

"Then why did those hunters try to kill me back in Gorman?"

"If we'd wanted you dead, then you'd already be in the ground," she said. "They were sent to bring you to me, but then that fool with the dagger tried to finish you."

"You killed him." Aden remembered his unseen benefactor with the cross-bow.

"No, someone else intervened. We don't know who." The frustration writ into her features left little doubt that much was true.

"The all-knowing Order?" Aden enjoyed the opportunity to mock her.

"I'd mind your tone," she said. "The Mordani Triumvirate considered having me kill you and deliver your head to Ostice. That would certainly be easier."

Yes, that sounded very much like the Order's triumvirate."So what changed their mind?"

"Just be grateful they did and leave it at that. "She paused for another sip of that wine. He finally noticed the bags beneath her eyes. Yes, she looked plenty tired. No wonder she had such a sour disposition. Judging by the smirk on Will's face as he watched her, he enjoyed hearing her vent. "You've gotten sloppy. Ambushed by children, your shakta stolen, and too great a fool to realize when you've been poisoned."

Will laughed outright at that, earning a glare from both Aden and the woman in red.

"When I require you to speak, Will, I'll let you know," she said, adding venom to his name.

"My apologies." His smile widened despite his words. What was so damned funny? "Pray continue."

She ignored him and focused her anger on Aden. "Someone wants war between our home and the Astesian Empire. We want to know who and why."

"All I want is my shakta back, the bounty on me removed, and the Order out of my life."

She smiled at that, a dreamy expression that looked beautiful on her face and strangely out of place.

"Shaktas belong to members of the Order. Even if the Order granted you amnesty, which they won't, they'd never let you walk free with your shakta. The seas will sooner burn before that happens."

She grunted, a queer sound, and she stumbled. If Aden hadn't been watching her this whole time, he'd have damned her for drunk, but she hadn't had nearly enough wine for that to happen. Will set his glass down and stood behind her.

She turned on Will. Her glass of wine dropped to the floor of the tent as she reached for her shakta, but she tripped and fell into him. Will grabbed her by the wrist to keep her from her shakta and covered her mouth with his other hand. Her muffled screams faded quickly, and her eyes rolled up into the back of her head.

Aden spotted Will's wine glass on the floor. The line of red wine hovered just beneath the rim.

Will let go of her, and she dropped to the floor of the tent.

"You poisoned the wine," Aden said. No wonder he'd been laughing at her jab.

"Thankfully, she'd purchased a competitor's product." Will leaned over to admire his handiwork. "Wouldn't have had the heart to do that to one of my own."

Aden slammed his fist across Will's jaw. The hit knocked Will down next to the unconscious hunter. The punch stung his knuckles, but that felt good.

"You let them use me, you fucking bastard!" Aden said.

"Keep your voice down!" Will said in a hushed voice. "I didn't know."

"Did you poison me, too?"

"No." Will held up his hands as if to beg off another hit. He showed some brains by not trying to stand. "For a long time, I wasn't even sure you didn't know who was giving me the jobs I passed onto you. She never admitted to being part of the Order, but I figured it out when I found the shakta in her clothes." Aden didn't have to ask how he managed that, not with Will's way with women. Of course, that also explained his disinterest in the woman. He remembered that well enough when she'd played with him in the Get Lost. What person outside of the Order would want a hunter in their bed? "I didn't say anything to you, because if you did know, then my giving away what I knew would have gotten me killed. I didn't know if I could trust you."

"And I don't know if I can trust you." Aden towered over Will and considered finishing this.

"We have a chance to leave here," Will said. "We can do this with her or on our own. I leave that choice to you."

"You think we can just walk past those other hunters? You really think it that simple?"

Will's smile returned. "Don't you?"

Aden considered that a moment. Could he really trust Will after this?

"She won't stay unconscious very long."

Aden cursed as he offered his hand to Will. "Get up."

"Smart man."

Aden glared as he tightened his grip on Will's hand. "I want every detail, everything she said, everything you figured out from the day you met her. All of it, or I swear I'll show you why they called me the Cold Shoulder."

"You'll have it, but I'll warn you now that it won't give you much."

"Let's start with her name."

"Rhea," Will said. "At least, that's what she claims. Never offered more."

"Ever hear the others call her that?"

"They never used their names in front of me."

Aden suspected as much. Members of the Order rarely used names, even with each other. He'd have to chance it. "Just keep your hole shut."

Will saluted, apparently taking Aden's command to heart.

Aden knelt next to Rhea and pulled out her shakta. "This will really piss her off."

Will laughed, and even if he didn't say it, he appreciated the poetry of the punishment. Aden slid her shakta into his jacket where his usually resided. Even if it wasn't his shakta or one he could use, just having it there made him feel a little closer to whole.

"Let's go." Aden took a deep breath before he walked out the tent's door.

"Have it your way!" Aden shouted. A hard chill had hit the oasis with the falling of the sun. The two hunters Rhea dismissed were both standing outside and turned with startled expressions as Aden and Will walked past them. He silently prayed these two really despised Rhea as much as the earlier eye roll had suggested. "One of you should punch her 'high and mightiness' in the throat." Aden made little effort to lower his voice, as if he wanted her to hear him. "Acts like she's one of the damned triumvirate."

An uncomfortable silence followed Aden as he and Will kept walking for the stables. He struggled to keep his face empty of fear, but his mind's eye only saw those two hunters withdrawing their shaktas and killing him and Will in the back. Just as he thought to take off into a run, the two hunters stifled their laughter. Praise the gods!

"Argus!" Aden knew this hand would be the trickiest to play.

The old stable hand shifted his one good and rather wide eye onto Aden. He hadn't been expecting commands from "little Aden Murai," and the tone Aden was using promised nothing but orders. Dellem looked equally startled, sitting on his arse by the stables with the two other hunters beside him.

"The witch in there says to get her courser ready and all this shit packed," Aden said.

"What?"

"We're headed for Ostice." Aden tried to sound pissed about it.

He stopped in front of Dellem and was close to telling the man to get on his courser when inspiration struck.

"All right, constable," Aden said. "Time to make your choice. You either ride with us to Ostice, or these two split your chest open with their shaktas." The proclamation surprised the hunters almost as much as Dellem.

"What! Why you lousy piece of shit."

Gods, so much for a brilliant idea. Dellem looked incensed. Aden feared Dellem might actually refuse out of spite. He knelt down, trying to make his face that of a man who promised death. He leaned close and hoped Dellem wouldn't shove him back.

"Play along or you'll get us killed." Aden kept his voice as soft as he could manage lest the hunters hear him. The only question was whether he was too quiet for even Dellem to understand what he'd said. Aden stood back up and offered the cruelest smile he could manage. Dellem stared up at him dumbstruck.

Aden crossed his arms. "Well?"

The hunters smiled down at Dellem and pulled out their shaktas.

"Fine," Dellem said, "I'll go, but you better sleep with one eye open from here on out—boy."

"I'll keep that in mind." Aden snapped his fingers at Will. "Get on your courser. Move it!"

Will mounted his courser with the appropriate haste. Aden did the same, but attempted to act more casual about it. He nearly gave it all away as he looked down into Argus' blue eye. The man had Aden's courser by the reins. Aden's gut roiled as he met the old stable hand's gaze. Argus wasn't buying into this, and he looked a breath away from calling him on it, too.

"What?" Aden laughed, hoping it didn't sound as forced as it was. "Did you really think I'd left the Order?"

Argus paled at that and his obvious fear made Aden laugh for real.

"No one ever leaves the Order," Aden said. "I would think you'd know that better than anyone."

He never had liked Argus. The man treated hunters like shit, probably because he couldn't be one anymore. The chance to cut the man down to size had never come when Aden was in the Order, getting the chance now that he was gone made the cut all the sweeter. Argus let go of the reins to Aden's courser as if he'd been holding a hot coal.

Aden kicked his courser into a brisk walk. "Don't fall behind, Dellem." Aden managed the cruelest tone he could, one worthy of a man named the Cold Shoulder. "I'll only go looking for you one time. I can promise you that."

He took the nearest turn he could find in the tent city's streets. Once he knew the hunters were gone from view, he spurred his courser into a sprint. Will laughed and cheered on his courser as if drunk. Aden felt just as merry. His smile wouldn't go away. He didn't envy those hunters when Rhea woke, and that thought alone kept him laughing even an hour into the night with the oasis falling deeper into the western horizon. Rhea would want him skinned alive, but he already had a plan for that. By Dark! He was even looking forward to seeing her again.

15

Aden's Name

Aden and the others stopped later that night, after exhaustion had worn away their giddiness at outwitting Rhea and her hunters.

They made camp off the road on the far side of a dune. Will didn't indulge in a smoke this night, clearly not wanting to do anything to help the hunters find them.

Aden pulled out Rhea's shakta and spun it in his hand.

"She's going to be pretty pissed that you took that," Will said without any of his usual mirth.

"Just wish I could use it." Aden slid it back into the sheath sewn to the inside of his jacket.

"Can she use that to find us?" Dellem asked.

"Yes and no." Aden knew the Order considered divulging a shakta's workings grounds for execution, but he'd earned that punishment several times over. "She needs a mage to do that, and even if she had one, it's not as simple as it sounds. There's a risk to the owner of the shakta."

"What kind of risks?"

"Dellem, any magic involving a person's soul has risks."

"That especially true for women?" Dellem asked. Aden knew why. He was all too familiar with the stories.

"The idea that women carry the seed of life and that magic might corrupt that seed? The Order claims half the abominations in the West came from the offspring of women whose souls were fractured by magic. It's nothing but a wagon full of lies passed on by old men to keep women in their place."

Dellem must have heard the buried anger lacing Aden's words, because he kept silent, answering with only a nod.

Aden held onto that anger as he directed his attention to Will, a threat clear in the two words he spoke. "Your turn."

"She came to me about three years ago. I'd already noticed you within the Get Lost and had seen you picking up a job here or there. I already suspected you were a hunter, but I didn't realize she was. Said she wanted to hire you. One rule: you weren't to know the jobs came from her."

"How long did it take you to figure out she was with the Order?" Aden asked.

"Took me almost a year. She started taking jobs of her own to justify her presence, but they were rare. Always small, local things that wouldn't take more than a day. She plays hard, too. Only got full-blown drunk one time—both of us did. She made a pass at me that night, and I ignored my better demons and took her up on her offer. I happened to wake before she did, so I went through her things to learn what I could.

"She's careful. Doesn't carry anything on her that would incriminate her, nothing but that shakta, but that was enough for me."

"She tracked me there," Aden said more to himself than Will or Dellem. They'd found him within a matter of weeks. So clever and careful he'd been, and they could have snuffed him out at any time.

"Don't feel too bad," Will said as if he knew Aden's thoughts. "You should know better than anyone. You people are trained to find anything you choose to seek. That's why every kingdom in the East and West has laws to kill you hunters on sight."

"Except for Mirite, of course." Aden smiled at the thought of home. Much as he didn't miss the Order, he longed to see his country again. The kingdom sat along the border with the West, the only people with the guts to live that close to the land of the damned.

Will rolled his eyes. "Well, since the Order works for Mirite, of course not."

"So what was that business back in the Oasis?" Dellem asked. "You said you'd planned to look for any of your contacts. Was your rendezvous with Rhea planned?"

"No, I definitely wasn't expecting to run into her there," Will said. "They'd left Gorman to look for you. If anything, I expected them to be a lot farther ahead of us or headed elsewhere."

"Why is that?" Aden asked.

"Because I'd convinced her that you'd left. She came for you after word hit the streets in Gorman about the bounty on you."

"But she already knew I was being framed, didn't she? That's how you knew."

Will's smile, though hard to see by only the moonlight, widened at Aden's observation. "Exactly. Want to guess why she hadn't come for you sooner?"

"She was waiting on instructions from the Order."

Will nodded. "Took the messenger hawks that long to travel to Mirite and back."

"But he was sleeping in your tavern," Dellem said. "How the Dark did she miss him?"

"I hid his courser at a neighboring inn. Told her he'd left without a word." Aden remembered Will's stable hand getting the coursers ready. He must have sent the boy to get his from the other inn.

"Surprised she believed you," Aden said.

"Why wouldn't she? Two of her hunters had just attacked you. Most people with any sense would have left town. You, you idiot, passed out in your room."

"Didn't have much choice," Aden said. "That poison still had a good hold of me."

"So back to the oasis." Dellem sounded like he thought Will was dodging that part of his confessional, and Aden wondered the same. "How'd you get caught?"

Will had to recognize what Dellem was inferring, but he just kept smiling.

"There's a tavern that floats around the oasis called the Hide and Seek. Good place for information traders to hook up. One of her hunters, one I hadn't seen before, was in there. He got Rhea, and they ambushed me as I was leaving."

"Don't look like you put up much of a fight." The memory of finding Will lounging on that rug in Rhea's tent still warmed Aden's rage.

"Four hunters against me?" Will shook his head. "I know my limitations. Besides, I was hoping to see what I might learn."

"Did you learn anything?" Aden asked.

"Rhea didn't share much," Will said. "She only wanted one thing."

"Me."

"Right," he said, "but I've got a feeling there's more to this than we realize."

"Wouldn't surprise me," Dellem said. "Something's got those hunters running scared. I might not know anything about the Order, but I do know when people are nervous."

"Rhea was definitely anxious. Way she was acting in that tent, even before Will's potion got a hold of her..." Aden shook his head. What he wouldn't give for the complete picture. Perhaps running away from the hunters hadn't been the wiser choice, but to stay with them only led to one place, an execution by sh akta.

"Well, if you gents will excuse me," Dellem said as he stood. "My bladder is getting anxious, too. Wasn't made for riding coursers. I'll take the first watch if you boys want to sleep."

"Much appreciated," Will said.

"Wake me in two hours," Aden said. "I'll take the rest."

Will shook his head. "Better make it me. You still aren't at your best, I think. You need the sleep more."

That rankled Aden a bit, but he wasn't going to refuse four hours of sleep compared to none.

As Dellem stepped away for a privacy, Will spread out his blanket. "Tell me something, Aden."

"What?"

"You ever see that woman before?"

"Rhea? I don't think so. Don't remember her within the Order, and gods know, I'd remember a woman who looks like that."

Will grunted.

"What?"

"She definitely knows you." Will started laughing. What was so damned funny now?

"I would say that much is obvious."

"No," Will didn't even pretend he was trying to quell his laughter, "it's not that."

"Then what the Dark is it?"

Will sprawled on his blanket. He looked up at the stars as if they would dance for him. "I don't usually advertise such things, but the night I had with Rhea... wasn't my name she was moaning."

"What the Dark? What do you mean?" Aden stammered the words. "Me? She said my name?"

"I don't know anybody else walking around named Aden."

He stared at Will. The dog was lying. He had to be lying.

Then Will turned his head to look at Aden and laughed even louder. "Relax, Aden. Not as if you have to marry her."

"She really called out my name?"

"On my mother's honor," Will said.

"Did your mother have any?"

"Enough."

"You're certain she said my name?" Aden asked.

"Several times, actually."

Aden sat on his blanket dumbstruck even long after Will had laughed himself to sleep. He hadn't a clue who this woman might be, didn't recognize her from any other he'd ever known, and she was crying out his name within her drunken fantasies. He hoped some of this would make sense after they reached Ostice.

16

The Best Way into a City

They rode hard and fast the rest of the way through the Aiman Desert. They stayed off the road whenever possible. People choked the roads as they neared the imperial capital, and the desert gave way to fields of grass so green that not even night could conceal how vibrant it was. Water which had been murderously absent now flowed about them like the walls of a maze that led to the ocean.

Their last night traveling to Ostice, Will led them well off the main road until they reached a plantation. He negotiated with the owner to let them sleep in the barn. Faint light flickered from the windows of the main house as they settled in for the night.

"Enjoy your rest, gentlemen," Will said as he sat next to the barn's open door, having volunteered to stay up for the first watch. This far from the main road, they didn't consider it likely the hunters would find them, but they weren't taking any chances. "Going to be a hard day tomorrow."

Dellem grunted in a manner that warned Will's remark understated their situation. The constable had wasted little time unfurling his blanket to rest on it.

"I've not been to Ostice," Aden said. "What will we have to deal with?"

"Nobody gets inside that city without going through a gate and getting checked. Paranoid bastards," Dellem said. "You can bet it's worse with the emperor murdered."

"The entire city is built on an island," Will said. "Doesn't leave a lot of convenient ways to get inside unnoticed."

"No army has ever breached its walls." Aden knew little else of use about the city, though. When he'd been with the Order, they'd trained him for assignments closer to home and in the smaller kingdoms that lived uneasily between Mirite and Astes. Most of what he knew came from idle talk in taverns, and when people spoke over ale and wine about Ostice, they always discussed the aplettsars, the most expensive and highly skilled prostitutes in the East. Only in Ostice could someone legally pay for a prostitute, but few could afford the price.

"We need a way into that place." Despite the edge to Will's voice, he juggled in one hand a pair of small rocks he'd found by the door to the barn. "Suppose we could stuff you inside a barrel and hope they don't search it that closely."

"I can tell you right now that won't work," Dellem said. "Spent enough time in the Astesian Army to know that much. When they lock down that city, nothing's sacred. They'll search everything going in and out, even the crack of a baby's bottom if they think they'll find something there."

"So how do we get inside, oh wise engineer?" Aden suspected if any of them might have the answer, it was Dellem.

"The best way to go?" Dellem rubbed his jaw as he considered that and then winced. "You won't like it, and there's no guarantee it won't be patrolled, but I know a way that might work."

"Do tell," Will said.

"Easiest way to get into a city is always the same," Dellem said. "You crawl up its arse."

The next day, Will negotiated with the plantation owner to leave their coursers stabled there. Considering the way Dellem planned to get them into Ostice, their mounts wouldn't do them much good anyway.

By the time the sun had risen to its zenith, Aden took his first look at the outer walls of the capital city. Two thin stretches of land provided bridges across the fresh waters of the Kamarayen River where it spilled into the salt waters of the southern ocean.

"Reputation has it you won't find a better-designed aqueduct system in the East," Dellem said as they stood on the far end of the western land bridge. "Fresh water feeds into several points along the northern wall, and every bit of sewage drains out into the ocean from the southeast and southwest corners. That's where we go in."

"Why not just go in where the water does?" Aden asked.

"They place grates on all those points. The holes in the grates are too small for us to fit through."

Will, a cigar resting precariously between his lips, cocked his head to walk away from the city. "What makes getting in the shit holes any easier? Wouldn't they grate up those, too?"

"Practical matter," Dellem said. "Debris collects and blocks up those grates. Not as big a deal or as difficult to clean where the water goes in, but where everything goes out—that's another matter."

"No one wants to walk through all that filth except us," Aden said.

"Pretty much," Dellem said. "The grates at those two points would keep out a small boat, but the holes in those grates might be large enough for a man to get through. Couple problems with that."

"The guards on the wall," Will said.

Dellem nodded. "That's one."

"Means we do it at night," Aden said.

"Right," Dellem said. "Other problem is that there's no guarantee the holes in the grate will be big enough for us. Long way to swim to find out we gotta try another way."

"What about once we're inside the aqueduct?"

"If we get that far, things get trickier." Dellem glanced over his shoulder at the island city as if to spy the answers Aden wanted. "I've never seen any maps of those aqueducts. The stuff I know about them comes from just looking at the place with an engineer's eyes and word of mouth. Do they patrol the aqueducts? I don't know. Guards on the entry-exit points? Don't know that either."

"Guards on those entry-exits to the aqueducts sounds more likely," Aden said.

"Doesn't mean they don't do the occasional patrol," Will said. "Still, I'm more worried about making it across the water unseen. There's no way we go unnoticed in a boat, not even a small one, and I'm not the best swimmer."

"I get by," Dellem said, "but it's been a good many years. Not as young as I used to be."

Aden sighed. He knew where this was going. "These people aren't looking for you two."

Will and Dellem stopped walking and looked back at Aden. He waited for a wagon loaded with wine barrels to roll past before he said more. The driver, whipping his large mirden, cast the three of them a dirty look. The mirden snorted its irritation at being whipped, but the sound of it lacked any conviction. Been hauling too many wagons for too many years.

"We don't want anyone to know I'm inside the city, not even any of the imperial candidates you might negotiate with," Aden said once the wagon had passed, "but we want them to think you two are bargaining my hide to the highest bidder."

"Your point?" Dellem asked.

"They'll be more likely to suspect I'm in the city if no one can account for you two going in by the gates."

"True enough," Will said. "Only one reason for the two of us to sneak in there is if we smuggle Aden in at the same time."

Aden looked back out towards the river. "I'm a good swimmer, too. By myself, I've a good chance of getting in there the way Dellem is talking."

"We need a way to regroup once we're inside." Dellem sounded less than pleased with this, even if it was partly his idea.

"What about the Black Dog?" Will asked.

Dellem let loose a low whistle. "That's one expensive inn," he said. "Big one, too. You aren't going to find any bounty hunters looking for him there."

"My thinking, too," Will said.

Dellem patted Will on the shoulder. "Glad you're paying for it."

"So how many aplettsars are you friendly with in this inn?" Aden asked.

"Just two," Will said, not ruffled a bit by Aden's taunt, "and both worth every coin."

"Women like that would probably make my heart give out." Dellem laughed.

"I only slept with one. The other aplettsar was a man I took to dinner to get some pointers."

Aden shook his head. Yes, that sounded exactly like the kind of thing Will would do. "All right," he said. "So you two go in by one of the gates, and I'll make my swim at sunset."

"We'll have a hot bath waiting for you," Will said.

"Word of warning before we commit to this plan," Dellem said. "Let's not forget the current. Swimming to those grates will be hard enough with the flow of water in your favor. If the holes turn out too small for you and you can't find a way to pry them open, swimming back won't be easy."

"Unless you two have any other ideas, it's all we've got." Aden looked over his shoulder at the city and the dark blue waters surrounding it. Despite Dellem's warning, he feared the swim would be the easy part.

17

The Swim

The warm waters of the Kamarayen River embraced Aden as he started his swim. The sun had just set with violent hues of red and orange fading from the western horizon. Much as he would have preferred to swim without the restriction of clothes, he couldn't easily carry his leathers any other way. The water felt good even as it invaded his boots, but he knew that would change once he got out of the water. That was assuming some sharp-eyed archer on the city's walls didn't pierce his back with an arrow.

He started far enough upriver that no one from the city or on the road would see him entering the water. The current made his swim easier. Despite his boasts, he'd gone quite a few years since he'd done much swimming. As a child, he'd spent half his waking, summer hours escaping to the Zwilang River. His old mentor had called his love of swimming a useless pleasure, but one could hardly expect a creature more cat than man to appreciate the feel of a cool lake on a summer day.

Memories of the old fellow soured his enjoyment of swimming, but they focused his thoughts. The ache in his chest owed nothing to the exhaustion of his swim. A mentor, yes... but he'd been more of a father. Part of why Aden left the Order was because of the old cat. He wanted to believe his mentor was honored by Aden risking his life to cut ties with the Order, but deep down, the part of his soul and mind that his mentor had molded constantly scolded him.

A hunter grown sloppy only dishonored a mentor. Aden swore to make it right, to prove himself the best student—the best hunter. Fulfilling that vow started once he made it inside Ostice and cleared his name.

He rested his arms and legs, allowing his body to float along the current and see how much farther he needed to swim. That's when he heard the splash of an oar. The sound of it reached him as if the oarsman might have slapped his head. He jerked about, expecting to face a boat at his back but found nothing there. Then he spotted the dark outline on the open waters. He'd forgotten how easily sound traveled over water, and this windless night only made that more so. The boat's outline grew more defined. The damned thing was rowing straight at him. An Astesian twenty-arm, he decided, making it too small for anything other than a patrol boat. He spotted a woman on the deck, leaning against the carving of a sea serpent that adorned the bow. The lookout hadn't spotted Aden yet, but as she got closer, even a bat with a blindfold wouldn't miss him.

Too far to swim for the city walls, he decided. No chance of outrunning the boat or swimming out of sight. Instead, he dove beneath the water's surface and swam towards the boat.

Clouds obscured the moon to little more than a dull glow, but it was enough. He could still see the shadow of the boat as it passed over him, the motion of the oars muted to a gurgle as if the lake had a stomach to upset. As the moonlight vanished from sight, he felt his lungs demand air. He'd thought he could last longer, and in younger days, he might have. If he tried to hold his breath until it was safe to come up past the boat, he'd never make it. With the boat still above him, he played a gamble.

The curve of the boat's belly concealed him from view as he surfaced alongside. He muffled his gasp for breath as best he could. He grinned at his cleverness until a slave's oar smacked him across the head. He managed not to cry out or tumble back into the water, but he was so dazed that he didn't realize the boat was almost past him until the stern was right beside him. He inhaled deep and plunged back beneath the waters.

Fear he'd made too much noise pushed him to stay underwater, even when the gurgle of the oarsmen's efforts had disappeared. Only once he couldn't last another second did he race back towards the sky. He twisted about as he broke the surface to face the direction of the boat. *All the better to see the arrow aimed at your stupid head*, he thought.

To his relief, he saw the boat had traveled far enough that the guard on deck couldn't possibly see his head bobbing about like an apple for an archer to target.

Luckier than I deserve. His muscles ached and burned, so he floated on his back to rest. The current carried him, helping him regain some of the ground he'd lost, but he couldn't let it take him too far. Do that and he'd find his fool self floating out to sea. Much as he loved to swim, he'd rather die with a sword shoved up his arse than drown.

Now that he knew the patrol boats were out there, he paused more often as he swam the rest of the way to make sure none of those boats were heading towards him or the direction he was heading. The last thing he could afford was to race against another one of those boats. He needed his strength for once he made his final approach to the city. The current would work against him at that point, so he couldn't afford to be exhausted from racing another patrol boat.

The city's outer walls touched the waters, not exposing a single bit of land for him to climb onto for rest. Stir up too much water fighting the current, and the lookouts on the wall would spot him for certain.

The waters turned rougher as he neared the city's walls. He could make out the shapes of the guards on the walls as some marched by and others simply stared outward in hopes of spotting something more interesting than waves. The last thing he'd expected was the current to push him closer to the city, but as he neared, a large wave caught him unprepared and flung him the last few meters.

Aden panicked as he struggled for control. Any effort to conceal his presence was abandoned as he tried to avoid crashing into that wall. At the last second, he gave up and threw out his arms as if to hug the city. He arched back as far as he could. His knees struck the wall. Pain shot up his legs, a mirror blow hammered into his chest. That he spared his head the same punishment came as small comfort. The blended fresh and salt waters splashed up into his open mouth, drowning out his cries until the same water was spewed out in a series of coughs that ripped at his lungs and throat. The thunder of the surf slapping against the city's brick borders drowned out his panicked cries and saved him from the arrows that would almost certainly have rained down from the guards atop the wall.

Once his head cleared, he worked his way around the outer walls of the city towards the grates blocking the exit points of the aqueducts. His neck ached as he looked back and forth from the top of the city's walls to the indefinite shapes of patrol boats on the lake. Would be just his luck to make it this far and get caught, but none of the city's sentries spotted him as he reached his destination on the southern side of Ostice.

He never thought the scent of shit could smell so sweet. Perhaps that overstated it, but he welcomed knowing his swim had neared its end. Once he made out the metal bars of the grate, he felt a surge of excitement empower him to cross those last few meters.

"No." The word came out more as a gasp of weary breath as he reached the grate. The holes barely offered enough room to stick his head through them. He grabbed onto the bars and jerked on them as hard as he could, hoping they might shake loose by some divine intervention. He received his miracle, but not in the way he expected. As he pulled on the metal bars, the lower half of his body was drawn towards the hole. He expected his feet to hit the submerged portion of the grate, but his feet kept going forward. Could it really be this simple? He kicked about and found a large hole in the grate. He ran his hand down one of the vertical bars and found where the metal had been broken off. Just before the break, the bar curved inward as if something from outside had punched its way into the city's sewers. He wondered how long this hole had been here. Given the opening was hidden beneath the water, it might have gone undetected for a while. No way to know for sure, but at least he had his way into the city.

One deep breath, a duck underwater, and he emerged within the sewers of Ostice. The tunnels were rounded like giant pipes, which he supposed they were. The place stank worse than a skunk's arse, but after a moment, the shock of the stench wore off.

He climbed out of the water onto an elevated walkway. The water in his boots created a sloshing sound with each step. He never understood how being immersed in water fully clothed felt pleasant when walking with water in his shoes disgusted him.

The tunnel he started in led to a large intersection.

"Just perfect," he muttered to himself.

He hadn't a clue which way to go or how he was going to get out of here. Something was wrong, but he couldn't place exactly what until he noticed some passages appeared more brightly lit than others. Just within the interchange, five fresh torches burned. They wouldn't bother with the torches, certainly not this many, unless they patrolled this place and often.

He decided to go with one of the more poorly lit tunnels. The torchlight dimmed to the point where he saw the light of the next torch as little more than a wink. The passage appeared to go on forever. He might find himself on the far side of this island city before he discovered a way out.

When the passage reached its darkest point, he didn't realize the walkway had ended until it disappeared from beneath him. He dropped into the foul water and thrashed about until he found his footing. He swallowed the tainted water as he struggled to grab onto the walkway. He retched up the water and more as he clung to the brick path.

A laugh trembled out of him. "So that's what piss tastes like."

Something warm and big brushed past him in the water. He scrambled onto the walkway. A growl echoed through the passage. He'd heard quite a few tales traded over childhood campfires about monsters feeding off the filth and fools in city sewers. He'd never believed those stories, but that growl reverberated into his bones.

After he steadied his nerves, he continued his trek through the dark. He moved more slowly now; one fall into the water was enough. He wanted to pretend the thing that brushed against him was nothing but flotsam, but whatever it was had reacted to him, had shifted in surprise at the contact. He shivered and cursed.

The next torch beckoned, and he looked forward to standing in its glow until the light ahead split into two flames. One remained steady while the other bobbed about and grew larger. He stood stock still, almost hypnotized by the movement of the light until he realized what he was seeing. The second torch was moving closer and held by a man. He considered running back the way he'd come, but after the first spill, he no longer trusted his footing. He decided to bluff and prayed for a guard without a suspicious nature.

"Who goes there?" Aden bellowed once he assumed the torchlight was close enough for the person to see him.

The guard jumped back with a squeal. Aden laughed as the guard reached for his sword with the torch still in his hand, then realized what he was doing and swapped the torch to his other hand. The sword sang with a stutter as it was freed from its wooden scabbard.

"Name yourself," the young guard said, then added as if it was an afterthought of the utmost import, "in the name of the, um, emperor!"

Aden held back the rest of his laughter. His old mentor's wisdom reminded him that even a dull mind can kill with a sharp sword.

"Dellem Arkreus." Aden knew better than to use his name, the most wanted man in the entire Astesian Empire. He put his age and height to good use. One look at this pitiful guard told him all he needed to know. He was dealing with a boy in borrowed armor. Little surprise the city guard would stick their junior-most members with this duty. "I've been with the guard seven years, you little shit. You never heard of me? What the Dark is your name, or do I just call you 'Little Shit'?"

That confused the guard plenty. His mouth worked as if he might force up the words he couldn't find.

"Gods!" Aden said. "Speak!"

"I—I'm Gardon Mustart," he said as if uncertain of his own name. Aden pitied him.

"Mustart, eh? Well, this is your lucky day."

"Yes, sir."

"Do you even know where you're going?" Aden asked.

"Yes, sir." Mustart smiled. "Main line for the west end. I was going south."

"You poor kid, they've been sending you down here a lot, haven't they?"

Mustart laughed with him. "Yes, sir."

"Well, to be honest, I'm more lost than a virgin in a brothel. Been a long time since they sent me down here. Even took a bad spill, so I guess that makes me more wet behind the ears than you." Aden pointed to his leather armor. "So do me a favor. How do I get out of here?"

"Closest exit point is the Castine Street interchange." The guard fumbled with the torch again as he sheathed his sword. As he stepped closer, his eyes took in Aden's leather armor for the first time. "You're not in uniform."

"I sure as Dark don't plan on walking around smelling like a damn sewer," Aden said. "They got a problem with me being down here in my old leathers, they can kiss my arse."

Mustart laughed at that. "Got to remember that next time they send me down here."

Aden laughed with him. "Lead on."

Mustart knew his way through the sewers better than Aden could have dared hope. If he hadn't been so worried about arousing the guard's suspicions, he'd have asked him to slow down. Even better, the guard babbled on so much that Aden never needed to speak a word. He just grunted in the appropriate places.

Aden might have made it out of the sewers without a drop of blood spilled. Unfortunately, Mustart wasn't the only guard on patrol down there.

18

The Wraith

Aden spotted the new torch approaching much as Mustart's had. He didn't think he could play the same trick twice, not unless his escort had a twin brother.

With Mustart's back to him, Aden slid one of his daggers free of its sheath.

"Wow," Mustart said, "they've got a lot of us down here tonight."

Aden took a look at Mustart's armor. He might slide his dagger beneath the back plate and sever his spine. Or he might go the simpler route, slit his exposed neck. He could do either, toss him into the water and hide before the one approaching them was any the wiser. Only problem was that he liked this k id.

"Gods," Aden muttered as he adjusted his grip on his dagger.

"What's that?" Mustart asked.

Aden slammed his fist as hard as he could into Mustart's temple. The guard crumpled to the ground like a heavy blanket.

"Who's there?" The other guard sounded older and more experienced. "Answer me now!"

"Gardon Mustart!" Aden knelt over Mustart. "Got a prisoner here. Give me some help."

"On your feet!" the guard shouted. No, this one wasn't falling for Aden's bluff.

Aden picked up Mustart's torch from where it fell and flung it at the second guard. The guard dropped his torch as he held up his armored arms to block the thrown torch. Aden borrowed Mustart's sword and swung it at the other guard like a club. Already off balance from the torch, the sword slammed into the guard's stomach and knocked him into the water.

The guard cursed and screamed as he thrashed about. He refused to give up. With his sword still in hand, the guard chased after Aden from the water and swung at his legs. Aden parried the attack, but the guard's swing came at an odd angle. The sword buried into Aden's boot and scraped his ankle. Aden thrust with his borrowed sword. The point struck the guard's chest plate but didn't pierce it, only shoved the guard back.

Aden limped down the walkway, trying to put some distance between them.

"Stop!" The guard shouted something more, but the same growl that Aden had heard before drowned out his words. The growl didn't come from beneath the water. Aden turned in time to see a black shape surface in a filthy shower right behind the guard.

The guard turned and screamed. Black, leathery wings unfurled. A pair of hands grabbed the guard's face and chest. Hundreds of tiny, sharp teeth in those hands gnawed off the guard's nose and bit through the chest, then burst out the back.

Aden forgot to run as he watched the monster dine on this man. It roared with victory as its hands bit off chunks of flesh, muscle and bone. The creature wore no clothing, only that smooth, black skin. A single, massive eye, a blue light that glowed from the iris which surrounded a catlike pupil, looked at Aden. He knew from experience that an opening in the back allowed that same eyeball to peer behind it, too.

The blue eye turned to Mustart. Aden ran to the guard he'd knocked unconscious and grabbed him. For such a short, thin man, Mustart's armor made him damn heavy. No chance of carrying him. Aden dragged him by the armpit.

"Wake up!"

Mustart didn't stir, so Aden ran as best he could. He forgot the pain in his ankle. How close was the damn door out of here?

The monster in the water ripped another piece out of the second guard's stomach then tossed the corpse aside and spit out the bits of unwanted bone. Sparks flew from the dead guard's armor where it struck the wall.

Aden looked over his shoulder. The black creature roared as Aden dragged away its dessert.

"Wake up, dammit!" Aden had left both torches where they'd fallen. The dim light made the walkway hard to follow. Water splashed onto the path, making his footing worse. He looked right and left for the way out, but all he saw was shadow and brick. "Wake up!"

Mustart said nothing, and the monster roared. Aden would never outrun it. He considered dropping the guard and running for it. The boy probably wouldn't return the favor had he known who Aden really was, but Aden couldn't bring himself to abandon him to that monster.

Aden dropped Mustart. He placed himself between the guard and the beast. Water exploded left and right with each step of the large creature, its mass more than twice that of Aden's.

Borrowed sword in hand, Aden asked himself why he was doing this. All this trouble to get here only to give up his life for an incompetent guard he'd conned into leading him out of these damn sewers. If he could get past those massive arms and stab the wraith in the eye, he might have a chance.

"Stay back!" The monster's roars almost drowned out Aden's shouts. "Just back off!"

To his shock, the black monster stopped. The silence of its stillness scared Aden more than its earlier roars. The sword shook in his grasp, much as he tried to keep his hands still.

"I said back off!"

That large eye's cat-like pupil narrowed on him. Then the last thing Aden ever expected happened. The monster stepped back. Then another step followed, and it kept backing away until it disappeared into the dark. A gentle splash let Aden know it had slipped back beneath the water's surface.

Aden dropped to his knees and gasped for breath. "Thank you," he whispered, "Oh, thank you, gods." Even then, he couldn't make his hands release their death grip on the sword.

"A dar'jiat wraith." Naming the creature made it no easier to accept what he'd seen. He didn't want to believe it, but he'd seen it. Not just any wraith either... the same damn one that killed his attackers in Crestnal. Now, he knew it hadn't merely happened upon those two boys. The wraith must have been ordered to spare him, maybe even protect him. Whoever controlled the wraith actually wanted Aden kept alive, and that order had given Aden power over the wraith, enough to make it retreat from an easy meal. Once the wraith's owner learned that, he'd make sure to take the advantage away.

The next time—and there would be one—Aden would be forced to fight.

19

The Black Dog

Aden's generosity to Mustart ended once he found his way out of the aqueducts. A set of stone stairs led up to a door. He forced it open and found himself in a moonlit alley next to some elaborately designed building. He dragged the guard up the steps and out onto the street. He propped him up against the side of the building. Someone might try to mug him, but he doubted that. As tense as this city must be, even the most foolish thief would think better about picking a guard's pocket, conscious or otherwise.

"Thanks for the help." Aden placed a hand on the unconscious guard's shoulder. "Sorry about your comrade."

He waited at the edge of the alley, looking up and down the street before walking out onto it. Deathly quiet. A glance at the moon suggested he'd taken much longer than he'd expected. He'd lost more than half of the night. Even Will would probably be worried by now, assuming he wasn't taking advantage of the local aplettsars.

Even this late, Ostice appeared unnaturally deserted. The city leaders must have enacted a curfew to keep order during the transition of power. He was considering which way to go when he saw the statue in front of the building where he now stood. The carving depicted a nude woman with a dog crouched at her feet as if to strike in her defense.

"Castine," Aden whispered, awed by the glow of moonlight upon that pure white figure. He remembered the guard had said they were near the Castine

Street exit. The statue and dog reminded him of Miriam and her pet. He'd emerged next to a temple devoted to this goddess, one of the newer ones.

He knew little about Castine or her followers. The Order had tried to infiltrate the Church of Castine shortly before he left. Their hunters were killed for the effort. According to the Order, the religion bore more resemblance to a cult than a church, but too many powerful people belonged to the new religion for the Astesian government or any other to dismiss or ban it. The size of this temple and the name of the street suggested the so-called "goddess of retribution" had gained an even stronger foothold within the Astesian Empire during the past three years.

The shadows of back alleys concealed him as he travelled across the city. He worried that the Black Dog Inn might not permit him entry given the hour and the curfew. Come to think of it, they might balk at the smell of him. He trusted Will to have covered for him, but his venal companion had made no promises. The bastard would probably leave him to his own devices just for the fun of watching Aden make a fool of himself.

At least Will and Dellem had given him good directions for finding the inn. Even at night, he found the Black Dog after he reached one of the major roads. They'd said the Black Dog was big, and they hadn't exaggerated. The building stood five stories tall, with each level slightly smaller than the one below it, reminding Aden of a pyramid.

The first signs of life he'd heard since finding his way out of the aqueducts whispered to him as he neared the front doors. He hurried inside and was caught in the frog-eyed gaze of a servant boy.

"Can I help you, sayer?"

"I'm meeting some friends here," Aden said, grateful to have found a child "guarding" the door.

"You smell like my dad's dog." The boy wrinkled his nose.

"Really?" Aden thought smelling like a dog must be a step up from a sewer.

"My mom says he smells bad, because he's always sitting in his bungs."

Great, Aden thought, *I smell like dog shit.*

"My friends should have a bath waiting for me," Aden said. "You got a room for Will October?"

"I don't know, sayer," the boy said. "I just run food up to the rooms when they tell me to. My mom's the overseer. I'll get her, if you want, but please don't tell her I was standing here. Don't want her to know I was hiding by the door. You know?"

Aden smiled. Children avoiding responsibility: a great universal truth. He suspected even the parents of the West, no matter what manner of beast they might be, suffered the same trials.

He winked at him. "I'm glad you noticed me while you were passing by, so busily working."

A mischievous grin appeared just before the boy ran off to fetch his mom. An overseer was what he'd called her. Probably the Astesian equivalent of a head servant.

He'd hoped for a woman worthy of an aplettsar, but the prize for his patience fell a far cry shy of that dream. She'd pulled back her hair in the current fashion, wound about a thin stick that pointed up and to the back. The extra hair, and there was plenty of it, spilled down behind her from the top of the stick. The fashionable style didn't match the hard lines of her face. A woman with at least a decade more than Aden's twenty-five years, she made it clear without words she wouldn't deal with any trouble.

"My son was wrong." Her eye twitched as if the sight of him offended her. "You smell worse than my husband's dog. We don't tolerate worthless vagabonds who haven't the sense to visit a bathhouse before stepping over the threshold. Now, get out."

Aden's eye was the one twitching now. "Overseer," he said, doing his best to sound respectful, "I'm meeting guests of yours who should have a bath waiting for me. My room is already paid for."

"I don't care if you're meeting the city minister and offering half the empire's treasury," she said, her voice shrill without being raised. "Get out, because the only room I'll see prepared for you will be in the jail."

"I'm meeting a fellow named Will October." Where the Dark was Will? Was he standing around the next corner getting a good laugh? If so, now was the time to end the joke.

"There is no guest here by that name," she said.

"He was traveling with another friend," Aden said before she could force him away, "Dellem Arkreus."

"Get out!"

Aden wanted to stand his ground, but he couldn't risk it. If she sent for a sentry, then he'd end up with more trouble than just a trespassing charge. Where were Will and Dellem? He stopped out onto the front steps of the inn as the door shut behind him. Will had given him some spare coins before they'd separated, and now he knew he'd need them. Had someone caught Will and Dellem? No one would even know to look for them. He'd have to puzzle over that one later, because he didn't dare linger in the open. Best to find another inn and fast.

He made it about ten feet from the front steps when the overseer's shrill voice once more called to him.

"Lord Shakta!"

Those two words petrified him. He turned to look at her, and any effort to hide his surprise was wasted.

"My apologies." She struggled to hold her head high, reminding him of a soldier at attention. "Your room is being prepared as we speak."

They stared at each other, and only once Aden realized she appeared as intrigued to discern what he must be hiding did he relax. Surely Will wouldn't have told her his name was Shakta, not even with his twisted humor. If Will hadn't, then who? He nearly refused the room, but if he didn't take this room, then he might find himself on the streets all night. Could he manage that without running into a sentry? He doubted it. He was lucky he'd made it this far without being challenged.

Aden climbed the steps back into the inn. The overseer never took her eyes from him. She made him feel like a wild animal that had wandered its way into the city. Did she realize he was wanted for the murder of her emperor? She didn't appear frightened, merely curious.

"Please follow me," she said.

They walked into the common room which was lit only by candle light. He saw more shadows than faces, but even in the thin light, he could make out the layers of fabric cast about the walls and over tables like multihued waves in a storm. A few eyes glanced his way, but none lingered. These people feared being seen, just as he did. People with their own secrets. No wonder Will had picked the place.

The overseer led him to the stairs, which spiraled upward from the center of the common room. As he climbed, he saw the rooms here included interior balconies that looked down on the common room. To Aden's surprise, his escort didn't stop until they'd reached the fourth floor. An imagined phantom brushed the hairs on the back of his neck. He turned in time to see a shadow of movement from one of the balconies, but whoever was watching him disappeared behind a layer of dark purple curtains and into the apartment. Perhaps he was just being nervous, but Aden doubted it. Someone had granted him entrance, and for certain, it wasn't Will or Dellem.

"Are you hungry, sayer?" the overseer asked.

"Your kitchen is still open?"

"It never closes." Pride twinkled in her eyes as she looked back at him. You'd think she owned the place.

"Some salted agon meat and ale." By the Gods, he'd gone long enough without ale. If his adventures this night had proven anything, it was that the poison had worked its way out of his body.

"I will have it brought to your room. I trust you will want your bath first."

"Gods, yes." Was there ever a doubt?

"My son is bringing the hot water." The way she said it left little doubt the duty was meant as a punishment for her son.

She opened the door to his room and led him inside. His only baggage was what he wore and carried in his heart. The room turned out more spacious than he'd expected. He hoped he found Will, because he didn't have near enough coin for this. Tapestries of the ocean covered the walls to the right and left. The bed, positioned within the center of the room, looked large enough to accommodate five bodies. He wondered how often that many people shared it.

"Will there be anything else, sayer?" the overseer asked as she opened the door.

"No, this will be fine."

Once she left, he searched the apartment to make certain he was alone. He found no one in ambush nor any concealed peepholes. A few minutes later, the boy he'd met at the door arrived. With many grunts and groans, the child poured the hot water into a round bath set within the floor. The water still boiled within the bucket, even as the boy added it to the cooler water of the bath.

"If you need more hot water, just ring the bell." The boy pointed to a blood red rope that disappeared into the ceiling. The boy didn't need to say how much he hoped Aden wouldn't ask for more hot water.

"What's your name?" Aden asked.

"Shevin."

"You've a good mother. I can see she loves you very much."

"Can be awful mean sometimes." Shevin gave the bucket a vindictive rap. "But she's good to me and Dad."

"I'll let her know you were very courteous to me," Aden said. "I'm grateful for her hospitality."

Shevin laughed at that. "The mistress didn't leave her much choice. Told my mom if she didn't get you before you left, she'd send her running after you, curfew or no curfew."

"The mistress?"

"Lady who owns the place."

"Mayhap I'll get to meet her," Aden said. "What's her name?"

"Mistress Sersas." He lowered his voice. "She's an apple star."

"Yes, I've heard of those. Thank you, Shevin. Now, off with you before my water gets cold, and I have to send for you again."

"Yes, sayer." Shevin scampered out the door.

Aden doused the candles in his room. Faint torchlight danced through cracks in the drawn curtains leading out onto the balcony that overlooked the common room. He removed a dagger from his jacket. He peeled off his clothes, still sickeningly slick from his toxic dip within the aqueducts. The warm water felt good between his fingers as he noisily splashed it about, but he resisted the desire to slide into the bath and cleanse his body. Instead, he pulled out one of his daggers and positioned himself by the door and waited.

The door never opened, nor did he see how his uninvited guest entered. The intruder wore a heavy cloak, and the fabric's folds rubbed against each other. The silhouette of the hooded figure passed between him and the balcony's curtains. He grabbed the intruder by the arm and tossed them onto the bed. They shrieked like an eagle shot by an arrow as they struggled to get up, but he pinned them face down as their arms flailed. A dagger appeared within one of their slender hands, but he slapped it from their grasp.

"Stop struggling or I'll let you suffocate." He kept his voice calm. Few things sucked the fire out of a panicked victim than an attacker's indifference.

A muffled cry of defeat answered him. He looked around to make certain no one else had entered while he struggled with his intruder. As best he could tell, they were alone.

He turned them over and gripped them by the throat. Aden pointed the tip of his dagger between their eyes.

"You look well, Miriam, or would you prefer I call you Mistress Sersas?"

She looked different and not just because of the darkness. The woman had painted her skin so that it sparkled like gold. The once matronly, village clothes she'd worn were replaced with a violet-blue dress that created the illusion that it might spill to the floor if she stood.

She stopped struggling as he pressed the tip of his dagger against the bridge of her nose. "Do you plan to kill me?" she asked.

"That depends on what you're doing here," Aden said, "and how well you answer my questions."

20
Miriam's Answers

Miriam's eyes focused on the dagger as Aden gently pressed the tip of the blade between her sender eyebrows.

"I will answer any question you have," she said, "but answer one of mine first."

"And what is that?"

"Where is Dellem?"

Miriam's question made him hesitate, because it was the last thing he expected her to ask. "He was supposed to meet me here."

"You damned fool! If they see him here, they'll kill him and me."

"Why?"

"You! Once they see him here, they'll realize he's seen you. They'll kill him and come for me."

"Who are they? Who are you working for?"

"I serve the emperor," she said.

"That's a lie." He fought the urge to snap her neck. "You stole my shakta and helped frame me for your emperor's assassination."

"I was deceived, just as you were. For centuries, the aplettsars have served as spies to the emperor. I thought I was working on his behalf, assigned to watch over you until they finished with your weapon."

"Then why did you let me leave unchallenged?" He squeezed her neck more tightly but made sure he left her enough air to speak.

"I only thought they wanted the shakta. Letting them keep it seemed even better. I didn't know about the emperor's murder until after you'd left."

He couldn't decide if she was lying to him again, but he didn't have anyone left to trust. He relaxed his grip on her throat and eased back the dagger. "Dellem was supposed to meet me here."

"He never made it," she said. "I would know if he had."

"The people who framed me have killed almost anyone who came into contact with me. So why spare you and Dellem?"

"They didn't kill Dellem, because they didn't know he spoke with you in Crestnal. No one was supposed to even know you were there."

"Did you hire those boys to attack me?" Aden asked.

"No, someone else must have. They weren't supposed to take a knife to you." She made that sound as if that was the only offense committed against him.

"How did they even know I was going to kill Orin in the outhouse? I didn't discuss that with anyone."

"I don't know that. All I know is that those boys were supposed to deliver you to me alive along with your shakta."

Aden was getting dizzy trying to keep all of this straight, but what those boys had done finally made sense. "They were double-crossing whoever hired them," he said. "Ambitious little bastards were probably going to make off with my shakta and sell it to the highest bidder."

"Most likely," Miriam said. "Have I answered enough?"

"Not near enough." He released her anyway. "Who's controlling the wraith that killed them, Miriam? Is it you?"

"Wraith?" She sat up fast as a dart aimed for the ceiling. "What are you talking about? A dar'jiat wraith?!"

"What do you think killed those boys?" He crossed his arms as he glared at her. Did she really expect him to believe she was this ignorant?

"A wraith that far east?" She sat up on her elbows to look him in the eyes. "That's ludicrous."

"Farther east than you know." With each step, the pain in his ankle reminded him of his encounter with the wraith earlier tonight. "I just saw the damn thing in the sewers."

She didn't respond to that, at least not with words. The doubt in her eyes let him know she trusted him as little as he did her.

He decided that if she was going to try another attack on him, she would have done it the minute he released her. At least she acted genuinely surprised about the wraith. She also seemed more worried about Dellem than anything else. The constable would like that.

"Stay there." Aden placed his dagger on the floor beside the bath, to keep it within reach. He slipped into the hot waters and groaned with relief. "You explained why they didn't kill Dellem. Why are you still alive?"

She laughed. "I'm one of the most well-known aplettsars in Ostice."

"Then why use you for that business in Crestnal? You were there for months."

"Before I became an aplettsar, I was a healer." She spoke of both professions with the same pride. "Not many aplettsars can make that claim, and not every aplettsar is a spy. We never discuss such things amongst ourselves, so we never know which of our peers is more than a sex worker."

"They've killed an emperor," Aden said. "I hardly think these people would shy away from adding you to their list of the dead."

Miriam fumed at that. The woman had more of an ego than he'd ever expected.

"They're keeping you around to frame in case they don't get me." Now that Aden had figured that out, he decided Miriam might be telling him the truth about her part in all this. He lowered himself in the water up to his neck. "Disappeared for weeks, rendezvoused with an assassin in Crestnal just before the assassination, and known well enough to make for sweet gossip... Wouldn't be difficult to concoct a motive either. How many times did you service the emperor?"

She sighed and rubbed her forehead, pushing back her hair. "Yes, a crime of passion would work well for them, whoever they are. If that's what they really wanted, then they wouldn't have asked me to let you live."

"I messed up their timeline by waking up early." If the emperor was murdered here in Ostice, then he'd made it to Gorman almost as fast as a messenger hawk. They'd counted on him not reaching Gorman until days after he did, maybe even hoped to arrest him in Crestnal.

"How long before a successor is named?" he asked.

"The Council of Regents announced the four candidates today. Next week, they select the new emperor."

"Doesn't leave us much time."

"Us?" Her eyes drifted to his dagger for a moment.

"They won't wait much longer to come after you," he said.

"They have Dellem."

"Would they bother keeping him alive?"

She shrugged. "I can't guess how they think, but I would let him live until I knew whether you valued his life enough to bargain."

"Who are they?"

She answered with a shrug.

"I don't believe you." He picked up the dagger and pointed it in her direction. "Someone told you to go to Crestnal."

"I never meet face-to-face with my contact, and I suspect he's dead now."

She sounded too certain of that. "If you've never met—"

"I left a message for him when I returned from Crestnal. There was no reply, and I later discovered my message was never retrieved."

"Wait." He stood in the bath, his grip on his dagger tight as he considered leaping out to grab her. "You knew about the wraith. You had to."

"I knew nothing about a wraith until you told me just now."

"Tell that to the Cavanagh family." He still remembered their gnawed bodies. "You used Amella Cavanagh's body to replace yours when you burned down your home in Crestnal."

Miriam answered with a blank expression. "Make sense," she said. "What is this business about the Cavanaghs and what fire?"

Aden told her about the wraith killing the Cavanaghs and how Amella's body was used to trick people into thinking Miriam had died in the fire. She stood and paced like a caged cat, despite the threat of the dagger in Aden's hand.

He didn't want to believe she was ignorant about all this, but he doubted even she could be this good of an actress. *Fooled you pretty damn well before, didn't she?* his old mentor's voice chastised him.

"Nothing was ever said to me about that," she said. "Nothing."

"Where is my shakta, Miriam?"

"Probably being held by the Imperial Guard somewhere inside the palace. You'll never get to it, not without an army to fight your way in there." She waved off the notion for the absurdity it was. "Was Dellem alone?"

Aden smiled. Was it possible Miriam was carrying a torch for the constable? He supposed so, but it didn't give him any more reason to trust her.

"Dellem was with a friend of mine, a tavern owner from Gorman named Will October."

She stopped pacing. Her eyes narrowed at the mention of Will's name. The son of a bitch definitely got around.

"How do you know him?" Aden climbed out of the bath. The water was turning tepid, but it had done its job. He felt much better. Certainly, he smelled better.

"The aplettsars have suspected him for a spy for some time, but we don't know who he works for."

Will, a spy? "I've always gotten the impression he was available to the highest bidder."

"No, there's a method to what he does. We simply think he's allowed a long leash to conceal his ties."

Aden grunted, trying to consider that. Will didn't strike him as idealistic enough to be a patriot for any cause or country, but the more he learned about Will, the less he really knew. He wondered if Will was even still alive.

"Will and Dellem were supposed to get a room here today and wait for me. Did either of them ever show?"

"No," she said. "It's fortunate you asked after Dellem. I was curious why someone would show up for a room well after the curfew, so I listened from around the corner as my servant ran you off."

"You didn't recognize me?"

"I couldn't see you, but when I heard you mention Dellem's name, I recognized your voice. I wasn't certain it was you, though, because I couldn't imagine what foolish notion would have possessed you to come to Ostice."

"Didn't have much choice." He abandoned that line of thought. "I have too many questions, and all the answers are here. Who's in charge of the aplettsars?"

"I don't know." She held up her hands to stave off his rebuttal, which must have been obvious from the way he'd scowled at her. "None of the aplettsars know. I have theories, but we haven't time for those."

He agreed with that. He wrapped a towel around his waist and walked over to the bed.

"We need to work our way up the chain," he said as he sat on the bed. "Surely you have some kind of plan for getting a message to and from your superiors if your contact is killed."

"Instructions do exist for this sort of thing," she said as she resumed her pacing, "but I've no idea who to trust."

"We don't want someone we can trust." Aden slammed his fist on the bedside table. "We want the bastards behind this. Find them, and we'll probably find Dellem and Will, too."

"We're more likely to find ourselves in a cell beside them, if we aren't careful."

Aden thought they'd be lucky to live so long.

"Very well," Miriam said after a long silence, "if we're going to do this together, then you'll need something proper to wear."

"Something proper? Just where are we going?"

"The palace."

21
Regent Aphestin

"Something proper" hardly fit Aden's opinion of his clothing, what little of it there was. Miriam could have at least given him a shirt. The only thing he wore from the waist up was a thick, gold chain wrapped about his neck like some damned dog collar. A black, silk sash was wrapped about his waist to top off a baggy pair of gold pants tucked into a pair of the nicest black boots he'd ever seen. He'd gladly hand over the pants when this was over, but he hoped to make off with the boots.

He felt like a fool strolling down the streets of Ostice like this and even more so for doing it in broad daylight. His eyes darted about, looking for street thieves. Miriam had placed up to four rings on each of his hands. He'd heard of thieves who'd cut off a hand for less than what he was wearing.

"If you wore any less," Miriam said, "no one would believe for an instant you were an aplettsar." What little sleep they'd gotten hadn't helped her mood. From the moment they'd gotten ready for this, she'd been critical and impatient. The woman was scared. A person didn't fake fear very easily, certainly not masked f ear.

"How much less can a man wear and be seen in public?" he asked.

"You'd be surprised," she said with a critical laugh. He wondered if she was simply having fun at his expense. She was certainly wearing more than he was. The clothes she wore amazed him. The thin, sea green fabric flowed about her. She looked like an ocean breeze made flesh. The outfit covered most of her body and yet created the illusion of indecency with just enough flesh showing in all the right places.

The brief walk from the Black Dog to the palace educated Aden on life in Ostice. As they walked past the market, three people made offers on Aden. A fourth person followed them for several blocks and made a handsome offer for the pair of them.

"We haven't nearly as many aplettsar men as there are women," Miriam explained.

"Why not?"

"There's a length requirement."

"You can't be serious," he said, laughing until he realized, "Spirits burn. You're serious."

"I wouldn't laugh, if I were you," she said, most definitely not sharing his amusement. "There's a reason I'm hiding your small prize in those loose britches."

"Shit."

He still had trouble adjusting to this new version of Miriam, or rather Mistress Sersas. To his surprise, Miriam had turned out to be her real first name. He still saw her as the motherly woman he'd met in Crestnal, but he couldn't ignore her sexual power. Men stumbled on their feet as she walked past them. She didn't come near the prettiest woman he'd ever seen, but she carried an air of confidence he'd never seen in another woman. Miriam could probably intimidate Rhea.

"Are you certain you want to do this?" Miriam asked him as they neared the palace.

They'd gone to some efforts to make him look as different as possible. His hair had gone some time without a cut, so they'd slicked his hair back and tied it off into a pony tail. They'd also shaved off his beard, which really pissed him off. If an Imperial Guard recognized him for the most wanted man in their kingdom, then he deserved to catch him.

"We don't have a choice," he said. She'd offered to come alone, but he didn't trust her that much.

He knew very little of this city. For all the information the Order of the Hunt possessed, most of his training had been directed towards defending the border against the West. He'd heard the palace in Ostice was the size of a small city, and judging from the outer wall of the palace, that was true enough.

The outer wall was dark grey brick piled twice as high as the tallest building he'd seen thus far in Ostice. To conquer this city required two sieges, first for the city and second for the palace. No small task. Adding to the challenge was a deep trench dug around the entire outer wall of the palace. A fence surrounded the trench, and a damn good thing. Anyone falling into that thing was good as dead. A wide bridge connected the palace grounds with the rest of the city. From what he could see, the bridge looked as if it just pulled back into the ground beneath the front gates. Despite the emperor's assassination, the gates were open. Eight men, armed with halberds, stood guard. He wondered if that was the normal number assigned to the front gate. He suspected there were more he couldn't se e.

One of the guards stopped them before they crossed the bridge. He must have been almost as tall as Aden. Mean looking son of a bitch, too. Aden was tempted to ask if his face doubled for the bridge in his off time but thought better of it. Bridge Boy smiled to them in that unfriendly way that said he'd rather cut out your tongue and fry it than trouble himself with the effort of an intelligent conversation.

"What's your business here?" He leered at Miriam and then laughed as if he'd made a joke.

"We need to see Regent Aphestin."

That wiped the smile from the guard's face. "Yes, ma'am. Who should we tell him is here?"

"No one."

"Let 'em pass," the guard said to his peers.

Aden waited to say anything until they were through the gate and walking a discreet distance from the guards.

"No one?" he asked.

"It's the second password," she said.

"The second? What was the first?"

"Regent Aphestin," she said. "There's no regent in Ostice with that name."

"Do the guards know that?" Aden asked. "Bridge Boy looked ready to drop a load in his armor."

"I'm not sure who they think he is or what they do once they've been given the proper passwords," she said. "I do know that Aphestin is derived from Malaphestino."

"The three-headed god of death," Aden said. Yes, that probably encouraged ample rumors, enough to scare the guards and keep them from asking questions. "I take it you've never done this before."

"No," she said, "I've never had to. I only know what is supposed to happen."

Aden had expected the palace grounds to be choked with buildings just like the city that surrounded it. Instead, fields of grass with sparsely placed trees greeted them. The emperor's palace, a wide structure with dozens of spires that shined like polished marble, stood in the center of the grounds. The dirt path they walked on led there, but Miriam turned left onto a smaller path leading to a less impressive building made from the same brick as the outer wall. The trees grew dense around this building. Golden curtains covered the windows, making it difficult to discern anything about this structure or its purpose. Aden wondered if that was on purpose.

"What is this place?"

"It's where the emperor's mistresses live."

Yes, definitely on purpose.

"Where to now?" Aden asked.

"The garden on the far side," she said, her teeth almost clinched as she spoke, an undercurrent of emotion there he couldn't quite make out.

"Take it you're pretty familiar with this place," he said.

"Yes," she said. "I was once the emperor's favorite."

Bitterness. That was the emotion in her voice.

"Once?" he asked. If she didn't want him to pry, he didn't doubt she'd tell him to shut it.

She afforded him a sideways glance, an irritated one, as she answered. "You suggested last night that I could be framed for hiring you, that it would appear the act of a scorned lover."

"So, things went beyond a matter of business with the emperor."

"Not for me, but it did for him."

Aden let out a low whistle. "I think I see the problem."

"He became obsessed, even suggested he could have his wife killed so that he could marry me," she said. "I should have ended it sooner, but I made my fortune from the reputation I gained as his favored aplettsar. I was too young to realize my reputation would only increase with the rumors that followed from our split."

"Surprised he didn't try to kill you or ruin you," Aden said.

She smiled at that. "He did try."

They said nothing more as they walked around the building. Aden heard nothing coming from inside it. He supposed with the emperor dead, the place had little purpose until a successor was named.

He let out a low whistle as they reached the far side of the royal brothel. "Not bad," he said. "Not bad at all."

Plants typically held little interest for him. Even he couldn't ignore the beauty of this place, though. He couldn't name a single flower, but he didn't see any color absent. Neatly trimmed bushes stood twice his height and sectioned off the garden much like walls to a house. Four small water fountains surrounded a much larger one. Water leaped from one fountain to the other creating arches that reflected the morning light as tiny rainbows along the footpaths.

"A good time of year to visit," she said without any enthusiasm. She'd probably seen this place enough times to rob it of its luster. Aden didn't indulge his admiration for long. Those walls of bushes created far too many places for an assassin to hide.

"Now what?" Aden asked.

"We wait."

They waited until midday. Aden fought to stay alert, but one could only maintain such a careful watch for so long. They settled upon a bench facing the larger water fountain. More than once, the rustle of a bird's feathers had raised his concerns. His search of the gardens found nothing but nature at play and brought him back to the bench to wait.

"I don't like this," he said. "They want to wear down our nerves."

"It's working," Miriam said.

"Tell me," Aden said, giving in to the need for distraction, "if you and the emperor were on such ill terms, why would you work for him as a spy?"

"It's complicated, but it's part of what spared me from his anger. Years of practice made me quite good at stealing secrets."

"You were too valuable a spy to kill?" Aden asked.

"Perhaps," she said, and she sounded more unconvinced than her choice of words suggested. "I told you I had suspicions as to who heads the aplettsars. I think the one who does is also obsessed with me."

Aden laughed. "Another client?"

She looked at him as if he was mad. "Gods, no. That one—"

Aden raised a hand and shushed her. He'd heard something move, something far too big to be a bird. Aden got to his feet and moved towards the sound.

"Come no further, or we will leave and order the Imperial Guard to kill you both on sight." The voice came from the far side of a brush wall.

That got a smirk out of Aden. Those damned guards were supposed to kill him on sight anyway, so that didn't make for much of a threat. Best to let the one talking not know that—yet.

"Who are you?" Aden asked.

"Who are you?" The stranger's voice rested on that rare border of man or woman. Aden hoped he could figure out that much with the more he or she said. "You are no aplettsar. All that spares you is that she is."

Miriam stood and walked in the direction of the voice. "I believe my messenger has been killed or captured. He never retrieved my last letter."

"Found dead several weeks ago in the trench around the palace," the stranger said. "You were gone for some time. We suspected you dead as well. We are intrigued to find you here."

"I was given orders to go to the town of Crestnal," she said, and Aden could already tell by the way she said it that she knew exactly what the reply would be.

"We gave no such orders."

"Then someone outside of the aplettsars has learned our glyphspeak and far more."

The stranger didn't answer right away. Aden wondered if that meant the stranger believed her.

"Who is this?" the stranger demanded. "He still has not given us his name."

Aden tensed. A dagger was concealed within the pants he wore, but he couldn't draw it easily. The bushes looked too solid to simply dive through, too. He'd tested the strength of their branches earlier to be sure.

"Perhaps what I want would be better," Aden said.

A flicker of movement could be seen through the bushes. A hand raised, a finger held up as if to mark off the point being made. "True... perhaps."

"You have something of mine that was stolen, and I want it back."

"Wooden, white, and full of life?" The stranger rattled off the words like some child's song. "Yes, we do have it. Many would have you."

"He did not kill the emperor," Miriam said. "I can speak for him."

"Tut-tut-tut," the stranger said. "No, that will not do. Your word is compromised. Gone too long, your messenger murdered, and legs spread too far."

Miriam rolled her eyes at the insult. "Those legs have stolen many secrets for you, including the emperor's. I've earned better than this."

"You earned enough for us to spare your life," the stranger said, "and barely that."

"You already know I didn't do it," Aden said. "You would have bound me in a cell by now if you did. What is it you want?"

The stranger's sharp intake of breath made Aden less certain of his assumption. "We only doubt a hunter would drop his weapon, unless you have managed a motive we cannot see."

Aden hesitated to say this next part, because one might assume it only implicated him. "Your emperor wasn't killed by a shakta, not mine. No one can use a shakta except its owner."

"Tut-tut-tut," the stranger said. Aden would have sworn the bastard was amused by all this. "No, a shakta killed our emperor. No doubts there. None."

"How would you know?" Aden asked. Damn it! He needed something to bargain with, something to clear his name.

"We," the stranger said, hesitating as if the word felt wrong to them. "We would know. We know the shakta's power. A hunter killed our emperor. If not you, then another."

Aden held back a curse. He didn't want to debate politics.

"You are a hunter," the stranger said, but the tone didn't imply accusation as much as musing.

Miriam and Aden exchanged glances, surprised by the stranger's abrupt statement. Aden looked around the garden, seized by the fear this stranger was trying to distract them from some ambush.

"Your point?" Aden asked.

"A hunter for the hunter," the stranger said. "We want you to find them."

"I have terms."

"Tut-tut-tut!" The stranger laughed. "You have nothing with which to bargain."

"I need my shakta," Aden said, "and I want my friends released."

A sharp intake of breath answered the demand. "We can deliver your shakta, but we cannot release those we do not have."

"Dellem Arkreus," Miriam said. "If you wish to have your true assassin, then you will give him to us."

"We do not have him."

"You can't expect us to find the answers we need without someone to help us," Miriam said. "The city guard keeps records of all who enter this city. We need to see this and verify the two we seek are here."

"Go where you normally leave your messages and ask for our room. Someone will come for you tonight."

"And my shakta?" Aden said.

He heard the smile in the stranger's answer. "So eager to have it back. What a wondrous toy it must be. Yes, the one we send will have it."

Without another word, the stranger left. Aden was tempted to chase after him, find out who they really were, but he might not get his shakta if he did. Gods be praised! Tonight, his soul would be made whole again.

22

So Close

Aden enjoyed the more respectful stares of the guards at the palace gates as he and Miriam left. He feared the added scrutiny might make them recognize him, but no danger of that existed, not while he shared in Miriam's company. None of them seemed inclined to waste their time on a half-clad man while a woman of her caliber was there.

To his surprise, he found himself somewhat immune to her bewitchment. She offered plenty for a man to enjoy, he respected Dellem too much. The old soldier's love for this lady didn't seem unrequited. That he didn't entirely trust Miriam also dulled some of her luster.

"You haven't said anything," Aden said as they made their way down the street.

"What do you mean?"

"Did you recognize Regent Aphestin's voice?"

He watched her as he awaited her answer. The confusion he saw there answered his question well enough.

"I'm not even sure that was a man or woman. Possibly, they were neither." She shook her head. "I didn't sense the voice was forced, but who knows? I am less certain than I was before who that was."

"So how will we—"

"Not now!" she said, then looked somewhat apologetic. "I need to think on this."

Nothing more was said until they approached a tavern a few blocks from the palace. Not the most expensive place by far, Aden decided, but not so pitiful as to beg why a woman of Miriam's apparent social standing would venture here.

Aden looked for a sign but didn't see one. He might not have thought it a tavern if not for the people going in and out. "This place have a name?"

"The You Know Where," she said.

Aden blinked. "That's the name?"

She laughed, but without any humor in it, probably too distracted by her impressions of Regent Aphestin. "Many years ago, it was called the Mischievous Lady. A name it well-earned."

"We're going to a brothel?" Aden could think of worse places to wait.

"Not exactly," she said. "It's far more than that, but its reputation for depravity made the Mischievous Lady a place with which no self-respecting noble wished to be associated. They never referred to it by name. People would say, 'We'll meet you-know-where,' and after a while, the new name overtook the old."

"Cute," he said, "but doesn't that defeat the purpose?"

"Certain things are no longer as taboo as they once were," she said. "The You Know Where is considered respectable these days."

He grunted as he thought on that. "So where do folks go for the depraved stuff?"

She looked at him as if the answer should have been obvious. "The Black Dog." Her place, of course.

"Before we go in," he said, "let's take a walk around the place."

"I already know every way in and out," she said.

"You do," he said. "I don't. Do you know which room we'll be in?"

"Not for certain," she said. "I can tell you all the rooms are upstairs."

"No windows wide enough to climb out," he said, reminded of the shop in Gorman where Rhea's men nearly caught him.

"And there's only one set of stairs," Miriam said. "You have to go past the bar to get in or out."

"So once we're upstairs, we've nowhere left to run," he said.

"They could have more easily killed us on the palace grounds and disposed of us." Miriam's point sounded true enough. The palace was huge, and if anyone there was worried about being associated with any of this, then her messenger wouldn't have found himself at the bottom of that trench. Of course, that assumed whoever Regent Aphestin was hadn't lied about all of that.

"No stables," he said. "Just a hitching post. Guess this place doesn't cater to the out-of-town people."

His observation amused her, judging by how the left corner of her lips curled. "Oh, they don't discriminate," she said, "but they don't get many who stay more than one night, if that long."

They ventured inside with Miriam taking the lead. Aden resisted the urge to check for the dagger strapped to the inside of his thigh. A move that odd would give away the weapon. First thing he planned to do once they got into that room was pull out that dagger. He'd had enough of this costume.

The tavern turned out more crowded than he'd expected. Even Will's place didn't do this well during the daytime.

The bar covered the entire right wall with every seat claimed. Aden counted three people working behind the bar with enough alcohol in its many forms to keep this crowd happily drunk for weeks.

Miriam slipped between two men at the bar. They gladly made room for her as she smiled to them. Without a spoken word, she let them know she was unavailable for the night but that they wouldn't be forgotten when she was. Aden had marveled at her transformation from Miriam to Mistress Sersas.

The bartender wasted no time coming to her. She arched her body forward, the movement provocative and Aden envied the bartender's view of her.

Get a grip on yourself, idiot, he scolded himself. For all he knew, she planned to slit his throat at the first chance. She'd come into his room with a knife last night, hadn't she?

He couldn't hear the exchange, but he knew when Miriam had invoked the name of Regent Aphestin. The bartender's eyes finally got out of her cleavage and found her face. He snapped his fingers, drawing another bartender away from the drink he was preparing. The second bartender brought a key to the first. From there, the key found its way into Miriam's fingers.

She turned away from the bar with a smile cast over her shoulder to her admirers, which included the bartender despite his shaken nerves. Aden couldn't deny a certain pleasure in escorting her away from the crowd.

The upstairs turned out more cramped than expected. The narrow hallway made it impossible for him to pass Miriam. The room she led him to was the next to the last on his left.

As soon as he walked through the door, Aden went straight to the window. He'd been right. Slim chance of either of them making it through that narrow opening. He checked the neighboring rooftops, but he didn't see any vantage points for an archer on the neighboring buildings.

This place turned out more luxurious than expected, considering the small space. He'd thought the room would offer little more than a bed. Far from it. Expensive fabrics, some thin silk with others made of sturdier stuff, hung from the ceiling in a variety of places around the large bed. Some might mistake them for decoration, but his imagination didn't require much help to consider all the ways an aplettsar might bind a customer with them.

He searched the walls and ceiling for any spy holes and found nothing.

"What are you doing?" Miriam asked.

"Making sure this room is safe," Aden said.

Miriam settled into a gold-painted chair, which matched the sheen of make-up applied to her skin. She might have passed for a statue of some revered queen from ages past upon her throne.

"We're as safe here as anywhere in Ostice," she said.

Aden thought that made it anything but safe. That didn't stop him from dropping onto the bed. Gods, he was tired.

"Any chance that 'Regent Aphestin' might be behind this?" he asked.

"If I knew who they were, then I might say, but I didn't recognize that voice," she said, "not exactly."

"What do you mean?" He sat up.

She looked out the window from where she sat. "That stranger's 'tut-tut-tut'," she said doing a fair imitation of the stranger, "reminded me of Regent Monast. He's the only one I know who does that, but the voice and accent sounded nothing like him. The accent resembled Lady Kleska. She's from a northern province of the empire, and few in Ostice share her accent."

"The accent changed more than once, though," Aden said.

Miriam nodded but added nothing more.

"Who is Regent Monast?" Aden asked.

"He's the military advisor to the emperor. If there's anyone in a position of power we can trust, then he's the most likely."

Aden rubbed at his face, trying to not to think of how little he had slept. "Why do you say that?"

"Boyhood friend to the emperor," she said. "No one was closer to him. He hasn't a large enough purse to make a bid to replace him either. More importantly, he has a bad habit of speaking his mind which hasn't made him any friends. Outside of the emperor, he has no allies—none with any political power."

"In other words, he hadn't anything to gain by the emperor dying."

Miriam smiled. "Exactly."

"What about the lady you mentioned?" he asked.

Miriam's smile disappeared. Before she could say anything, a shriek from the streets below sent Aden jumping to his feet and running to the window. Miriam squeezed past him for a look. A man was sprawled out on the street. His chest was ripped open as if his heart had burst. People scattered, their screams reminding him of the assassin in Gorman who was killed trying to knife him in the back just a week ago. Only this time, the killer hadn't used an arrow.

"A shakta," Aden said. "Stay here!"

He slammed open the door to their room and ran out into the hallway.

"Move!" He shoved a drunken man on the stairs to the side. The crowd within the main room was pressed against the windows, drawn by the dead man's earlier scream, but a fight between two gamblers was forcing their attention back into the tavern.

The door out was blocked by people running out for a closer look while those who'd already seen it tried to force their way inside. Aden took advantage of his height and size. He shoved people aside like a dog digging a hole in the ground. Over the heads of the people in his way, he saw a man dash out from between two buildings and to the body. He wore the black mask and dark green hood of a hunter. Why would he expose himself just to inspect his kill?

Horns sang in the east, announcing the city guard was coming this way. Aden freed himself from the crowd. Then he saw why the hunter had risked a closer look. The hunter pulled something slender and white from the bloodied jacket.

Aden's chest hollowed out at the sight of his shakta, and to see another holding it filled him with a jealous need. This close, he could feel the life within it call out to him as if equally desperate to be made whole.

The hunter looked up at him, and the eyes he saw within the mask's only holes made Aden stumble. The man's right eye was a normal blue, but that left one... No normal sea of white filled the socket, only a massive, yellow iris. Even without seeing the mouth, Aden knew the bastard was smiling at him.

Aden ran as fast as he could, but he was too far away and the hunter too fast. The hunter thrust Aden's shakta into his jerkin and pulled out his own, a battered looking brown stick the length of his forearm.

He heard the thrum of the shakta as the hunter awakened it. The hunter pointed it at Aden and unleashed two strands, meant to surround him from the right and left. They coiled like snakes, then struck. Aden rolled beneath the attack and came back up to the left outside of the attack. The hunter stared, stunned by what he'd just witnessed. Now was Aden's turn to smile.

He wanted the hunter to try another attack with his shakta, but instead, the hunter dashed back for the alley. Aden glanced at the body as he passed it, but he didn't recognize the man. Riders on coursers appeared a few blocks to the east. The city guard was almost here.

Aden ran into the alley and saw the hunter racing down it.

"Stand and face me, you fucking bastard!"

The shakta awakened again and ripped the back wall of a house down to crush Aden. Too late to stop, Aden dove for it. The only thing that saved him was that none of the bricks hit his head. His legs took the worst of it, but the old wall crumbled before it could land on him. That didn't stop the bricks from hammering his legs. He dodged enough of the wall to pull himself out.

The hunter's shakta ripped into the ground where Aden had been prone. Dirt showered up into the air as the magical strands drilled into the dirt. The bastard would have ripped out Aden's heart.

Aden forced himself to his feet and charged down the alley. The hunter had gained a good lead on him, but he was running to a dead end. Aden roared to force his thoughts from the pain in his legs. He didn't want to give the hunter another chance to attack him with that shakta.

That familiar thrum of power, not so much a sound but a sensation that not even most hunters could sense, warned Aden he was too late. He strained with his mind to sense the attack he knew would come, but that never happened. The hunter stopped at the dead end, a two-story tall, brick building. Strands of life shot out of the shakta, not at Aden but into the sky. They latched onto something and pulled the hunter up off the ground. With the shakta's aid, he ran up the side of the building.

"No!"

Aden grabbed his right pants leg and ripped it open. The golden fabric drooped to his foot, exposing the dagger he'd concealed along the inside of his thigh. He grabbed the weapon and threw it. The small blade buried into the hunter's back, just below his right shoulder blade.

The hunter cried out. The pain shattered his concentration and the shakta's strands evaporated. He grabbed for the wall, but the brickwork didn't offer any handholds. Gravity attacked him. The hunter aimed his shakta at the ground and tried to slow his fall, but he hadn't enough time to complete the complex arrangement. He landed on his stomach with a pained whimper.

Aden didn't give him a chance to recover. He kicked the hunter repeatedly in his side. The grunts that answered his assault sounded like music and released all the frustration Aden had held back ever since he lost his shakta. The power of those emotions caught him off guard, clouding him to anything short of making this man hurt. He didn't recognize the "sound" of the shakta until just before its strands hammered into his stomach. The air rushed out of him as the shakta sent him flying back. The most basic of attacks with the shakta, but it was enough to send him into the nearest wall. His head cracked against it. He dropped to his knees, too dizzy to focus on anything.

By the time Aden's head cleared, the hunter was gone along with Aden's shakta. Aden stayed there, on his hands and knees, and an anguished cry erupted from the hollows of his chest and echoed against the walls of the alley.

23
Doors and Deals

The sun was nearly set by the time Aden found his way back to The You Know Where. He relied on the frenzy of the evening crowd to conceal the condition of his clothes. He was forced to hold up his pants leg as he walked through the tavern and hurried up the stairs.

He shoved open the door to the room without a knock or any warning. In hindsight, he realized he was lucky Miriam didn't shove a dagger into him.

"Where the Dark have you been? What happened?"

Aden answered with narrowed eyes. They might have intimidated her if all else about him hadn't resembled an over-whipped mirden. He sat on the foot of the bed and let his shoulders slump.

"A moment longer, I would have left and assumed you dead," she said, her voice lashing at him with little effect.

"He is a hunter," Aden said, "but not one I've ever seen. One of his eyes... wasn't human." That yellow eye... What manner of creature was that?

"We can't stay here any longer." Miriam stared out the window. Blood still stained the ground and likely would until a strong shower washed it away. "I don't think we should risk the palace again. I don't think there would be any point."

"Why do you say that?"

"The man your hunter killed was Regent Monast," she said.

"Shit," he whispered. There went the one man Miriam had thought they could trust. "Someone else must have been in the garden, heard him arrange the meet here."

"We are out of options," she said. "We either stay here and wait to die, or we run."

"No," Aden said, "we aren't finished yet."

"And what do you propose?" she asked, her words clipped with anger.

"First, we go back to the Black Dog." He glanced out the window. "I can't go around dressed like this."

"And if they're waiting for us at the Black Dog?"

"If they wanted us," Aden said, not bothering to wait for her, "then they would have already ambushed us here."

He pulled open the door, only to have it rip off its hinges. The door crashed into him and knocked him facedown to the floor.

"Not a word," an all too familiar voice said, the threat directed more to Miriam. Aden tried to shove the door off his back, but it pressed down, nearly squeezing the breath out of him. He could sense the life strands of a shakta holding it in place.

A pair of dark red, leather boots stopped just to his right. Her pants creaked as she knelt down. "Aden," Rhea said, her voice strained with anger, "where is my shakta?"

"Not here," Aden said. He forced as much confidence as he could manage into his voice. "Like being ripped in two, isn't it?"

"Where is it?!" She sounded out of control, just the way he'd wanted her, just the way he felt.

"I'll give you your shakta, but I expect something in return."

She slammed her foot down on the door. He heard something crack, and he couldn't decide if it was the door or his back. "You'll live!" she said. "That's reward enough!" She held her foot there, pressing down until she forced a groan out of him.

He gasped as she lifted her foot off the door.

"You don't plan to kill me anyway," he said once he'd swallowed enough air to do it, "so if you want that shakta, then you help me find mine."

"Mine first," she said.

"I want your word," Aden said, "your word that you'll help me get my shakta back, and I want the Order out of my life."

She knelt down again, low enough this time for him to look into her pale, blue eyes. They looked hard enough to pass for diamonds. Any other time or place, he might have considered them beautiful, and even in this awkward position, he couldn't help but recall Will's story of how this woman had called out his name in a drunken passion.

"And what's to stop me from going back on that word?" she asked.

"You won't," he said with a devilish smile that would have shamed Will October himself.

The hard lines of Rhea's anger faded from her features. "I can't offer you your freedom from the Order. That's between you and the Mordani, and we both know what those three would say."

"Then help me get my shakta, and give me a day's head start," he said. "We both want this assassin found, and I've seen him... today, in Ostice."

"Who is he?" she asked.

"No," he said, "first I want your promise."

They stared into each other's eyes for a long moment. He clung to the sympathy he found there, prayed it was enough to save him.

"My shakta back first, or the assassin we hand over to Ostice will be you," she said, her voice harder than her gaze suggested.

"I'll take you to it as soon as you get this door off my back," he said.

She stood, hiding her face from his view. He lingered there, waiting for her answer.

He heard her sigh, and he couldn't help the smile on his face, because he knew he'd won.

"No," she said.

"No?" Aden shouted. That was most definitely not what he'd expected her to say after that sigh. "What the Dark do you mean, 'No'?"

"You return my shakta for sparing your life," she said, "but in return for helping find your shakta, you return to the Order."

Aden roared in vain. He couldn't free himself from the position they'd pinned him.

"Letting you loose, even for a day?" she said. "The triumvirate would take my head as easily as yours for that. Your only chance is to return to the Order of the Hunt. Refuse this offer, and the Mordani will order every hunter to kill you on sight, assuming we don't just kill you here and now. Do you really want to keep running?"

"Why don't you go fuck a sword?"

Miriam laughed, the first sound she'd made since Rhea and her hunters had stormed into the room.

"Be silent!" Rhea said.

"He's not going to give you what you want," Miriam said. "Trust a woman who's pried darker secrets than that from dozens of men. I know that tone. That's a man unwilling to yield. He'll sooner cut open his own chest than go back to your Order."

"I said to be silent!"

When Rhea knelt again, Aden didn't see any more sympathy there. One of his old mentor's few alcohol-induced proverbs came to mind, *Never fuck with a woman who wants to fuck you.*

"We need each other," she said.

"We need our shaktas," he said, eager to piss her off with that reminder. The humorless stare she directed at him assured him he'd hit his mark, for better or worse. "If we find my shakta, then we find the assassin. He has it."

"Then we work together to find him," Rhea said, "and when the task is done..."

"...we'll see which of us is faster," Aden said.

She nodded with a confident curve to her red lips. A shift of her eyes directed the hunter holding Aden down to release the door. Aden felt the door lift off his back. He dragged himself back up onto his feet.

He glanced at Miriam to make certain she wasn't harmed. Not only did she appear unhurt, but she looked amused as she watched him and Rhea.

24

Back into the Sewers

An hour after the sun set on Ostice, a bell chimed from the palace. The sound echoed across the entire city and into Aden's bones. Miriam had told him to expect it. The chime warned citizens to stay indoors, and Aden considered the bell alone one damn good deterrent.

"The gods must keep a bell like that ready to usher in Kalle-Al," Rhea said.

"The End of All Things," Aden said, somewhat amused by her observation. They'd been waiting in the alley behind the Black Dog for the city's curfew to begin.

"Where is my shakta?" Rhea asked for what must have been the thirteenth time since they left The You Know Where. That he'd been asking the same question about his shakta for a week now didn't give him much sympathy.

He didn't say anything, just started walking down the alley. Even with Will's directions, he'd wandered a bit on his first night in Ostice, trying to get from the sewer to the Black Dog. Trying to track his way back to the Temple of Castine turned out easier than he'd expected. That the temple ate up an entire block helped.

"What the Dark are we doing here?" Rhea asked. She was staring with disgust at the statue of Castine.

"Getting your shakta," Aden said.

"Tell me you didn't hide it in there."

"No, it's in the sewer beneath the temple."

"You put my shakta in a sewer!"

"Wanted you to have to get a little dirty to get it back," he said.

She tried to slap him, but he swatted her hand aside with his forearm. Her left fist hit him in the stomach, but his leather armor absorbed most of the hit. He pinned her to the wall of the temple and knocked aside two more strikes. She moved a lot faster than he expected, but he got the impression her heart wasn't really in it.

"How did those boys manage to ambush you?" she asked.

"Like you said, I'd gotten sloppy." He let go of her and took a step back.

"They wanted you dead."

"Those boys came close to it." He wondered why she felt the need to discuss this here.

She shook her head. "I mean the Mordani Triumvirate."

"Surprised they didn't try."

"We thought you could be more useful alive. You were still hunting, one of our best, and now they could use you without any official ties."

"That's worked out well, hasn't it?" he said with enough sarcasm to choke a courser. Served the arrogant bastards right. If he had his way, he'd kill all three of them. "Was it your idea or theirs?"

She shook her head and laughed. "Actually, it was Argus' idea. Said you were too good a hunter to lose."

Aden laughed. "I'll enjoy lording that over the one-eyed bastard next time I see him." He didn't think the old courser master had it in him to give any hunter a compliment.

"Why did you leave?" she asked. "No one knows, not even the Mordani. What can you possibly get out of this kind of life? It's meaningless."

"It's my life." His hand shook as he pointed at himself. "Those bastards have used me!"

"The Order of the Hunt serves a noble purpose. We preserve the border and ensure peace with the West."

"Your Order murdered my mother."

She obviously didn't know what to say to that, and he didn't wait for her to think of something.

"Let's get your shakta." He walked over to the same door he'd used last night and pulled it open. "We won't have to go far, but best to keep quiet."

"The city guard has been patrolling the sewers," she said.

"I'm more worried about the assassin wraith that's down there."

"What!"

"Whoever is behind this is also using an assassin wraith." He'd taken a perverse pleasure in holding back this bit of news until now. "I saw it last night when I used the sewer to get into the city."

"We should have brought my hunters!" She stood her ground just at the threshold as he descended the steps into the sewer.

"We're going to need Miriam," Aden said. "Best to keep your hunters where they are, watching over her." He didn't share the fact he didn't entirely trust Miriam. Rhea would have definitely told them to spy on her, and he was counting on them doing just that. Of course, he didn't trust her hunters either. At least he knew the wraith would eventually try to kill him. The hunters, he'd waste too much time wondering if they were about to betray him.

"I wouldn't want to face an assassin wraith alone, even with my shakta," Rhea said. "What fool would?"

He went down the steps. If she wanted her shakta badly enough, and he knew she did, then she'd follow.

Despite his bravado, Aden wasn't pleased about going back into the sewers either. One spill into the city's watered down piss was enough. An orange glow wafted across the concrete walls. Fresh torches had been lit. The city guard hadn't given up its patrol.

"These men are scared," Rhea said, pointing to all the lit torches.

"The wraith ate one of their guards last night."

He wondered if they'd found the remains of the guard. No matter what, he felt certain the guard had increased its patrol. Whether they were looking for him was another matter. If Little Shit had told his superiors about his encounter with Aden, then these guards might be watching for him.

"Damn," he said as he stopped along the walkway.

"What?"

"There weren't this many torches lit last night."

Rhea just shook her head and shrugged as if to ask why that should matter.

He cleared his throat. "Last night, there was only one torch lit in this section."

"The torch is your marker for finding my shakta?"

"Yes."

"Idiot," she said, growling out the word like a cat. "If I wouldn't have to smell you the rest of the night, I'd shove you in that water."

He wondered if she'd considered the smell of her shakta. After a day in the aqueducts, he suspected her weapon would need a lot longer than another day to lose the smell of this place, if it ever did.

Even without looking, he felt her glaring at him as he crouched his way along the walkway. The brickwork was broken up at the wall's base, another reason he'd chosen that spot. The hole was just large enough to completely hide her shakta, but with the added light, he realized the wall was littered with such holes where water splashing over onto the walkway had eaten away at the brick.

"At least this light should deter the wraith from showing," Rhea said.

Aden grunted his agreement, wondering if the one holding that monster's leash knew about last night's encounter. Was IT the hunter who took his shakta? The Order hadn't known much about how the wraiths and their masters' relationships worked in his time with them. He doubted that had changed much in the three years since.

He also wanted to know what dark sorcery had given the hunter that inhuman eye. Aden suspected the hunter was nothing but another pawn, little more important to the overall scheme than the wraith hiding in these aqueducts. Of course, that didn't make him any less of a threat.

"Do you hear that?" Rhea asked.

Aden stopped walking and listened. Distant voices, coming from somewhere ahead of them, echoed through the aqueducts. He heard at least two men.

"They're patrolling in pairs," he whispered. "Shit! Back the way we came."

"Not without my shakta," she said. She refused to move, leaving him no room to get past her and back towards the Castine Street entrance.

"We can come back once they pass," he said.

"No, we're close." She could sense it. One look at her told him that. She had a glassy, distant look in her eyes that did nothing to hide her desperation to be reunited with her shakta. He wanted to shove her in the water and leave her.

"Dammit," he said. "Let's hurry."

He ran from torch to torch, attention divided between the holes in the base of the wall and the direction from which those voices were approaching. Why was this taking so damned long? Hadn't he been closer to the exit when he hid her shakta?

"There!" He spotted the hole, and even in this different light, he knew its shape was right.

The approaching voices stopped. "Who's there?"

"Gods," Rhea said. "Quick! Get it!"

"Stand straight, raise your arms and name yourselves!"

Shit! They weren't sending the junior members of the guard down here tonight. Aden reached into the hole and felt around for the shakta. His fingers brushed against the ribbed stick but it rolled out of reach. "Oh, gods!"

"I said stand straight!"

"Dammit, Aden, what are you doing?"

"Can't reach it!"

He heard the guards running. A look up warned him he'd miscounted. Not two, but three... and all with swords drawn.

25

A Leap of Faith

Rhea leaped over Aden as he struggled to get her shakta free from the hole at the base of the aqueduct's wall. Torchlight reflected off the short swords that Rhea drew. She twirled them before she parried the first guard's sword. A second move slit his gut right-to-left. A shove sent him sprawling into the other two guards. One slipped into the water, but the other jumped back in time to stay on his feet. The remaining guard's sword clash against Rhea's swords, the rhythm reminding Aden of a fast dance.

One of Aden's fingertips tapped against the stick. The shakta rolled again. "Gah!" The weathered brickwork cut into the back of his hand as he forced his fingers deeper. He placed one finger flat against the shakta. He rolled it close enough to place two fingers on top. Another roll, then another, and he had it.

He heard one of Rhea's swords bounce off the aqueduct's wall, knocked from her hand by the remaining guard.

"Rhea!" He yanked the shakta free from its hiding place and threw it up to her.

She spun out of reach of the guard's sword and snatched the shakta out of the air. A blue light, invisible to all save Aden, flared out of the black stick as it found its proper owner. Rhea crouched beneath another swing of the guard's sword. Three vibrant strands spiraled out and drilled through the guard's heart.

Water erupted to Rhea's left as the guard who'd fallen in swung at her back. The strands of her shakta's life force retracted, seeking a new formation. She wasn't fast enough, but Aden was. His thrown dagger slashed across the bridge of the guard's nose. The guard dropped his sword as he tried to protect his eyes. Rhea's shakta, the strands formed into a razor-thin blade, sliced off the guard's head. The head hit the water with a high-pitched "plop." The body fell into the water a second later, sending small ripples across its dark-green surface.

"Come on!" Aden ran for the exit. "There might be more."

"I'm more worried about the blood attracting the wraith."

They emerged back into the alley and slammed shut the door to the aqueducts. They only stopped running when they were in sight of the Black Dog.

"You're good," Aden said, after he'd caught his breath. "Never seen a better burrow formation."

He felt her gaze on him, like spiders crawling up his back. "What?"

"You're not just saying that." She'd been hunched over with her hands on her knees but stood and even took a step back from him. "You can actually see the strands. Can't you?"

"I saw how neatly you dispatched that guard," he said, attempting to deny her accusation.

Judging from the way she studied him, looking him up and down as if she might see some malformation on his person to explain how he could see what no one else could. "There were plenty of rumors about you in the Order," she said. "I saw you catch one too many hunters by surprise back when you were training."

"How could you have seen me?" he said. "I don't remember you, and I couldn't have overlooked you if I tried."

She smiled at that, apparently taking his statement as a compliment. "I wasn't allowed to train with you or the rest of the shateen. That didn't mean I couldn't watch."

He considered her name as he studied her face. Blond hair, blue eyes, take away a few years and fatten that face to a little girl's round cheeks.

"Rheanna Miskhai?"

Her smile faltered. She hadn't expected him to guess it.

"No," he said, "I suppose they wouldn't have let you train with the rest of us. Wouldn't be the first time one of the Triumvirate's children was assassinated by a 'training accident'."

"My father has always been overprotective."

Aden grunted, preferring not to share his thoughts about her father. He looked up and down the alley where they'd stopped.

"We should get back to the inn." He made it one step before she brought him to a stop with one question.

"Why did they kill her... your mother?"

"That's between me and your father," he said. "Now, let's get inside before we're discovered."

He didn't wait for her, just sprinted for the inn. She kept up with him and nearly passed him as they neared the Black Dog.

They made it inside, going through the servants' rear entrance. Little Shevin waved to him as he and Rhea walked past him in the kitchen.

Aden patted him on the shoulder. "Busy night?"

"Yes, sayer," he said with a wide grin. "My mom says we're making a lot of money off the curfew."

"Where's Mir—I mean, Mistress Sersas?"

"Went upstairs."

"Thanks," Aden said.

One look at the crowd gathered in the Black Dog's atrium affirmed what Shevin had told them. Even with all the customers speaking in hushed voices, they were loud enough to let Aden and Rhea speak without any worry of being overheard as they went upstairs.

"You insist we need this woman," Rhea said, "but you haven't said why."

"She's an aplettsar and one of the most successful in Ostice," he said. "That gives her access to people and their secrets."

"In other words, you have no idea how we can use her."

"Her being used to detain me in Crestnal wasn't coincidence," he said as they climbed the stairs. "Anyone who came into contact with me within Crestnal or knew I was there has been killed except for her and Dellem Arkreus. They could have just as easily used a lesser-known healer to do the job, then killed her once they were done."

"You think she's involved with the ones framing you?"

"That or they want something from her. Might even want to use her connection to me against her, possibly a personal vendetta."

"Either way," Rhea said, "she knows who's behind this, even if she hasn't figured it out yet."

"Exactly."

They split once they reached the fourth floor. Rhea headed for Aden's room. Most of her hunters were in there.

One Rhea's men had been ordered to watch and "protect" Miriam. Aden wanted to make sure she was all right and ask her a few questions before Rhea got a chance to ask some of her own.

He knocked on the door to Miriam's room, but no one answered, not even a question as to who was knocking.

"Aden!" Rhea ran up to him. "They're all dead!"

He turned back to Miriam's room. A dark red line formed a crooked path from beneath the door. When he opened the door, the trail of blood widened along the floor, beginning at the broken body of Rhea's hunter. His chest was split open, arms and legs broken and bent as if formed with three joints each instead of one.

Aden rushed into the room. It opened up into an office. He checked behind what was left of her desk and then glanced into her attached bedroom. "Miriam's not here." He held a dagger in each hand as he searched the rest of Miriam's home.

The life awakened within Rhea's shakta, ready for an attack, as she knelt to examine the body on the floor.

"Your hunter's work." she said.

The bed and the rest of Miriam's furniture were thrown about.

"Was my room like this?" Aden asked.

"No, the kills were more efficient," she said from the other side of the room, "all three of my hunters in there were strangled to death. It's as if they never saw the attack coming."

"He wanted Miriam alive. She made him fight to get her." Aden walked back to the hunter's body and lifted the flap of his jacket. "Never even drew his shakta."

"Neither did my other hunters." She lifted the bed's mattress for a look beneath it, possibly checking for Miriam's body, which wasn't there.

"Who else knew your hunters were here?" Aden asked.

"No one," she said. "I didn't even know we'd be here until we found you at The You Know Where."

"The bastard must have been watching us the entire time," Aden said. "Never really left after I chased him."

"Who is he?"

Aden described him as best he could with that horrific eye and shakta resembling a small piece of varnished driftwood.

"I don't know of any hunters like that," she said. "Sounds more like a 'borrowed man'."

"Men who steal pieces of the dead to rebuild their own bodies? I've heard of them, but to carry a shakta? I can't see how that's possible. Shadow can't mix with Light."

"You're assuming borrowed men require Shadow Magic," she said.

"Stealing life from another body?" Aden laughed. "What else could it be?"

"We can debate that later," Rhea said. "This place isn't safe. If they've made their move to take Miriam, then you're next. I just don't understand why they waited this long."

Aden shushed her. "Listen." The buzz of conversation that drifted up from the atrium had vanished. In its place, they heard a single voice. Too far away to discern any words, but the tone left little doubt to the speaker's occupation.

"The city guard," Aden said.

"Grab his shakta and hood!"

Aden bent and pulled the dead hunter's shakta from his jacket and ripped off the hood sewn into the back of the collar.

Rhea ran out to the balcony. She was looking over the edge and down into the atrium as Aden ran out of the room and to her side.

"They're climbing," she whispered.

"Did you get the others' shaktas and hoods?"

"No," she said, "we have to get them. There's already too much evidence to tie the Order to this assassination. Let them find and identify four dead hunters within their city, and any hope to prevent a war is gone."

"How far have they gotten?"

"Third level," she said.

They dashed down the stairs. The shouts from the guards' commander became more distinct. "No one is to leave their rooms, or they will be arrested!"

"Hurry!" Rhea shouted as she ran into Aden's room.

The guards feet pounded like a squad of swift drumbeats. "Stop!"

Aden followed Rhea into his room and kicked the door shut. "Throw something in front of that door!"

She fumbled for her shakta, having already grabbed one of the fallen hunters' weapons. She threw it down and pulled out hers. The strands of life shot out and wrapped about the bed. The mattress and frame held together as she flung them towards the door. The door cracked open an inch before the bed slammed it shut, propped up at an angle.

"Hurry!"

Aden grabbed the nearest hunter's jacket and threw it on over his own.

"What are you doing?" Rhea demanded.

"Not now! Just get that hood off!"

He tore off the third hunter's hood and took his shakta. The door shuddered as the guards threw themselves or something heavy at it.

Wood splintered, but the door held. "They're cutting their way through!" Aden said.

The way the bed was propped left enough room for someone to get in if they could make an opening large enough in the base of the door.

Rhea held the dead hunter's hood and shakta in one hand and her shakta in the other. "How did Miriam get in here before? You said there was a hidden door."

"Drop your weapons and surrender while you still can!" A guard shouted all too clearly through the widening hole in the door.

"No time!" Aden grabbed Rhea by the arm as she was shoving the dead man's hood and shakta into her jacket. He pulled her over to the window, kicked it open and dove out with her in tow.

"Aden, no! I've never done this!"

The sloped roof sent them sliding to the edge. Despite her protests, her shakta exploded into life. They were already in free fall as the strands shot forth, seeking something to latch onto.

"Don't let it go taut too fast!" Aden's arms wrapped tightly about her waist. If she tried to instantly stop their fall, she'd dislocate her shoulder for sure. Rhea screamed her fear and frustration. He looked up and saw the three strands reaching skyward.

"Find something!" he shouted.

"Hang on!"

The strands coiled tightly, and the end stabbed through the wall of the inn. He felt the strands anchor onto something. "Not too fast!" he said, but the ground was too close.

Their descent slowed, but they still hit the ground hard. Aden stayed limber as his feet hit the street, collapsing into place, but having Rhea land on top of him didn't help.

They didn't move for a moment. They sang a duet of groans. Rhea recovered first. "You fucking idiot!" She crawled off him.

"Later." He struggled to his feet. They'd landed in the alley. Wouldn't take the guards long to find them.

"Need a place to hide," Rhea said as they ran down the alley.

"They'll be searching the inns," Aden said as he waved for her to follow him, "but I've got an idea."

26
Questions in the Dark

Aden's eyes had adjusted as best as they could manage, but he could barely discern the outline of his hands unless he held them close to his face. The nearest light came from a torch at the turn of a neighboring passage. The guard hadn't been lazy, Aden had just tossed the torches that were in this section into the water. At least if someone decided to patrol in this part of the aqueducts, Aden and Rhea would see the guards long before the guards saw them.

"We can't stay down here forever," Rhea whispered. They had barely spoken, not wanting to risk their voices carrying.

"No, but this is probably the last place they'd think to look for us. They might be patrolling the sewers, but they won't search them in force unless they know for sure we're here."

They'd run until they found an entrance to the aqueducts. Aden had worried they'd have to make it all the way to the Castine Street entrance but they found a way in just a few blocks from the Black Dog. He couldn't tell how long they'd been underground. Tracking time without a sky was damn near impossible.

"No point in moving until we figure out what to do next," Aden said.

"We need a way to figure out who's behind this," Rhea said.

"Will thinks it's someone making a bid for power here in Ostice."

"Makes sense, but which one? Damn politicians. Last I heard, there are four people vying for power."

"Whoever it is has got Will, Dellem and Miriam, locked away somewhere."

"You're assuming any of them are still alive," she said.

"Doesn't make sense to kill your hunters and not just leave Miriam's body there if the plan was to kill her."

"Shhh!"

They didn't speak for several minutes. Aden strained to hear what had worried her, but he didn't notice anything. He knew better than to ask.

"Thought I heard a splash of water," she said, "a ways off."

He had told her about the dar'jiat wraith, that it had responded to his commands last time, but neither of them wanted to test that again. Dousing the torches certainly didn't help their chances of avoiding it. With the rest of the aqueducts lit up, the dark might draw the wraith to them. "Let's hope it was just the tide changing," he said, "affecting the currents in here."

He didn't need to see her face to know that wasn't a convincing theory.

"Any chance Argus is inside the city?" Aden asked.

"No, we rode ahead on our coursers. The plan was for him to wait outside the city with the wagon once he got here. Is that your way of saying we're so desperate, we'd even turn to a courser master for help?"

"He might be an ass boil, but he's a good fighter, even without a shakta."

Back when Aden had been in the Order, he'd taken part in the weekend spars. No shaktas or any other weapons were allowed, and the fights weren't limited to hunters. Anyone with coins to gamble could take part. For an old man, Argus could put up one hell of a fight. He was infamous for planting his opponents on their faces and telling them, "Kiss the marble. Easy money." Argus had beaten him down to that red, marble floor more than once when he was a boy. Shakta or no, Aden and Rhea could do far worse for help at this point.

"I'm not even sure if Argus has reached Ostice yet," Rhea said, "and I don't plan to risk going through the city gates to check."

Aden wondered if she was more worried about getting caught herself or if she expected him to run the instant he was out of her sight.

"What about Will and Dellem?" she asked. "When and where did you last see them?"

"We parted ways on the road, leading into the city's front gate," he said. "That was two days ago, middle of the day. I didn't ever see them actually enter the city. I went a long way up the river to wait for nightfall and swam in through the sewers. For all I know, they never even made it through the gates. If they did, then it wasn't the guards who caught them."

"You're assuming the man you and Miriam spoke to wasn't lying."

"Pretty confident he wasn't." Aden was still uncomfortable using the word "he." That voice had been so odd. "If they got inside the city, then they were taken before they ever made it to the Black Dog. That wouldn't have given the one who caught them much time."

"Probably an hour, at most," she said. "I just don't understand why anyone would have recognized them. You're the one everyone is after. For all we know, a jealous lover saw Will and decided to get revenge."

Aden laughed with her. "Possible, but then that wouldn't explain Dellem being missing," he said, then stopped short. "They didn't recognize Will. It was Dellem."

"We've overlooked somebody." The way she said that made it clear she agreed with his theory.

"Someone back in Crestnal." He tried to think of anyone that had stood out while he was there. "Gods! Except for Dellem and Miriam, there was only one other person who came into contact with me long enough to warrant being killed. The priest. Will was right—damn him! He said there was something odd about the priest not being dead."

"But why wasn't Dellem killed?" she asked.

"Miriam never told them he came into contact with me. She was protecting him."

"So who was the priest? What was his name?"

Aden just shook his head, a wasted gesture given the darkness. "He never said, and I never asked." He pounded his fist into the wall. "Dammit!"

"Then we start with the church," she said. "Do you remember which one he belonged to?"

He thought back to the church in Crestnal. "Had four sigils: mountain, fish, flame and cloud."

"Essentialists," Rhea said. "Pretty common for a farming town in Astes."

"Suppose if I made my living off the amount of sun and rain I got, I'd be an Essentialist, too," he said with a shake of the head. "Never put much stock in religion, though."

"You carry a weapon empowered by something unseen, your very soul, and you doubt in a god?" She sounded more amused than offended by his declaration.

"You don't?"

"Suppose I doubt it, too. The Order doesn't encourage much interest in religion beyond reconnaissance."

Then in unison, they both said, "Learn what kind of gods people bend to, and you can bend them to you." They laughed.

"You do miss the Order, don't you?"

"I miss my mother more."

"Did you even know her?"

"Never got the chance," he said. Her question had killed the brief levity and yet somehow he couldn't bring himself to take offense at her curiosity. He decided to change the subject before she did manage to say something that would anger him. "A priest whose name we don't know, only his chosen church... what do we do with it?"

"We're in the heart of the Astesian Empire," she said with a smile in her voice. "Perfect place to start."

"How long you think we've been down here?" he asked.

"Considering how tired I am?" she said. "I'd guess we only have a few hours until sunrise."

"Probably," he said. "Let's try to sleep. You first."

"Would like to say I've slept in worse places, but I don't think I have."

He heard her shifting to lie down. He hoped she didn't take long to fall asleep. That concrete slab wouldn't make it easy, but the longer she took to sleep, the longer he'd have to wait for his turn. Her heavy breathing a moment later assured him she wasn't having any trouble at all.

"Good night, Rhea," he whispered.

27
Two Churches

They found a public bathhouse in what might well have been the worst neighborhood in all of Ostice. Aden had endured far worse since leaving the Order, but for Rhea, the place was only a tiny step better than swimming in the aqueducts.

"Can't decide if I smell better or worse," she said as they walked out of the bathhouse and into a midday sun. She grabbed a handful of her long, blond hair and brought it up to her nose. "I'm telling you I can still smell that damn sewer in my hair."

She held up her hair for Aden to sniff and make his own assessment. "Don't smell anything."

"You've gone into a sewer three times in the past two days. If you have anything left in that nose that works, I'd be shocked."

He laughed because she was probably right. She smiled, and he found it hard not to smile back. He heard his mentor's voice gearing up to scold him, and promptly told "Ol' Whiskers" to shut up. Wasn't he allowed to enjoy himself just a little? Gods knew Will always managed to. *And look where he is?* his mentor managed to warn him despite Aden's best efforts.

Her expression turned to confusion as she stopped to look around them. "Wait. This isn't the way to the Essentialist Church."

"No, there's something I want to see before we go there," he said.

They continued in the direction he'd chosen until they came within sight of the western gate. The gate opened up onto the busiest street in the city. Seven coursers could stand nose to tail and still not cover the entire width of the road. That didn't prevent a clog of vendor carts, mirdens and people.

"Best you don't get too close to that gate," she said.

He followed her advice. Thanks to Miriam, he looked different from any posters that might be hanging around, but that was hardly a guarantee.

"This'll do," he said, then gestured for them to head east down the road.

"For what?" Rhea asked. "I don't understand."

"What's our theory?" he asked rhetorically. "That someone recognized Dellem as he and Will were walking from the gate to the Black Dog."

"Yes?" she said, looking for whatever it was he was hoping to see.

"Let's just walk awhile," he said.

They made their way down the street until they reached the middle of the city. At the center of the large intersection, an exaggerated statue of some long-dead emperor reached up into the sky with his sword. A small, diamond-shaped pool of water surrounded the statue. Three boys laughed as they ran past. They were throwing a toy disc amongst themselves. Aden let the boys get by, then stopped near the statue and looked north and south along the intersecting street.

"So why are we stopping here?" Rhea asked. She crossed her arms and rested her weight on her right leg. The tight leather armor showed off the curve of her hips and Aden smiled as he admired her.

"Well?" She tapped her index finger on her forearm.

"Don't you see it?" he asked.

"See what?"

"Think about it. Which way is the Essentialist Church?" He pointed north along that intersecting street. "And where is the Black Dog?"

She turned her head to look south in the direction of the Black Dog. "You're right. That doesn't make sense."

"Not if the person who recognized Dellem was at the Essentialist Church."

"So you think we're wasting our time," she said.

He shook his head. "Just saying that it doesn't make sense. I can't think of any reason for Will and Dellem to go past the Essentialist Church after they entered the city."

"You saw the traffic on this street," she said. "Who's to say this priest wasn't out for a walk when he saw Dellem? Dellem might have recognized him, made chase and gotten caught."

"Doesn't feel right to me," Aden said.

"So what? We don't go to the church and look around?" she asked. "What?" He could hear a growl to her words. He felt just as frustrated.

"I don't have any better ideas." He shrugged. "We still have to check, but I think we're missing something."

Aden's observation darkened their mood as they traveled north. The crowds around them increased as they worked their way against the tide of people entering the city through its northern gate. Halfway down the road, they came to the Essentialist Church. Aden had to admit to some disappointment. A far cry from the smallest building he'd ever seen, but compared to the Church of Castine, which he'd seen the other night, this place was a hovel. A small garden with a wide fountain occupied the front of the church. The building was constructed from grey brick, little different than the buildings on either side. All that set the church apart, other than the garden, were the statues and carvings along the flat rooftop's edge. A tall pair of doors stood open as a weak invitation for anyone who wished to walk off the street.

Aden let loose a low whistle once they walked through the front doors. What the church lacked on the outside was made up for on the inside. The church reached the entire length over to the next street. Light spilled in through hundreds of tiny windows along the top of the walls. Artwork decorated every bit of wall not occupied by a window. He recognized some of the references, including Kalle-Al with Setinac, the Great Dog of the Gods, leading the legions of the damned out of the West to herald the End of all Things.

"That is one ugly dog," Aden said.

Rhea laughed. "How would you look if five gods ganged up on you, ripped off part of your tail and dropped half a mountain on you?"

"Good point." Aden laughed. "Suppose he's looking pretty good considering."

"She. Setinac was a bitch."

They exchanged playful grins as they walked down the aisle. The scent of melted wax wafted down to them. Chimes danced along the ceiling. The murmurs of priests gathered in a circle within the eastern knave sang to their gods, praying for loving tears to water the crops of their followers. Aden took a moment to realize the hymn wasn't literal, but a plea for more souls to join their congregation.

A priest garbed in a gold, velvet robe stepped away from the prayer group. The smile he offered looked sincere, but Aden had never liked salesmen. That these men traded in the currency of souls didn't improve his impression of them either. He knew they'd be lucky to get out of here without enduring some long sermon on why they were doomed to reside in the Dark if they didn't give over their souls to the Gods.

"Welcome, sayer and sayla," the priest said "Gods guide you both to the Light. How may I service you?"

"The Light shine on you," Rhea said. "We need help with a letter."

The request took the priest by surprise. Her request surprised Aden, too, but he managed not to let it show. He kept his eyes on those gathered within the knave to see if he recognized any of them.

"What kind of letter, sayla?" the priest asked.

"My companion's mother recently died." Rhea pointed at Aden. "She was traveling with us to Ostice, but when we stopped in Crestnal, her heart and body could go no further."

"I'm so sorry." The priest touched Aden's arm. "I can think of few losses more painful."

Aden nodded but said nothing. Rhea's ruse was touching a little too close to his true feelings which he didn't want to share with some strange priest. She wanted to fool this priest, and so she was relying on a bit of truth to make the deception work.

"Thank you," Aden said, unsure what else to add without overstepping his place and ruining whatever gambit Rhea had planned.

"We had to bury her in Crestnal, you see," she said. "It wasn't an easy choice. We weren't sure it's what she would have wanted, but she didn't wish her body taken by flame."

The priest nodded. "No, not an easy decision."

"It wasn't, but your priest there gave her a beautiful burial. His words gave us so much comfort, and we wanted to let him know—to thank him. We'd like to send him a letter, but—well, we don't know how to reach him."

"I don't understand," the priest said. Even Aden was a bit lost with this one.

"He never told us his name, and," she paused, working her hands together as if to rub something into her palms, "you see, we don't know how to write."

The priest took her hands into his. "Sayla, it is all right. I would be honored to help you both with this letter."

"Do you know what his name is?" she asked.

"I'm sure we can find out."

Her eyes looked wet with the promise of tears. "Thank you." She held to the priest's hands as if they were a rope to pull her from the rapids in a storm.

Aden had to fight back the smirk tugging at his lips. The priest was buying her story, top to bottom. *And what makes you so sure she's not doing the same thing to you?* his old mentor's voice asked him. He forced himself to stop staring at her and look back at the priest.

"Thank you," he said to the priest with an uncomfortable smile. He'd play his part for now and remember not to have his back turned to Rhea when this was all finished.

28

A Familiar Face

Aden and Rhea sat with the priest at a long table in one of the church's back rooms. The priest called this their dining hall, and the smell of baking bread drifted in from the kitchen in the courtyard. The entrance to the church had proven more deceptive than they had realized at first.

"The church started out small, but we grew over time. As need required, we added on to the original structure until we owned almost the entire block," the priest said as they waited together. He'd sent a page to fetch some paper and ink, in addition to looking up which priest was assigned to Crestnal.

"The buildings along the front didn't look like part of the church," Aden said.

"No, we've never been able to obtain those properties. The church being here, in addition to the street being midway between the northern gate and center of the city, has always made business too good."

"A few of them looked abandoned, though," Rhea said.

"Yes." The priest attention shifted to the top of the table as his hands tightened their grip on one another. "Hard times for us all."

"For the church, as well?" Aden asked, doing his best to sound surprised in hopes that would encourage the priest to share more. He wasn't that interested, but it was best to keep the man's thoughts focused on anything other than him and Rhea lest he have time to become suspicious of them.

"The Astesian Empire was never intended as a monotheistic society," he said with obvious dislike for that fact. "With hard times, there have come several other religions claiming to know the way."

"I noticed the Church of Castine has grown quite a bit since I was last here," Rhea said feigning a tone of disapproval.

The priest sighed. "I fear so, but let us speak on more pleasant matters. Tell me more about yourselves. What brings you to Ostice?"

Aden smiled sweetly to Rhea, a silent message to remind her that she was the lead in this dance. She smiled and hesitated. Shit! She hadn't thought this out yet.

"Priest Destam," a young boy said from the door to the dining hall. Thank the Gods!

"Yes, page," the priest said. "Ah, excellent. You have the paper and ink."

"Yes, sayer." The page set the requested items on the table. Aden noticed the boy's eyes shifting all over the place with discomfort. What the Dark was going on? Aden kept a smile on his face, but placed a hand on Rhea's leg beneath the table as a warning to be ready to move.

"What is it?" the priest asked the nervous boy.

"Sayer, I wanted to make sure it was Crestnal you were asking about."

"Yes, it was," the priest said with a look to Rhea who nodded her assurance.

"Well, I asked the Priest of Records, and she said we don't have a priest there yet."

"What?"

Aden ignored the priest's exclamation. "What do you mean 'yet?' Who was there?"

"Well, Priest Acclastus was there, but he died a few months ago. And well, we just haven't had anyone to send yet."

"But there was a priest," Aden said, "a man."

The priest sitting at the table looked back and forth from the page to Aden. He finally settled on the page. "You made it clear you were asking about Crestnal?"

"Well, yes."

"I don't understand," Rhea said. "There was a priest. Your sigils were on the church."

The priest cleared his throat. He appeared as genuinely startled by this as they were. "Page, that should be all for now. I'll summon you, if needed."

"Yes, sayer." The page bowed and hurried out. Aden guessed the boy was wondering if all this would somehow get him into trouble.

"I'm sorry," the priest said, "and I feel awkward to ask such a thing, but are you sure you have the right church?"

Aden and Rhea walked out of the church having suffered several apologies by the priest. His sincerity almost made Aden feel guilty for their deception.

"Are you positive that priest was an Essentialist?" Rhea asked.

"I'm positive that's what he was pretending to be."

"Which leaves us exactly where we started," she said.

"Perhaps," he said.

She glanced at the businesses around them. "We'll need to find a different inn for the night."

"Let's head towards the Black Dog for now," he said.

"We can't stay there."

"No, but that's not why I want to go that way."

Rhea smiled. "Oh? And just why are we going that way?"

"Same reason I wanted to go by the gate. Someone saw Dellem and recognized him."

"You assume."

"Don't have any better ideas yet," he said, "so let's take a walk."

"And see if we can get someone to try and abduct us?"

He laughed. "Something like that."

They reached the fountain in the center of the city. The children at play had been replaced by a pair of minstrels, a man with a flute and a woman armed only with her voice. He smiled as she winked at him. "I suppose we should check the brothels," Rhea said with a disapproving grunt. "We might find Will there."

"Not likely," Aden said. "This city doesn't allow brothels, not the traditional kind, and I think Will values his stones a bit too much to risk them on anything other than a free ride or an aplettsar."

They didn't say anything else for several blocks. Aden focused on the people and the buildings. Nothing stood out. None of the faces looked familiar. He'd given the priest in Crestnal little thought at the time. He wondered if he'd even recognize the man if he walked right up to him.

"The Church of Castine," Rhea said as they neared it. "They're obviously doing much better than the Essentialists."

"Lot more impressive looking, isn't it?" He gazed at the statue of the woman with her faithful dog at her side.

"Lot busier, too."

A steady stream of people flowed in and out like dutiful ants on a hill. Aden noticed several wore dark red, hooded robes that belted at the waist and stopped just above the knees. He assumed the ones with the robes must be the priests or whatever title the Church of Castine granted such people. Only a few wore the hoods up, but even with the hoods up, the faces were easily seen. Aden had never understood the practicality of a hood. The only way to wear one so that it hid the face forced the wearer to lose almost all of their peripheral vision.

One of the priests coming out of the church walked by him and Rhea. Aden saw the young man's narrow face, and a chill hammered into his back. The priest had a beak-like nose and thin eyes. The half-hearted attempt at a beard even followed a familiar pattern. Aden recalled the drawing Dellem had made of the two who attacked him in Crestnal, and he felt certain this man was related to b oth.

Aden grabbed Rhea by the forearm. "That one," he whispered. "Follow him."

Was this what happened to Dellem and Will? Had the old constable also seen this man, recognized the connection to the two boys in Crestnal and followed?

"What is it?" Rhea asked as she pulled her arm free of Aden's grip. "Who is he?"

"His face," Aden said. "He looks just like the two who attacked me in Crestnal. I'm certain of it."

The priest led them back in the direction from which they'd come. "Hold my hand," Aden said, "and smile."

She did smile, but the expression wasn't forced. "Clever," she said. Even if the priest noticed them following in his path, he wouldn't be as likely to think twice about two "young lovers" out for a walk. Rhea played it well. When she drifted close to him, she whisper up into his ear. "This is the same direction as the palace," she said, "isn't it?"

"I was thinking the same thing."

Her thumb rubbed against his, and he squeezed her hand. *Easy to forget this is just a lie,* his mentor's voice nagged him, *isn't it?* He'd never held a woman like this. The intimacy of simply holding a beautiful woman's hand surprised him. The feel of her calloused fingers forced him to realize how lonely he was. He only connected with people he needed to survive; he used them. The truth hollowed out his chest with regret. Where was he going?

"The palace," Rhea said without a gesture to the priest as he walked through the front gate. "Can we follow?"

"No," Aden said. The guards said nothing as the priest passed them. One even nodded a greeting. "Just keep walking."

"They didn't challenge him," she said.

"So they know him," Aden said. "We need to find out who he is and who he's going in there to see."

"I'll ask the guards." She let go of his hand.

"Are you crazy? You'll make them suspicious."

She laughed, not sounding the least bit worried. "No, I won't, not if you just keep on walking without me."

"And what makes you think they'll tell you anything?"

"Simple," she said, "I'm a woman."

"Good point." That she was a good-looking woman certainly wouldn't hurt.

"Now, give me a kiss and circle back to the fountain. I'll meet you there."

He was going to ask the point of a kiss, but her lips were already wrapped about his lower lip, giving a light pull. Her hand wrapped about his neck, holding him there and stroking through his thin layer of hair. The moment ended too damn fast. His heart beat painfully against his breastbone, and the urge to pull her back for another kiss nearly bested him.

"Rhea, be careful. Separating like this is dangerous."

"I'll be careful." She walked back to the gate. For this to look right, he needed to be gone, let her look like a girl flirting out of sight of her lover. *Leave her alone,* he told himself. He couldn't help but worry, though. Every time he let someone out of his sight, they didn't come back.

29

The Lost Soul

The minstrels were gone by the time Aden made it back to the fountain. He wondered if the city guard had run them off. This must be the place everyone picked to meet. He'd seen several groups of people come together and then leave.

The more he waited, and Rhea was taking longer than he'd expected, the more he puzzled over what they'd just seen. The two that attacked him were related to that priest, assuming he even was one.

"Miss me?" Rhea said. She appeared out of nowhere, startling him from his thoughts.

"Where have you been?"

"I'll take that as a yes," she said. "The guards were eager to help."

"And?"

"Sept Leader Arraset Loman," she said.

"Never heard of him," Aden said.

"Well, I have." The way she said that left little doubt this was the worst of bad news.

"That bad?"

"He has the ears of every ruler north of the Antolis River, including the kingdom of Nescat."

"Does Nescat even have an official ruler anymore?"

Rhea laughed without any humor in it. "The civil war?"

He nodded. Even separated from the order, he'd heard talk in taverns about the strife in that small kingdom.

"Who do you think incited the war? Our spies, those that are left there, claim Loman provided the church's treasury as a war chest for the current regime. Loman always picks the winning side of a war."

"Sounds like he makes the winner," Aden said.

"Exactly, and doesn't seem like he's betting on you now does it?"

He rubbed his forehead, sensing a headache brewing behind his eyes.

"We need to find a place to stay," he said.

She looked over at a pair of the city guard walking through the intersection. "Perhaps it's time to consider getting out of Ostice."

"We still have one advantage. They don't know what I look like now." He ran a hand over his smooth, beardless chin. "That gives us a little time."

"The problem is that Miriam knows, and we don't know who has her. That's an advantage for someone else."

Aden pointed down the street and started walking, taking her hand into his as they had before. "All the more reason to find a place and quickly."

"Where were you thinking?" She looked down at their hands, then smiled up at him. Those lips formed a pretty smile, too. He supposed they didn't really need to play the part of young lovers now that they weren't following Loman. The feel of her bare hand gripped within his was just pleasant.

"Oh, now that is perfect." Rhea laughed as she realized where he was taking her.

"Noticed it when we went by here earlier."

The Lost Soul might well have been the cleanest inn Aden had ever seen. The white exterior looked so pure it hurt the eyes. Of course, its most endearing trait, at the moment, was the property directly across the street from it.

"Now, we just need a room with a window facing the Church of Castine." Rhea obviously approved, judging by the way she continued to smile at him.

"Shall we?"

The inside looked about the same as the outside. Aden had never visited such a well-lighted inn, nor one so crowded and quiet at the same time. A large, square bar occupied the center of the first floor. Decorative arches quartered off the area surrounding the bar. An odd sort of natural segregation could be seen. Those to the left half were clearly the ones better off. "Guess we know where we belong," Aden said.

"Mm-hmm."

They ventured to the right side. A poorer class of people occupied the tables on this side. One family wore the wide-brimmed hats indicative of more southern kingdoms. Another man at the bar had wrapped his head in a green scarf, a custom of the borderland's native tribes.

"The Church certainly draws all kinds," Aden whispered to Rhea. She nodded her agreement.

They forced their way into one of the few openings at the bar. Even with three people working the long bar, Aden and Rhea waited several minutes before any of the tenders noticed they were waiting.

"And what'll you have, sayer, sayla?" The tender wore his sleeves rolled up as if to compensate for the droopiness of his weary eyes.

"A room," Aden said, "preferably one facing the church."

The tender grinned, his eyes shifting from Aden to Rhea and back. "Getting married tomorrow evening?"

Aden's throat dried up. Rhea's response didn't help.

"How did you know?"

The tender was obviously enjoying the panicked look on Aden's face. Did they really need to keep holding hands now?

"The monthly mass wedding ceremony always draws in a lot of people from out of town. Lucky for you, one couple just got cold feet." He leaned a little closer to whisper. "The groom caught his wife-to-be in their room with an aplettsar. So yeah, we've got a room if you two want it."

"That's lovely." Rhea squeezed Aden's hand and leaned her head against his shoulder. Oh, Gods. "Well, not the part about the aplettsar. Poor man."

"Nah, he was a piece of courser shit." The tender waved over one of the inn's staff, floating between tables. "Lady definitely traded up on that one."

Aden managed a nervous laugh. He didn't notice much else between the bar and the room as the young girl in a white uniform led them upstairs.

"It's perfect." Rhea hugged Aden after they entered the room.

"If you need anything, just pull on the bell." The young girl rocked on her heels by the door.

"Um, dear..." Rhea canted her head towards the girl and cleared her throat.

"What?" He looked over at the girl and then suddenly realized what Rhea was trying to tell him. "Um, thank you." He dropped a few coins into her hand. "Ow!" Rhea kicked him in the foot. What the Dark had he done wrong now? She did another one of those throat-clearing things. Great, the tip must not have been good enough. He dropped a few more coins into the girl's hand. He looked back at Rhea with an exasperated expression. Damned if she didn't look pleased with herself.

"Best wishes tomorrow," the girl said as she walked out, closing the door.

"Dark, woman," Aden cursed. "Will didn't loan me that much money."

She walked over to the bed and spun around before falling back onto it. "Relax, I just don't want my food covered in servant spit because you don't tip well." She issued this melodramatic sigh. "Are we going to spend the rest of our lives arguing about money?"

"Oh, you're funny." He walked over to the window and opened the shutters just enough to look out at the front of the church. The statue with the woman and her dog dominated the view as parishioners and the many members of the congregation flowed in and out of the church. What the Dark was there to do in a church in the middle of the week that warranted that much foot traffic?

"Well, I've plenty of money, if we need it. Unlike you, I haven't spent the past few years scratching by." She sat up. "Don't give me that look. I didn't tell you to go live like some vagabond, begging for work. That was your choice."

"Do me a favor," he said as he looked out the window again, "go sleep with an aplettsar. It'll save us the trouble of a divorce."

She got a good laugh out of that. "At least the bed's comfortable."

Up until the point they got "engaged," he'd have probably agreed.

They took turns sleeping and watching the people going in and out of the church. A lamplighter was igniting the street lights across the street about the time the sky was turning shades of red and purple. He wondered if he had any chance of recognizing anyone coming from that church. Even if he did, what was he going to do? He still hadn't pieced all of this together. All he had was a religious nut good at picking rulers, a handful of people he didn't even know vying for power in Ostice, a hunter with a monstrous eyeball who'd stolen his shakta, and some weird-voiced politician running the spies within the aplettsars who might or might not be dead.

He heard a rustle of sheets to his left. The shriek from Rhea as she stood and stretched hurt his ears.

"This isn't getting us anywhere," he said.

"We haven't given it that long."

She came up beside him and looked out the window. He could feel the residual warmth of the bed clinging to her.

"Don't think we have that long," he said. "We don't even really know how much time we do have or who we're looking for."

She walked back to the bed and sat down. "Well, I had a thought." The way she smiled at him left little doubt she was pretty sure she had something clever.

"We're certain Loman is connected to the ones who knifed you in Crestnal, right?"

He nodded.

"And we know Loman has a history of picking the winning side when it comes to political struggles, so what we need to find out is who Loman and the Church of Castine supports."

He blinked in surprise as he took in that idea. "That makes sense."

"I've been known to have a good idea once in a while."

"All right, great spymaster," he said, "how do we find out who he's pulling for?"

Her head wobbled with her uncertainty.

He laughed as he held up a hand to save her the trouble of finding an answer. "I got this one, but it'll cost you a few coins."

"A few coins?" She emptied five gold coins from her purse into her hand. He was reminded of the first night he'd seen her in Will's tavern, when she'd lost her wager at the dart boards. "Is that enough?"

"One gold should do it, actually." Gods! He'd meant a few coppers.

"One gold?" She arched her eyebrow so high, looking at her face made his hurt. "What kind of informant do you know in Ostice that will talk for one gold coin?"

"One who doesn't know he's being paid for the information," he said, palming the coin from her hand.

He stretched as he stood from his chair. "Keep an eye on the church. I'll be downstairs, getting a drink."

"A drink?" The question had a growl behind, suggesting she was wondering if he'd just hoodwinked her into buying him an ale.

"Trust me." He said each word very precisely, then walked out.

The Lost Soul's downstairs looked and sounded more like a tavern now that it was night. Even if these were religious people, alcohol had a way of making quiet people louder... and alcohol always flowed more freely at night.

"Brandy," Aden said once he found an opening at the bar, "and leave the bottle."

The tender he'd talked to earlier was still there. He'd counted on that.

"You look nervous," the tender said as he poured Aden's drink.

Aden feigned a nervous laugh. "She keeps talking, and I'm starting to wonder what I've gotten myself into."

The tender laughed. "If I had a woman like that in my room, I know I wouldn't spend all that time talking."

"You think that's my choice?" Aden downed half the brandy poured for him. "Dark, man! If I could part those legs of hers with anything less than a wedding vow, you think I'd be here?"

Aden and the tender both laughed at that.

"Not even a member of the church, are you?"

Aden shook his head. "Haven't admitted to it yet. She keeps talking about it, though. 'The Church of Castine says this,' and 'The Church of Castine says you shouldn't do that.' If I don't figure out what the deal is with this church before tomorrow morning, I can probably kiss her goodbye."

"If I had a gold coin for every man who came through this place with that same story, I'd be rich."

Fighting down a smile took everything Aden had. He couldn't have asked for a better opening than that.

"Tell you what." Aden placed his gold coin on the bar. "If you'll tell me what I need to know, then this coin is yours."

The tender snatched the coin between his fingers and tapped it on the bar. "Leena, I'm taking my breather early." The serving girl behind the bar scowled.

"Don't come back drunk this time," she said.

The tender laughed as he snatched an empty glass. He pointed to a table just behind where Aden was standing.

"You a member of the church?" Aden asked as they sat.

"Technically." The tender slid his glass forward. "Kind of a job requirement. The Church owns this inn. Needed the job pretty badly, so if they'd said I had to piss on my own back, I'd have found a way to do it."

Aden nodded. He could appreciate that. After going enough weeks with little more than soup to fill a belly, he'd felt just as desperate.

"So what is the deal with this church anyway?" Aden poured some brandy into the tender's glass.

"Basically, they believe that all the old gods are dead. The goddess Castine slew all of them, a revolt among the gods."

"That why she's called the Goddess of Retribution?"

The tender nodded. "In the first age, the Gods carved up the world, forming the Great Divide and the rivers used to define the twenty-three kingdoms. Each God laid claim to a kingdom."

"Wait. Twenty-three? Don't you mean the thirteen kingdoms?"

The tender leaned forward. "You see, that's part of what the traditional churches have left out, the ten kingdoms of the West. The division of the West and the East was forced upon us by the gods' greed. The gods and their kingdoms warred with each other during the second age. Castine led the second generation of gods in a revolt and destroyed all of the old gods, bringing the second age to an end. She killed the old gods for their greed, vowing to once more restore peace and unity between the East and West. This third age is all about breaking down the barriers created by the old gods and the wars they forced upon our kingdoms. The ultimate promise of the Church of Castine is a fourth age, a golden era of unity for all manner of life with no more wars."

Aden busied himself with the brandy. He sipped at his glass and topped off the tender's each time the man paused in his explanation for a drink. He hoped the mundane task hid how startled he was by this ridiculous distortion of history. The West and the East had never known peace. What a load of shit.

"Nothing wrong with peace." Aden feigned a smile and raised his glass as if in a toast.

"Damn straight." The tender laughed and downed his latest shot of brandy.

"Can see why it's so popular," Aden said. "My fiancée was saying some of the neighboring kingdoms don't care for the Church of Castine, something about banning it or something like that."

"Yeah, it took a while to catch on in Ostice. The emperor called it a cult, even after his wife joined. Savvy bitch, that one."

"Really?"

"Lady Kleska? Oh, yeah. Word has it that lady was running the kingdom behind her husband's back even before they got married."

Aden fought to keep his face straight. Lady Kleska. He recognized the name. Miriam had mentioned that one, but she'd never explained that Lady Kleska was married to the emperor.

"Imagine the church is a little nervous about the assassination. Would think they're worried about losing her as a powerful advocate, that sort of thing."

"Not if she becomes empress." The bartender laughed. "She's one of the four candidates. Bet you anything she's got enough dirt and bribes on the rest of the regents to make sure she's voted into power, too. Most of the regents are part of the Church. Don't think any of the other candidates are."

"Just who are the other candidates?" Aden asked. The tender seemed on quite a roll, the sort who liked the sound of his own voice.

"Heard Regent Dardane, General Gelleran and Lady Biyerra made the cut."

Aden grunted. None of the names rang a bell except for General Gelleran. He'd heard of her. "Three women and one man," Aden said.

"Dardane hasn't much of a shot at the throne either. Looks like we're guaranteed an empress. First time that's happened in close to two centuries."

"What's wrong with Regent Dardane?" Aden wondered if that might seem an odd question, but the tender was too busy sipping brandy and blabbing to give it a thought.

"Dardane the Dreamer?" The tender just laughed as if that should explain it all. Aden shrugged. That got another laugh out of the tender who held up a hand for Aden to wait until he'd calmed down. "Businessman, y'see. Pretty successful one for the most part, but he got all obsessed with this legend of a golden temple in the Aiman Desert. Emptied his treasury funding one expedition after another. Word has it he owes money to more than half the regents. He'll be lucky if he ever pays back one of them."

"Surprised he's even one of the four nominees," Aden said.

"Idiots he owes probably hope he'll get in power so he can pay them back with the kingdom's treasury. Damn dim chance of that, if you ask me. He becomes emperor, then why would he give a shit what these bastards think he owes them."

Before Aden could say a thing, someone slapped the back of his head.

"I can't believe you!"

Aden turned to see Rhea standing there with her hands on her hips. She glared at him with that eyebrow of hers arched high again.

"I'm upstairs all this time waiting on you and you're down here drinking with the bartender!" She marched off with a frustrated growl.

The tender laughed loud enough to hurt Aden's ears. His promise to stay sober on his break had been an empty one. "Oh, I think you're gonna get it pretty bad, my friend."

"Tell me about it." Aden hurried after Rhea. What the Dark was her problem now?

He caught up with her near the base of the stairs over by the back of the inn.

"What took you so long?" She glared at him.

"I was getting our infor—"

"Save it," she said. "I just saw Loman leave the church with an escort."

"An escort?"

Rhea nodded. "Two large men, each armed with a sword. The curfew bell can't be far off. Whatever he's doing must be important to risk being caught out after the curfew."

"Let's hope so," Aden said, "because we're about to risk the curfew, too."

30

Uninvited to the Party

Aden and Rhea ran out the rear servants' door of the Lost Soul. They managed to avoid the notice of the kitchen staff, working in their separate building. The street itself was all but deserted.

"Which way were they going?" Aden asked. How much of a head start did Loman and his men have?

"There they are." Rhea grabbed Aden by the wrist to slow him to a walk. Aden spotted the outline of a small group a few blocks ahead of them. The three men passed beneath the glow of a street lamp. Aden recognized the dark red robe indicative of the church's parishioners.

"Stick to the middle of the street." Aden pulled her over with him. The street lamps were placed along the edge of the road. He hoped being in the middle of the street might make them harder to see. They passed a few other people, despite the approaching curfew.

"Where do you think they're going?" Rhea asked.

"Might be the palace, again," Aden said. So far, they were headed in that direction. A meeting with Lady Kleska, perhaps?

If they were headed for the palace, then Loman and his men would be turning right in just a few blocks. Instead, they cut left and well before the fountain at the center of the city.

"Definitely not the palace," Rhea said.

They ran for the intersection where they saw Loman turn. Aden peeked around the corner. Would be just their luck if Loman's guards had spotted them and were waiting to pounce. One look assured Aden they hadn't been discovered. He saw the three they were following still walking down the street at the same pace.

"Where are they going?" Aden asked.

"I don't know, but we've definitely figured out where the money in Ostice is."

Aden had to agree. He'd seen villages the size of the mansions they were passing. To his surprise, the foot traffic had picked up, along with a few carriages. One passed them that looked gold-encrusted.

"A party?" Aden couldn't think of anything else that made sense.

"With the curfew in place? That doesn't make sense," Rhea said. "As important as he is, I'm surprised Loman's not using a carriage like these others."

Aden nodded. "Maybe it's just not his style. Might think it makes him stand out or something. Who knows? Priests do all sorts of stupid things."

"I suppose."

Even with Aden's limited relationship experience, he recognized when he was being politely told he was full of shit.

"They're going through those gates up ahead," Aden said. The carriage went first, followed by Loman and his guards. A pair of tall men, each armed with a halberd stood watch at the gate. They were dressed in what Aden took for a more ceremonial version of the armor he'd seen the city's guard wearing.

"Shit," Aden whispered. "Other side of the street... fast." He recognized one of the men standing watch at the gate, "Bridge Boy" from the palace.

"Do you think he recognized you?" she asked.

"More worried about him recognizing you." He moved to her left to hide her from Bridge Boy's view. Aden didn't notice Bridge Boy looking in their direction, but on his last glance he spotted a decorative name plate on the outer wall and whispered the name more to himself than to Rhea. "Monast."

"What?" Rhea asked.

"I think I just figured out what's going on." He took her by the arm. "Let's get out of here, before those guards start to wonder why we aren't going inside."

He took another glance towards the mansion. He couldn't see into the court-yard, but he could see people chattering away with each other on the balconies. No laughter and no boisterous gesturing. Everyone acted just the way they should for a wake. The house must have belonged to Regent Monast, the poor bastard who got his chest ripped open as he was returning Aden's shakta to him.

"You two, stop there!"

Aden spotted Bridge Boy and three other guards walking straight towards them. So much for getting past unnoticed. Aden and Rhea ran for it.

"I said stop!" Bridge Boy was pissed. Someone sounded a horn to summon more guards. Just perfect.

Aden sensed the silent hum of Rhea's shakta in her hand.

"No!" Aden grabbed her wrist.

Openly use a shakta and these guards would tear up the damn city before morning to find them, and Aden and Rhea weren't likely to make it into the sewer to hide a second time. "Just run!"

She jerked her arm loose. "Trust me!"

He saw the trio of strands emerge from the black stick in her hand, and an unexpected rush of envy nearly got the better of him. If he thought for one instant her shakta would work for him, he'd snatch it from her and knock her to the ground for those guards to capture.

She didn't miss a step, didn't even bother looking over her shoulder. He glanced back and saw the strands of her shakta sweep across the street. Bridge Boy was the closest, only a few steps back. His foot tripped on one of the shakta's strands. Tall as Bridge Boy was, he took out two of the other guards when he fell. The fool with the horn got caught in mid-blow. He sounded like an angry tabuck punched in the gut.

The only one still on his feet jumped over the others. Bastard was fast, too. Even in metal armor and carrying a tall halberd, the guard was gaining on them.

"This way!" Rhea turned right onto a cross street.

The guard threw his halberd like a spear, aiming straight for Rhea's back.

Aden struck the wooden pole of the halberd, knocking it just enough to the left to spare Rhea. The collision knocked him off balance and sent him sprawling onto the street.

Rhea shouted his name, a warning just before the remaining guard drew his sword and was on him. Aden's training asserted itself. He leaped to his feet, spun to the side, snagged the guard's sword arm and flipped him to the ground. He kicked the guard's head hard enough to knock the fight out of him.

"Let's go!" Aden yelled.

The other guards were already on their feet again. Aden and Rhea had gained a good lead, though. They made it to a back alley. Hidden from the guards' view, Rhea used her shakta to help them scale the side of a warehouse.

Collapsing onto the rooftop, Aden heard the guards running down the alley with that shrill horn sounding again.

Rhea was still catching her breath. "They'll be hunting for us all night. We'll never make it back to the inn."

"Well, it could be worse." He didn't need to look to know she was glaring at him. "At least we're not back in the sewers this time."

She hit him on the chest as they muffled their laughter.

31

Trading Demons

Aden and Rhea traveled across the rooftops as far as they could manage. That let them make it to one of the main roads. By that time, they'd lost several hours and found several new friends, all made of stone.

"I'm telling you, that's a mountain massale." Rhea pointed to the catlike statue looking down the southeast corner of the theater where they'd finally stopped to rest. "Just look at the wings."

"And I'm telling you, that's a western wernrolt."

"Wernrolts have wings like bats!"

"Keep it down." They'd spent the past hour guessing at what each statue on the theater's roof was supposed to be. "I think they just got the wings wrong."

"Oh really?"

"That thing has its eyes in the front. A massale isn't a predator, but the wernrolt is."

"Well maybe they got the wings right and the eyes wrong."

Aden shook his head. She really was a stubborn pain sometimes. He sat down beside her beneath the shadow of what they'd already agreed on as a mythological death dog.

"The patrols seem like they're finally letting up," Aden said, eager to give up their game of *Name the Statue*. "Haven't seen a guard pass by in a while."

"Doesn't mean they've stopped checking the inns."

"Glad we slept when we did." Aden wondered how safe it would be to go back to the Lost Soul. He'd been worried enough when it was his face that might be recognized, but Bridge Boy and the rest of the guards at the palace gate had gotten a good look at her. She'd be easy to spot and easy to describe.

"We need to figure out our next move," she said.

"Don't suppose you'd listen to me if I told you to save your arse and get out of Ostice without me?"

She smirked. "Sounds more like saving your arse from the Triumvirate."

"Don't I have enough problems without them?"

"Seems we both do."

He didn't have anything to say to that. The air over them had turned too heavy with their troubles. He'd spent the past week or so doing nothing but running. The time had passed to take the offensive, but how?

"Aden, something doesn't make sense to me."

He wondered if she was about to pry into his past again but didn't try to interrupt her.

"You said the wake back there was for Regent Monast, the one who was killed while bringing your shakta to you... that he was most likely the one you'd spoken to in the palace garden."

"Actually, I've only Miriam's word on that, but what's your point?" He couldn't figure out where she was going with any of this.

"So how did the hunter with the strange eye know that Monast would have your shakta?" Her question left him with a blank look on his face as he realized what she was suggesting. "He can't use your shakta, so the only reason I can see that he'd want it is to keep you from regaining it. But that also means he had to know Regent Monast was bringing it to you."

"You think it proves he wasn't the one in the garden?"

"All I think it proves is that he was answering to someone else," she said. "I also think he was set up. The hunter wasn't just sent there to keep your shakta from you. I think he was there to make sure Monast died. Don't you think it's odd for a regent to be playing delivery boy?"

Aden suspected he could find several other theories that might fit, but what Rhea was saying felt right. His old mentor had always been one to trust instinct.

"Let's say all that is true," he said. "How do we use that to our advantage?"

"Who do we know is in the palace? Who do we know already has ties to the Church of Castine? Who do we know has reason to want her cheating husband dead, a husband who also disagreed with her ties to the Church of Castine?"

"Lady Kleska, the emperor's widow." Aden nodded his agreement. "And Regent Monast was a lifelong friend to her husband. If she was behind her husband's death, then she'd have reason to fear Monast helping us."

Aden stood and patted the back of the death dog. "Then we know our next move. We need to ally ourselves with the emperor-hopeful who hasn't a chance of winning."

"And just who is that?"

The answer made Aden smile. "A dreamer."

Daylight brought Aden face-to-face with one of the hardest things he'd ever done.

"This is a woman's shirt, right?" He tried to imagine how this clothing would look on Rhea, but he just couldn't do it.

The merchant scowled at him with a face more wrinkled than a slept-in shirt. "Sayer, that is a girl's dress."

Aden wondered if he'd do better to find another shop, but this was the first one he'd found, the closest to the theater where he'd left Rhea. The assumption that the guards would have eased up in the morning light hadn't proven true. He noticed more of them walking the streets than he'd seen any other day since arriving in Ostice.

"What about this?" Aden held up a dark green shirt with one of those curved necklines. He figured it wouldn't hurt to draw some attention to her neckline and away from her face. The cleavage would be a nice change. He'd been tempt-ed to pick up the red shirt, but he figured it was best to avoid that color.

"What about the shirt, sayer?" the merchant asked.

"Well, I mean..." Aden stumbled over his words. "It is a woman's shirt, yes?"

"Castine save us," the merchant grumbled with another roll of the eyes. "Sayer, just tell me what it is you need and if you actually have the coin for it."

"Yes, I have the coin." Would be nice to have some coin that wasn't borrowed from someone else for a change. "She's this tall," he held his hand level with his eyes, "with a thin waist, really nice curves and a great pair of... uh, well... you k now."

"Breasts, sayer?" The merchant went for a third roll of the eyes, as if he spent most of his life with his eyes in motion. "Ostice nice or Gorman nice?"

"Huh?"

"In Ostice, the perfect breast fits in a wine glass."

"Oh, um, well what about in Gorman?"

His eyes narrowed with disdain. "That would fit in a mug made for ale."

Aden wondered what the man had against large breasts. "I'd say she's some-where between those."

"Very well then." The merchant rifled through the table stacked with pants. "That shirt you have should do fine, and that should go very nicely with these." He pulled out a loose pair of black pants with some kind of silverish, shiny stuff going down the sides.

"Are those flames?" Aden asked.

"Flowers, sayer."

"Probably better to get something a little less shiny. How about that dark grey pair?"

"Just the one outfit?" the merchant asked. "Perhaps the lady would also like something less-suited for manual labor?"

"What about a jacket?"

"I was thinking perhaps a dress." The merchant offered a sarcastic smile that bordered on creepy with that wrinkled face.

"No, I need a jacket for her, something with a deep pocket on the inside. You have anything like that?"

Eye roll number four wasn't encouraging, but the old merchant found a leather jacket that seemed to work. Or rather, Aden decided it would work.

"Will there be anything else, sayer?"

Aden wondered why the merchant didn't just say to please get out of his shop?

"Only if you know where I might find Regent Dardane," Aden said.

The old merchant's eyes narrowed enough to smooth out his brow. "What do you want with the regent?"

"He owes me some money," Aden said, recalling the man's reputation for his debt, "and I mean to collect it."

The merchant pocketed the coins Aden had given him. "You'll need the tenacity of Castine herself to manage that. He lives in the Silver District on Jalasper Street, and if you actually get the foul soul to show himself, remind him he still owes me twenty golds. I sold him a leather waistcoat two years ago, and he never finished paying me."

"That'll be a pleasure." Aden picked up his purchases and headed back out onto the street. He was plenty pleased with himself. He'd gotten Rhea's new clothes, some for himself, and learned where to find Regent Dardane all at the same time. That should make Rhea happy.

"What in the Dark did you do?" Rhea struggled into her new jacket. "Were you trying to buy the ugliest clothes in Ostice? This is a jacket for a little girl."

"Would you keep it down?" Aden said. They were in the alley behind the theater. She already looked quite different by the time he got there. She'd braided her hair so that it reminded him of a laurel, the excess hair hanging down her back like twin tails.

"And what are you wearing?" she said. "That ridiculous outfit Miriam put you in at least looked like someone did more than stitch together some leftover material from a bed sheet."

He didn't know what her problem was. He'd gotten himself a dark yellow shirt, grey pants and a new leather jacket. "The whole point is not to be noticed. Do you want the city's guards looking at your face?"

"No, but we're trying to get this regent as an ally. He's never going to take either one of us seriously looking like we crawled out of the sewer."

"Technically, we didn't crawl out of the sewer. We walked out."

Rhea slipped her shakta into its new home. "You are completely missing the point."

"Are you done?" Aden pointed towards the street. "Seriously. We're standing in an alley. If a guard sees us here, these new outfits won't make a difference. Better to get lost in the crowd while we can."

"Fine," she said, "let's go."

At least she hadn't complained about how much he'd spent.

"I can't believe you gave that man three golds for these cheap rags."

"Actually, it was four."

"Four!"

She stormed out onto the street. His longer legs made it simple enough to keep up with her, though. She looked pissed about that, too.

They didn't say anything for a while. They navigated the crowded streets until they reached the Silver District. Aden had expected the houses to shine, but they didn't look any different than the others he'd seen. These were simply bigger brick houses with larger yards. Like the "Monast" house, most of these had name plates on their front gates. Some of the name plates looked more elaborate than others, part of the social competition between the city's rich. That made recognizing Regent Dardane's house a simple task.

"That has got to be the gaudiest thing I've ever seen," Rhea said.

The fence, more decorative than defensive, came up to the middle of Aden's chest and was made of a strange metal material with a mirror-like quality. The house was a three story, pillared monstrosity that tested the length of the property, leaving little room to walk between the sides of the house and the neighbor's fences, no doubt taller to hide Dardane's property from view.

"Not much in the way of security," Aden said. "Not visible anyway."

"Gate wide open, no guards on it," Rhea said.

"The roof?"

Rhea canted her head towards a tower on the right side of the house. Over the edges of the roof, they could just make out movement. "Archers."

"How very discreet. No way to cross that lawn without being spotted. No cover either."

"Probably have dogs or dreiters," Rhea said.

Aden suspected the latter. Those lizards moved damn fast and bit even harder. Their thick skin made them hard to kill, too. The way dreiters blended into their surroundings, a person couldn't hope to see them until it was too late.

"Haven't come this far to walk into a place like that," Aden said.

Going to Dardane, trying to make him an ally was risky. Men who needed money, and lots of it, didn't always make for the most reliable allies. Their choices were pretty limited, though.

"Then what?" Rhea asked. "Either we go to Dardane, or we run."

"No, there's a third choice," Aden said. "Dardane comes to us."

Shortly before midday, a carriage rolled out the front gates to Regent Dardane's estate and turned towards the main road.

Traffic forced the carriage to stop at the intersection, drawing more than a dozen beggars.

"Get out of here!" the driver shouted. He swatted at one of the more aggressive ones, making it clear none of them would get any coins out of him. They didn't really care, because they'd already been paid.

Rhea had given each one of them a copper for keeping the driver busy. Aden had waited at the corner most of the morning and rushed the wagon as he saw the beggars doing their job. He hoped Rhea was moving just as quickly, or this could go bad very quickly.

Aden jerked open the door on his side and jumped inside.

"Gods above!" The shout came from an older, thin-boned gentleman, garbed in a black suit. He sat in the forward-facing seat. A second man with thick, muscled arms that strained his jacket sat across from the first. That one jumped up and pulled back his arm to strike Aden. The carriage's other door opened, distracting both occupants long enough for Aden to land a hard punch to the larger man's temple. Rhea climbed into the carriage and sat across from the older gentleman as Aden shoved the unconscious one out of his seat.

Rhea pointed her shakta at the regent. "I trust you know what this is," she said. If his look of wide-eyed horror wasn't confirmation enough, then his seizure-like nod was.

"Good," Rhea said. "Tell the driver to get moving."

"Dr-driver, move along!"

They heard the driver's muffled curses at the beggars who'd still refused to take the hint. The carriage started moving a second later.

"Not a word, regent," Rhea said.

"But—"

The life strands shot out of her shakta, wrapped about the regent's throat, and shoved him back. "I said—not a word." She held him with the shakta a moment longer, until she was satisfied her point was made.

"Do you know who I am?" Aden asked.

The regent shook his head.

"My name is Aden Murai." The regent's mouth gaped, about to utter something, probably a plea to spare his life, but a glance to the shakta must have reminded him he was supposed to stay silent. "I'm not here to kill you, regent. I'm offering you a chance to eliminate one of your competitors for the throne here in Ostice. We know the Church of Castine is conspiring to place Lady Kleska on the throne. She framed me for your emperor's assassination. I've come to Ostice to clear my name. I'm offering you a chance to work with me to find the evidence I need.

"We both know what implicating Lady Kleska in her husband's murder would do for your chances to be named emperor."

The regent's gaze shifted from Aden and Rhea to that shakta aimed at him. He looked too petrified to give a damn about anything other than getting out of this carriage alive. Aden wondered if this man could really do a damn thing to help him. How did a man like this manage to con so many out of their money?

"Regent Dardane," Aden said in a voice hard enough to force the regent's attention to stay on him, "I'm offering you a chance to rule this kingdom. What do you say?"

The man's attention returned to the shakta as he answered in a shaky voice. "I can speak now?"

Aden nodded.

"I'm just an accountant." The old fellow then pointed at the larger man on the floor of the carriage. "He's Regent Dardane."

Aden looked down at the man he'd hit. Now that the large fellow's fist wasn't aimed at him, Aden realized he was dressed in a much finer suit than the accountant's. He was also wearing one very expensive looking ring on his left hand, too.

"You knocked out the regent?" Rhea looked at Aden like he was an idiot.

"He was going to hit me." He shrugged. "Thought he was a bodyguard."

They sat in the coach as it traveled through Ostice. An instruction from the accountant kept the driver from stopping. Other than the buzz of the city life, only an occasional sigh broke the silence as they waited for Dardane to wake.

"He is breathing, right?" Rhea asked after a while.

Aden put his hand in front of the regent's mouth and felt for his breath. "He's alive."

"Just how hard did you hit him?"

Aden shrugged.

"He hasn't gotten much sleep lately," the accountant said.

Rhea nudged the regent with her foot, but he still didn't wake.

"So where were you going?" Aden asked the accountant.

"Oh, he was taking me back to my droffa while we finished discussing his finances," he said.

"Droffa?" Rhea asked.

"Where he works." That was one bit of Astesian terminology Aden recognized. "Heard his finances aren't the best."

"Quite the mess," the accountant whispered with pride, "but he's got more to work with than you might imagine. Quite the clever man. You'd never know how well off he is. Puts on quite a good show that one, but you didn't hear that from me."

They all shared a polite chuckle which led into yet another awkward pause. The accountant adjusted the cuffs of his sleeves. Rhea spun her shakta in her hand like a small baton. Aden settled for tapping his foot to some catchy tune to which he couldn't recall the name. Damn he hated when that happened.

"A wonderfully cool day, wouldn't you agree?" the accountant said.

"Oh, gods spare me." Aden kicked the regent's leg. Bad enough to wait for the bastard to wake, but to be forced into small talk with someone who probably thought daggers were nothing but oversized steak knives... "Wake up!"

The regent groaned, then yawned. His eyes opened, a confused expression that focused on Aden and quickly sharpened. He scrambled to get upright, but Aden planted a foot on his side to push him back down.

"Relax, regent," Aden said. "If we'd wanted you dead, we wouldn't have waited for you to wake, now would we?"

"There are some who prefer to do it that way," the regent said. "If you don't want me dead, then what do you want?"

"I want my name cleared." Aden removed his foot from the regent.

"So, you're the emperor's assassin, aren't you?" The regent laughed as he sat up.

"I didn't kill your emperor."

"Of course you didn't, but that's not important, now is it?" The regent sat next to his accountant. He looked over at Rhea with a confident smile that reminded Aden of Will and not in a good way.

"Word has it the emperor's wife is going to replace him," Aden said.

"So I've heard."

"How would you like to see her executed?" Rhea asked.

That definitely got the regent's attention. "Are you offering to assassinate her, too?"

"Only politically," Aden said.

"We know the Church of Castine is behind the emperor's assassination," Rhea said. "And I think we all know how close Lady Kleska is to the Church."

"You think the Church of Castine and Lady Kleska murdered the emperor?" A slow smile shown on the regent's face, like a child caught with his hand in the cookie jar and still getting away with it. "You have proof?"

"We've seen the real assassin," Aden said, "here in Ostice."

"I can see why you would want another blamed," the regent said to Aden, then looked over to Rhea. "So what is your stake in this?"

"My homeland is being framed in order to start a war. We didn't send one of our hunters to kill your emperor."

The regent crossed his arms, leaning back in his seat as he shook his head. "For a hunter, you are very naïve. You think killing our emperor is the only reason the Astesian Empire would wage war on your lands?"

"We defend the borders of the East." Rhea sat up straight, chin thrust out. "We are protectors."

"You are also spies and manipulators," the regent said. "Some would say you're not as bothered by the ethics of the Church's actions as much as you fear the competition."

"Trading demons is always dangerous, regent," Aden said.

"Is that a threat?"

Aden couldn't figure out this man. On the one hand, he seemed eager for what Aden and Rhea were offering, and yet acted as if he didn't want or need their help.

"I left the Order of the Hunt a few years ago. Decided I'd had enough of them manipulating my life. I traded demons, and I can't say I like my new one any better. Trust me. You're better off staying with the demon you know."

"So you think if I let Ostice ally itself with the Church of Castine that I'll find it worse than the Order of the Hunt?"

"I think we both know what your emperor's opinion would be," Aden said.

The regent laughed in agreement as he pointed a wagging finger at Aden. Obviously not a man who was among those crying at the emperor's funeral.

"So," the regent said, "let's drop off my accountant at his droffa, and then you and your lovely ladyfriend can tell me how you plan to prove Lady Kleska conspired in her husband's murder."

32

The Back Door

After an order from Regent Dardane, the carriage stopped near a tall building a few blocks from the palace. The regent climbed out with his accountant to have a word with him.

Rhea pressed her ear against the side of the carriage, trying to hear what was being said outside.

"What are they saying?" Aden asked.

She shook her head. "Can't make out anything. Too many people chattering out there, and I think they've walked too far from the carriage.

"I'm not having a good feeling about this Regent Dardane." Aden was kicking himself for this. They had very little choice now, but he hadn't considered what a sleaze this man would have to be to have avoided all those debts for this long. Still, that might work in their favor. Criminals offered the best access to any foreign land, because they'd already figured out how to get around those in power. The problem was that you couldn't afford to forget the nature of the people you were working with.

"If we want to back out now, then this is the time," she said.

Aden shook his head. No, they'd ride down this path a little longer, and see where it led.

The carriage door near Rhea pulled open and Dardane climbed back in. "So, tell me how you think we can prove Lady Kleska is a conspirator in the assassination of her husband."

"The real assassin is still in Ostice," Aden said. "We need to track him down."

"And just why should I believe this 'real assassin' will expose Lady Kleska? If he doesn't, then once she's in power, she can 'prison pardon' him."

"Prison pardon?"

The regent laughed. "The prison of Baladair has more than its share of assigned cells that hold no one."

"Lovely." Rhea rolled her eyes.

"If we find him, we find all the evidence we need," Aden said. "I trust that a man such as yourself has his share of eyes and ears in this city."

"Throughout the Astesian Empire and beyond."

"Then it shouldn't be hard to find our man in Ostice." Aden couldn't hold back a smile. Maybe this would work after all.

"Just how do you plan to stop this man when you haven't your shakta?" the regent asked.

"I have mine." Rhea held out hers. "That and we have other advantages."

"Really?" The regent didn't look convinced. Even Aden wondered what "advantages" Rhea was talking about. Was she bluffing, or did she have an edge she'd yet to admit to him? He certainly did know how to pick his allies: a power-hungry debtor and a lady who wanted to drag him back into the Order of the Hunt. Then there was Will, Dellem, and Miriam... wherever they were.

"I have a man with many contacts, the kind I wouldn't normally want to be seen with." The regent relaxed, looking out his carriage's side window. "I'm taking you to meet him now."

"Who is he?" Aden asked.

The regent didn't answer right away, and even though nothing in his expression changed, Aden could sense a sudden tension. "It's probably best I let him introduce himself. As it is, I'll have to go in first and see if he'll even meet with you. I don't suppose you can afford an information broker?"

"Depends on how much he's asking for." Rhea sounded pissed, in that false-polite way. Regent Dardane didn't seem to notice.

"Driver!" Dardane shouted. "I said the back entrance!"

"Yes, sayer," the driver's muffled voice answered.

The carriage jerked to a halt.

"Gods," Dardane muttered. The carriage made a hard right turn, overcompensating for having nearly missed the back alleyway.

Aden looked out the window, trying to figure out where they were. He'd seen a lot of this city, but a good portion of it had been at night. He prided himself on having a good sense of direction, but he wasn't certain where they were. The alley itself didn't offer anything that would help, only that it definitely wasn't a residential district. The wall to Aden's left was flat, white brick that seemed to stretch for the entire block with only a few doors.

"Wait here." The regent climbed out and knocked on the nearest door, a nondescript wooden one, polished dark enough to pass for black. The door cracked open, permitting whoever was inside a chance to see the regent. The regent gestured towards the carriage.

"What's he saying?" Rhea asked.

Aden shook his head. "Too far away. Doesn't sound like whoever he's talking to is pleased, though."

"This doesn't feel right."

"The man's a criminal," Aden said. "Just keep your shakta in hand and where they can see it. Whoever Dardane is taking us to, he'll think twice before taking on a hunter."

"A pair of hunters," Rhea said with zeal.

Aden smiled back at her. "I haven't been a hunter in a long time, and I'm not going back."

"Then what's the point of all this?" Rhea pointed towards the regent, still quarrelling with the unseen doorkeeper. "Why go to all this effort to clear your name in Ostice when you'll still be walking under a death sentence from the Order? I don't want you dead, Aden."

"Too late for that." He took her free hand into his. She really did have nice hands. "I made my choice when I walked away the first time. If I go back, the Triumvirate is going to want to know why I left. When they find out, I'm as good as dead anyway."

"Why? There's nothing your mother could have done to earn her death that would mean the same for you."

Aden let go of her hand. "My mother didn't deserve to be murdered."

"Fine," Rhea said. "She didn't deserve to be killed, but there's no reason they would want you dead except if you refuse to come back to the Order. Why else would they want you dead?"

"He's going inside," Aden said. The regent looked back at the carriage and held up his hand for them to wait before the door closed behind him. Aden kept his eyes focused on the door, not wanting to look back at Rhea. He didn't need to be thinking about his mother, not right now. If he wasn't careful, he'd be taking that last boat ride across the River of Souls to see her.

Rhea touched his arm, forcing him to stop his brooding. "Aden, the triumvirate doesn't have to know about your mother. You have my word that I won't tell them, no matter what happens."

Aden turned on her, ready to yell at her what shit that was. The way she looked at him kept his yap shut. He wasn't prepared for the sincerity in those blue eyes, and her grip on his arm felt much warmer. The strange thing was that her eyes weren't soft. They were hard, resolved. Most of all, she trusted him, even though she had every reason not to. All his instincts screamed to pull her close and kiss her, and if they'd been granted another moment's peace, he might have mounted the courage to do it.

A shift of her eyes warned him the opportunity was lost. The regent knocked on the door to the carriage and pulled it open.

"He'll see you," Dardane said. "Let's be quick about it. He's not known for his patience."

Aden looked back at Rhea and nodded to her. She held up her shakta and gave it a playful spin.

They climbed out of the carriage and hurried through the door. Wooden boxes were piled up along the far right wall of the large room. Aden assumed this space was for storage.

"Where's your man?" Aden asked Dardane.

The regent was closing the door they'd just entered. "He'll be joining us in a moment."

"Where's the one he was talking to?" Rhea whispered to Aden.

Other than the boxes, he only saw a torch and two sets of stairs. One set led up while the other, on the opposite side of the room, led down.

"I'll go get him." Dardane hurried up the stairs. His footsteps faded away. Aden looked over his surroundings, considering the possible routes of escape.

Rhea stepped in the direction Dardane had gone. "I hear singing."

"I don't hear any—" He stopped as soon as he heard it, too. The music was faint, but he could make out a stiff chorus of voices, dozens or maybe hundreds, coming from somewhere above them. He was reminded of the pretty minstrel at the fountain he'd seen yesterday, but these singers didn't sound half as skilled. "What are they singing?"

Rhea didn't answer right away. She slowly turned to face him again. He watched as her face changed from confusion to horror. She ran past him for the door they'd used to come inside.

"It's a wedding hymn!" She tried to open the door, but it didn't budge. "It's the mass wedding!"

They were in the Church of Castine.

"Stay back!" she shouted and held up her shakta.

The flutter of large wings offered their only warning. Aden and Rhea turned just as the large shadow landed beside them. One of the wings swatting at Rhea's arm and knocked her shakta to the floor before she could form a defense.

If they'd doubted their attacker was a dar'jiat wraith, its roar confirmed it. The twin warble coming from its hands held a seething rage.

Aden snatched one of the small swords from Rhea's back. The wraith's arm thrust at him like a snake strike. He dodged the attack and swung at the arm, catching it before the wraith could pull back. The blade lodged in the wraith's black, tarlike skin and ripped out of Aden's grasp. The wraith shrieked but didn't retreat. That huge, glowing eye turned on him.

Rhea blocked a strike from the other arm using her remaining short sword. That sharp-toothed hand snapped at her throat, but only bit on the blade of her sword. The short blade snapped in half. The wraith growled and spit out the top half of the sword.

Aden and Rhea retreated a few steps. The wraith didn't move, standing above Rhea's shakta. Damn thing knew the shakta was a weapon and that it belonged to Rhea. The only edge they had was that it couldn't touch the shakta without the light magic in it burning the wraith's flesh. Aden drew two daggers. "Rhea!" He pointed to his eyes, cuing her where to aim her daggers. As she reached for hers, he threw his, one aimed for the wraith's large eye. The wraith swatted the dagger aside with a snicker, but the feint had the desired effect, making the wraith protective of its eye. The second dagger went low, but Aden's target wasn't the wraith's feet. The blade hit Rhea's shakta, knocking the black stick into the wraith's feet. Smoke erupted from a pink, open wound in that black fles h.

The wraith's wings flapped violently as it jumped back, far from the shakta. Before the wraith could recover, Rhea struck its eye with another thin blade of metal. Aden ran for her shakta, his boots sliding across the smooth floor. His heart thundered like a storm against his ribcage. He struggled to keep his eyes on that damn shakta and not the wraith he expected to rip into his chest with one of those sharp-toothed hands. He snatched up Rhea's shakta. The wraith roared as it charged him. Aden threw the shakta to Rhea and retreated from the wraith.

The monster's large, flat feet shook the room with each step as it charged forward. Aden looked over his shoulder. One of those deadly hands rattled forward like a snake launching into an attack. Aden tried to dodge. His footing failed him, sending him to the floor, just under the wraith's strike.

Both of the wraith's arms shot forward. Aden scrambled to get back on his feet, but he couldn't move fast enough. He felt something slither about one of his legs. "No!" The leg jerked hard to the side, and his body slid across the floor but not in the direction he'd feared.

He looked down at his leg and saw the three threads of soul light from Rhea's shakta pulling him to safety. The strands released him, but his momentum sent him sliding past Rhea.

She stood her ground. The fool woman was going to take on the wraith. "Rhea, no!"

She didn't answer. Her shakta's strands wrapped around the wraith's leg but couldn't get a grip on it. The dark magic that animated this beast repelled the light magic of the shakta's strands. The wraith chuckled as it unfurled its wings again, ready to pounce. Rhea's lips curled into a snarl as she jerked on her shakta. She wasn't trying to grab the wraith's leg, though. The strands burrowed into the open wound Aden had already made. The wraith shrieked as the unprotected innards of its foot sizzled.

The black mass fell forward, but that huge, winged body didn't crash onto the floor. Its fanged hands bit into the floor and braced its fall. Using only its healthy leg, the wraith jumped straight at Rhea.

Aden had already scrambled to his feet, running for her. He grabbed the broken blade from the sword the wraith had bit in half, but he knew he was too late.

The wraith flew at Rhea. Her shakta's life strands whipped back, trying to find some new formation. One of the wraith's hands snapped at her heart. She spun right as the hand's mouth bit down just short of her chest. The closed hand brushed against her and sent her to the floor as its second hand snaked in for a strike. Rhea screamed as its fangs buried into her right shoulder, blood spraying outward. Her shakta fell from her hand.

The wraith's free hand reared back for a strike at her heart. Aden grabbed hold of the sword still buried in that arm and pulled back on it. He ducked underneath the arm, too close for the wraith to attack him with its hands.

The edges to the shattered bit of sword cut into his fingers as he buried it point-first into the wraith's eye. A shrill, wounded cry deafened Aden as that large, glowing sphere caved. Light blue goop splattered onto Aden's arm just before the wraith stumbled back from Aden. The filthy eye goop, hot as boiling water, leeched onto the sleeve of Aden's shirt and burned against his skin. He ripped off the sleeve, dropping it to the floor.

The wraith wasn't coming back for more. The beast retreated on all fours with a long series of pitiful warbles. The damn thing wasn't dead, probably not even permanently blinded. The heat of its eye would melt away the metal of the improvised dagger soon enough.

"Aden!"

The terror in Rhea's voice made him jump. She wasn't on the floor anymore. Instead, two threads of soul light, wrapped about her neck, wrists, and legs, held her up against the ceiling. Aden followed the trail of those twin threads to the one holding the shakta. The hunter with that monstrous yellow eye glared at him.

"Make a move against me, and I'll rip her apart," the strange hunter said, then added with arrogant amusement, "little Aden Murai."

"Gods," Aden whispered. He knew that voice, but it was Rhea who named him first.

"Argus?" The anger in her voice was sharp enough to cut a man's soul. "You fucking traitor!"

Argus pulled off his mask. Aden had never seen the courser master without his eye patch before now, and he wondered just how long that monstrous eye had been hiding behind the leather patch and just how long he'd been carrying that crippled shakta with just its two strands.

"Why?" Aden asked.

"How long has it been for you, boy?" Argus laughed with contempt. "A week? Longer? You can stand there without your shakta, and you have to ask why I'd do anything to get back a piece of my soul?"

Aden saw a pair of shadows descend the steps behind Argus. Regent Dardane and the Church's sept leader Loman walked side-by-side.

Loman raised his hands and clapped them in a passionless, formal manner. "I don't know which of you to applaud most. Dardane for delivering you both, Argus for capturing you, or perhaps you, Cold Shoulder. I have never seen a man with anything less than a shakta injure a wraith."

"I had hers." Aden spared a glance up to Rhea to make sure she was still all right. "I don't suppose there's any chance you'd let her go since you've got me?"

"You suppose right." Loman strolled beneath Rhea. "She's not going any-where. A daughter of the Mordani Triumvirate in my grasp..." Loman spun around with a laugh.

Aden considered his options while the church leader gloated. If he could reach Argus and disarm him quickly enough, Loman might cushion Rhea's fall.

A low growl from behind him changed his plans. He looked over his shoulder. A large brown dog, crouched as though to pounce on Aden, waited at the side of a tall, slender man. "You hurt my wraith." The man wore a black, leather mask to match the rest of his armor. Aden recognized it as Western in its design, the kind worn by most wranglers, men who mastered all manner of beast in the West. Even if he couldn't see the face, he recognized this fellow by the right hand missing its pinky finger.

"The priest from Crestnal," Aden said. So this was the one holding the wraith's mystical leash.

"Very good." The wrangler stroked his large dog's back. "I trust you remember my little dr'schund."

The wrangler clicked his tongue and the dog's snout lengthened. The rest of the canine's body followed suit, flesh rippling and fur thickening until its mass had doubled, its back as high as the wrangler's shoulders.

"I liked Castine better when she came up to my knees."

"So did Miriam." The wrangler laughed.

"Is she still alive?" Aden asked.

"For now," Loman said. "I trust you're carrying more weapons. Put them down now, and we'll let you live."

Argus tightened the soul strand around Rhea's neck. Her eyes widened as she gasped for breath but found none.

"More importantly, little Aden," Argus said, "she'll live."

Aden wondered that they even bothered offering it as though he had a choice and dropped what daggers he had left onto the floor.

33

The Traitor's Tale

Argus used his shakta to bind Aden's hands behind him and did the same to Rhea.

Sept Leader Loman led the group up the stairs, stopping at a landing with a single door. "Put them in the closet," he said as he straightened his robe. "We'll question the young woman after I've finished with the mass wedding."

"I'll be happy to help with that," Argus said.

"No, I don't trust you to restrain yourself." Loman pointed sternly towards Argus, then turned to the beast wrangler. "Make certain he puts these two away unharmed."

"I should leave before someone recognizes my carriage," Regent Dardane said.

"True." Loman smiled to him. "You've done well. My people will keep the Cold Shoulder here until the time is right for you to reveal his capture."

Aden blocked the regent from going back down the stairs. "Why, Dardane? Why would you betray your people?"

"Betray them? I'm saving my people. After every blade of grass in your home-land of Mirite has been burned to ash and your people killed or enslaved, the Astesian Empire will stand unopposed in the East."

"You really think the West will uphold any agreement you've made with them?" Rhea said. "Your people might not wear the shackles, but you'll be slaves, just the same."

Dardane smirked as he walked past them both.

"Put them away," Loman said as he continued up the stairs.

The wrangler opened the door and stepped aside. Argus pushed Aden and Rhea inside with his shakta. They stepped into a narrow corridor with brick walls. A single torch burned at the far end. Aden counted three doors of steel bars on each side. The doors belonged to some of the smallest cells he'd ever seen, each with only enough room to sit on the floor if a person held their knees up to their chest. Little wonder Loman had called this "the closet."

Argus pointed to the first cells to his left and right. "I'm sure you recognize these two."

"Dellem," Aden whispered as he looked into the left cell. The old constable didn't answer, nor did he look capable of it. Dellem's left eye was swollen shut. Crusty trails of dried blood ran down that side of his face along his throat to his heavily-bruised chest. He'd been stripped of his shirt and boots.

Aden expected to see Will in the cell to the right. Instead, Miriam was crouched on the floor. She didn't look as ill-treated. Her sea green dress, the one Aden had last seen her wearing, was tattered and dirty, but her body looked unharmed. She didn't say anything, opting to glare at Argus as Aden and Rhea were ushered past her.

"Get in there." The life strands to Argus' shakta shoved Aden and Rhea into the two cells at the end of the corridor. Aden turned around as soon as the strand released his hands, but the door to his cell was already shut.

Argus glared at Aden. "If I had my way, you'd already be dead, you little shit."

"Trust me, Argus, the feeling's mutual."

"Aren't you even curious?" Argus asked. "Hm?"

"About what?" Aden didn't want to listen to the bastard gloat, but letting the traitor rant would probably answer more than a few of his questions.

"Oh, for instance, why you?" Argus leaned against the wall next to Rhea's cell and tapped his shakta against the bars to her door. "What about you? Want to know why I love watching this boy suffer?"

Rhea didn't answer. Aden wanted to strangle the life out of Argus, but the bars on his cell were too close together for him to get a hand through them.

Argus glance over his shoulder at Rhea. "You recognize the name K'lara Staarns?"

Aden could just make out Rhea's glare in the dim torchlight.

"You see, K'lara Staarns was a hunter. Damn good one, too. Earned herself a death mark, though, didn't she, Little Aden?"

"You don't deserve to speak her name," Aden said, more to goad him on than anything else.

"K'lara was trained by the same cat-man that trained this boy. Guess Meertak always did have an eye for talent." Argus laughed at that point, as if he'd just made a joke. "Well, some say he loved her like a daughter, even if she wasn't one of his fur-covered kind. Yeah, the tall cat's little girl was charged to hunt down an assassin who killed one of the Triumvirate. Didn't kill him, though. Oh no. Meertak's little 'daughter' went and fell in love with that assassin. Together, they ran and hid from the Order in the West. Bad as all that was, that wasn't what really earned her a death mark. Isn't that right, Aden?" Argus kicked his cell d oor.

"Argus," the beast wrangler said in a warning tone from just outside the closet's door.

"Relax." Argus didn't take his gaze from Aden. "Just having a nice, little conversation about old times. No harm to anyone in that."

"She didn't deserve a death mark," Aden said, less to defend his mother and more to get the traitor back on the track of his story. *Give me something I can actually use, Argus.*

"The fact you're here is reason enough for her to be dead," Argus said. "You see, Rhea, this here is K'lara's baby boy. That's how she earned her death mark. Stupid bitch got pregnant and wouldn't get rid of the abomination in her belly. Her mentor—Aden's mentor hid him when he was a baby and then brought him into the Order once he figured it was safe. Miss him, don't you, boy?"

"I still don't see why you give a damn about any of this," Aden said.

"Oh, yeah?" Argus leaned in close and pointed at that slitted, inhuman eye. "Get a good look at this, boy. Your mom cut out my old one. Four of us were sent into the West to kill her and your father. Two of 'em died killing your mom and dad. The third didn't make it out of the West alive... dar'jiat wraith got him. Me? Lost my shakta making it back into the East. Sacrificed everything to kill your traitorous mother, and how did the Order repay me? Refused to help me get my shakta back. Let a piece of my soul rot in the fucking West and told me I could stay if I'd shovel up their coursers' shit. Some reward, huh?

"That's what I got for doing your mentor's fucking job. He should have been the one to hunt down your mother and kill her, but the cat couldn't bring himself to do it. That's all right, though. I paid him back and then some."

The smile on Argus' face was enough to make Aden want him dead right then and there.

"What did you do?" The words came out as cold as the rage burning inside Aden's heart. He'd spent half a year hunting for his old mentor in the West before giving him up for dead. He never found a body, though. Never found out what really happened to him.

"I knew how bad your old mentor wanted to believe your mom wasn't dead, so after the West offered to give me back my shakta, I had them start a rumor she was alive. Soon as he left to find her, I let them know. Even helped them catch him. All those years, I'd hoped to pay him back, and the only regret I had when I got the chance to torture his furry, fucking ass was that he could only die one time. They tortured him good, and how he kept silent, refused to answer their questions as long as he did... I'll never know how he did it, but he broke. Everyone eventually does, and that's when I found out about you."

Argus started laughing and even when he continued talking, he couldn't stop his laughter.

"Oh, when I found out about you, I wanted to dance. Your mom put on a damn good show before we killed her. She cried and cried about her little boy, saying you'd been stillborn... your body all twisted by the sorcery on her soul from getting her shakta. Damn, she was good, but your mentor let the cat out of the bag. I had another chance to not only even the score, but to get one up on your mom and mentor both. I planned to sucker you into the same trap once I got back, but you were already gone looking for Meertak. Nearly did give you up for dead in the West, but then Rhea found you in Gorman. Triumvirate wanted your head on a spike for running, but I conned them into keeping you alive.

"You see, no one else gets to kill you—nobody but me."

Aden's hands shook, eager for the chance to crush Argus' head in his hands. Aden had killed a lot of people. Every kill he made for someone else, for country or pay. Until this very moment, he couldn't have named a man he wanted to kill just for himself.

"You're right about me being an abomination, Argus." His heart pounded high in his chest, hard enough to make him feel faint. "Now let me tell you something I know about you. You can betray every oath you've ever made and kill as many people as you want, but your soul still isn't whole. I can see the strands to your shakta—the shame that no one but the two of us can see. Two strands—just two. Your new friends in the West broke it, didn't they? All that dark magic they probably threw at it trying to figure out how your shakta works... Finally realized they were wasting their time but figured as long as you'd been separated from it, you'd be desperate enough to settle for even a sliver of what you'd lost."

Argus didn't say anything this time. Aden took some satisfaction in seeing the glare in both his eyes.

"Tell me, Argus." Aden slapped his hand against the bars on his cell. "Does it hurt to use that broken shakta? I bet it does."

"Oh, yes, like fire running underneath my skin, and worth every bit of pain." Argus leaned against the cell door, his eyes looking up into Aden's. "Bet you miss your old mentor, the big kitty cat. Don't you, little Aden? Bet you'd give anything to see him again, to look him in the eyes. Well, I can give you half your wish." Argus just looked up at Aden and started laughing. "Hm? See anything... familiar?"

The horror of just what Argus was saying made Aden's mind spin. That borrowed eye Argus had hidden all this time was stolen from his mentor.

Aden kicked his cell door as hard as he could. The metal bars rattled, but not enough to hurt Argus, just startle him. "Fucking bastard! I'll rip out your other eye with my bare hands!"

"Your bare hands?" Argus laughed. "Oh, that's right. Can't use your shakta, can you? I'd tell you where it is, but I like the thought of you wondering."

Aden hit the door one last time with his fists.

Argus saluted him with his shakta as he walked away.

"Argus!" Rhea shouted. "If you're the one who killed the emperor, then how is it you never left Gorman? You never had enough time to make it here and back."

Argus stopped without turning back around. "Smart girl," he said, "but I did kill him. Figure out that one, and you'll know how the West is going to conquer the East."

He walked out without another word. Then the beast wrangler clicked his tongue. In walked Castine, looking just as she did that first time Aden saw her in Crestnal.

The thought of that small town stirred his memory of when he was attacked.

"Hey, wrangler, tell me something," Aden said. "What does 'Jha veet est. Bayot,' mean?"

"Is that what those two mortayvans said before they stabbed you in Crestnal?" The wrangler sounded amused. Whatever it meant, he obviously got whatever the joke was.

"Yes," Aden said. "What does it mean?"

"It means, 'Kiss the marble. Easy money.' This means something to you?"

"Just Argus being cute." Aden shook his head. Those were the words Argus always said when he beat someone in a sparring match back in the Order.

The wrangler didn't say anything else. He closed the door, leaving them to Castine's company.

"He paid those two boys in Crestnal to kill you," Rhea said.

"Maybe. Dark, he might have even been there and got run off by the wraith." He hadn't even been able to see the two boys that were there, and he couldn't see Argus giving up the kill to someone else like that, not after his little speech. Argus could have easily been there without Aden ever seeing him. Probably why Loman didn't trust Argus alone with him now. "A safe bet, though, he was the

one in Gorman who took out that assassin... the one who came after me in the st
reets."

This was just as Will had warned Aden. Argus had played the long game with Aden, waiting until there was no getting out of the traitor's noose.

34

The Bride and Groom

Aden stared at the small dog outside his cell. Even if he could find a way to open his cell door, there was no getting past that furry guard. Castine looked just as she had that morning in Crestnal in Miriam's house, but the dr'schund could transform in an instant into something far more monstrous and deadly. Any escape plan required a way to kill that shape-shifting beast, and the only way to do that would be to rip out its heart.

They weren't going anywhere.

"Is it too much to hope you two let yourselves get caught as part of an elaborate rescue plan?" Miriam sounded exhausted. He wondered how much sleep she'd gotten since being taken from the Black Dog by Argus.

"'Let ourselves get caught' describes it well." Rhea sat down in her cell and kicked her door. "Still working on the rescue plan."

"Has Dellem said anything?" Aden asked.

"Very little. Just enough to know—"

Aden cut her off. "Mind your words. Anything we say will eventually make it to the wrangler."

"What do you mean?" Miriam asked.

"Our little 'friend' here," Aden said. Castine just sat on the floor and watched the torch's flames dance. Those big ears shifted each time one of them spoke, though. "Dr'schunds share a connection with their master. The wrangler can read her memories later and learn everything we say. I'm assuming you were given her as part of your 'cover' in Crestnal. They were keeping tabs on you."

"If we actually do get out of here, will the wrangler know it when it happens?" Rhea asked.

"No, doesn't work that way. He'll have to collect her memories later." Aden tried to think of a way to ask about Will without coming out and directly naming him. "Did Dellem say if he'd seen anyone else being held in here?"

Given the pause in Miriam's answer, she understood what he was really asking. "Just him and the three of us. Dellem recognized Loman somehow."

"He looks like the two boys who attacked me in Crestnal," Aden said as he studied the door to his cell, trying to find any way of forcing it open. "Might have been his brothers."

"Not likely," Rhea said, she gave her cell door another lame kick. "Forgot you left the Order before we learned about his kind."

"His kind?" Aden sat up.

"Mortayvans." Her cell door rattled a bit as she tried to force the door open with her legs. Didn't look or sound like she was having much luck. "They're a kind of shape-shifter. They feast on the body of a living person and steal their appearance."

"That is vile," Miriam said.

"Rhea, can you make out anything useful about your cell door?"

"Three hinges on the outside. Might could pry out the bolts in the bottom two hinges but not the top one. They haven't gone cheap on the brickwork either. Don't see much dust breaking loose when I'm kicking it."

Aden reached his fingers through an opening in the bars. The top hinge was too close to the ceiling. No way to pull out the bolt. Ceiling had probably been built after the door was installed. Person who designed this "closet," as Loman had called it, knew what they were doing.

"Small opening along the bottom." Aden slipped his fingers out to wiggle them but quickly drew them back as Castine yapped and snapped after him.

"They use that to slide food into the cell," Miriam said. "Only bread and small bowls of soup, so far."

"I don't recognize the lock on this door either." Aden could tell some kind of key was required, but he'd never seen a lock that looked as complicated and stubborn as this one. Some locks were simple enough to pick with a boot lace, but he'd need better than that to get out of this.

"What if you—" Rhea stopped short as Castine jumped up and growled towards the door to the closet. The little monster doubled in size before its paws touched the floor. She crouched, ready to strike.

Aden realized Argus might be coming back to make good on his threat to kill him. He kicked at his cell door, only getting a loud rattle. Bracing his back against the wall and his feet on the door, he pushed with all his strength but the door wouldn't give.

The door to the closet opened. Castine pounced. Aden heard the ring of a drawn sword. Castine yelped and a spray of blood drew a red line down the middle of the closet. The dr'schund's body landed on its back and rolled back onto its paws. Blood dripped from her mouth as a growl gurgled from the back of her throat. Aden tried to see who'd wounded Castine, but the closet was too narrow and too long.

Aden considered telling whoever was out there that they needed to cut out Castine's heart to kill her, but he still didn't know if it was someone trying to save or kill him.

"Come here, little girl," a deep, raspy voice whispered in a soothing tone. "Come on."

The swordsman drew closer. Aden didn't yet recognize their voice, but they definitely weren't Argus.

Castine circled once. Her mouth and upper chest had nearly healed from the first cut. She hunched back a few steps, right in front of Aden's cell.

"No, no," that cautious voice taunted Castine. "Make your move. Come to me."

The point of the sword came into view first. The torchlight reflected on the surface of the twin-edged blade. Then Aden saw who it was.

"Will October," he whispered to himself.

Will didn't look at him as he spoke, just smirked his acknowledgment. He let the sword's point linger a heartbeat between Castine's light brown eyes. Then he tapped her snout as a taunt.

Castine pounced, going straight for his throat. Will couldn't match her speed, but he swung his sword just right. The dr'schund's body impaled itself on the sword. He used her momentum to swing her over his head and onto her back, right behind him. Will put all his weight onto the hilt, driving the blade straight through her chest and into the floor. She writhed and yelped but every move only worsened her predicament. Will had buried the sword too well and the pain had Castine too distracted to try changing her size.

"You've got to rip out her heart," Aden told Will.

"Don't want to waste her blood that fast." Will's voice still sounded raspy, and he looked more pale than usual. "I'll have you out of there before she can get loose."

"Not sure you've got that much time." Aden kept his eyes on Castine, in case she freed herself and attacked Will again. "Never seen a lock this complicated."

A click came from the lock. Will pulled the door open and turned to Rhea's cell.

Aden swung the door back and forth as if to confirm it really was open. "How did you do that?"

Will looked over his shoulder at Aden as if he was insulted. "Aden, please. It's me."

"What happened to you and Dellem?" Rhea asked as Will opened her cell.

"We can kiss and tell once we're safe and popping the cork on a bottle of Baron Arnold's merlot."

Will walked back to Castine. He pulled out a long dagger and impaled it through Castine's throat. A shrill cry attested to Will's skill with the blade, and the dr'schund stopped writhing. Instead, the large dog twitched as its eyes rolled in their sockets as her body could not.

"By the way," Rhea said as she stepped out of her cell, "nice suit." Now that Rhea mentioned it, Will was dressed even better than usual.

"Oh, yes, meet my bride." Will pointed towards the door to the closet.

"Bride?"

Knowing Will, Aden expected a tall redhead with enough cleavage to keep five men happy at once.

"Nikayla, will this work?" Will asked as he stepped over the impaled Castine.

"There should be enough life in it." Nikayla walked into the closet. Even wearing a white corset and light blue skirt, she fell a far cry from Will's usual company. She only came up to Will's shoulders. Her straight black hair was trimmed short. She wasn't sexy, even if she was somewhat pretty. The most unusual feature was her violet eyes. If anything, Nikayla's stern demeanor resembled a cat that had its tail stepped on one too many times. She placed one of her small hands on the door to Dellem's cell. "Just get him out and be quick a bout it."

"You could at least say please." Will brushed past her in the narrow corridor. "This is why I pulled us out of that mass wedding before those priests married us."

"Enough joking. Get him out." Nikayla knelt beside Castine and then looked up at Aden and Rhea. "Shouldn't you two be guarding the door?"

Rhea looked ready to protest until Nikayla pulled out a dagger with an ugly-looking blade. Aden wondered if the woman was threatening them, but then she placed the point against the dr'schund's belly.

"Aden!" Will waved him over as he opened Dellem's cell door. "A hand here."

Dellem stirred as Aden and Will pulled him out. Dellem's movements were limited to a few winces.

"Gettin' too old for this shit," he muttered.

"If we hurry, you'll be running out of here faster than the rest of us," Will said.

"Wait." Rhea worked her way past them to watch the door.

A low growl came from Castine. All eyes turned towards her. Her body rippled, starting to grow. She'd finally calmed enough to figure out a way to free herself.

Nikayla pointed at Dellem. "Bring him to me now!" The dagger that had been buried in Castine's throat fell to the floor, as if something from within her body had pushed it out. She bared her teeth, then roared as she swung her head back to attack Nikayla.

Will's escort thrust her dagger into the dr'schund's chest. Castine yelped as the blade cut into her just above her heart. The blow knocked her head back to the floor. Nikayla ripped out the dagger and plunged it a second time before Castine could recover. No more shrieks accompanied the blows. The dr'schund was reduced to ragged breaths.

"Set him down," Nikayla said, "and don't touch him, no matter what."

She reached into the opening she'd created in Castine's chest and ripped out its heart. Blood and severed veins dripped down Nikayla's arm as she held the large muscle within her palm.

Aden felt as if his stomach might revolt. He kept telling himself not to breath or notice the stench of the dr'schund's insides.

"Let go of him," Nikayla said, her voice distant as if focused on something none of them could see. "Dellem, this will hurt."

Aden and Will set him down in front of Nikayla and quickly stepped back. Dellem laughed weakly. "Can't be much worse than the past few days. Get Miriam out."

With a shocking speed and unexpected strength, Nikayla shoved Dellem against the wall. She placed the dr'schund's heart above Dellem's. The dagger in her hand glowed with the same light Aden saw when a shakta was used. He wondered if the others could see it, or if it was only him.

Nikayla stabbed the dagger through the heart and into Dellem's chest. The old man's mouth dropped open as if to scream, but he didn't seem able to take a breath to do it. Miriam shouted Dellem's name as she shook the door to her cell.

Aden saw the glow of the dagger illuminate the heart and then spread over Dellem's entire body. Nikayla ripped the dagger free and the glow faded from Dellem. Blood stained his chest where the dagger had pierced him and Castine's heart.

"It's safe to touch him now. Get him up." Nikayla wiped the blood from her dagger and slipped it back into its sheath beneath her skirt.

"Gods," Dellem said. "Never felt this bad and good all at once."

Will laughed as he touched the place where the dagger had cut into Dellem's chest. "Not a mark on him."

"You doubted me?" Nikayla arched an eyebrow, and it was difficult to tell if she was really offended or teasing Will.

"You've never worried about being gentle." Will stopped in front of Miriam's cell. Those brown eyes darkened as they focused on the aplettsar. "So, Aden, if this is what you call 'motherly,' then I hope to one day meet a woman you consider wanton."

"We hardly have time for you to play games, Will October," Miriam said. "Now, let me out."

Will didn't move. "Aden, it's your neck. You decide."

"Let her out, Will," Dellem said. The old constable was already standing without any help from Aden or Nikayla. Whatever she'd done to him had worked.

Will ignored Dellem and turned his head to look at Aden. "Leave her or free her?"

Going by the looks traded between Miriam and Will, they didn't require introductions. Was there a woman anywhere he hadn't bedded or pissed off? Or both?

"Let her out, Will." Aden hoped he wouldn't regret the decision, but he assumed if Will truly knew a reason worth leaving her, then he wouldn't be making it an option.

Even standing there to watch, Aden couldn't figure out how Will was unlocking these cell doors. He supposed it didn't really matter, but it just served as another reminder there were things about Will he didn't know.

"Rhea and I got in here using a rear door," Aden said, pointing towards the stairs. "Probably the quickest way out."

"Sounds better than anything I had in mind," Will said.

"What about my shakta?" Rhea asked. "That bastard Argus has it."

"I thought he had it?" Will pointed to Aden, but then shook his head as he held up his hands. "Never mind. I'm starting to think you hunters could lose trees in a forest."

"You're not really catching us at our best," Aden said.

Rhea grabbed Will by the arm. "I'm not leaving without my shakta."

"I didn't risk my life getting in this place to rescue you two," Will said. "I was only expecting to find Dellem. Do you even know where in this place this Argus is? No, I didn't think so."

Aden stopped Rhea before she could protest again. "The longer we stay, the more likely we are to end up back in there." He placed his hands on her shoulders. "We'll get it back, and when we do, Argus is going to regret taking your shakta."

"Shall we?" Will sounded less than patient.

"Let's go," Rhea said.

Aden took the lead. They didn't have to go far to make it back to the storage room where they'd faced the wraith. He worried the door would still be braced, but he'd assumed it wouldn't be since the regent had most likely used it to get to his carriage. The door opened without so much as a creak of resistance, and as simple as that, they were back on the streets of Ostice.

They ran out of the alley and down the side street of the church. Will ran in front, leading them straight down that road for several blocks. When they came to one of the city's main streets, Will stopped and leaned against a black street pole. In the daylight, his pale complexion was even more noticeable. His breathing was labored. Will closed his eyes and wiped a thick layer of sweat from his brow.

Nikayla stepped up to him and roughly gripped his face. "Look me in the eyes," she said.

Will complied without a protest or pithy comeback. Not a good sign.

"You need to rest," she said.

Will removed her hands and stood straight. "You're standing here with blood on your hands and your skirt. Dellem looks little better. We can't stay outside any longer than we can help it. I'll rest when we get to your home."

Nikayla placed a hand on his stomach, causing Will to wince. "I think your stitches have held. Keep pushing yourself, though, and you'll start bleeding again."

"What's wrong with him?" Aden asked.

"What isn't? Run through with a sword, fell from a roof."

"Nothing a glass of wine won't cure." Will started walking again without looking to see that they were following. "We stay with the alleys where we can. It'll take longer, but it's safer. Let's go."

Aden looked from Will to Nikayla. He'd never met a witch. Women who dared to wield magic were executed without trial. The Order of the Hunt wiped out most of them in ancient times in the name of securing the safety of the East. Given all that, he wondered how well Will knew this witch and just how likely she was to help a pair of hunters. He hoped she would, because if he and Rhea had a chance of getting back their shaktas, then they needed Nikayla to do it.

35

The Witch

Aden and the others followed Nikayla into the alley behind her row house. A short, lavender fence defined the boundaries of her back yard. Her house and most of the neighboring homes looked clean and tidy.

A group of children ran around them playing a game of tag. One of the boys, who looked about five years old, stopped in front of Dellem.

"That's a lot of blood, sayer. I once fell and split my lip open and got blood all over my shirt. My mom made me take a bath. You should probably take a bath, too."

Miriam had stayed close to Dellem ever since they escaped the Church of Castine. She smiled to the boy. "You are very right. I'll have to get him inside and take care of that right now."

The boy nodded and seemed close to saying something else equally insightful until a girl ran up behind him and tapped him on the shoulder. "You're it!"

"That's cheating!" The boy chased her down the alley.

Miriam's behavior now resembled the way she'd acted in Crestnal, almost motherly. Dellem smiled to her, but there was no missing the hesitation in the way he looked at her. It was impossible to know which was more the façade, Miriam the healer or Mistress Sersas. Aden wondered if even Miriam knew who the real her was.

Nikayla led them through the gate to her back yard. Aden and the others kept their feet on the hexagonal bricks that formed a path from the gate to the back door to avoid stepping on her garden. Herbs, tomatoes, and leafy trastus covered most of her yard. A pair of wooden chairs, painted the same lavender as the fence, were set beneath an awning that ran the width of her house.

Nikayla held open the door to her house and waved for them to get inside. "Hurry before anyone else notices all of you and asks questions."

Aden hesitated when he got his first look at Nikayla's living room. The walls were painted a pleasant shade of beige with lightly stained wooden furniture. He didn't notice any clutter within her home. Filmy-thin, white curtains provided privacy while allowing in plenty of natural light. Mirrors hung in several places to help distribute that light. The only thing that seemed unusual were the crystals hung in a few places. Aden suspected they had a function beyond decoration.

The normalcy of Nikayla's house unnerved Aden more than if it had lived up to the grim picture of cobwebs and human skulls that centuries of folk tales insisted belonged in a witch's home. That was how others felt about a hunter the first time they met one. Most expected some freak or monstrosity; they expected Argus. In Aden's experience, what made people most uncomfortable was to see how perfectly normal a hunter really was.

Will cursed as he stumbled and grabbed onto the railing of the stairs. Nikayla and Aden grabbed Will's arms to support him.

"Damn, stubborn fool," Nikayla muttered.

"I'd say you haven't usually complained," Will said, "but you always have."

"Help me get him upstairs," Nikayla said to Aden. She had Will's right arm over her shoulders, but Aden felt as if he was carrying all of Will's weight.

"Wait." Nikayla looked down at the three guests standing in her living room. "You." Rhea, Dellem, and Miriam all looked up at her. "No, you... the aplettsar."

Miriam stared back, looking uncomfortable at being singled out. "Yes?"

"Pour him some water and put some honey in it." Nikayla led Aden and Will the rest of the way upstairs. "Don't go mounting him either. He needs to rest."

Aden heard Will laugh under his breath. Once they reached the second floor, he whispered, "Aren't you being just a tad hyp—"

"Shut up." She sounded plenty pissed. Even Aden was startled into keeping his silence. Nikayla was one of the shortest women Aden had ever met, and she was quite possibly the most intimidating person he'd ever encountered. While her lavender irises might be rare, the way they assessed everyone and everything they latched onto exposed an intellect he'd encountered in few others.

They took Will into what must have been Nikayla's bedroom. She pulled back the sheets before Aden sat Will down. "I can handle this part myself," Will said. "If I can strip off my clothes when I'm three sheets to the wind and still bed a lady, then this should be nothing."

Nikayla shooed Aden out of the room. "And close the door."

Aden didn't close the door all the way. Nor did he go downstairs. He stopped at the top of the stairs as he listened to Will.

"The things I have to go through to get into your bed."

"Dammit, stop it." Nikayla sounded ready to add to Will's injuries. "Can't you just stop being Will October for even one moment?"

"It's not that simple, and you know it." There was an awkward pause before Will spoke again. "Your door isn't closed all the way."

Aden scrambled down the stairs before Nikayla could see him. He managed not to catch any creaky steps, not an easy thing for a man with feet as big as his.

"Did the witch chase you back downstairs?" Rhea said with a teasing lilt to her words.

"Something like that." Aden noticed Miriam and Dellem sitting together at the kitchen table. Even whispering to each other, they couldn't disguise the tension between them. He felt sorry for them. At one point, he'd thought those two might have a future together, a strange one to be certain, but looking at them now, he doubted it.

Aden pointed to the large, red stain on Rhea's shirt. "How's the wraith bite?"

She gingerly rolled her injured shoulder. "Looks worse than it is. The wraith's teeth didn't go too deep."

"That's a relief, so how good a climber are you?"

She groaned. "I forgot about our armor." They'd stashed it on the roof of the theater. Getting back up there without her shakta wasn't going to make that an easy task.

"Don't worry," Aden said. "I'll take care of that."

"I'll not argue." She sat on the sofa and put her feet up on the coffee table.

"What are you doing?" He gestured for her to get back up. "We need fresh weapons. While I'm making like a spider, you need to buy us some swords."

She groaned again as she stood. "Suspect this witch's neighbors would snitch in a heartbeat, so we better get back here before the curfew."

"I'll wager Argus is already looking for us."

Her body stiffened at the mention of the traitor. "Most likely."

Aden remembered the last time they split up, and he wasn't any more comfortable about it this time. Waiting until morning to arm themselves wasn't an option, though. Argus and his allies would be plenty pissed, and they wouldn't let the curfew stop them from hunting down Aden and Rhea again.

The sun was already set by the time Aden returned to Nikayla's house. The children were no longer playing in the back alley as he pushed open the gate to the back yard. He grunted as a shot of pain ran through his back. He'd cursed the dar'jiat wraith at least a dozen times since he'd finished climbing the back of that theater to get their armor.

"What happened to you?" Nikayla's voice startled him and stopped him in his tracks as he stepped beneath the awning of her back porch. Little wonder he hadn't seen her. She was sitting in the shadows and covered in a black blanket to fight the slight chill in the air.

"I forgot the hard part about climbing." Aden dropped the sack holding their armor onto the porch.

Nikayla arched an eyebrow, which he took as her invitation to elaborate.

"That getting back down is when things get tricky." He lowered himself into the only other chair on the porch, grunting as he did so. Getting back up wasn't going to be easy, but at this point, he didn't really care. "Halfway down, I lost my grip and landed on my arse."

Aden heard a huff of breath from Nikayla. The closest thing to a laugh he'd heard out of her thus far.

Despite his fall on the way down, he'd impressed himself. That wall hadn't offered much in the way of handholds. Not many people could have made that climb, and given the injury to Rhea's shoulder, he was glad she hadn't tried it.

The wind shifted and he caught the scent of mint in her small garden.

"Surprised you aren't inside," he said.

"I'm not used to so much company."

"And yet you live in a city." His observation went without reply, unless one counted her negligible shrug. "Is Rhea back yet?"

"Yes."

Aden winced has he leaned back into the chair.

Nikayla looked out into the alley, though it was hard to tell if her violet eyes were focused on anything.

"So how long have you known Will?" he asked.

She ignored the question, didn't so much as turn her head to look at him. She just stared out at her garden as if she was considering what might be ready to harvest and if there were weeds to remove.

The last hints of color in the western sky had faded when Nikayla finally spoke. "Your back still hurts?"

He nodded.

"Sit up." She stood and moved behind his chair. She gripped his shoulder at the base of his neck and slid the other hand down the length of his spine. Once she neared the bottom of his back, pain shot through his tailbone.

"Shit!"

"Easy enough." She sounded as though she was talking to herself more than him. "I'll numb the pain first."

She pressed on two points along the back of his neck. The results were subtle, but he realized the chill in the air was gone from the neck down. He tried to move his arms, but neither responded.

Her face brushed against the left side of his head. That's when he realized just how vulnerable he was.

"Let me make something very clear," she whispered. "Don't ever ask me about Will October again. His past has nothing to do with you or this insanity between the East and the West. If you want my help, and we both know you need it, then leave his past and mine alone."

Nikayla released her hold on him and picked up her blanket from her chair. She didn't wait for him to answer, because they both knew he didn't have a choice. All she'd done was state her terms.

"Dellem is cooking dinner," she said as she folded up her blanket.

Aden fidgeted with all his fingers just to reassure himself he had all his feeling back. He'd never experienced anything like that, and he hoped he never did again. He stood and picked up the bag of armor.

He was surprised to realize there wasn't any pain in his back when he stood. "You fixed my back." He stood a little straighter just to make certain.

"You sound surprised."

"Don't you have to rip out some bird's heart or something to do that kind of thing?"

"If I manipulate the life strands, yes," she said. "Fortunately, not everything requires magic. I just applied pressure where it was needed."

"Thank you."

He wondered if the healing was a peace offering. Part of him really wanted to know just what it was in Will's past she was protecting, but he needed Will and Nikayla's help a lot more than their life story. Mayhap he'd get to satisfy his nosey nature one day, but he had to live through the next few first.

36

The Rest of the Story

Will seemed more like his usual self as Dellem served their dinner. Aden wasn't sure what Dellem had cooked, but it had red meat in it, and that was enough for him to be happy.

"This, ladies and lords," Will said as he held up a dust-covered bottle of wine, "is by far the finest merlot you will find anywhere in the East. I could espouse the fine balance of the peaches and strawberries contained within this wine, but frankly, that's just wasting time best spent drinking it. Some first for our hostess." Will poured some into Nikayla's glass and whispered something to her that produced a private smile.

Will made the rounds filling the rest of their glasses. There was something odd about sitting at a table in a nice house, sharing a meal over fine wine, and trading tales of murder and conspiracy.

Aden went first, telling of how he'd encountered the dar'jiat wraith in the aqueducts, found Miriam at the Black Dog, and gone with her to meet the strange head of the aplettsars.

"Regent Aphestin," Miriam corrected Aden when he'd mispronounced the name. "It's derived from Malaphestino, the three-headed god of death."

"I've heard rumors about Aphestin," Will said over his second glass of merlot. "Can't say I trust most of what I've heard. One fellow claimed that Aphestin wasn't mortal, a being neither man nor woman, who cannot die. Even came across a written reference to them in a document some three hundred years old."

"Aphestin might be in bed with the Church of Castine." Aden paused to finish off a rather spicy piece of meat and wash it down. "He set up our meet with Regent Monast, the emperor's military advisor. Argus used the opportunity to kill Monast and steal my shakta. There's no way Argus could have known he'd have my shakta unless Aphestin sent that information to him.

"After that, Rhea and her hunters found me. I took her to get her shakta back. I'd hidden it in the sewers." Aden found it difficult not to smile.

Everyone at the table started smiling or chuckling, everyone but Rhea.

"I don't see what's so funny about that." She sat a little straighter. She was tall for a woman, but sitting next to Aden negated the affect. Her comment just made them laugh even more.

"Anyway," Aden said once the laughter had waned, "by the time Rhea and I got back to the Black Dog, her hunters were all dead and Miriam kidnapped."

"That one you call Argus did it." Miriam said as she ran her fingertip along the rim of her glass. She looked over at Aden. "I think they'd expected to catch you then, too. He had that wrangler with him and that damn dog."

"Explains how your hunters got killed so easily," Aden said to Rhea. "They wouldn't have questioned Argus being there, and they wouldn't have expected him to have a working shakta to use against them either."

"I just don't see why they waited that long to try to catch you," Rhea said. "Why then? Why not at the You Know Where or the Palace? Catching you would lock in Lady Kleska's bid to succeed her husband."

"The Church of Castine doesn't want Lady Kleska in power." Will walked over to Nikayla's wine rack. "Do you have another 323 merlot?"

Nikayla smiled to Will as she shook her head. "Sadly, no, but there's a 294 near the bottom." Seemed these two shared a love for wine. Another piece of the puzzle Aden knew he'd probably never put together.

"Will, how can you be so certain the Church doesn't want Lady Kleska in power?" Aden asked. "They've been using her to run things in Ostice and throughout the Astesian Empire for years now."

"Exactly." Will pulled the bottle Nikayla had suggested from her wine rack. "Why ruin a good thing? Things must have soured between Lady Kleska and the Church. The emperor was a well-known nymphomaniac, more obsessed with his cock and private harem to bother with running the empire. For all of Lady Kleska's faults, she's done a good job overseeing things. I can't see her compromising her empire for the Church."

"This is true." Miriam traced the rim of her glass. She avoided looking at Dellem with the discussion touching on the emperor. Aden wondered if the constable had any idea how Miriam's past was so closely tied to the dead ruler. "Lady Kleska isn't a woman guided by her passions. In her own way, she was obsessed with me and the rest of the aplettsars, couldn't understand what it was about us that gives us so much power over others."

Will uncorked the bottle of merlot and refilled Nikayla's glass before his own. "She's equally fascinated with the sway of religion over others," he said. "I imagine Loman exploited that interest to give his church a foothold within Ostice, but to really gain power over the empire, Loman needs a true puppet as emperor."

Miriam stopped playing with her wine glass and leaned forward. "How do you know that?"

Will chuckled. "Sorry, I might be giving up some of my secrets tonight, but none of my trade secrets."

"So that's why the Church of Castine wants Regent Dardane in power," Aden said, wanting to get the conversation back to the real matter at hand.

Will sat down. "That's my assumption. Dardane's affiliation with the Church of Castine explains a lot of things."

"How so?" Rhea asked.

"Well, let's consider our enemies' actions," Will said. "Why not simply take Aden and Miriam at the Palace? The obvious answer is that doing that would give the credit to Lady Kleska."

"But how did Argus know about my meet with Monast at the You Know Where?" Aden asked.

"Regent Aphestin, named for some 'three-headed god'," Will said. "To me, that suggests a triumvirate runs the aplettsars. Dardane is most likely one of them. Monast was probably part of the 'Aphestin Triumvirate,' too."

"Dardane is a debtor and a traitor." Rhea shook her head. "How could someone like that ever end up in charge of a group of spies?"

"Simple." Miriam paused to sip her wine. "Dardane is one of the emperor's illegitimate children. One of those well-known secrets the regents are expected to pretend they don't know, but it's also how he's managed to avoid paying most of his debts. Word has it the emperor had tired of covering for him, though, and paying for his ridiculous treasure-hunting expeditions into the Aiman Desert."

"And if Dardane gets in power, he's free of all those debts." Aden recalled the information he'd gotten from the bartender at the Lost Soul. "Probably how the Church of Castine got him to join with them."

"The point is that Dardane would have learned Aden was with Miriam when they went to the Palace," Will said. "Again, consider our foe's actions since that meeting. Dardane could have set up Monast at the You Know Where because he knew about the meet. He also learns Aden is with Miriam, meaning he's most likely staying at the Black Dog. That night, Argus and the beast wrangler make their move, killing Rhea's hunters and capturing Miriam."

"Why not take me at the You Know Where?" Aden asked.

"Too public, and since you're seen running from Monast's murder—another assassination with a shakta—you take the blame for that, too."

"Also makes Monast a potential scapegoat who can't defend himself," Dellem said.

"Exactly."

Aden shook his head. In hindsight, going to the Palace that day had been the worst move he and Miriam could have made. Dardane might have even been the one they'd spoken to in the gardens.

Will pulled out a cigar and leaned forward to light it with one of the candles on the table.

"Don't you dare stink up my home," Nikayla snapped.

Will winced. "Sorry, forgot."

Aden's eyes widened. Rhea and Dellem looked just as surprised. Their reactions didn't go unnoticed either.

"What?" Will asked as he put away the unlit cigar.

"Never seen you pass on a smoke for anyone," Aden said.

Will laughed. "That's because no one ever asks."

Aden had his doubts about that but didn't see a point in debating it. "So what happened to you and Dellem?"

"Ah, yes." Will laughed. "Shall I kiss and tell, or do you want the honors, constable?"

"I'll start, and you can finish." Dellem sat up and looked a bit uncomfortable with everyone's attention on him. "After we got into the city, we spotted Loman walking into the Church of Castine. Looked too much like those boys back home to be a coincidence, so Will and I went inside to see what we could find out."

"You went inside?" Rhea asked in disbelief. "What possessed you?"

"Well at the time, we didn't realize who Loman was or that he was the head of the church," Dellem said. "Public place, my lady, so we didn't see the danger in what we were doing until it was too late. Probably would have gotten in and out without any trouble, but that fake priest—"

"The beast wrangler?" Aden asked.

"Yes, him." Dellem sounded like he wanted to spit out the mention of him. "Happened onto him once we were inside. Chased him, but didn't take long before he found some friends and they were chasing us. We made it out of the church, but they didn't give up, even after we ran inside some inn along the canal. Cornered us on the roof and that's when the swords came out. I went down before Will. Sorry about that, lad."

"Not your fault," Will said. "I didn't last much longer. We were outnumbered. Took a sword through my stomach, then fell off the roof into the canal." He shook his head, looking angry with himself at the memory of how it happened. "If I hadn't fallen into that canal, I'd probably be ashes in an urn about now."

"If you hadn't come to me when you did, you'd have been dead anyway," Nikayla said in a hushed voice.

Will reached over and took her hand as he whispered a thank you to her. Then he turned his attention back to Aden. "Soon as I was well enough, I went looking for you at the Black Dog to get your help rescuing Dellem, but you weren't there.

The other guests were still talking about the men Argus killed and how you two had taken a dive out a window and still managed to get away. Assumed Rhea had caught you, and that you were probably halfway to Mirite.

"Anyway, Nikayla and I snuck into the church posing as a bride and groom in that mass wedding. Wasn't very hard to slip away with that large of a crowd and go looking for Dellem. Got quite a surprise when I found you and Rhea in there with him."

"Well, this has gotten a lot bigger than the Astesian Empire," Rhea said. "The Church of Castine seems to be allied with the West."

Nikayla raised her hand and waved off Rhea's observation. "The Church of Castine is the West."

Her declaration left the rest of them silent. No one so much as moved to pick up a glass or take a bite of their food.

Rhea found her voice before the others. "Just how do you know that?" The question clearly had more do with the fact a simple witch knew this before the rest of them, people skilled in the art of espionage.

"I've known it, because the Church of Castine as good as admits it. This asinine notion that Castine has destroyed all the old Gods, that she will unite all the kingdoms of the East and the West in an age of peace... This is not some glorious and blessed event. This church is selling people on the idea that Kalle-Al, the End of All Things, is not our doom but our deliverance. The Church of Castine is selling the East its own death."

Aden thought of the painting in the Essentialist Church that depicted Kalle-Al.

"But in the prophecy of Kalle-Al," he said, "the destruction of the East is brought about by some great dog, Setinac."

Nikayla nodded. "Consider the statue in front of the church. Everyone assumes Castine is the woman, but she's really the dog at the woman's side."

Will downed the rest of his glass and set it on the table. "This is why Regent Monast was assassinated. When Dardane is put into power, he will name a replacement. He would have had to do this anyway in order to secure control of the Astesian military, but now he can do it without anyone questioning his motives."

"That's why they want war with Mirite," Rhea said. "With all the treaties that exist among the kingdoms of the East, a war between the Astesian Empire and Mirite would draw all of them into the conflict. The West will use that war to weaken the armies of the East."

"That and to wipe out some of the smaller kingdoms," Will said. "Save the West the trouble."

"And when the West finally does send their armies against us, they'll already have us surrounded." Aden leaned back in his chair and rubbed his head, aching with the weight of his part in all this. All because he'd let those two boys ambush him outside that fucking outhouse in Crestnal and lost his shakta.

37

Following the Thread

Dellem threw two more logs into the fireplace. He attacked them with a poker to build the flames as high as they would go.

"I think that's as good as I can get it for you," he said to Nikayla.

"That should work." The witch gestured for Aden to join her by the fireplace. She knelt down before a small table that Aden would have mistaken for a footrest. A potted plant, a rather gnarled looking thing, was set atop the small table along with a mortar and a pestle.

Aden knelt on the opposite side of that table. The height discrepancy was somewhat humorous.

"In what hand were you holding your shakta when it was created?"

"My right." He was surprised she knew that made a difference. Not even many mages outside of those employed by the Order of the Hunt knew that.

She rolled up her right sleeve. "Physical contact will be very important, both in this world and the other. Roll up your left sleeve. When we start our walk, you must keep hold of my hand at all times."

"What happens if I don't?" He wiped the sweat from his brow and pretended it was because of how close he was to that large fire Dellem had built.

"If you let go of me in either world, your soul will be severed from your body."

"You mean I'll die."

"Worse," she said. "Only your body will die. Your soul will never find its way to the River of Souls. At best, you'll become a ghost, occasionally touching this world but never a true part of it again."

"Don't let go." Aden took a deep breath. "Got it."

The others didn't look much more comfortable with this than he was. Rhea had offered to go first, but they'd all agreed Aden was the better choice. Despite her offer, Rhea stood with Miriam over by the window near the front of the house, about as far from Nikayla as she could get. Will, on the other hand, stood at Nikayla's side as if to protect her.

"The rest of you, do not touch us for any reason. You could..." She stopped and somewhat smiled. "Just don't touch us. It would be bad."

"You ever done this?" Aden asked.

"I've walked along the life threads many times," she said, "but never to track a hunter's shakta."

Aden glanced at the potted plant. "Thought you had to rip out something's heart?"

"Manipulating the life threads does require a sacrifice." She uprooted the plant from the pot. The dirt that had served as its home peppered out onto her wooden floor. "Some plants actually work better than animals. If you've ever tried to kill a weed in a garden, you know just how violently some plants hold to life." She stroked one of the uprooted plant's yellow blossoms. "The holphus flower makes a very good sacrifice, but you can only use it if you destroy it completely. You need a strong fire for that."

She plucked a few of the yellow petals and dropped them into the bowl of the mortar. The pestle in her grip, Nikayla pounded the petals into a fine yellow powder.

"Are you ready?"

In his head, the answer was *No, definitely not*, but given there was little choice, he said, "Yes."

She took some of the yellow powder and spread it on the palm of her right hand and the bottom of her fingers. The sight of her yellow hand reminded him of a child getting ready to fingerpaint. "Now do the same to your left hand."

He did as she instructed, surprised to find the powder was sticky, more like a fine paste. Covering his hand nearly exhausted the remainder of the pounded petals.

"That will do," Nikayla said. She picked up the rest of the holphus flower and tossed it into the fireplace. "Now, just hold my hand and close your eyes. I'll do the rest."

Good, Aden thought, *because I don't have a damn clue what we're doing.*

He shut his eyes. Even through his eyelids, he could make out the flickering of light from the fireplace to his right.

Just earlier this night, Nikayla had rendered him helpless. He swore to never let that happen again, and yet here he was taking her by the hand, trusting his soul's fate to her.

Gods, how long was this going to take? Then he realized something had changed, and he couldn't place just what it was, not right away. The light of the fire no longer flickered, replaced with a constant glow.

Nikayla squeezed his hand. "You can open your eyes. We're here."

He wasn't certain what he expected, but as he opened his eyes, he saw nothing different. They were still sitting in Nikayla's house. Everyone was watching them as they had before, but as he looked more closely, he realized none of them were moving. Their bodies all had a faint glow similar to the life strands he saw come from his and others' shaktas. The crystals he'd noticed hanging from the ceiling glowed as brightly as the fire. Lines of that light-blue life energy spilled out in all directions. Then he looked at the fire and realized why it no longer flickered. The fire was as still as a painting, the flames captured in mid-dance, but as he looked a little longer, he just barely made out the movement of the flames.

"Things move more quickly here," Nikayla said.

"More quickly? Seems as though everything is moving more slowly."

"Let me put it this way," she said. "From our perception, we could stay in this world for what feels like days, but when we return, only minutes will have passed in the mortal world."

"So we're moving more quickly?"

"Yes, and that's fortunate. We have a long walk ahead of us. There's a thread of life that extends from your shakta hand to your weapon. That thread is the connection that keeps your soul whole. You are never truly parted from your shakta, but distance weakens the thread. You won't be able to see it, but I can tell by just how faint it looks—"

"Doesn't look all that faint to me." Aden looked at the thread coming out of his palm and going out the back wall of the house. He lifted his arm and watched in fascination as the thread pulsed with each movement.

Nikayla stared at him. "You shouldn't be able to see it?"

"I can always see the shakta threads when a hunter uses them. That's not something I'd prefer many to know."

"Well, that will make things easier for us. If you can see it more clearly, then I will let you take the lead." A quizzical look passed across her face as she looked from him to Rhea. "Can you see her thread?"

Aden looked over to Rhea and realized he'd nearly overlooked the thread because her arms were crossed. The thread ran from her hand and out of the front of the house behind her. "Yes, I can see it."

"Praise the Gods," Nikayla whispered. "This will spare me from doing this with her."

"I didn't think witches believed that business about magic being more dangerous for women."

She looked at him as if he was a fool. "It's dangerous for anyone."

"So now what?" Aden asked.

"Now, we stand," she said. "Take it slowly. You'll need some time to adjust. Until you do, the vertigo might drop you on your knees. If you stumble and lose hold of my hand..."

"Say no more." Aden took in a deep breath to steady himself. "All right, let's do this."

Standing proved just as difficult as promised. The world just didn't seem to move right, as if cut into millions of pieces that couldn't all shift at the same time.

"Aden? Are you all right?"

He didn't answer right away, still waiting for everything to feel normal. "Aden?"

"Am I standing straight or leaning a little to the right?"

"Leaning," she said, as if that should have been obvious, "and I'd feel a lot better if you'd stand straight now."

He righted himself and let out a breath he'd been holding. "Okay, I'm good."

"Let's take a few, small steps." Nikayla moved to his side, turning him to face the back of her house and in the direction of his life thread.

Turning around didn't cause him any troubles. He supposed that made sense. After all, he'd have probably noticed the disorientation while looking around the room when he was sitting down. Those first few steps turned out more difficult, though. Walking wasn't all that hard, but everything shifted in a way he wasn't accustomed to, as if it was all flat.

"This really gets easier?"

"Stay here long enough, and you'll likely fall flat on your face when we go back."

When they stopped by the back wall of her house, Aden glanced over his shoulder at the place they'd been sitting.

"Wait," he said. "Where are we? Our bodies?" He saw the small table where they'd been sitting. Will stood off to the side, but Nikayla's body wasn't there. "Shouldn't our bodies still be there or something?"

"Our bodies are still there, but you can't see them while we're here." She sounded amused.

"So how do you know we're just our souls walking around here and not our bodies, too?" he asked.

"Look closer." She pointed back towards the table. "You might not see our bodies, but you can still see our shadows."

Sure enough, he could see the black outlines of their bodies across the floor as if they were still sitting there. He looked over at the wall he was standing in front of and realized neither he nor Nikayla were casting a shadow on the wall as they should have.

"So, are we able to use the doors? I mean, how do we get out?"

"You cannot affect anything inanimate, so we can't use the doors. We'll have to walk through the wall."

He held up his free hand near the wall. "Feels cold."

"Wait until you go through it." The tone of her voice made it clear it was worse than he knew. She squeezed hard on his hand. "Like the walking, this will get easier the more we have to do it. Hold tightly to me."

They stepped forward, and he'd initially feared more what it would look like, what he would see once his eyes went through the wall. All he saw was darkness, and that original fear was erased by the cold—as if standing within a block of ice. His breath rushed out of him, and the gasp to replace that lost air in his lungs found nothing for what seemed a long time. Hard as he tried, he fell to his knees on her porch as he made it out of that frozen hell.

"It will get easier," she said in a soothing voice. "If we are fortunate, there will not be many more walls to go through."

"What if the strand goes through a person?" He forced himself back onto his feet.

"It won't," she said as she led them down the alley. "Have you ever been walking along and tripped for seemingly no reason?"

"You're telling me that's someone's life thread I'm tripping on?"

"Well, you're probably just being clumsy, but it does happen."

"Ah."

The life thread to his shakta didn't turn out very considerate. The damn thing refused to just go straight down the middle of a street. On the bright side, by the time they made it to the city gates, he'd become an expert at walking through walls.

"This is going to be a problem," Aden said as they passed through the gates.

"Getting you out of the city to recover your shakta?" Nikayla said.

"More than that," he said. "We're talking about getting me out of the city and back in a second time."

They didn't say much as they traveled the path of the thread. The city of Ostice turned into a small shadow to their backs. Aden's head ached, confused by this night that wouldn't end. He'd noticed the moon had moved very little.

"Am I right in thinking we're making better time than we would if we were making this walk in the real world?" Aden asked.

"This is the real world." Nikayla sighed with obvious impatience for his thickheadedness. "But yes, our spirits move more quickly than our bodies. A single step here can be the equivalent of several in the physical world. In fact, one can merely think their spirit-self from one place to another in an instant."

"So why don't we do that now?" Anything to shorten their walk through this flattened view of the world sounded good to him.

"We can't do it, because we don't know where we're going."

The shakta's life strand moved off the road as they neared the Aiman Desert. By Aden's estimate, getting this far would take almost an entire day, but he couldn't be sure.

"Why bring it out here?" Aden said, more to himself than Nikayla.

"To keep it from you?" She shrugged.

"Maybe, but they're going to need it. That's going to be part of the evidence against me. Dardane will want to present both me and the shakta."

"Then bringing it here makes even less sense. The regents are set to vote in four days. That doesn't leave much time to catch you and bring that back into Ostice."

"I don't know," he said. "They might want me to come here, using it as bait for a trap." He didn't believe that, though. Why bring him this far into the desert for a trap they could set more easily within the city?

Aden stopped in his tracks. A shiver ran up from his right hand and shook his whole body.

"What is it?" Nikayla's voice sounded urgent.

"Like a death dog's shadow fell across my grave," he said, "only a damn cry stronger than I've ever felt that. Did you feel it, too?"

She shook her head. "Wouldn't have even noticed something was wrong if I wasn't holding your hand and noticed you tense up."

"Could someone else be here?" he asked. "In this spirit world, I mean?"

"Yes, that is possible, but unlikely. The risk to my life is just as great as it is to yours. I can guarantee you no other witch would do this for you, and any mage would charge you a small kingdom's treasury."

"Why do you think I haven't tried this until now?" Aden said.

They continued along the path of the life strand, and Aden felt they were getting closer. Gods, he hadn't felt his shakta's presence this strongly since the last time he'd held it in his hand. More than once, he caught himself flexing his fingers as if to grip that white, ribbed stick of wood.

Aden spotted a glowing light coming from just over a sand dune. "There."

He wanted to run, but given the height difference between him and Nikayla, she'd never keep up. He wasn't about to risk losing his grip on her hand, either. No point in finding his shakta if he wouldn't be alive to hold it.

They reached the top of the dune. The light came from a campfire, frozen still like the one in Nikayla's fireplace. A mirden slept, still hooked up to its wagon. Two men dressed in the robes of the Church of Castine sat at the front of the wagon while two other men were lying next to the fire. His thread led to the far side of the fire.

"There it is." Someone had shifted the sand to create a small mound and set his shakta on it. He reached towards that bit of his soul. Something about the glow of light from it made his shakta seem so much more real than anything else in this flat world. "Can I touch it?"

"You can't touch the wood, but you might—Gods!"

"What?" He looked up at Nikayla. She wasn't looking at him or his shakta. Her gaze was on the two men lying next to the fire. Now that he wasn't so focused on his shakta, he realized these men were not sleeping. They were dead.

"Each one has his hands and feet bound by a single rope," he whispered to himself, taking in the details to figure out what did this to them and why. "Something bit open their throats. Haven't been dead very long, but judging from the rope burns, they've been held captive for a while." He pulled Nikayla along with him as he took a closer look. "There should be more blood."

He felt Nikayla shake, then saw the revulsion on her face. He considered pointing out she wasn't squeamish when she was holding that dr'schund's heart in her hand earlier.

"Whatever bit them drank the blood," she said.

"They weren't bit by an animal. Must be a drayken," he said, but Nikayla didn't respond. "It's a dark mage, and sure as Dark isn't human."

"I know what they are," she snapped, "but where are they? And why would they be out here?"

"Well, something that butt ugly can't exactly go walking down a civilized street." She was right, though. He looked at the scene before them and kept asking himself the same question she'd just asked. "He was doing something with my shakta. Must have required magic, which would explain these two bodies."

"Sacrifices," Nikayla said.

Aden turned his attention back to the two sitting on the wagon. "So why are those two just sitting there? They haven't even unhitched the mirden?"

"They aren't planning to stay very long."

"I think you're right." Aden realized the two men were looking in the same direction. "They're staring at my shakta."

"No, they're not."

A shadow in the shape of a drayken led away from the fire, but there wasn't a body to cast it. The drayken was in the spirit world with them.

"We have to get back! Now!" Nikayla ran up the hill. He tried to make her stop, but she turned out much stronger than he expected.

"Nikayla, wait!" If he lost his grip on her, he was dead. "Let me try—"

The drayken didn't give him a chance. A blur of black flesh and random patches of yellow fur landed between them and the fire.

"Down!" Aden fell backwards, taking Nikayla with him, just as the drayken pounced. He wondered if he'd break Nikayla's fingers in her body with the grip he had on her soul's hand. Their backs hit the sand. Aden kicked up and nailed the drayken in its stomach. The dark mage stabbed down with its elongated forefingers, but Aden's kick kept it out of reach and sent it flying past them.

Aden didn't bother to see how it landed. Damn things were like cats, always landing on their feet... or rather hooves, in this case.

"Move!" Aden yelled at Nikayla.

"I'm trying!"

They heard the drayken's howl, something between a cat and a dog. It was going straight for where they held hands. The drayken was trying to trap Aden's soul in the spirit world by breaking their connection.

"Hang on!" Aden jerked Nikayla off her feet and spun her in a circle just as the drayken passed. Nikayla screamed. One of the drayken's overgrown forefingers raked across his back.

He heard the drayken snicker as it leaped away.

Nikayla cursed. "Don't do that again!"

Aden tugged her back into a run. "Can't you cast some spell to kill it?"

"I need a sacrifice to power the attack! You feel like killing yourself?"

"Point made!" He dodged the drayken's next pass, jerking Nikayla to the right with him.

"Where are you going?" Nikayla asked. "We can't dodge him like this all night!"

"Over to the fire!"

The drayken appeared before them, as if from nowhere. Must have been doing that shifting trick Nikayla had mentioned. It grabbed their arms and snapped at their hands with its snout. Aden buried his fist into the side of its snouted head. It yelped, just standing there, knocked senseless.

"Go!" Aden yelled.

Aden and Nikayla lifted their hands up over the drayken's head and ran for the fire.

"You can't burn him, Aden!"

"Not planning on it." He looked over his shoulder to see the drayken shaking its head. "Would he be the same size in the real world?"

"This is the real—"

"Dark, woman, just answer the question!"

"Yes!"

He hoped she didn't trip, because this was going to be damn close. That was assuming what Aden had planned would work.

They jumped over one of the sacrificed bodies. Aden heard those hooves take a pounce on the ground. Damn thing was coming for them fast.

He saw his shakta and planted his hand down on it. He could feel his soul there as solid as Nikayla's hand and the drayken's jaw.

His mind connected with the shakta. The three strands shot out the tip, curved around and spiraled through the space where the drayken's body was sitting in the physical world.

The drayken howled, its spirit plunging for their hands again. The soul faded into nothing, reduced to an invisible, cold shiver passing through their arms. Its body appeared where it must be in the physical world, along with chunks of flesh, bone and brain which could be seen trapped in midair in the spiral pattern of his shakta's attack.

"Get an eyeful of this, bastards," Aden said to the Church of Castine's acolytes. His shakta's strands retracted, then shot back out to deliver the same manner of death to them. He didn't care how fucking petty it was, he enjoyed watching their heads explode. They wouldn't be delivering his shakta or any sacrifices to anyone else.

Nikayla dropped to her knees, seemingly out of breath.

"You all right?" he asked.

She nodded, then after a moment said, "If you'd asked me, I would have told you there was little chance that would work." She cradled her brow in her free hand. "I'm glad you didn't ask."

Aden laughed.

"Why did you go after its body and not its soul?" Nikayla asked.

"Figured the body wouldn't be a moving target," Aden said. "What I can't figure out is how it knew we were here."

"I don't think it did, not exactly." She stood with Aden's help. "I believe they were bringing your shakta to the drayken to find you."

"Basically the reverse of what we're doing. Makes sense. They couldn't easily bring the drayken to the shakta." Aden wished there was a way to question the two people who'd been sacrificed, but even if they'd still been alive, there was no way to get answers from them, not while Aden and Nikayla were in this shadow of the real world.

"At least my shakta shouldn't be going anywhere," Aden said. "If I leave right away, maybe I can get it before the Church even realizes what's happened to their men and the drayken." Gods, he wanted that so badly, that it made his chest hurt with the desire to have it back. He just wished he could pick it up here and now and take it with him.

"We should get back to Ostice," Nikayla said.

"Any chance we can do that shifting from one place to another trick you mentioned?"

She shook her head. "If we don't shift in unison, your soul will be severed from your body."

"So we're walking."

They didn't discuss anything on the way back. Aden obsessed over his shakta sitting there in the sands of the Aiman Desert undefended and abandoned. He wondered how long the drayken had been this far into the East and why it had chosen that spot. He couldn't answer the questions, no matter how many times he asked them.

When Nikayla broke the silence between them, they were standing in front of her home.

"Do you see Rhea's thread?" she asked.

"Yes." The silver-blue light ran out the front wall of Nikayla's home.

"Let's see where it leads."

After following his thread, tracking Rhea's seemed odd. His thread had moved with him in this spirit world, but Rhea's remained still. How long had they been here? His mind felt fatigued, but not in the way that one requires sleep. That didn't make sense to him, but he wasn't trained in this kind of magic.

That reminded him of how Nikayla had known it mattered which hand he'd been holding his shakta when he'd gone through the ceremony for it. "How is it you know so much about shaktas?"

"Your Order doesn't keep its secrets as well as it likes to believe." She must have seen he was about to ask another question about that, because she cut him off. "That's one of those things that you don't need to know about me."

"As you like."

Rhea's thread went across the street from Nikayla's home and through several houses.

"Might still be at the church," Aden said. "This is the same direction."

They stepped out the side wall of a house and onto an intersecting street, which is where they found Rhea's shakta.

"Shit!" Aden almost fell backwards as he emerged right in front of Argus. Close to two dozen men, armed with swords, were following Argus to Nikayla's house. Judging from the pose of their frozen bodies, they were moving quickly.

"They're almost on us," Aden said.

"We have to get back and get everyone out of my home."

"Isn't there anything we can do here to stop them?" If only they could somehow attack them.

"We can't do anything to them." She pulled on his arm to run for her house.

An idea came to him, and he gave in to her wish to run. "What if we have Rhea use her shakta from here, the same way I did against the drayken?"

"Not enough time to bring her over!"

They ran through the front wall of her house. Nothing appeared to have changed. The fire might have shifted slightly, but not by much. Everyone stood where they'd been before he and Nikayla had left.

"What do we do to get back?" Aden asked.

"Sit back down in the same place and the same position."

"Does it have to be exact?" He hadn't even given a thought to how he'd been sitting.

"No, just so that you're in roughly the same space," she said in a rushed voice.

They got down on their knees on opposite sides of the table.

"Close your eyes so I can do this," she said. "Don't let go of my hand until I tell you to."

He shut his eyes. He was tensed, ready to move the moment she gave the word. It was bizarre to think that Argus' attack was frozen in this place, and yet in the physical world, they'd only have a few moments. They had to warn the others and make a run for it.

The firelight he could make out with his eyes closed didn't seem to waver. He'd almost given up on that happening, opened his mouth to speak, but then the flickering began.

"Wait," Nikayla whispered.

Were they back or not? No, the light was moving too slowly. The light got faster, though. Then his right leg shifted on its own, as if his soul was being forced back into the same position as his body.

"We're here." Nikayla sounded weak.

Aden jumped to his feet. He started to run for a look out the front window. "We have to get—!" Then he fell flat on his face.

"Aden!" Rhea and Dellem ran over to him and helped him back up. Nikayla had warned him about this.

"It's Argus," Aden said. "He's got two dozen men with him. We saw them two blocks from here. If we hurry out the back, they might not catch us."

"Will you be all right?" Will asked Nikayla.

She held onto his arm but didn't look happy about needing the help. "It will pass after I walk a bit."

Aden ran for the back door. "Hurry!" The fall seemed to have knocked him back to sorts.

"I've got our weapons," Rhea said.

"What about the fire?" Miriam asked. "Should we put it out?"

"No point and no time," Aden said.

"Dellem, here." Rhea tossed a sword to him. The constable caught it by the hilt and ran out the back with Miriam.

Will helped Nikayla out the back. She looked like she was having more trouble readjusting.

"Did you find your shakta?" Rhea asked as she handed Aden a sword.

"Yes." He nearly told her that Argus had hers, but knowing Rhea, she'd take on Argus here and now. She'd get herself killed.

"What is it?" Rhea asked.

"Nothing. Let's go."

Aden looked towards the front window. No movement out front that he could see. He followed Rhea out the back door and closed it behind them. Nikayla had them heading in the opposite direction from where they'd seen Argus. The bastard would probably try to surround the front and back of Nikayla's house before making his move.

They all stopped once they were out of the alley and Nikayla's house was gone from view.

"So you found your shakta in the Aiman Desert." Will sounded as excited by that news as Aden.

"Means we have to get out of Ostice," Aden glanced down the street they were on to watch for any sign of Argus or his men.

"Well, you won't have to go through the sewers this time." Will led them down the street and into another alley. "With a little bit of commerce, we'll take you out the front gates."

38
Barrel Full of Joy

Will's solution to get Aden out of Ostice turned out to be his favorite answer to any problem: wine.

Aden, Rhea and the others stood next to a wagon loaded with four large wine barrels. A few torches barely lit the inside of this storehouse.

Rhea, back in her red leather armor, fidgeted with the bracer on her left forearm. "What's keeping him?" Will had disappeared into a neighboring building where the storehouse's owner lived.

"Negotiations." Miriam paced enough to create a small path in the dirt floor.

"At least we got away," Dellem said.

"For now. Will has taken us to one of the city's most well-known smugglers. If this hunter Argus knows anything about Ostice's underworld, then he will look here."

"He is good," Aden said, somewhat dispirited. "Found us at Nikayla's before that drayken could have sent word we were there."

"Still don't see how he managed that." Rhea climbed on top of the wagon, inspecting the barrels, probably out of boredom more than anything else.

Aden walked beside her, but stayed on the ground. "Doesn't really matter how he did it, but it probably means he knows Will and Nikayla are helping us."

Miriam stopped in her pacing for a moment. "All the more reason Argus will check here."

Will entered by the rear door. "My ladies and lords, our chariot out of Ostice awaits." He'd changed clothes, his usual finery replaced with a brown sack of a shirt and dirty-looking blue pants. An irritated grunt, too loud and deep to come from a person, sounded from out back. A moment later, two men came in, each with a thick rope tied to the harness of a large mirden.

"Dellem, borrow one of those gent's cloaks," Will said. "I want you riding in the back. Nikayla, you'll be up front with me."

Rhea stared down at Will from the back of the wagon. "And what about the three of us?" she asked, pointing to Aden and Miriam.

"Seems you three are the ones most likely to be recognized, so you get to ride in the wine barrels." Will hopped up onto the back of the wagon. He climbed over to the middle two barrels and flipped one of them open.

"Hidden compartments." Aden was impressed. The insides of the barrels were padded for comfort, too. "What's to stop them from opening those barrels and finding us inside?"

"For starters, these two middle ones are the only ones for smuggling people. The rest of the barrels are real."

"But what if they look inside these two?" Rhea sounded far less confident in Will's plan.

"Relax," he said, "these two barrels are the ones they're guaranteed not to check. We're going to place a row of three on top of these four, then two on top of that. Won't make it all that easy to get you out when we get far enough outside the city, but it'll be worth it."

"But you only have two barrels," Miriam said, arms crossed.

"I'm afraid two of you will have to ride together."

Miriam strolled over to the front barrel. "Seeing as the two hunters are dressed to match, I'd hate to break up the pair."

"Nice of you two to volunteer." Will slapped Aden on the back and whispered. "Don't do anything in there I wouldn't."

"But—" Aden wanted to point out that the two ladies combined barely took up the same amount of space that he did by himself, but he could already tell that was a fight he'd lose.

"Aden, ladies," Will pointed to the barrels.

Aden climbed up onto the back of the wagon. "After you, Rhea."

"What happens if they try to sample the wine that's supposed to be in this barrel?" Rhea asked as she stepped inside the barrel. Her red leather creaked as she got comfortable.

"Don't worry. It's all taken care of." Will grinned as if he was thinking over a private joke.

Rhea didn't look any more convinced than Aden was, but she shifted to make room for Aden. He set his sword down on the opposite side of the barrel.

"Try not to make too much noise while you're entertaining each other in there," Will said as Aden climbed inside.

"Funny," Aden said, without sparing on the sarcasm, "very funny."

Will shut the barrel, trapping the two of them inside, facing each other in the dark. They both had to fold up their legs to where their thighs were almost flat against their chests. Aden hoped this wasn't going to take too long. Dark, he just hoped the damn idea worked.

Only a slim amount of light made it into the barrel, through very thin slits in the bottom half. Aden assumed that was so they didn't suffocate. They heard Miriam climb into the second smuggler's barrel. The additional wine barrels Will had told them about were quickly piled on top of them. That made the inside of the barrel that much darker. He could barely see the outline of Rhea's body across from him.

Something thumped against the side of the barrel.

"Play nice in there, you two," Will said, his voice muffled. "We're moving out now."

The wagon creaked back and forth. There was a crack of a whip, a mirden's deep mewl, and the groan of the wagon as it started to move.

"Whoa." Aden grabbed the sides of the barrel.

"How far into the Aiman Desert are we going?" Rhea whispered.

"Too far."

Even with the padding inside the barrel, they felt each bump in the road. The streets of Ostice had seemed much smoother when they were walking them.

Aden hoped the wagon wouldn't draw Argus' attention. They were well after the curfew. Aden had pointed that out to Will, but he'd insisted the curfew would only work to their advantage. Aden didn't see how that made any sense.

They weren't far from the gates, though. That definitely worked in their favor.

Aden took a deep breath and let it out very slowly to calm his nerves. Rhea's fingers brushed against his before resting on top of his hand.

"Relax," she whispered.

He took her hand into his own. "You, too."

They didn't say anything else as the wagon bumped and bounced its way down the road. How could something so weighted down jostle this much?

The wagon turned left, and Rhea fell into Aden with a squeal that she quickly swallowed. Aden laughed, but fear of discovery forced him to keep it quiet.

Aden listened for any sound of movement on the street, a sign of attack, but if any existed beyond their barrel, he couldn't hear it over the sloshing load of wine all around them. It was like riding blind in a bubble beneath a stormy sea and about as stressful.

The wagon jerked to a stop, with a weary growl of the mirden.

"What's this?" The shout must have come from one of the city's guards.

"Just getting an early start, sayer." Will was difficult to understand from where he sat at the front of the wagon.

"Manecks certainly has some balls sending out a shipment at this hour." Another one of the guards, Aden assumed. "There's a damn curfew, fool."

"Manecks said he was worried his nighttime friends' purses were getting too light because of the curfew," Will said.

"Damn right there," someone grumbled from just outside their barrel.

Aden and Rhea didn't dare move or speak. He squeezed her hand, and she squeezed his in answer.

"You don't look like one of Manecks boys."

"Just hired me this week." Will was right outside their barrel now. "Which one of you is Garver?"

"That's me."

"Manecks said to give you this." Even through the barrel, Aden recognized the sound of coins jingling in a bag. "For the toll, of course."

"Nice," the guard said. "What else you got for us?"

"Thirsty?"

"Dark, yes," one of the guards said. The other guards echoed his sentiment. Another yelled for a pitcher.

"Little sample of the red?" Will asked as he patted Aden and Rhea's barrel. What was that fool trying to do? Get them killed!

"Sounds good to me," Garver said. "Fill her up." That got a lot of cheers from the other guards.

"We keep our finest red hidden in this one." Will laughed along with the guards.

The palm of Rhea's hand went slick with sweat.

"Here we go!" Will said.

A slight tremor ran through the barrel as someone gripped the stopper on its side. What could he and Rhea do? They were stuck. No way out and not a damn thing to do to save their happy arses.

Something creaked, probably Will turning the stopper for the fictitious contents to pour out. To Aden's surprise, he heard the "glub glub" sound of liquid coming out of the barrel. He even felt it at his back, more vibrations in the wood.

After a moment, they heard another creak and the barrel went silent.

"Damn, that's good," Garver said. Some happy banter followed, along with a refill of the pitcher. Aden feared the barrel would run dry trying to fill that pitcher a second time. Their luck held, and by the time Will cracked the whip on the mirden to get them moving again, the guards' spirits were sufficiently lifted. All Aden could think was that if he'd tried half that shit Will just had, he'd get thrown in a cell.

Only Will.

Not long after the wagon started moving, Aden heard Will singing.

"What is that song?" Aden whispered to Rhea. He figured by now, they ought to be far enough from the city to at least whisper.

"That mirden's turd is singing *Barrel Full of Joy*," Rhea said. "When you get back your shakta, you hold him down and I'll kick him."

"Why do you get to kick him?"

"'We keep our finest red hidden in this one'," she said in a purposefully poor imitation of Will.

"All right, you have a point," Aden said, "but I can kick him and use my shakta to hold him at the same time."

"Fine, we both get to kick him."

The bumps in the road worsened the longer they traveled. Thanks to the cramped quarters, Aden kept smacking the back of his head against the top of the barrel. Every time the wagon slowed, he hoped they'd finally reached a place where Will and the others would let them out. Another whip crack and a mirden's protest dashed his hopes each time.

The damn wagon finally jerked to a halt. The Gods only knew how long they'd been stuck in this barrel.

"He better not crack that whip again, or I'll let the mirden stomp on him," Rhea said.

"You really do have quite a vicious streak in you."

"And don't you forget it."

The next sound they heard was the footsteps around them, ropes undone and barrels shifting above them.

"Careful there, Dellem." Aden could hear the strain in Will's voice. "Believe me when I say you don't want to drop any of them."

"Why is he being so careful?" Rhea asked.

Just then, Aden heard the thick growl of a courser, followed by two more. The mirden issued a panicked groan. What was going on?

"You are early." Aden didn't recognize the man's voice, but he knew the sound of distrust.

"Manecks couldn't safely keep the shipment in the city any longer," Will said.

Torchlight once more shown through the slits in the barrel, just enough for Aden and Rhea to see each other's faces. Rhea looked just as confused. A loud sniff, a courser no doubt, came from just outside their barrel. Who the Dark was out there?

The mirden made this panicked sound. Aden heard a lot more movement around the wagon. Probably meant a lot more than just three coursers, too. No wonder the mirden sounded nervous. Was probably worried those big cats were going to eat it.

"And what's this?" the one on the courser outside their barrel asked. He sounded plenty pissed, too. "I was expectin' seven barrels, not nine." The accent sounded familiar, but Aden couldn't quite place it.

"Relax," Will said as he tapped on Aden and Rhea's barrel and then Miriam's. "These two are for someone else. It's all the damn security in Ostice. Having to do double-duty with our shipment. Not easy getting past those guards these days, you know?"

"Oh? Just what's in these two?"

"Just a wine shipment for the Thoran Oasis," Will said.

"Wine, huh? Right. And just who are you, pretty boy? Never seen you before."

"Your shipment is on time, sayer," Will said. "If you'll just k—"

"The shipment is fuckin' early! My wagon won't get here 'til sunset, dammit. You expect me to just give you a thousand Nescatian silvers—you, who I don't know from goddess Astra's left tit. And you think I'm goin' t'sit in the open with seven barrels full of vastrium just waitin' for some damn Astesian patrol to come along!"

Vastrium! No wonder Will had wanted Dellem to be careful with these barrels. The Astesian Army considered that one of its most prized weapons. Just a bucket full of that that stuff could punch a hole the size of a boulder in a castle wall. Considering the coin being traded, these men must have been arms dealers from Nescat. Aden wagered they were planning to sell the vastrium to the highest bidder in the civil war up there.

"Fine." Will sounded like he was done with civility. "Dellem, load them back up. Keep your damn coin, sayer. Gods help you when your customers find out you've lost your supplier and can't deliver."

"I got a better idea." Aden heard someone draw a sword, then several more of the same. "What say I keep my coin, the vastrium, whatever you got in these two barrels, and let you walk back home? Then again, maybe I'll just fuckin' kill you and save Manecks the trouble."

"It's your mistake to make, but I think you'll want a look at what's really in this barrel before you make that decision." Will tapped on the barrel with Aden and Rhea as he said that.

One bloody damned awkward pause followed Will's challenge. The only sound Aden heard was the heavy breathing of that courser just outside their cramped hiding place. Aden didn't dare move and neither did Rhea.

"Fine," the weapons dealer said, "let's unload this fuckin' wagon and see what you've got."

"Dellem, let's—"

The arms dealer cut off Will before he could finish the order. "No, I don't trust you." He barked out some orders in his native tongue. Aden wasn't fluent, but he knew enough of Nescat to recognize he was ordering his men to get on the wagon and unload the vastrium. "Any tricks out of you and I'll shove this sword down your throat until you're kissin' the hilt."

"As you like," Will said.

Rhea and Aden looked hard into each other's eyes. He could see her steeling herself for what they had to do next. They shifted carefully within their confines as they picked up the swords they'd brought with them. That Will had chosen their barrel instead of Miriam's told them all they needed to know. They were going to have to fight their way out of this. As Aden and Rhea waited, he drew a line across his throat with his fingers. Aden wasn't cuing Rhea to be quiet, though. Judging by the way she nodded her agreement, she knew exactly what he was saying. The explosive liquid about them sloshed as the weapons dealers unloaded the barrels resting above them. Aden tried to ignore his fear that one of those idiots climbing on the wagon might drop a barrel of vastrium and kill them all. He focused on Rhea. They continued making their silent gestures until they'd agreed on their strategy.

They heard several hands grab their barrel. The men outside tried to move it, but the barrel didn't budge. Damn things must have been built into the back of the wagon. Aden heard the men outside bickering in Nescat. Rhea tapped his knee three times. He nodded his agreement; there were at least three just outside their hiding place.

"They can open them just as easily on the wagon," Will said. "There's a latch near the bottom."

The arms dealer with Will translated the orders for his men. Aden readied his grip on his sword. He heard one of the men on the wagon grab hold of the latch and pull. Ignoring the ache in his legs and the crick in his neck, Aden sprung from the inside of the barrel first, taking a blind swing at the men on the wagon. One screamed just before the sword sliced open his stomach. A second fell off the wagon with a minor wound to his side. Rhea took the third, shoving her sword's point in just below the ribcage and up into the heart.

Out of the corner of his eye, Aden saw Will take advantage of the surprise. The one atop a courser, holding a sword to Will's chest, gaped as he saw three of his men being cut down. Before the arms dealer could make another move, Will grabbed him by the wrist and twisted it so that he dropped the sword. Will yanked him off the courser and pinned him to the ground with his arm behind his back. Will produced a dagger into his free hand and stabbed it into his captive's neck.

The arms dealer got up onto his knees, grasping at his throat. Blood spilled over his fingers and down his shirt.

"The value of courtesy," Will said, "cannot be overrated."

Aden counted off five more arms dealers, not including the one he knocked off the wagon. That one was crawling away, apparently too busy holding to his wound to even think about drawing a weapon. The others rushed towards Will. Two of them were on coursers.

Aden jumped onto the dead man's courser. The large cat snarled but followed its training and heeded the wishes of its rider. He kicked his new courser into a charge, meeting the other two. He started with the one to his left. With a practiced swing of his sword, he parried his opponent's attack and slit open the back leg of the courser. The large beast fell onto its side, skidding across the sand and sending its rider flying.

The second courser rider wouldn't go down so easily. That one didn't risk a charge. His cat hissed and growled its challenges to Aden's ride. The cats stalked one another in a graceful circle. Aden's cat bared its teeth. The sounds of swords striking by the wagon threatened to distract Aden. He wondered if the others were all right, but he kept his eyes on his opponent. The other rider kicked his courser into an attack. Aden did nothing to prompt his courser. The cat, far more than its rider, always knew its best defense. His foe's courser pounced as prodded, exposing its throat. Aden's courser curled around and bit open the other's throat before it bounded away. Blood spewed from where Aden's courser had bitten. The cats started to circle again, but this time the other courser stumbled. Aden's cat attacked, going for the rider. The weapons trader screamed, a dreadfully shrill cry cut short as Aden's courser bit off the man's head.

The other courser fell to its side. Its front paws struggled for purchase in the sand, but the efforts failed, reduced to slow swipes, leaving bloody lines to mark the place it died. Aden's courser growled as it waited for its former companion to stop moving.

Will, Rhea, and Dellem were still standing by the wagon and didn't look a bit inclined to come near the coursers.

"Come on." Aden tugged on the courser's reins and led it back to the wagon. The cat stopped and crouched for Aden to dismount.

Will wiped the blood from his sword. "I really do have to talk to Manecks about the company he's been keeping."

"Your negotiating skills could use some more practice, too," Aden said. "Were you trying to piss him off?"

Will shrugged. "How far from here is your shakta?"

"By wagon," Nikayla said from the front of the wagon, "I'd say we'll be there about midday."

"Probably could cut that time in half on these coursers."

"Only three of them left," Rhea said. "None of them look well cared for either. Rules out riding double back."

Aden's new courser looked about the best off. Its brown hide had a good shine, and its eyes were clear, focused.

"You two go ahead." Will walked over to the unloaded pile of vastrium. "I don't plan to leave these here. We'll reload the wagon, burn the bodies and follow."

Rhea mounted a dark brown courser that had slept through the whole business. Everything about the animal screamed "indifference." Aden wasn't surprised by how much Rhea had to kick it in the side to keep it moving.

Truth be told, Aden wasn't all that comfortable making this ride without Nikayla to make certain he was going the right direction. They were in the middle of a damn desert, after all. He also realized he wasn't seeing his surroundings as well as he had in the spirit world. The world, despite its flat quality, had been easier to see, the sky not so dark. Aden and Rhea said nothing, at least not to each other. Rhea issued more than a handful of curses to her sluggish, stolen ride. During one of her rants, Aden looked back at her and saw sunrise was near. The eastern sky had taken on that pale quality that promised sharper and more varied hues.

"How much longer?" Rhea asked.

"I think we're getting close," Aden said, slowing his courser to let her catch up.

"Define close." She looked eager to redirect the scolding she'd been giving her courser to Aden.

"As in after sunrise, but not by much," he said, "and don't ask me to define 'much'."

Judging by the way she smiled, she'd been planning to ask.

"Wasn't expecting this to happen," she said.

"What? You didn't think we'd find my shakta?"

She regarded him with a sideways glance. "I didn't think I'd find myself in a situation where you had your shakta and I didn't have mine."

"Scared I might tie you up and run?"

Rhea nodded.

"Relax, Rhea, I'm not going anywhere until this is done."

"Define 'done'." One look at her made it clear she was teasing him.

"Done—as in get your shakta back, kill Argus, destroy the Church of Castine, and restore order to the East."

"Oh, is that all?"

"What? You don't think I can do all that?"

"I think Argus will be lucky if I don't rip his heart out before you get to him." She sounded serious, too. "Do you even have any idea how you're going to manage all that? You ask me, we'll be hard-pressed to get our shaktas back, much less stop the Church of Castine from gaining power in Ostice."

"I've got a few ideas." He embellished with wiggle of his eyebrows.

"Really? You actually have a plan?"

"What? You think Will is the only one who knows how to put together a plan?"

"Forget Will." She eyed him suspiciously. "Just what have you got planned?"

"You'll just have to wait and see." He could tell she didn't believe him, but that was fine. A few ideas had come together while he was riding with her in that barrel, but he still wasn't sure how to pull off any of it.

"Wait." Aden pointed to the next dune. "That's it. Just over that hill." He kicked his courser into a run. His shakta was waiting just over that pile of sand. He shouted victoriously as his courser leaped to the top of the dune. Then he pulled the courser to a stop.

All he saw was sand. No shakta, no bodies, no mirden.

"Are you sure this is it?" Rhea asked as her courser stopped next to his. "There's nothing here."

Aden climbed off the courser. "It was here!" Even to his ears, he sounded like he was trying to convince himself.

"You weren't expecting us to get here this quickly," she said as she dismounted her courser and followed him

"It was here!" He struggled through the loose sand of the dune as he walked down. This had to be it. Where had it all gone? "I killed a fucking drayken with it!"

"A drayken?" Rhea turned around, suddenly spooked. The sun wasn't fully risen, not that a drayken couldn't survive in the daylight. They just didn't like it. "Look at this place, it's—"

"It was here!"

She grabbed his arm. "Aden, calm down. I was trying to say that someone has swept the sand to hide any tracks. Just look at it."

She was right. He could see a pattern in the way the sand was disturbed. Wind didn't do that, but you wouldn't notice any of this if you weren't really looking for it. He'd been so pissed about his shakta that he hadn't even thought about that. *Calm down, fool,* he scolded himself. *Calm down and think.* He walked around the area where he remembered seeing the fire and his shakta.

"They rushed it." They'd taken the time to clear away the obvious signs, the tracks and the ashes of the fire, but he could still see the tiny mound where the drayken had placed his shakta. They hadn't bothered to do more than brush over it with whatever they'd used.

"We came from the direction of the city," he said, "so wherever they've gone, it's not back to Ostice."

"I'll check the surrounding area for tracks." She ran back up to the coursers and mounted hers.

The sun edged over the top of the dune, painting the dark sands a fiery orange. Aden knelt by the small mound where his shakta had been. He glanced to where the wagon would have been. How had someone cleaned away all of this so quickly? How had they known?

He looked up to the next dune and saw what he needed. Even if someone had smoothed out the tracks, they couldn't do anything to hide the displacement of the sand. All the other dunes had smooth surfaces. This one had a jagged quality to it where the wagon and mirden had gone. He walked over to the dune and could see they'd tried to hide the wagon's tracks, but they hadn't gone beyond that hill of sand. Beyond that, the tracks were visible again.

"Aden," Rhea shouted down to him from the top of the first dune. "I found the tracks of a wagon from the direction of the main road, but only one set."

"I found another set leading away." He scrambled back to his courser and mounted. "They took the wagon northwest."

"Wonder how far," Rhea said. "Looks like a whole lot of nothing out there."

"Can't be too far." He kicked his courser into a run. The tracks offered a clear path in the daylight. The heat slapped the sweat out of them and the terrain didn't offer any relief. The loose sand turned to hardened, cracked rock that brought them to a cliff.

"Where the Dark could they have gone?" Rhea asked. "I haven't seen any trails leading down into that ravine."

"I'll go left," Aden said. "You go right. We'll meet back here."

Rhea's courser moved more enthusiastically than it had in the night. Aden went in the opposite direction and found a path that led down. He could see where the wagon and probably several others had carved their tracks into the road.

He considered going back for Rhea but decided against it. Halfway down into the ravine, he saw some movement in the shadows along the base. He recognized the shape of a mirden and its wagon. The wagon continued along the base of the cliff, then disappeared into it.

Aden turned his courser around and hurried back. Rhea took a while to come back. He didn't wait for her to stop. Aden kicked his courser to walk back towards the dunes.

"You must have found something," Rhea said. "I hope so, because I didn't."

"There's a cave in the base of that cliff. Saw a wagon go into it."

"Surprised you didn't try to go after your shakta."

"Was tempted, but I've got a bad feeling that cave might be something bigger than we were expecting."

Rhea kicked her courser to fall in beside him as they headed back towards the others. "Just what do you think you've found?"

"Regent Dardane's dream."

39

Dardane's Dream

Will and his wagon of vastrium were waiting at the sanitized clearing.

"How good a look at this cave did you get?" Will asked.

Aden was lying on the ground with his eyes closed. Gods, when had he last slept anyway? Even the sand made a good mattress. "Couldn't risk getting too close." Aden yawned. "All I know is that the bartender said Dardane has been searching for a temple in the Aiman Desert for years. I'm willing to bet there's a lot more than that wagon inside that cave."

"What? You think there's an actual temple in that cave, some kind of treasure?" Nikayla sounded skeptical, and Aden agreed.

"Probably not, but I'll bet my last coin there's something important in there—something other than my shakta."

"Do you have any coins?" Rhea asked. Aden looked over at her and saw her rather satisfied smirk.

"I still have a few left," he said, pausing to clear his throat before he muttered the rest, "from what Will loaned me."

"So you're really betting Will's last coin." Miriam traded a conspiratorial smirk with Rhea.

"Fine. Yes," Aden said. "The point is there's probably something important in that cave."

"What kind of defenses could you see?" Dellem sat on the back of the wagon and looked about as tired as Aden felt. He'd slept some, but whatever recharge

Nikayla's magic had granted him, it demanded a lot of rest to help his body finish the job.

Aden shook his head. "The best defense they have is the approach itself, not to mention the big fucking desert that's all around it. No way to get down there unnoticed. That's assuming they have someone who keeps watch at the mouth of the cave. Didn't see anyone outside."

Dellem looked at their sparse surroundings. "If that's where the drayken had been staying, then why did it meet the church's followers here?"

"Meeting them halfway, I imagine," Will said. "They're running out of time, and so are we."

"Three days until the Council of Regents vote," Miriam said. "Knowing the church, they'll make certain Dardane wins that vote even without Aden, but I suspect it will be a slim victory."

Will leaned back against one of the wagon's barrels and crossed his arms. "It will be a suspicious victory that won't give him much real power, not as much as the Church needs him to have. Even with the Church's help, the man will waste the next few years trying to establish a strong power base."

"Couldn't we just sit tight then, out in the desert?" Dellem shrugged. "After all, if they don't have Aden, then they're weakened."

"Yes, but only temporarily, constable," Will said, "and Aden's value to Dardane won't end just because he's been named emperor. If he captured Aden days into his new reign, it would secure his power almost as well, if not more so."

"And we have to assume Argus will figure out we're here," Nikayla said. "The only explanation for him finding my house before is that he somehow learned of my connection to Will. Chances favor he knows I'm a witch, too. If he didn't before he found my house, then he'll probably figure it out once he searches my belongings."

"Then we'd better get moving." Will hopped back onto the front of the wagon.

"I'm too tired to ride that courser." Aden groaned as he stood and made a good showing of his stretching. "Anyone else want to use it?"

No one did. Rhea already had her courser and opted to keep riding it. Nikayla stayed up front with Will. Aden tied his courser to the back of the wagon and then climbed onto the back of the wagon, next to Dellem. "Mind some company back here, Dellem?"

"Not a bit, lad."

Miriam sat on the back of the wagon with them.

"And what shall we talk about?" She smiled to Dellem, the expression nervous. Normally, Aden would have felt like a third wheel, but he'd hoped for this arrangement.

"I was hoping Dellem might share some of his war stories with us."

One look at Miriam let Aden know she was suspicious of his motives, but that didn't stop Dellem from talking. The constable sounded glad to have something comfortable to fall back on for conversation, and Aden was glad to see the two of them finally relax a bit around each other.

The wagon made good time, crossing the desert to that ravine. Aden even managed a quick nap. His brain was wrapped in a sleep-deprived fog, but the sensation passed after he walked a bit.

"Can't get down there with the wagon," Will said. "Too wide for that path." He'd positioned the wagon almost directly above the entrance to the cave.

"Think we should knock and see who answers." Aden grabbed an empty water skin from the front of the wagon.

"More like see 'what' answers," Rhea said.

Aden went to one of the barrels on the wagon and filled the water skin with a load of the vastrium.

"Don't drop that." Her smirk left little doubt Rhea was teasing, but she did take a few steps back from him as she said it.

"Keep your eyes sharp, Rhea."

She must have figured out what he was doing, because she got onto her stomach right up against the edge of the cliff. "Let her fly."

Aden spun to build some momentum and flung the water skin as far as he could.

Rhea whisper a children's song. "Fly little lightning bug, how far can you fly?" She didn't sing any more than that, because that's when the vastrium hit the ground and exploded. Even as far away as he was, Aden felt the ground shake, all the way up into his legs.

"Four with swords already out the door," Rhea said. "Loose formation, too. Smart. Don't want to all get blown to bits. Looking up here, but I don't get the feeling they saw the water skin. Wait. Looks like one—no, two western wernrolts. Ahem, note the batlike wings."

Aden sighed. She was still stewing from their debate over that stupid statue on top of the theater.

"They shouln't be able to fly this high," Aden said.

"No, but that garnet scryhawk can."

"Shit." Aden got up and ran back to the wagon. "Will, got any bows and arrows in that wagon?"

"No, what is it?"

"Scryhawk headed this way."

"Let me deal with it." Nikayla climbed down from the wagon and knelt on the ground. She pulled her dagger from her belt, pushed up her left sleeve and slit down the back of her forearm. Wasn't a deep cut. "Only requires a small death," she said before closing her eyes. Her head canted left and right as if looking for something.

"It's heading this way," Rhea said in a warning tone that they needed to do something now.

"Avoid killing it, if you can. Doing that will give us away." Aden realized in hindsight that the bow and arrow wouldn't have been an ideal solution.

"I'm not killing it," Nikayla said in a distant voice. She ground her teeth together and sweat beaded upon her brow. "There you are!"

Aden looked back over the edge of the cliff. He could see the bird climbing.

"Won't be much longer before it sees us," Rhea said as Aden crouched next to her at the edge.

"He won't," Nikayla muttered, though it was hard to tell if she was talking to them or herself.

Aden heard the bird screech and dive out of control. Nikayla's eyes stayed shut, but she was smiling as she let out a long and steady breath. The scryhawk tried to climb again, but it lost control of its flight and swooped back down.

"It's giving up." Rhea looked at Aden then back to Nikayla.

"Got tired of fighting the wind." Nikayla sounded satisfied with herself as she opened her eyes and stood.

"Aden, we've got two of those guards heading for the path that leads up to us." Rhea crawled back from the edge and then got to her feet.

"What about the others?" Aden asked.

"Walking back to the cave, by the looks of it."

"Perfect." Aden drew his sword, then grabbed Nikayla by her uncut arm. "Come on. Let's put that blood to some use. The rest of you wait here."

Will looked a bit surprised at seeing Aden and Rhea taking control like this. Aden enjoyed that. Wasn't often he did something Will seemed unable to predict.

"While they're climbing, they can't see the top half of the trail that leads down," Aden said. "I want you to lie down and not move until I tell you to. This is good."

He helped her down onto her back. "Find a comfortable position so you won't be tempted to move," he whispered. He wiped some blood from her forearm and smeared it on her face. As he ran back up the trail, he looked back to see she'd chosen a prone position on her back.

Rhea, having waited at the top of the trail, waved for him to hurry. He felt his heart pounding hard in his chest. Damn, he'd forgotten how much he loved this feeling. He grinned at Rhea as he reached the top. They hurried to a spot on the cliff just past Nikayla.

After a moment, they heard footsteps on the trail as the guards approached Nikayla.

Aden couldn't make out everything they said, but he recognized a few words that were definitely Seronklin, the most common language among humans in the West. When he heard one of the guards warning the other not to get too close, Aden nodded to Rhea. They jumped over the edge of the cliff onto the trail just behind the guards.

Before the nearest guard could turn, Rhea had thrust her sword through his back and shoved his head against the cliff face. The guard collapsed as Aden slit open the other's throat. Blood sprayed onto the trail. The guard gasped for a breath, trying to scream. Aden grabbed the steel, spiked helmet off the guard's head and took another swing with his sword to finish him.

Nikayla had opened her eyes and crawled up the trail, still on her back. She stared wide-eyed at Aden and Rhea's precise butchery.

"This one should work for me." Aden looked back to Rhea, pointing to the guard she'd killed. "What do you think? Will or Dellem?"

"Definitely Will."

"Go get him," Aden stripped the armor off the guard he'd dispatched. "Nikayla, stay put. Keep an eye out for the other guards in case they check on these two."

He didn't wait for an acknowledgment, just struggled to get the guard out of his black armor. Bastard was tall, but still not as tall as Aden. He'd barely fit, but the brief advantage would be worth the trouble. By the time Aden was out of his armor and slipping on the guard's, Will had arrived. Nikayla had started dividing her attention between the trail below and getting the armor off the second guard.

"What took so long?" Aden asked as he slipped into the top half of the armor. He'd avoided untying the straps as much as possible, but given the size difference, that made it difficult to slip the leather onto his body.

"Had to help the constable." Will was already out of his clothes and slipping on the second guard's armor. "Wanted to make certain he'd be ready to roll when the time comes."

"Fine." Aden threw on the helmet, then snatched up the sword his guard had been carrying.

"I'll be right behind you two," Rhea said, "as soon as I see you go inside the cave. Try to leave some of them for me."

Aden laughed. "Right."

"Nikayla." Will grabbed her by the arm and looked ready to kiss her. Instead, he settled on a smile that she grudgingly returned.

"Try not to fall down this time," she said.

"I'll do my best, m'lady."

"Enough," Aden said. "Let's go."

He and Will ran down the trail with Rhea behind them. She stopped at the turn halfway down. Any further down and she'd be exposed for anyone in the cave to see her.

Now came the hard part. Aden and Will had to walk the rest of the way. *A man without immediate purpose walks with patience,* Aden reminded himself, recalling the haste he'd displayed in Crestnal when the time had come to kill Orin Gregane, the mistake that had gotten him into this mess to begin with.

"You'd better stay in the shadow of the cliff as much as you can," Aden said. "Neither one of these guards had a beard."

"They're going to be alert, too." Will slowed his step a bit to let Aden get ahead of him. Aden realized what he was doing and moved to place himself partially between the mouth of the cave and Will.

"You speak any Seronklin?" Aden asked. He hoped so, because his Seronklin wasn't good enough to fool anyone. A pity, because if he'd known more of it, he might have realized Argus was involved in all this as far back as Crestnal.

"Choi tote sabbae onklin." Will even spoke the Western speech with a flawless accent and then translated. "I speak many languages."

Aden looked back at him. "Just how many?"

"Enough to survive."

They didn't say anything more as they neared the cave. This close, Aden could see the cave entrance was entirely manmade. Looked as though someone had blown their way into this place, probably using the same kind of explosive as the one in their wagon atop the cliff.

Aden expected to find the other guards waiting just inside the cave, but the entrance was unguarded. This part of the cave only went a few steps into the cliff before it took a sharp right. Aden and Will exchanged confused looks and shrugged. Keeping their borrowed swords drawn, Aden walked around the corner and found the other guards were crouched on the ground.

The one on the left barked out a question in Seronklin.

"Ta," Will said, shaking his head.

The guard who asked the question narrowed his eyes. They widened as they realized Aden and Will weren't who they'd expected. A breath from shouting the alarm, Aden smashed his sword into the side of his head with the thick sword he'd taken from the guard.

Will dispatched the other guard with a swift slash of a dagger across the throat.

Aden thrust his sword through the other guard's chest. The guard stared back at Aden with a look of shock and recognition that he was dead, and when Aden ripped the sword free, the light behind those eyes went out.

They heard footsteps behind them and turned to see Rhea round the corner.

"Still no critters or wrangler." Aden shrugged as if to apologize for not saving anyone or thing for her.

"Let's hope that's all we have to worry about," Rhea said.

Aden heard the wernwolts barking before he even saw them. Their dark brown hides made them all but invisible in the cave's darkness.

"I've got this," Will said with obvious disappointment that no other option existed. These creatures' only crime were being placed in poor company, but they'd obviously been trained for attack. Will kissed the back of his hand and whispered an apology to the wernrolts. In two swift moves, he killed them. He knelt next to the wernrolts and tapped the top of their hands with the place he'd kissed the back of his hand.

"Down!" Rhea shouted. Aden ducked as she flung a dagger through the air. The blade intercepted the scryhawk which was plunging towards Aden with its talons raised, ready to dig into his face. The scryhawk shrieked as the dagger struck first and it dropped to the cavern floor.

The three of them ran down the sparsely lighted cavern. Aden wondered where the wrangler for those dead animals was hiding, and if he was alone. Just how many guards did someone place in a desert cave? And what were they guarding? Surely, this cave was hiding something more than just his shakta.

The passage led to an open door, flanked by waist-high pedestals with glass objects set atop each, a blood red bowl on the left and an orange sphere on the right. Aden recognized the symbols of the Western mystics. The color and shape held specific meanings, but he could decipher all that later.

They rushed through the door with their swords held ready. He'd expected to find a large room filled wall-to-wall with more guards. Instead, they found only one man in black armor, a beast wrangler, armed with a sword. The man was rambling in a panic on the far side of the large open space. Aden couldn't make out much of what the wrangler was saying in Seronklin, but he heard "open" issued as an entreaty more than once. The wrangler jumped and turned around, apparently finally aware he was no longer alone in this room.

"Where is my shakta?" Aden shouted, the words filled with all the long days of mounting rage and frustration he'd suffered to get here.

When the wrangler didn't answer, Will translated the question into Seron-klin.

The wrangler still refused to answer, but his eyes flicked to the right, towards a table with two benches.

Will lowered his sword and walked over to the table. The wrangler raised his sword in a threatening gesture and placed himself between Will and the table. "Ta! Ta! Ta!"

"Oh, please." Will sighed. "You don't even know how to hold that thing."

A whack of Will's sword disarmed the wrangler, with a clatter of metal as the wrangler's sword fell to the stone floor. Will leveled the tip of his sword against the base of the wrangler's throat. "Ta bache," Will said, and Aden suspected it must have been a warning to stand down, given his threatening tone.

Aden sheathed his sword and walked over to the table. He saw a half-eaten loaf of bread, several water skins and a flat, wooden box. He placed his hand on the box and took a deep breath.

"Please be in there," Aden whispered. His teeth felt as if they might chatter from the chill of nerves.

"Ta!" the wrangler shouted. Aden turned to see the wrangler lunge at him with a dagger in his hand. Will and Aden acted in unison. Will's sword sliced into the wrangler's back. Aden grabbed the wrangler by the wrist and twisted his arm to shove the dagger into the wrangler's stomach. The weight of the wrangler's body fell limp against Aden. He felt the pressure breath out of the dead man, with a whispered curse in Seronklin.

"You hunters really do need to improve your reputation." Will shook his head as he wiped the blood from his sword. "Any fool from the West with half a brain knows you hunters will kill him no matter what. You can't negotiate with a man when he knows he has nothing left to lose."

"Keeps things simple, if you ask me," Rhea said.

Aden let the wrangler fall to the floor. Will was right, though. Soon as he finished questioning the wrangler, he'd have killed him. *Never leave an enemy alive that might kill you another day.* The Order of the Hunt drilled that and the rest of their doctrine into every shateen.

He turned back to the box and touched the lid. He was certain he could sense his shakta in there and fearful that the feeling was nothing but wishful thinking. Would it even work? Had these bastards broken it as they had with the shakta they'd taken from Argus?

"Aden?" Rhea touched his shoulder.

He opened the box. That white, ribbed stick shined gently even in this dark cave. He reached into the box, not bothering to pull it out yet, just enjoying the feel of his shakta's ridges. Then he wrapped his fingers around it, felt his soul within the wood. His eyes closed as he lifted the shakta to lightly touch his bowed head. Now that he finally had it back, he realized just how terrified he'd been of never finding it. "Thank you," he whispered. He took a moment to realize he wasn't thanking any of the gods or even the two friends standing beside him. Meertak, his old mentor's ghost, had gotten him to Ostice. The whiskered devil's memory had taunted and lectured him to make it this far. He also realized that the knowledge Meertak was truly dead had silenced that voice.

My soul is whole again, he thought to himself, *and I'm going to do the same for you, old cat.*

"Aden?" Rhea gently squeezed his shoulder. "Are you all right?"

He opened his eyes to look at her and nodded.

Aden realized Will had gone uncharacteristically quiet. When he and Rhea turned to look, Will was staring down at the floor where the wrangler had been when they'd entered the room. There was a haunted look in his eyes, all bravado gone.

Because of the darkness, Aden hadn't noticed the design in the floor. The layout of the floor's stone tiles created an indentation in the floor, a hexagon formed from six triangular stones.

"He kept saying 'viat'," Aden said as he knelt next to the indentation.

"Open?" Rhea said. "Is this some kind of trap door?"

Will stepped back to let Rhea get a closer look. "I doubt that."

Aden remembered the glass markers outside the room and walked back out to get a better look at the items on the pedestals. Will and Rhea followed him to the doorway.

"I'm not well-versed in Western mysticism," Rhea said as she reached up to touch the red, glass bowl but stopped short of placing a finger on it, as if she expected it might burn her.

"The red bowl means the magic needed requires a blood sacrifice." Aden pointed back into the room at a stone bowl attached to the floor near the indentation. "Means whatever magic they're doing must be pretty powerful, though."

"And the orange sphere over here?" Rhea asked.

"Being the symbol on the left, that symbolizes the result of the magic. Orange is the color for land, and in this shape, it symbolizes the world." Aden leaned in a little closer and realized it wasn't just a glass sphere. "There's something inside." He hurried back into the room and grabbed a torch from off the wall. There wasn't much room left behind the sphere and the wall, but he positioned the torch close enough to shine its light through the sphere. "You see those red lines running through the inside? Red symbolizes blood."

"Blood within the world?" Rhea said with a dread that left Aden certain she was thinking the same as he. "Eskles ko tomela?"

That bit of Seronklin, Aden knew. "Veins of the world. That's how the wraith made it so far into the East. Might also explain how Argus got to Ostice for the assassination and then back to Gorman so quickly."

Will just stared into the room at the hole in the floor.

"It's a legend," Aden said. "Thousands of years ago, the dark mages of the West gathered all their power together and tapped into the life strands of the world itself. They built scrying pools at the points where these strands emerged into the surface of our world as entry and exit points."

Will's jaw clenched. "I'm familiar with the story. Didn't think the West was mad enough to start using them again."

Aden was surprised Will knew about that. Legend had it that ancient Western mages had scorched the lands in the West and East, killing hundreds of thousands in a matter of seconds when they mishandled the portals.

"Regent Dardane's expeditions must have found this place," Rhea pressed her hands together in front of her mouth as if to pray and let out a slow breath. "He might have been working with the West the entire time to find this place for them. They could send an entire army into the East, surround our armies from both sides."

"We need to leave." Will stepped back from the door, heading back towards the cave's entrance. "Now."

"Relax," Aden said. "As long as the gate's not open, we're safe."

"It's opening."

Thick, black liquid bubbled up from the center of that six-sided pool until it was filled. Then the black, fanged hand of a shadow wraith emerged.

"Time to leave," Aden said. Will and Rhea were already sprinting back towards the entrance. Aden caught a glimpse of the wraith's glowing eye, then took off running. The monster's twin warble chased them down the cavern. Aden looked over his shoulder. The damn thing was already out of the pool and racing after them.

They reached the turn into daylight with the wraith drawing just within reach of them.

"Roll it!" Will shouted so loud that the echo in the cavern hurt Aden's ears. "Bloody damn roll it now!"

The wraith hissed as its hands snapped after them. Aden heard the sunlight sizzle the wraith's black flesh, and the dark creature retreated back into the cave as they reached the safety of the sunlight.

"Keep running!" Will shouted at Aden and Rhea.

Aden glanced back at the cave, caught a shadow of something falling from the sky. The next thing Aden knew, a hot wind as hard as a wall slapped against his back. His feet lifted off the ground and flipped him over. He felt his hand brush past Rhea's hair as they passed each other. Only just before he hit the dirt did he hear a thunder as loud as if the sky had split open. Hot pebbles rained down on him after he hit the ground. He only knew it because he felt them hit his back. The only thing he could hear after that was something like a chime that wouldn't stop.

He looked over to see Rhea drag herself up to all fours, trying to get on her feet. Will had landed to Aden's left and was already up on his knees looking back at what was left of the cliff.

If Aden hadn't been watching Will's lips move, he wouldn't have understood what he was saying over that nonexistent chime.

"Damn, that was fun."

40
Caught in the Rain

When they made it back up to the top of the cliff, Will gave Dellem a slap on the shoulder and a very loudly spoken compliment on his timing.

"When you said to 'roll it,' I thought you were telling us to run faster," Aden said as he changed out of his borrowed western armor to put back on his.

"A little more warning would have been nice," Rhea said from where she was lying on the back of the wagon, opting to get some sleep on the way back to Ostice. She didn't open her eyes as she spoke and even blocked the light with her forearm draped over his face.

"Sorry." Since Rhea wasn't using her courser, Will mounted it. "I had the constable ready one of the vastrium barrels near the edge of the cliff, just in case we needed it."

"With any luck," Rhea muttered, "that explosion killed the dar'jiat wraith."

"I hope so." Aden checked the saddle on his borrowed courser, opting to ride it instead of joining Rhea on the wagon. "Pretty sure that wasn't the same one we ran into at the church. Last thing we need is a second wraith."

Nikayla joined Rhea on the back of the wagon to get some sleep of her own. Miriam and Dellem took turns handling the reins up front.

As they traveled through the desert, back to Ostice, Aden nudged his courser to move up beside Will's. "If you knew about these stupid smuggler's barrels, then why'd I have to swim into Ostice?"

"Same reason we can't be riding back into Ostice with this wagon. This close to having left, those guards will suspect something. They like their bribe money, but they aren't fools. You'll have to figure out your own way of getting into Ostice this time, my friend."

"Looks like I'm going to have to get wet again."

"Would have thought you'd had enough of those sewers by now," Will said.

"Oh no," Aden said, "I've got a different way of getting in there now. I plan to do it like a hunter."

Will arched an eyebrow. "And after we all get back into the city? What then, hunter?"

Aden patted his shakta, resting snuggly in its sheath within his jacket. Gods, it felt good having it back there. "Then I have some people to kill."

The last hints of daylight had disappeared beneath the desert horizon when Aden and the others neared Ostice. They stopped by the farm where Aden, Will and Dellem had stabled their coursers. Aden's green courser was sleeping in its stall and yawned with indifference to see he had returned for it. The lazy cat smacked its lips as it righted itself and stretched away the sleepiness from its muscles.

Not far from where he started his original swim into Ostice, Aden entered the dark waters while the others continued to the city gates. Storm clouds cried a light mist as Aden started his swim, but as he neared where the patrol boats had been, the rain dropped in waterfalls. He had to work that much harder to swim through those rough waters, but the heavy rainfall made him all but invisible to the patrols.

Once he made it within sight of the city's walls, he pulled out his shakta. Pointing towards the wall, the strands shot out and hooked into the brickwork. He gripped both hands about his shakta and as he let the strands shrink, they brought him to the city walls like a fishing rod pulling in its catch.

Once he was hugging the walls, Aden's shakta strands released their grip and reached for the parapet. The climb up wasn't easy. The swim had his boots wet and the rain made the city wall as difficult to climb as a sheet of glass. The downpour kept getting in his eyes and threatened to break his concentration. Even with the ocean to break his fall, a drop from the top of the wall might kill him if he didn't hit the water just right.

His arms were burning by the time he'd reached the parapet. Once he felt safe enough to risk it, he used his shakta to help him make that last climb onto the path on top of the wall.

"You there!"

Aden looked up to see a guard running towards him with a halberd in his hands. With a thought, the strands from Aden's shakta shot out and wrapped around the guard's throat, choking him. The guard gasped as he dropped to his knees. The man held enough sense to recognize Aden was to blame for his condition. The guard raised his halberd, too far to reach Aden with it, but he could throw it.

"Sorry for this." Aden flicked his wrist, and the guard launched over the wall into the waters below. Aden controlled the descent enough to spare the guard's life and keeping him within reach of the wall. That was assuming the fellow knew how to swim.

Aden lower himself to the street with his shakta. The technique wasn't all that different from what Rhea had done when they escaped the Black Dog, only his descent was more controlled. Soon as his feet met the cobblestones, he retracted his shakta's threads and walked away. Best of all, no one would question his drenched condition when he reached his destination, not in a downpour such as this.

The heavy rain continued as Aden reached the Lost Soul. Meeting here had been Will's suggestion. Aden had expected it to be busier, but the crowd didn't sound as enthused as they had during his first stay. He supposed the mood of the crowd last time had more to do with the mass wedding planned for the next day; although, he suspected the weather and the pending vote for the next emperor also had something to do with it.

Aden was relieved to see a different staff behind the bar. Their enemies had no way of knowing Aden and Rhea had stayed here or that they would even think to use it as a place to hide in Ostice. Aden's old mentor would have approved of Will's choice. He'd been a frequent lover of the "hiding under your enemy's nose" choice of lodging.

He found Will, Nikayla, and Rhea at a table along the wall in the lower class side of the room sharing a bottle of red wine.

"Gods, I didn't think drowned rats came in that size." Will stood and slapped Aden on the shoulder. "Good to see you made it."

"The rain helped more than it hurt," Aden said as they sat. "Where are Miriam and Dellem?"

"Already in bed," Rhea said. "Those two have been through a lot. They're fortunate to be alive and whole."

"Guess I'll wait to go upstairs and dry off," Aden said.

"No need." Will poured a glass of red for Aden, offering a conspiratorial look as he said, "They're sharing a room."

Aden gulped down half the glass. Felt good on his cold throat, and he could tell this was strong stuff, too.

"So what's happening with our friends across the street?" Aden pointed his thumb in the direction of the Church of Castine.

"Quiet, but we did see Loman going inside shortly before sunset." Rhea pointed towards one of the larger windows which offered an excellent view of the church.

"We haven't seen Argus," Nikayla said. "What guarantee do you have that he's even in there? He might be out looking for you."

"I'm counting on that." Aden finished the rest of his wine. Will lifted the bottle to offer a refill, but Aden shook his head. Best not to overdo it.

"So where's our room?" Aden asked Will.

"Our room." Rhea smiled, probably enjoying the look of surprise on his face. "Come on, I'll show you."

"Get some rest." Will sounded serious, but he had a sly smile on his face.

Rhea took Aden by the hand and walked with him to the stairs. The feel of her fingers entwined with his reminded him of just two days ago when they'd followed Loman to the palace. Felt more like a week had passed since then.

"What?" Rhea asked. He didn't realize until she said something that they were just standing at the bottom of the stairs, staring at each other.

"Sorry, was just thinking that we work well together." He smiled and felt like an idiot, but in a way, he didn't really mind. "You?"

She smiled at his words, but then her expression sobered. Before she spoke, she glanced up the stairs. "Are you sure we can trust Dellem?"

The question startled him. Of all the things he'd expected her to say, that wasn't it.

"He hasn't given me a reason to doubt him." He lowered his voice to be as quiet as hers. "Why?"

"A while after he and Miriam went to their room, I went outside to the privy. I ran into him right here. He was coming in the door just as I was about to go outside. He was drenched pretty good, about the way you looked when you arrived. Claimed he was checking on the coursers."

"And you don't believe him?" Aden tried not to show anything he was thinking, but her suspicions about Dellem had his stomach in knots.

"I checked with the stable boys. They said they hadn't seen him in the stables all night."

Aden sighed, trying to figure out the best thing to say, something that wouldn't make her worry any more than she already was.

"I've trusted him this far, and if the man really was a danger to me—to us, then he's passed up plenty of opportunities to betray us."

"What about the way Argus found us at Nikayla's?" Rhea let that thought linger. The question did chip at his trust. Gods knew, he was placing a lot of faith in the old constable. If he was wrong, then he was as good as dead.

"I trust him. This close to ending this, I don't have any choice but to keep faith in all of you. Besides, aren't you the one who's threatening to drag my happy arse to the Triumvirate after all this is finished?"

"True enough." She stepped closer to him. "Sure you really trust me?"

His heart seemed to float on the waves of his nerves as he stared into her eyes. Her hand trembled within his grip as he pulled her the rest of the way to him. Their lips touched, a gentle brush. This wasn't their first kiss, but it was their first real kiss, one just for themselves and not for the benefit of others. Their eyes met a second time as their lips pulled apart. The second kiss abandoned hesitation with a third and fourth quick to follow. By the time they'd made it to the room upstairs, Aden had stopped counting. He wanted to forget all the shit in his life and enjoy this while he could. They struggled to remove their damned leather armor in their clumsy dance from the door to the bed. Her warm body burned away the cold rain he'd yet to towel off.

By the time they'd each suffered the little death, the rain drops on his body were replaced with sweat. His heart pounded within his chest so hard that it hurt, but he was long past caring if it shattered his ribcage. She'd been worth it. The room held a chill to it, but they didn't bother with the sheets. Only their bodies were tangled upon the bed. He enjoyed looking at her body, that perfect curve that ran along her thigh and up around her bottom. He could smell the rain in her soft hair as her head rested against his shoulder.

"I've dreamed of that most of my life," she whispered with languid weariness.

"I don't know why you'd want me," he whispered back, "but I'm glad."

She stroked his neck with her fingers. "You were forbidden."

"You were a woman training to use a shakta. Wasn't everyone forbidden?" Aden teased.

"Yes, but you were cute, and then you got tall."

She drifted off to sleep, rolling over onto her side of the bed. Aden watched her, the way her back moved with each breath. He found it hard to believe that tomorrow, they wouldn't be able to do this again. Even if this all worked out, if he got her shakta back, killed Argus, and stopped the Church of Castine, then they'd still end up with her trying to drag him back to the Order. In his imagination, he could see her running off with him, but he knew that was nothing but fantasy. Rhea was a devoted follower, and as much as he had been, he couldn't go back.

He reached over the side of the bed and picked up his jacket. The memory of her pulling it off and tossing it to the floor was hot and hazy. Reaching into the jacket, he pulled out his shakta and slid it under his pillow. He'd worry about tomorrow when it got here. Until then, he'd enjoy what was left of tonight.

41

Like Mother, Like Son

The silence woke Aden more than anything. His eyes opened. He'd fallen asleep looking out the window at the rain, but the rain was gone. Something in the glass moved, but it wasn't a drop of water clinging to the outside of the window. It was a reflection.

He wanted to warn Rhea, but he needed to be sure. He'd only get one chance, if he was right. All he did was firm his grip on his shakta beneath his pillow, keeping the movement as minimal as possible.

Then he heard that thrum of life, a shakta... but not his.

Aden rolled out of the bed as the strands of a shakta shredded through the mattress where he'd been.

The life threads burst from Aden's shakta in a spiral formation. He looked up to see the strands hammer into Argus' stomach, knocking him through the room's door and into the hallway.

Aden jumped over the bed and unleashed a narrower arrangement to rip open Argus' chest. Argus rolled out of the way, anticipating the attack.

Rhea was on her feet with a sword in her hand. They both knew of how little use that sword was against a shakta.

Argus screamed as he lunged at Aden. Those twin threads spun in a tight circle. Aden dodged Argus' swing and used his shakta to snatch up a chair and throw it. Argus sliced the chair into sticks before it could harm him.

Another attack from Aden got tangled in Argus' threads. Aden swung at Argus' head with his left fist, but Argus ducked and planted a kick to Aden's unprotected stomach.

Rhea attacked Argus from behind. Her swing never came close. Argus wrapped his shakta strands around her waist and flung her into the hallway.

Aden directed another burrow formation at Argus. The years spent apart from his shakta and then concealing that he had it didn't dull Argus' instincts. Argus wrapped his threads into a tight line, sword formation, and parried Aden's attack.

"You're too predictable, boy." Argus laughed. "Too much like your old cat man, thinking you're so clever to hide in a place this close."

Argus thrust his fist up for Aden's jaw. Aden dodged it and landed a punch of his own to the old hunter's head. They went back and forth, trading blows, each trying to keep the other too busy to use their shaktas.

Aden looked past Argus and saw Will and Dellem run into the room. Argus heard them and shoved Aden back. With a swing of his shakta, Argus plowed apart the floor. The four of them fell into the main room of the inn. Aden heard Rhea yell his name as he landed on a table. The table fell onto its side, sending him to the floor on his arse. Argus was just getting up onto one knee. Will was on the floor with Dellem buried between a shattered table.

"Will!" Aden shouted the warning as he attacked Argus with his shakta. The simple formation struck Argus in the chest and sent him through the air, across the room.

Will scrambled to where Argus landed. He swung down with his sword, going straight for Argus' chest. Argus swatted the sword from Will's grip with his shakta then tripped him. Will fell on top of him and landed a headbutt to him. Argus ripped Will off with his shakta's strands, flinging him to the far side of the main room.

Aden took the opening the instant he had it, but Argus dodged the burrow formation aimed at his head. He jumped to his feet and flung a table at Aden. Aden shattered it with his shakta.

"You're good, boy, but you can't play this game all night. I know how you think. How do you think those boys in Crestnal got the drop on you?"

Argus unleashed a whip attack, but Aden wrapped his shakta's strands around the whip formation. A hard yank sent Argus flying across the room and out the front window.

"Aden!" Rhea shouted to him. He saw her standing by the hole in the ceiling. She tossed his saddle bag down to him. He ran to it and grabbed his ceremonial uniform out of it. He'd not worn the black, blue and white raiment of the Order in more than four years, but he would today.

"Will, did you get it?" Aden shouted as he slipped on the uniform.

"Got it!" Will was already running upstairs to Rhea.

Dellem ran past Aden to the shattered window. "Don't see him out there."

"Probably going for help." Aden pulled the black mask and hood over his head. "Rhea, get dressed and get down here! Time to finish this." Aden ran for the door. "Dellem?"

"All ready, lad."

"Stay close to me until this is done." They ran out of the inn and straight for the church.

They hadn't run halfway across the street before Argus made his next move. Aden spotted the glow of the shakta strands coming from above.

"Look out!" He shoved Dellem aside and ducked to the left. The shakta strands cut into the street and then retracted to the top of that statue of the woman. That's where Argus was hiding.

Aden hit the statue with the full force of his shakta. The stone cracked loud as thunder, tumbling back into the front of the church. He'd hoped to hear Argus scream, but the sound of the statue breaking in the front wall of the church drowned out all else. The head of the statue broke off, rolled down the front steps and into the street.

"Well, if that doesn't bring the city guard running, I don't know what will." Dellem ran past the large head in the road.

Dellem was right. That didn't leave them much time to finish this fight with Argus.

"Let's knock a little harder." Aden grabbed hold of the statue's head with his shakta and flung it into the front of the building, creating a huge opening that exposed the sanctuary.

Aden and Dellem ran inside. They spotted Argus racing down the long, center aisle and past the pulpit, disappearing into the back of the church. Aden unleashed his shakta, tossing pews across the large room, shattering the many stained-glass windows and statues. Several dozen guards, servants of the church, ran into the room from where Argus had disappeared. Armed only with swords and crossbows, they didn't offer much of a threat. Aden snatched their bolts out of the air and their swords from their hands, tossing them aside before doing the same to the guards themselves.

"Damn," Dellem said, "doesn't even seem fair."

The floor opened like a newborn volcano, but instead of lava, the shadowy shape of the assassin wraith emerged.

"That evens the odds," Aden said.

The wraith's glowing eye narrowed on Aden. He could see the shape of the eye was slightly warped, not yet fully healed. The monster's growl sounded plenty pissed with Aden.

Aden spun the shakta in his hand. "I'll keep the wraith busy."

"You do that, lad, and I'll see to the guards that are still breathing." He gave the wraith a wide berth as he ran to the far right wall of the sanctuary where Aden had thrown most of the guards. That large blue eye didn't waver from Aden, though. Yes, it definitely remembered him.

The wraith leaped from the floor straight at Aden. Its twin mouths bared their teeth, eager to rip open his chest. Aden wrapped the soul strands of his shakta about an exposed support beam and pulled himself up into the air, above the wraith's attack. He landed on the support beam and looked down to see the wraith spin around in a tight circle looking for him. Its arms shivered, taking in all the scents in the air. That single eye turned up to focus on him. Its wings spread as it crouched, and then the wraith launched straight at him.

Aden grabbed hold of another support beam with his shakta and ripped it free. He was rewarded with at least one jagged-looking end. Aden jumped feet-first towards the wraith, wanting it focused on him. He flung his make-shift spear at the wraith, swinging it down with all the force of a catapult. The more pointed end of the wooden beam drove straight into the wraith's chest, knocking it out of its flight to plummet. The wraith's beast wrangler screamed from near where the pulpit had been. The wooden beam pinned the wraith, who issued a pathetic cry, the plea all the more pitiful as it could only manage the call for help with one of its mouths.

After releasing his "spear," Aden refocused his shakta to grant him a controlled fall. Just before he touched the floor, he was struck from behind. Argus' shakta sent him flying back towards the front of the sanctuary. Aden lost hold of his shakta as his body plowed into some of the shattered pews.

He scrambled for his shakta, but Argus was ahead of him. Aden saw the twin strands swat his weapon beyond his reach. Then those threads snapped towards him, wrapping themselves around his throat and tossing him onto his back. He tried to move, but Argus' shakta wouldn't let him. He could barely breath, getting light-headed as his vision blurred.

"You arrogant brat." Argus walked over to him and knelt beside him, just out of Aden's reach. Aden tried to grab the traitor, but even if he could have gotten his hands on him, the lack of air was weakening him to the point of lame swats. "Did you really think you could just come in here with your fucking shakta, tear up the place like a child having a tantrum, and then kill me? You really thought you could ki—What the fuck is so funny?"

If Aden could have gotten any air, he'd have laughed, but that didn't stop the widening smile on his face. Then he felt the strands around his neck ease just enough to let him gasp an answer to Argus' question.

"Wasn't—trying to—kill you."

"You should have." Argus leaned in close. "Because I'm going to kill you."

Before Argus could finish off Aden, a needle thin burrow formation shot through both his wrists. The instant the strands from Rhea's shakta pierced the second wrist, the formation ballooned. Both hands exploded off of his arms. Argus screamed as his hands, what was left of them, and his shakta dropped to the floor.

The twin strands from Argus' shakta vanished. Aden took in a deep breath and got back to his feet.

"No, Argus," he said in a rasping voice, "I didn't need to kill you. Just needed to distract you."

Blood flowed out from the stumps of Argus's arms. Argus stopped screaming as Aden slipped on a set of brass knuckles and shattered the man's jaw in a single punch. Argus moaned as he looked from Aden to Will and Rhea, as they walked up beside him.

"Nice work," Aden said to Will. "He never even noticed you'd taken it." Aden patted Argus' chest where he'd been holding Rhea's shakta captive.

"It's not the first time I've lifted something from a person's pocket," Will said with obvious pride. "Although, I've usually taken their purse, not a shakta."

Rhea pointed her shakta at Argus, not that he required any more warning to not move.

"We shouldn't linger," Will said as handed Aden his shakta, having retrieved it for him. "The city guard is assembling down the street."

"In a moment." Aden knelt beside Argus and pointed his shakta at Argus' eyes. He wished the traitor could have seen the strands as they slowly curled out from the tip of the white stick. Instead, he let them tickle the bridge of Argus' nose, cheek and forehead, around the eye stolen from Aden's mentor. Argus grunted, probably trying to scream. "Like mother, like son," Aden whispered. The strands stabbed into Argus. His screams only encouraged Aden to make this take that much longer, the strands burrowed deep until they cradled the base of his old mentor's eyeball, then ripped it out. Aden plucked the eye out of the air and let the strands retreat back into his shakta.

Argus stopped screaming, or rather trying to scream. Weak ragged gasps were all he could manage. He held the eye so that it looked down into Argus' remaining eye.

"Aden, that's enough." Will grabbed him by the shoulder. "We need to go—now."

"You and Rhea go ahead." Aden didn't look up at them. "I'm not done with him yet."

"I'm not letting you out of my sight." Rhea's words were cut short. Will struck the back of her head, knocking her out. He and Will had planned this ahead of time. She'd never believe it, but this was for her benefit, more than for Aden's.

"Get her out of here," Aden said.

"Been a pleasure, Aden." Will lifted Rhea over his shoulder and carried her to the back of the Church, probably heading for the same alley door they'd used the other day. Aden looked up towards the front of the church. He heard the shouts of the city guard and the pounding of their feet as they marched closer.

"Not much time left for us," Aden said to Argus, "but there's enough."

He still had his old mentor's eye looking down into Argus' remaining one. "Take a good look at Meertak's eye, Argus." Aden's body shook with his anger. "Take one damn good look, because it's the last thing you're ever going to see."

Aden made this one quick. Sympathy didn't enter into it, not even fear of the city guard interrupting. He just didn't want to give Argus a chance to look away from Meertak's stolen eye. Aden let the second eye drop to the floor. Argus screamed, more of a moan given the disaster Aden had made of his jaw. This time, Aden could tell the man was more than in pain. He was pissed.

Dellem walked up behind him.

"I trust the beast wrangler's dead?"

"Aye, lad," Dellem said. "I got him."

"Good."

Aden looked up at the sunlight spilling in through the gaps he'd created in the front wall. Long shadows that belonged to the city guard climbed those front steps.

"It's time," Dellem said.

"I know." He'd known this was going to happen, but now that the moment was here, he was scared.

Dellem stood behind him and placed the edge of his sword against the front of Aden's throat.

"I am Constable Dellem Arkreus, and under the authority of the Astesian Empire, I place you under arrest for the assassination of the emperor."

The guards entered as Dellem finished issuing the charge. Aden set his shakta on the ground. He was thankful for the mask that hid his face, because letting that piece of his soul drop to the floor, choosing to be separated from it again, hurt more than having had it stolen.

A woman, dressed in silver armor and adorned with the yellow and red braids of a general, stepped to the front of the group. She was an older woman with hard lines and strong arms. For a woman who'd lived most of her life at war, she'd held up well. He realized he'd never heard much about how General Gelleran looked, but then it was her victories in battle and her skill as a strategist that had built her reputation.

"Constable." She nodded.

"General Gelleran," Dellem answered. "The assassin, as promised."

"I must admit that when you came to my home last night, I had my doubts." She smiled to him, then looked down at Aden. "He is disarmed?"

"Yes, general."

"And this is our assassin?" the general asked.

"That's right, general." Aden found it harder than he'd expected to feign the arrogance and contempt he needed for this moment. "I killed your emperor."

"I'd mind your tone with me, assassin."

"He was hired by the Church of Castine and Regent Dardane," Dellem said.

"He looks more like a hunter from Mirite." The general ripped off his mask.

"He's not," Dellem said. "Turns out he's nothing but a common bounty hunter that was expelled from the Order of the Hunt years ago. Been working out of Gorman ever since, taking odd jobs. Was where the Church of Castine found him. They've been working with the West to put Dardane in power as a puppet."

"You have proof of this, constable?"

"Quite a bit, but I think that thing over there should be enough." Dellem pointed to the wraith's impaled body, slowly writhing as sunrise assaulted what was left of it. Aden smiled as he saw the look of fascination and revulsion on the old lady's face.

"Seems I'm once again in your debt, Arkreus." The general glared down at Aden. "And you, assassin," she paused as the back of her hand slapped Aden across his face, knocking the sense out of him for a moment. "The Astesian Empire owes you much pain." She stepped back to make room for her guards. "Take him!"

Aden made a good show of it, giving the guards plenty of trouble as they dragged him away. He looked over his shoulder before being taken outside. He saw Dellem pointing down at Argus and whispering something to the general.

42

The Final Gambit

Aden spent the next week in a cramped jail cell in Ostice. The second day, he heard the cheers as the regents chose their new ruler. His nerves, already strained from being without his shakta again, left him a fidgeting, pacing mess. He couldn't stop sweating as he waited to hear the shouts of the crowd say the name. If all went as planned, then Dardane didn't have a chance. If the man had a brain, he'd be halfway to the West by now, but if he was still here and managed to blackmail the regents or some other clever con... If that happened, then Aden's gambit with his life was for nothing.

Then he heard the crowd shouting the name of their new ruler.

"Gelleran! Gelleran!"

He dropped onto his cot and let out a long breath along with a prayer of thanks to the gods. Letting the general catch him had given her the edge. He just hoped she'd run the Church of Castine out of Ostice. Even in his cell, he'd heard the rumors make their way through the jail, hearing other prisoners talk about the dar'jiat wraith and other monsters found inside the church. He'd also heard his name mentioned more than once. The guards wouldn't let him out of his cell for fear the other prisoners would kill him. A man like Aden Murai couldn't simply die in his cell. The new emperor needed to make his death a spectacle.

The next day, Aden was loaded into a wagon and sent into the Aiman Desert to the prison of Baladair. The heat alone was enough to punish a man to death.

He found it hard to eat. The motivation just wasn't there, even without the food tasting like a wraith's armpit. The guards here also didn't risk letting him loose among the prisoners. Every prisoner here was already sentenced to death, so they didn't have anything to lose by killing Aden. All Aden could do in his cell was sit and sweat.

"Prisoner Murai!" The guard's shout startled the Dark out of Aden. He'd been on the verge of another nap when the bastard had disturbed him. This was one of the guards he didn't like. He'd been surprised to find most of them pleasant men, despite how hard their duties required them to be.

"Get up," the guard said. "You have a visitor."

Aden prayed it wasn't another inquisitor. He'd feigned resistance to answering their questions when they'd questioned him, but now he was just too damned tired, just wanted to say the same lies and shit and sleep until it was time for this torment to end.

"Aden?"

He sat up to stare at one of the last people he'd expected.

"Rhea?"

The guard held the door for her, closing it behind her. He stood and met her hug with an eager embrace.

"I was tempted to kill Will when he told me what you were doing," she said.

"Told you I could stop the West from taking over Ostice."

"That you did. You also said you'd destroy the Church of Castine."

"Did I?"

She looked irritated by his question, grudgingly answering him. "Loman's on the run, and so is the former regent, Dardane. As far as the Astesian Empire is concerned, the Church of Castine has been ruled an enemy to the public's welfare."

"On the run, huh? Nice to know they're getting a taste of what they did to me." He smiled as he studied her face. He hadn't expected to ever see her again, not without a shakta in her hand and the strands holding him prisoner. "You look good."

"You do not."

They sat on the cot, just holding hands. Aden was reminded of that first time he'd taken her hand into his. Another unexpected treat, one he sure as Dark wasn't going to pass up.

"I'm not as bad as I look," he said. "Just sweating off a lot of weight. I'm in a desert cell, after all."

His attempt at humor didn't get a smile from her. She leaned closer, her voice a whisper. "I couldn't risk bringing my shakta in here. That doesn't mean I can't come back tonight."

"And what?" Aden stopped her before she could say any more. "Dark, woman, do you want a war?" Keeping his voice to a whisper was hard to do. After all he'd been through, if Rhea did what she was considering, then everything he'd suffered through this past week would be for shit. And at the same time, he wanted to kiss her.

"You don't belong in here." Her hand squeezed his as if she meant to break his fingers lest he agree. "You know damn well Argus killed that emperor, and you had all you needed to prove it!"

"Yes, I could have proven that a member of the Order of the Hunt murdered the emperor of Ostice."

She jerked her hand free of his and slammed her fist against the wall. "They're going to execute you and Miriam in five days!"

"It's that or a war," Aden said, "and I sure as Dark—wait. Miriam? They're executing Miriam?" That damn well hadn't been part of the plan. How in the seven kingdoms had that happened? How did that even make sense?

"The day after you surrendered yourself, she confessed to working with you. Claimed she was your contact."

"Does Dellem know? Have you talked to him?"

"No, I haven't. He left the same day she was arrested," Rhea said. "I can get you out, both of you. Don't be stubborn about this. We could make it look like the Order just wanted to kill you themselves—"

"And what? The Order doesn't? Don't be naive. There's no difference in being in here and being out there, not for me. I've been living under a death sentence for three years."

Rhea didn't say anything. She just wrapped her arms around her stomach as if hugging herself for some sense of comfort.

"Rhea, I'm tired of running."

"What if—oh, gods." She paused. He couldn't tell if she was at a loss for words or just too pissed to speak. "What if I ran away with you?"

"You? Leave the Order?" He shook his head. "Don't think I'm not tempted by the thought of being with you, because I am, but you'd come to resent me. You aren't made for a life outside the Order. You still believe in them."

"And you don't?"

He reached for her shoulder, but she shrugged away from his touch.

"You don't want me to go back," he said, "because the only way I'm going back to Mirite is to kill the Triumvirate. They murdered my mother."

"Argus killed your mother," she said.

"Acting on the Triumvirate's orders. That's the same thing, and you damn well know it. If I had the chance to kill them, I'd do it and never regret it."

"You'd be killing my father."

They didn't say anything else, but they did hold hands again. She leaned against him, her head resting against his shoulder. He kissed her forehead and wished this could be like that last night they had together at the Lost Soul.

"I want you to make me a promise," he said. "I don't want you there when they kill me. It won't be pretty, and I don't want that to be the last way you see me. And I don't want you telling the Order my secrets—not about my mother or that I can see the strands or any of that. I get to keep those, dammit."

"I'm going to tell them what you did, though," she said. "They won't be writing you into their books as a traitor to the Order or the East. They're going to remember you for who you are... one of the best hunters they've ever had."

He rested his head against hers until one of the guards said it was time for her to go. She didn't look back. Rhea hugged him tightly, then turned and hurried out.

That turned out to be one of the hottest nights in his cell. He supposed there wasn't much room for cold air with his conscience beside him. He hoped Rhea would do as he asked. Most of all, he just hoped she wouldn't be in Ostice for the execution.

Days later, Aden and Miriam rode on a pair of coursers, the city of Ostice at their backs. Their executions were scheduled for this day, but they wouldn't be the ones dying.

Aden's plan had worked.

"You ready?" he asked.

"I've said my goodbyes and settled my affairs." She didn't look at him as she answered, just kept her eyes straight ahead. She looked quite different. Her long, brown hair had been shorn, coming down to just above her shoulders. Her face wasn't painted as she'd worn it in Ostice. In that respect, she looked more as she had when he first met her in Crestnal. Like himself, she'd lost some weight from all that time in a hot cell, and they both looked all the more pale for it.

"I'm more than ready to put this life behind me," she said. "Wouldn't have made that 'confession' otherwise."

Aden looked over his shoulder at Ostice. Even from this distance, he heard the cheers as the new empress and her people celebrated her triumph. Part of him wanted to see the executions, but that would have been dangerous, too much risk of discovery.

His only regret was that he wouldn't see Argus die, but with the hood over that traitor's face, the sight of his death wouldn't have been as satisfying. Rhea's attack had left him unable to speak and barely able to walk. Truth be told, there was something ironic about the actual assassin being executed, even if the crowd chanted the wrong name. He wasn't sure how Miriam's replacement had been chosen. He didn't want to know and didn't need to.

"Let's be on our way." He kicked his courser into moving. They were gifted with a cloudless sky for the start of their journey through the Aiman Desert.

More cloudless skies greeted Aden and Miriam as they rode into the town of Crestnal. The sun was descending, the blue of the sky being replaced by the harsh reds and oranges of sunset. Eager as they were to rest, Aden insisted on circling the town to make certain things were safe. After all he'd been through, he knew better than to assume even a place this out of the way was without threat.

They didn't go into town. Instead, they rode to Dellem's house on the outskirts. The constable ran out the front door. Aden smiled as Miriam slid off the back of her courser and ran to meet him. He'd assumed these two didn't have a chance of making it together. Being wrong could be nice sometimes.

"Took you two long enough." Will strolled out the front of Dellem's house.

"Got held up two days in the oasis," Aden said. "Sand storm."

Dellem and Miriam clung to each other. Aden didn't blame them. If Rhea had been here, he liked to think they'd probably do the same thing. He envied these two. They were going to enjoy the ending he'd have chosen for himself, if he could have had it.

"Let's get you two inside," Dellem said. Aden saw tears in his eyes. "Make you some dinner."

Aden and Will didn't need long to realize it was better for them to wait outside on the front porch with their glasses of brandy. Will smoked a cigar, too. Nikayla was right. Those damn things really did stink.

The front porch faced the sunset. Aden was glad to see the sun without having to feel it as much as he had in that desert cell.

"Had us worried for a while there," Will said.

Aden leaned back in his chair. "Just glad we were in the oasis when that storm hit."

"I was talking about your little plan for getting yourself arrested and 'executed.' Just how the Dark did you figure out Dellem would have any inroads with General Gelleran?"

Aden laughed. Was nice to finally one-up the wily Will October. "The benefits of being a hunter," Aden said. "Part of all that training includes a pretty heavy history lesson and profiles on all the most dangerous people we might face on a battlefield. General Gelleran is the best strategist in modern siege warfare. Seeing as Dellem was such a savvy engineer, I figured he must have served under her."

"Hardly a guarantee he'd have had any sway with her, though." Will took a sip of his brandy, then set the glass on the arm of his chair. "You're lucky he didn't do something in that war to piss her off."

"You have no idea." Aden looked over his shoulder towards the front door to make sure Miriam wasn't anywhere near it. Then he leaned towards Will, lowering his voice to a conspiratorial whisper. "As it turns out, Miriam isn't the only one in that house who's shared a bed with an Astesian ruler."

Will must have started on the brandy a while back, because he blinked a few times before Aden's words sunk in.

"Dellem? And the general?"

"That's empress now, thank you." Aden laughed.

"Why that dog." Will started laughing, too. "Old constable was holding out on us when we were trading war stories out here all those weeks ago." Will abruptly stood. "Oh, almost forgot. Stay right here. I'll be right back out."

Will disappeared inside the house. A moment later, he returned with Aden's shakta in one hand and a saddlebag in the other.

Aden snatched the shakta back into his hand. Gods, it was good to have it back. "Thank you."

"Seems only fitting you get it back here in Crestnal. It's where you lost it, after all."

Aden nodded. Was damn good to be whole again.

"So what's in the bag?" Aden asked.

"Your cut."

Aden undid the draw string. Even in the setting sun's light, he recognized the sparkle of gold coins. "Dark! That must be—must be, um."

"That," Will said as he sat in his chair again, "would be the equivalent of four hundred and sixty-eight Astesian gold coins, my friend. We split it evenly between you and Dellem. The reward on your capture had reached a thousand golds."

"Never thought I'd ever collect a bounty for turning myself in." Aden ran his fingers through all that money, the coins clinking like music. "Hey, wait." Aden looked back up at Will. "If it's split evenly, why haven't I got five hundred?"

Will cleared his throat and sat up. "Sorry, but after three years, you've built up quite a tab at my tavern."

"Ah, yeah," Aden ran his fingers through all those coins again. Damn that was some mighty good money. "Seems fair enough."

"Speaking of which, try not to use up all that coin in one place. Not bad money, but you can't retire on that either."

Sadly, Will was right enough there. Tempting though it would be to try, he knew he'd only get a few years out of even this much money.

"Well, I'm a far cry from retired."

"We'll have to be a bit more discreet in the future to give you some jobs," Will said. "Would hardly do to have one of the Order's hunters spot you, and we still don't know if Rhea is going back to Mirite or Gorman or somewhere else, for that matter."

"I appreciate that, Will, but I've already got a job."

Will's right eyebrow shot up. "You do? What job?"

"Let's just say Empress Gelleran was very impressed, and felt she could use a new spy that knows his way around the East and West."

"Imagine that'll pay well." Will raised his glass again.

"It's steady pay," Aden said. "It'll be nice to stop worrying about where my next

meal is coming from."

"So I imagine you're headed back to Ostice."

"Oh no, not yet. I told the empress I had some unfinished business to see to first." Aden grinned as he reached into his purse and pulled out the piercing he'd taken weeks ago from Orin Gregane's rotting corpse. "That merchant in

Salendar still owes me fifty silvers for this, and under the circumstances, I think he'll be paying me a hefty fee for unexpected expenses."

Acknowledgements

I started *The Cold Shoulder* as a fun side project almost two decades ago. When I entered into Aden's journey, I went in blind: no worldbuilding, almost no character profiles, nada. I wanted to write an epic fantasy with a main character in the vein of Bernard Cornwell's Richard Sharpe. On the surface, Sharpe is a common man prone to some boneheaded mistakes but also some brilliant military decisions.

Thanks to Sheri and our friends Katharine Herndon and Shawna Christos. They all served as my beta readers for this novel during its rough draft. We still fondly remember traumatizing a knitting group sitting near us at a Barnes & Noble when discussing the appropriate motions for stabbing someone.

I also want to thank Phillip Hilliker for the cover art that depicts Aden using his shakta. He created that for this story's original serialized release on Kindle Vella back in 2021 and now serves as the cover for the collected novel.

About the author

Bill Blume's love for the written word started in high school with an addiction to comic books that was later hijacked by novels such as *Frankenstein* and *Dragonflight*. His short stories have been published in many fantasy anthologies and ezines. Like the father figure in his *Gidion Keep, Vampire Hunter* series, he's worked as a 911 dispatcher for more than 20 years.

To learn more about Bill and his books, visit his website at www.billblume .net.